The Cherry Tree

The Cherry Tree

MARTIN GILLARD

Oswald
Badger

For John

Chapter One

November 21st, 1916 – July 12th, 1917

The old man took a final shallow breath and allowed the fever to claim him. The senior physician approached the bed, felt for a pulse, and turned to the young woman beside him.

"I regret your grandfather has left us all to grieve, Your Royal Highness," he said.

The news of Franz Josef's death was received with much sadness in Vienna and Berlin, and with much rejoicing elsewhere in Europe. And long before his coronation the new emperor, Karl the First, was known throughout the Hapsburg lands as Karl the Last.

Life ebbed, and life flowed. Minutes before Emperor Franz Josef died in the Schloss Schönbrunn, one of his newest subjects made his noisy entry into the world in the far north-western corner of the empire. Shortly after 9 o'clock on the evening of the 21st November 1916, in the Bohemian town of Cheb, Karolína Kovaříková gave birth to her only living child. She named him Tomáš.

Had the old emperor ruled for another 68 years, he would have placed little value on the arrival of this new subject. For Tomáš Kovařík was born a Czech, and Franz Josef's sympathies were always for his German-speaking subjects, and not for the 22 million Slavs who also happened to be ruled by the Hapsburgs.

To Tomáš's family, gathered together in the narrow, timber-framed house in the centre of Cheb, his arrival was a miracle. Karolína was now 28 years old and this was her third pregnancy, and the first to reach its full term. But as her son was placed in her arms Karolína's joy was mixed with anguish. It was seven months now since she had received news of her husband. In his last letter Pavel had not even been allowed to say where he was. Karolina knew only that after his leave in February he had been sent back to the fighting.

The war was insatiable - a miscreation, quickly swallowing up Austro-Hungary's youngest recruits. It took only six months before it had demanded the presence of a thirty-year-old teacher of mathematics to keep it fed. Pavel's conscription papers arrived one day in March 1915 and with them came a letter, ordering him to report to the recruitment office in his own school to collect the field-grey uniform of an Austrian rifleman.

"How in God's name can a Czech be expected to take up arms against his Slav brothers?" he had raged when he returned home with the brown-paper package under his arm. "Fight the Prussians or the Bavarians or the damned Austrians? Yes. Just give me the chance. But how can any Czech or Slovak be expected to fire on a Russian or a Serb? It's civil war, Kája."

Karolina and Pavel talked of him hiding in the woods by the lake to avoid the call-up, but the Austrian secret police had spies everywhere, and who knew what reprisals might be taken against his parents or against her if he failed to report? So Pavel put on the uniform of his Austrian oppressors, and boarded the train to Pilsen to join the other Czechs, summoned with him to form the Imperial 29th Infantry Regiment. As Pavel waved goodbye to Karolina at Cheb station, neither he nor she knew that inside her was growing the healthy baby they both had prayed for so much.

Karolína looked down at little Tomáš cradled in her arms. He was so beautiful. If only he could have been born at a better time into a better world.

In the continued absence of any news from her Pavel, Karolína listened to every rumour circulating in the town concerning the progress of the war. Every day she made her painful way to the New Town Hall on the east side of the main square to read the official bulletin posted in the long, glass-fronted case on the wall by the main doors. And every Thursday her mother, Magdaléna, her plumpness accentuated by her second-best dress, would insist on linking her arm and walking with her. Karolina dreaded Thursdays, the day the town clerk pinned up the week's casualty lists.

As they crossed the square and approached the glass case, the women knew if there had been a major offensive on one of the many fronts, for then the normal two or three white sheets would increase to five or six. Karolína would quicken her pace and focus on the middle sheet, halfway through the alphabet - K for Kovařík, P for Pavel, O for Otakar. And every week when she was sure his name was not there, the fear that held her would loosen its grip for a few precious moments, and she would turn and fall into the arms of her mother.

On July 2nd 1917 the Russians launched a fresh offensive against the Austrians in Galicia on the north-eastern border of the Hapsburg Empire. Ten days later the list of casualties in the case filled seven sheets, and this time the absence of Pavel's name did nothing to lessen Karolína's fear.

"I know he's dead, Máma," she said, as they turned and she half walked, half stumbled, back across the cobbled market square.

Magdaléna put her arm around her daughter's waist and pulled her close to her. "You must not say that, my child. His name was not there and you cannot give up hope, until there is no reason left for hope."

"But it's over a year now, Máma. I would have heard something if he were still alive."

"But it's even more likely you would have heard something if Pavel was dead, Kája. You know that."

"Do you think so, Máma? Do you really think so?"

"Of course."

"But Pavel doesn't believe in what he's fighting for, Máma. How can he survive when he wishes no harm on the people trying to kill him?"

"Your Pavel is a clever man, Kája. He will know how to survive."

They reached Lanek's bakery in the colonnade beneath the brightly painted houses on the west side of the square, and joined the end of the queue.

"These Austrians are at war with the whole world, Máma. He could be anywhere, France, Italy, Russia. Even Serbia or Romania. Who knows?" Karolina looked about her, her voice raised. "And who around here do you think cares?"

Magdaléna grabbed Karolina's arm and pulled her away from the women in the bread queue.

"Sshh, Kája. What are you doing? Do you want Tomáš to be without a mother as well as a father? For God's sake, child, keep your voice down. And you know you have to speak German when there are people around."

She ushered Karolína down a deserted side street leading through the old Jewish quarter to the river.

"No, Máma. I refuse to be forbidden to speak my own language. How can they say we're not allowed to speak Czech, even with our own family? What right do they have?"

"I don't know, my child," whispered Magdaléna, "but it is the way it has always been." She looked back to be sure no one had followed them. "I heard from Frau Staněk..."

"There you are, Máma. Why *Frau* Staněk? Why do you not say *pani* Staňková?"

"Very well, if you must. But keep your voice down, child. I heard from pani Staňková, the police in Prague are beating people in the street with truncheons for speaking Czech."

"Yes, I heard it too, but I didn't want to believe it. Do you know,

Máma, I never understood Pavel before... the way he hated having to teach his Czech pupils in German. He used to tell me most Austrians didn't even know there was once a Czech state... or that Cheb was an important Czech town when we had kings of our own." She rubbed the pain above her eyes. "When I think how often I lost patience with him... But I see now Pavel was right to say those things. When they take away our language, they take away who we are."

Magdaléna took her arm.

"Don't upset yourself, Kája. You can't change any of it. It's been this way for hundreds of years. And most people in Cheb are German now anyway. It's just the way of things."

"But that doesn't make it right, Máma. Why should we not be allowed to speak Czech? Why should every sign and street name be written in German?"

They paused on the bridge over the River Ohře. Karolína leaned on the parapet and looked down into the deep, clear water.

"You know, Máma, Pavel hated German names for Czech places. Eger for Cheb. The River Eger instead of the Ohře. He used to talk about all these things. It was so important to him and I never understood why. But if he has died fighting to preserve something he hated..." She lowered her head and wiped her eyes. "It will have been the worst thing for him."

"Don't torture yourself, my child. You must stay brave for the sake of little Tomáš."

Karolína turned and faced her mother.

"I swear Tomáš will grow up to be a proud Czech, Máma. I shall see to that. And I swear on Pavel's memory that I will never allow his son to be treated as second-best. Or to fight for something he does not believe in."

Chapter Two

April 9th – 10th, 1916

"*Christos voskres!*" The cry drifted across no-man's land, followed by a chorus of deep, strong voices returning the chant, "*voistinu voskres*". The sound was trapped under the day's fading light and hung over the battlefield.

"What is it, Sergeant?" asked a voice from the depths of the trench. "Are they coming?"

"Calm down, Vaněk," the sergeant called down to him. "It's probably nothing. Get some rest."

The eight new recruits under the sergeant's command had only arrived a week earlier, and already their number was reduced to six. Martinek had been killed by a mortar shell on Wednesday; parts of him, impossible to recover, still lay out in no-man's-land. And the next day Skála was shot.

The sergeant had warned the newcomers not to rest against the sandbags without checking for gaps, but the smiling young student from Prague had ignored the warning and leaned back to light a cigarette. The rising smoke told the Russian sniper where Skála was, and the small opening where a new bag had been laid in the night was all he needed to put a round into the Austrian trench, through the back of the boy's neck.

Vaněk and the others saw their friend catapulted forward by the force of the bullet and, huddled together on the floor of the trench, they watched as their sergeant sat with Skála in the mud, comforting him and trying to stem the pulsing stream of blood.

None of the recruits was yet nineteen and this was their front-line communion, as they witnessed Skála's struggle to suck in air through the flapping hole in his throat. After twenty minutes death had come to him as a friend.

"*Christos voskres!*" came the single cry again. "*Voistinu voskres,*" chanted the chorus.

"Is it another attack, Sergeant?" said Vaněk.

"I don't think so, son." The sergeant moved up on to the firing step and stood next to the sentry.

"What can you see through the periscope, Sedláček?"

Štefan Sedláček, a student of music in another life, strained his eyes

boots of Russian infantrymen. They had taken off their peaked caps and held them in front of them. The sergeant caught glimpses of the double-headed imperial eagle above the peaks.

"I... I'm sorry... I know very little Russian," he said. "*Christos voskres,* my friends."

"*Nazdar,*" replied one of the enemy infantrymen, employing the archaic greeting now popular again among Czech soldiers. "It's alright, brother," he said. "There's no need to be afraid. We are all Czechs, just like you. Our officers are Russian, but every man you see out here was born a Czech or a Slovak." He pointed to the insignia at the top of his sleeve above his corporal's chevrons: *1st Jan Hus Rifle Regiment.* "We only realised last night there were Czechs in the Austrian trenches too. We heard someone shout 'Happy Easter' to us. We couldn't believe it."

"That was young Sedláček," said the sergeant. He felt tensed muscles release his neck and shoulders.

"We've got a Sedláček in our trench too," replied the corporal. "Like the rest of us here he comes from Kiev in the Ukraine now, but his family came originally from Brno."

He turned and pointed to the dozens of soldiers who had left the Russian trenches and were now standing in the middle of no-man's land.

"Just about every man in the Jan Hus comes from a Czech family. Most of our people emigrated to the Ukraine fifteen years ago during the big lay-offs. These fellows here are in my section - Maly, Kraus, Hrubny and Martinek."

The sergeant took off his helmet and nodded towards the men.

"And my name is Beran," said the corporal. "Ludvik Beran. My family was originally from Prague."

The sergeant offered his hand. "My name is Kovařík. I am Pavel Kovařík, from Cheb."

Ludvík Beran took Pavel's hand and, as soon as the two men touched, they embraced, to the loud cheers of all the Czechs around them.

For two hours the 1,800 Czechs from the Austrian 29th Infantry Regiment, and the 2,000 Czechs from the 1st Jan Hus Rifle Regiment, stood beneath the weak morning sun in no-man's-land, celebrating the bond that transcended their uniforms. They shared cigarettes, food and coffee, and cursed the conditions under which they were all trying to survive.

But as the sun rose higher in the cloudless sky, they found it ever more difficult to ignore the horror that lay around them. The heat brought out the blow flies, which soon covered the bodies and parts of bodies, turning them into black moving masses. And the noxious smell that filled the air every day between noon and dusk gradually drove the men back to their trenches.

They did not stay there. They came back out to no-man's land with entrenching shovels and picks and stretchers, and side by side they dug communal graves. The flies rose in their millions, stubbornly refusing to give up the bounty they had enjoyed undisturbed for so long, and they harassed the men as they worked. But for five hours the men kept to their task, until every Slav body that had lain abandoned – Czech, Slovak, Ukrainian or Russian – was laid to rest.

Throughout that evening a delegation of officers and men from both sides sat and talked together in the Russian trenches. The Russian officers made bold proposals, and opinions were sought among the Czech soldiers. Conditions were laid down, and finally agreement was reached.

At eight o'clock the following morning the entire Austrian 29th Infantry Regiment, with band playing and banners flying, marched across no-man's land in Galicia and joined their Slav brothers in their long fight against the German and Hapsburg Empires.

Chapter Three

April, 1916 – Summer 1917

During his last week as a soldier in the Austrian army Pavel Kovařík sent a letter home to his wife. If he had known it would be the last he would be able to send her from the front, he might have tried to express more in it. As it was, he was only allowed to communicate by ticking prescribed options written in German.

I am in good spirits. I am not ill. I am not injured. Please send me … Pavel added '*books*'.

At the end of the letter he was allowed to add eight of his own chosen words, written in German in order to pass the censor. He wrote, '*I shall live and come home to you*'.

Karolína kept the letter as a talisman. She tucked it into the waistband of her skirts, and she would go nowhere without it. She sent Pavel three books with the covers and spare pages removed, to ensure they did not exceed the maximum weight allowed by the Imperial Army Postal Service. And, to give her husband even more reason to stay safe and to come home to her, she enclosed a letter telling him she was carrying their baby, which she promised him would survive.

As with all the mail sent to the soldiers of the Austrian 29th Rifle Regiment after the events of Easter 1916, Karolína's letter, the two books of poetry and the book on Fermat's Last Theorem were all destroyed by the Imperial Army Postal Service in Linz. In order to prevent any rumours of mass desertion amongst the ranks of the Czechs serving in the imperial armies, dependants at home continued to receive the soldiers' pay, but officially not one utterance was ever made about the regiment again.

Karolína continued to send letters until the summer of 1917, but when nothing came back and no news was heard of anyone in Pavel's regiment, she resigned herself to his death.

"It is the hardest thing to live continually with hope, Máma," she said. "It does not sustain me any more. For Tomáš's sake I must embrace the things I know are real in life, not the things that only might be. I have Pavel's love and I have his child, but I do not have Pavel. It must be enough."

And that night she put Pavel's last letter behind his photo on her dresser, and there it remained out of sight.

During the seven years Pavel and Karolína were married, their home was a rented timber-framed house by the bridge over the River Ohře. They were happy there, although at times both sensed privately that the house would only truly come alive if the sound of a child could fill its cosy rooms and narrow staircases.

Now, to Karolína, it seemed that without Pavel the house had lost its heart. She knew the problem was with her. If she could have kept alive a belief that he would be coming back, she could have preserved his presence in the house, but without that belief there was no sense of family there. And it was not what she wanted for their son.

Tomáš was such a happy boy. From the very beginning of his life he showed that rich combination in a child of reaching out with warmth to those around him, while being perfectly content within himself. And continually he delighted his mother, and amazed the older women of Cheb who had experience of these things, by the way he reached each stage of his development earlier than anyone had seen in any child before.

Karolína spent most of the summer of 1917 with Tomáš at her parents' chata in the woods outside Cheb. When the weather was fine, which it was on most days that summer, she sat Tomáš in his sling facing her and set out over the bridge outside their house on the road out of Cheb to the north. The signposts told a traveller the road led to the imperial spa town of Franzenbad but, as Karolína explained to Tomáš as she walked, to a Czech it was the road to Františkovy Lázně.

Tomáš, who by August was into his ninth month, would listen intently as his mother pointed out the plants and birds they passed on their journey, and he would chat back contentedly, mostly in a language of his own making, but sometimes copying a word he had heard from his mother.

"*Pták, pták!*" he would say that summer every time he saw a bird. And Karolína would kiss him and pet him and whisper to him, "You're the cleverest boy in the whole world, Tomášek. So much like your *tatka*."

She had been anxious that Tomáš might be deprived of the things she knew Pavel would have given him. Pavel was such a natural teacher. She knew he would have instilled in Tomáš a desire to find the truths contained in the world around him, and an understanding of the freedom that knowledge brings. But when she looked into Tomáš's face as they walked, and she saw the same sharpness and intelligence in his eyes as she had always seen in Pavel's, she understood that Pavel had already passed

11

to his son his most precious gifts.

A short distance along the road to Františkovy Lázně Karolína took a turning to the left along a well-worn track leading to the village of Skalka, where for centuries boatmen had carried travellers and goods across the River Ohře. Now the collection of cottages and inns was popular with hikers and with holidaymakers, who still came in the summer to swim off the sandbank on the wide bend where the river slowed.

To get to her parents' cottage Karolína had to turn off before she reached the village and go down a path into a forest of beech, oak and fir trees. The path was wide enough to allow a donkey cart along it, and after two hundred metres it opened out into a clearing next to a large carp lake. And that marked the end of her daily walk, for standing in the clearing was the chata of Karolína's parents, Michal and Magdaléna Štasný.

The log cottage had been built by Karolína's great-grandfather in the spring and summer of 1849. In later years the walls inside and out were plastered and whitewashed, the original wooden roof replaced with a pitched roof of red tiles, and outbuildings added to accommodate the workshops of the Štasný men - three generations of the best carpenters and furniture makers in the region.

Karolína's grandfather, in his turn, added a jetty to moor the rowing boat the family used for fishing trips out on the lake, and her father built an arbour where three people could sit and watch the sun go down behind the tall fir trees which skirted the lake on all sides.

This was the place where Karolína was born and raised. It was here Pavel came to court her, and it was where they celebrated with friends and family after their wedding in the Church of Saint Wenceslas in Cheb in April 1910. More than fifty people danced on the green in front of the chata that day, driven on by a Moravian band of cimbalom, double bass, clarinet and fiddle, and by the slivovitz Karolína's father dispensed from an oak barrel he kept by his front door.

Esther Lochowitz, Karolína's closest friend since primary school in Skalka, was her maid of honour and stood with her and Pavel under the single wild cherry tree which grew on the edge of the clearing. At great expense a photographer was brought from Prague, and one of the dozen pictures he took hung in the living room of the chata next to the large, green porcelain-tiled oven. The photograph showed three young people with their lives in front of them, staring confidently into the camera as they stood below a canopy of white cherry blossom.

"What are you thinking, Kája? You seem to be in a world of your own," said Michal.

"Oh, it's you, Táta. I was day-dreaming. I was thinking of my wedding day. Of Pavel, Esther and me having our photograph taken beneath this tree all those years ago. Do you remember?"

"Of course I remember. It was the proudest day of my life."

He reached down to his grandson sitting on the blanket next to Karolína.

"No, no, Tomášek. You mustn't eat cherries. I know they taste good but they have nasty stones in them. And when they've been on the ground they might have horrible maggots in them too."

Tomáš looked puzzled that his Děda would deny him these lovely bright-red objects that felt and smelled so nice, but he let it pass. And the next sensation he felt was a force, both wonderfully powerful but gentle, lifting him into the air.

"Come to your Děda, my little Tomáš. Kája, it will be dark soon. It's time for me to walk you home."

"Yes, Táta. I'll get our things from the house and catch you up."

Karolína kissed her mother, who had come out to wave goodbye, and hurried up the forest path to her father.

"You know you don't have to go home at the end of every day, don't you, Kája?" said Michal. "There's always a room for you and Tomáš here with us."

"I do know that, Táta. I have thought about it."

"Tomáš needs to feel the love of his whole family around him, Kája."

"I know. I can see how he thrives on it, being here with you and máma."

"Why not come to us then?"

"Because I'm afraid that if I give up my home with Pavel I shall be losing one more link with him."

"Kája, my precious, your greatest link with Pavel is right here now, asleep in my arms. That link cannot be broken, whatever is happening out there in the wider world."

"I know, Táta. I see so much of Pavel in my boy. He seems so sure of his place in the world, and yet he needs my love so much."

"Of course he does."

"I *shall* keep Pavel's link with Tomáš alive, by what I teach him. I shall tell him all the things his father would have told him."

"I'm sure you will."

"But I don't know how I shall ever explain the madness that grips our world now, Táta. How could anyone imagine such chaos in our lives?"

"Bohemia has always had its wars, Kája, but we always rebuild."

"But this is different, Táta. So much is changing. Did you ever imagine the Tsar abdicating, or the Germans fighting the Americans? How will we ever explain all that to our children?"

"I don't know, Kája."

"I hate this war so much. I hate what it has done to my family. Pavel loved the Russian people. And he loved the freedoms that France and America stand for. But he was forced to die fighting against them."

"Kája, you must stop saying Pavel is dead. It's not going..."

"It's no good, Táta. I know he's dead. I know how strong Pavel is, but I also know he couldn't survive such contradictions in his life. Fighting for the Germans against the people he admired most. He would prefer death to that. He resented the Germans. He didn't hate them. But I do now. I hate all of them."

"Kája, you must not talk like that. I understand your grief, but such bitterness isn't in your nature."

"It wasn't, but now I have it deep inside me."

Michal stopped at the end of the forest path and faced his daughter.

"Kája, your father is a simple man. But I have seen more of life than you. You talk about Pavel struggling with contradictions, but you are creating contradictions of your own. You cannot hate all Germans."

"I can. I do."

"No, Kája. Esther's husband is German. Can you hate him? Can you hate the German children you went to school with? Or the von Stricker family, who have done so much for us?"

"By allowing you to own Czech land which should belong to you anyway?"

"But the von Strickers have owned these forests for centuries, Kája. They didn't have to give your great-grandfather the freehold to his land. They did it because they are fair people. Because they wanted to give something back to the Czechs. And now we must be fair too."

Karolína said nothing. She reached out and took Tomáš. He opened his eyes and looked at her as she put him into his sling. As she started to walk with her father along the track towards the Cheb road, Tomáš opened his eyes once more and scanned his mother's face for a long time. At last she looked down and smiled at him, and only then did he allow himself to sleep.

"Perhaps you're lucky, Táta," Karolína said, "that you have two daughters. With me here and Zuzana happy studying in Prague, you know your children are safe. Imagine what Janek and Berta Kovařík are going through with three sons at the front."

"Is there any news of Teo and Petr?"

"Not for a month or so. They think Teo is in Italy, and Petr is probably in Serbia. But it's Pavel they're worried about most. With no news for 16 months."

"Do you see much of Janek and Berta?"

"Less and less now. It's not easy getting to Pilsen, and it upsets Berta too much to see Pavel's child. And they sense I've stopped believing their son is alive. It's too painful for all of us. And I see a difference in Tomáš when we've been there."

Michal put his arm around his daughter's shoulder and drew her close. Immediately she turned and buried her head in his chest and he felt her sobs.

"Just don't tell me any more not to hate the Germans, Táta," she said. "Just don't say it any more."

"My child, my child," said Michal, and he kissed the top of her head. "Don't think I cannot understand how you feel. A father fears for his daughters too."

He put his hands to her face and wiped away the tears with his thumbs. "Listen to me, Kája. You've done enough on your own. With little Tomáš here you've been as strong as any soldier has to be. For Tomáš's sake, let your máma and me help you now."

"How can you?"

"Bring Tomáš and live with us until this terrible war is over."

"I would have to give up the lease on the house."

"No, Kája. Keep the house. Go there when you need to. Perhaps one day..."

"You're wrong, Táta. I know he's not coming back."

"Whatever you say, my child. But for Tomáš's sake, don't let him feel your bitterness. A young child breathes in the mood of its mother, and once inside, these moods can be part of their character for life. Fight against your bitterness, Kája. For Tomáš's sake, fight against it."

15

Chapter Four

April 11th, 1916

Artillery and mortar shells exploded on the Austrian lines in the distance. Pavel looked back and admired the carefully worked-out plan. The first line of the Jan Hus was advancing across no-mans-land to occupy the Austrian trenches abandoned by his regiment. Within minutes a second wave followed the first, passing through the gap in the Austrian line and beginning a flanking movement in the open country beyond.

Pavel envied these men. His pleas to exchange his Austrian grey for Russian brown and join them in their fight was denied. With the rest of his now defunct regiment he was ordered by the Russians to stay in formation and keep marching, until the noise of the battle faded into a dull, indistinct rumble behind him.

After five hours breathing in the red dust kicked up by the long column of men, Pavel arrived at the railhead at Brody, a small town in the valley of the River Styr on the border of the Austro-Hungarian and Russian Empires. Here the men were at last allowed to rest in a park by the river and fill their water flasks, as Russian troops took up positions around the perimeter.

"Later today you will go in groups of one hundred to the railway station," a Russian officer informed them. "You will be taken to your new barracks to be issued with Russian uniforms and weapons. All Austrian weapons of any kind you will leave here at our collection points."

"What do you think, Sergeant?" asked Jan Vaněk. "It doesn't seem right giving up our rifles."

"No, it's alright, son," replied Pavel. He turned to the boys of his section sitting behind him on the grass. "It's best to do what they say. But when it's our turn to leave, make sure you all stay with me. Understood?"

They all nodded and Jan Vaněk and Štefan Sedláček shuffled closer to him across the grass.

At four o'clock in the afternoon Pavel and the six boys were ordered to stand and form up with the next group of one hundred. They were stripped of their weapons and marched to the railway station within a cordon of armed Russian soldiers. Nearing the station they heard men shouting and swearing in Czech, and the sound of stamping feet.

They were led away to the side of the station along the track between two more lines of Russian soldiers, standing with bayonets fixed. Pavel realised the commotion was coming from Czech soldiers further up the track, crammed into goods wagons, with doors bolted on the outside.

He turned to the Czech officer marching beside him. "Good God, Captain, they're treating us like prisoners of war."

"Stay with the men, Sergeant, I shall find out what's going on here." The captain, an army regular, pushed through the line of Russian soldiers to speak to their officer standing behind them. Pavel saw the Russian officer draw his revolver, point it at the captain and scream an instruction to him. The captain returned to the line next to Pavel.

"Keep the men moving, Sergeant, and make sure they do as they are told. You're right. These Russians are making no distinction between us or any other Austrian troops. All they see is our uniforms."

The doors of the next empty wagon were opened and prodding bayonets encouraged the men in front of Pavel to climb aboard. The men behind had to break step as a log-jam developed and they could only shuffle forward.

"Stop! Everybody wait a moment. This is not right," Pavel heard himself shouting.

The shuffling stopped and the men in front turned to see where the protest was coming from.

"We are not prisoners of war, men," cried Pavel. "This is not right."

He turned to face the line of Russian soldiers who stood less than two metres from him, with rifles at their hips and bayonets pointing towards him. He held out his arms to show his raised voice contained no threat.

"We are not Austrians, my friends. We are Czechs. Understand? *Český!* We are your Slav brothers. This is not our uniform."

He threw down his kitbag and tore at the buttons of his tunic. He hurled the tunic onto the stones by the track, and kicked it towards the Russian soldiers. The Czech soldiers started to cheer as Pavel took off his boots and threw them down too. Off came his soldier's breeches as the Czechs around him and on the train shouted and whistled encouragement.

Pavel stood in his woollen vest and long-johns. He stepped forward and spat on the Austrian uniform at his feet. Now some of the Russian soldiers were laughing too, as Pavel kicked the discarded clothes along the track.

"Zkurvený Rakušáci! Fuck the Austrians!" someone shouted from behind him, and another loud cheer went up and several more Czech soldiers started to tear off their tunics.

There was a loud crack and smoke drifted up behind the Russian soldiers. Everyone fell silent as a tall figure in a brown greatcoat and a brown cap with red officer's band strode through the ranks of his men with a revolver in his hand. He shouted an order and, when no one responded, he screamed it at the top of his voice.

"*Odentyes! Odentyes!*"

"Men, the Russian officer is insisting you keep your uniforms on," the Czech captain said calmly. "He would like you to pick up your tunics."

When no one moved, the Russian officer took two steps forward and raised the revolver to the side of Pavel's head.

"*Odentyes ili zastrelyu yevo!*" screamed the officer.

"If you don't put your tunics back on, men, he says he will shoot Sergeant Kovařík," the captain said more urgently. "Do as he says."

"It's alright, Captain. Getting rid of those Austrian rags is a good thing to die for," Pavel called to him.

"No, Kovařík. Don't be a fool. Put your tunics back on, men."

The Czechs carried out their captain's order, while the Russian officer kept his revolver pressed against Pavel's head. A Russian soldier was ordered to collect Pavel's clothes and put them in a pile at his feet.

"*Vozmi odezhdu i syad v poezd!*"

"He wants you to pick up your things and get on the train, Kovařík," said the captain.

Pavel slowly turned his face towards the Russian until the barrel of the gun came to rest in the middle of his forehead. He looked into the Russian's eyes.

"*Nyet,*" he said.

The Russian cocked the trigger. Pavel looked up. A single cloud drifted across the pale-blue sky. He thought of his parents and his brothers. And he thought of Karolína. He hoped they would forgive him. He closed his eyes and waited. He heard a voice.

"No, Sergeant, no! We won't let you do it."

Pavel opened his eyes and looked down. He saw Štefan Sedláček at his feet, scrambling to pick up the discarded uniform. Tears ran down Sedláček's cheeks.

"You must not leave us here, Sergeant. You promised us you would get us home."

"I can't, Štefan."

"Yes! Yes, you can, Sergeant." And Sedláček took Pavel's hand and led him away from the Russian officer. The Russian kicked Sedláček as he walked by and laughed at the sight of a grown man in his underwear being led by a tearful boy.

Pavel looked into the faces of the Russian soldiers as he walked along their line towards the open doors of the wagon. They jeered and laughed too as he passed them.

"So these are our Slav brothers, Štefan," he said, "to whom we Czechs have turned for centuries to be our saviours from the Germans. This is a lesson we must never forget."

The men remained locked in the wagons as the train took them east. Any fear they may have felt about their uncertain futures was banished by their anger at the Russian betrayal. And any sense of despair was turned to defiance as their camaraderie grew, fuelled in part by the retelling of Sergeant Kovařík's performance, both heroic and comic, at the goods yard in Brody.

The men shared what little food they had and the water some had collected from the River Styr. In one corner of Pavel's wagon soldiers used bayonets to dig out a hole in the hardwood planking to fashion a latrine. And together they all reached agreement on how best to seat fifty men in a space measuring only nine metres by three, once a generous allowance had been made to isolate the sanitation area.

After ten hours, at two in the morning, the train stopped, and the captain peered through a gap between the doors.

"We are in Kharkov, men," he announced. "I know Kharkov. It's a big city. Maybe the Russians are going to stick to their promises after all."

The Russian officers had promised much on the evening of the Sunday truce, desperate as they were for the Czechs to abandon their Austrian trenches. The men would be given three choices if they came over to the Russian side. They could put on Russian uniforms and fight the Austrians, or they could choose to work in a factory or on a farm. Most intended to fight.

"There are plenty of factories in Kharkov, men," said the captain, "and the whole area is surrounded by wheat fields and farms."

"What about those of us who want to fight the Austrians, sir?" someone asked.

"Well, I'm sure they must have army barracks here too. Maybe the Russians are going to do the right thing by us after all."

But within a minute of the train stopping, Russian troops lined the platform facing the wagons, and stood once again with rifles at their hips and bayonets pointing at the train. When the men in the cattle trucks realised they were not going to be allowed to get out, and they were to receive none of the food and water being taken on board, nine hundred pairs of feet and fists began to stamp and pound on the wooden floors and sides of the wagons. Gradually the men found a common rhythm, creating the sound of ancient warriors beating swords against their shields prior to battle. Then a chant began in unison with the beating.

"Ruský mizerové! Zkurvený zbabélci!"
"Ruský mizerové! Zkurvený zbabélci!"
"Russian bastards! Fucking cowards!"

Some of the noise escaped into the night, but most of it was trapped beneath the roof of the station and became a physical presence around the Russian soldiers on the platform. They looked at one another with panic on their faces, staring at the rattling bolts which stood between them and the fury that was on the train.

The tall Russian officer, who had been so mocking in the goods yard at Brody, strode up and down with his pistol in his hand, shouting at his men to stand firm. He turned to face the train and on his order his men raised their rifles to their shoulders. He fired three shots from his revolver into the air and at last the noise of the warriors stopped. But for the Russian officer it was replaced by something far worse. Laughter. The Czechs laughed and whistled at his puny response and a new chant began.

"Střílejte! Střílejte! Střílejte!"
"Shoot! Shoot! Shoot!"

The Russian officer waved frantically to his men to get back on the train. They lowered their weapons and scurried away from the barrage coming at them from the wagons. The Russian waved frantically again, this time towards the front of the train in an urgent forward motion. The whistle blew, the train jolted, and a huge cheer went up. Only when they reached open country did the cheering stop.

As the euphoria of their victory subsided, Pavel and the others drifted into sleep. When Pavel awoke, the captain informed him the train had passed through Kursk.

"We're heading north, Sergeant. It looks likely they're taking us to Moscow."

Chapter Five

May 10th, 1917

"The Minister will see you now, Professor Masaryk. May I take your hat and coat?"

Tomáš Masaryk took his watch from his waistcoat pocket and studied it long enough to demonstrate that the time he had been kept waiting had become an issue to him. The floor and the walls of the Russian Ministry of War in Petrograd were lined with marble, and even in May they still held the cold.

"I understand how busy Minister Kerensky must be in these difficult times," he said, and he handed the young functionary his thick black overcoat and grey trilby hat.

"How would you like me to announce you to the Minister, Professor?" asked the young man.

"Sir, one day soon you will have no need to put that question to me. I am the President of the Czecho-Slovak National Council. The representative of a proud nation in waiting. Please announce me as such."

"I see. Thankyou, Professor. Please come with me."

Masaryk felt the stiffness in his legs as he followed the young man down the long corridor. He removed his pince-nez spectacles and massaged the bridge of his nose before replacing them. He smoothed the long white moustache which extended into his trimmed white beard and pulled back his aching shoulders. He had turned 67 in March and there were times recently when he had begun to feel the weight of those years. But that weight was as nothing compared to the burden of responsibility he had taken upon himself over the past two and a half years of war.

They stopped in front of a pair of double doors which extended four metres upwards between two marble columns. The two soldiers standing guard on either side of the columns came to attention. The young man knocked, the doors were opened, and Masaryk was led across another hallway into a large circular room where a small figure sat behind a desk in front of a window overlooking the River Neva. The functionary coughed.

"Professor Masaryk, President of the Czecho-Slovak National Council, Minister," he announced.

Alexander Kerensky rose from his desk, approached Masaryk and reached out his hand.

"Professor Masaryk. What a pleasure it is to meet you finally."

Masaryk knew prior to the meeting that Kerensky was only 36 years of age, but it still came as a shock to see such a youthful figure in a position of such power. Only the dark rings beneath Kerensky's eyes and the premature flecks of grey in his hair betrayed the impossible nature of the job he had been asked to do. Masaryk knew such strain often made men indecisive, and understood his task would not be an easy one.

"The pleasure and honour are mine, Minister," he said. "I am very grateful that you should see me so soon into your new appointment."

Kerensky ushered Masaryk to a chair covered in red velvet next to a low table dominated by an enamelled, silver samovar. Kerensky sat facing him. The functionary filled two cups with tea and then sat behind Masaryk with a pen and notepad.

"I understand, Professor, that you spent the early years of the war with our allies in England and France," Kerensky said, passing Masaryk his tea.

"Yes, that is correct, Minister. Thankyou. As one of the opponents of Austria's alignment with Germany in this war I was forced to flee my homeland in 1914 and settle in Switzerland."

"But you spent the whole of 1915 in England."

"Yes. And last year in France. But my task, my duty, since the war began has remained constant, Minister. And it is the fulfilment of that duty that has compelled me to seek this meeting with you today."

"And how would you define that duty, Professor?"

"To persuade, to convince the major Allied Powers that a key aim of this war must be the complete disintegration of the Austro-Hungarian Empire, and at war's end the establishment of a free Czecho-Slovak state."

"And what response have you received from our British and French allies?"

"I am pleased to say, Minister, that France, England and now our new ally, the United States, have all agreed to recognise the Czecho-Slovak National Council as the true representatives of the Czech and Slovak people currently living within the boundaries of the Hapsburg Empire. And my hope, indeed my expectation is, Minister Kerensky, that our Russian Slav brothers will do the same."

"And do you speak with the consent of the Slovak people too, Professor?"

"As I am sure you are aware, the Vice-President of the Council is General Štefanik who represents the Slovak people. I speak with his consent."

"I understand Štefanik has recently been appointed a general in the French army."

"Yes, in the air arm, Minister. General Štefanik is a fêted hero in France. It was he who arranged the meeting with the French President, Monsieur Briand, which has proved so constructive."

"I see."

Kerensky leaned forward to squeeze lemon into his tea and then sat back again to study his visitor.

"And what form of government would you intend for your new Czecho-Slovak state, Professor?" he asked.

"From what I know of you from reading your speeches, Minister Kerensky, I aspire to the same form of government for my people as do you for your own. You supported the overthrow of the Romanov dynasty as I support the overthrow of the Hapsburgs. You in the Duma, and I in the Austrian Assembly, have always spoken out for universal suffrage in a liberal democracy and a social programme which protects the peasantry and the industrial workers. If you will allow me to say so, I see us as natural allies."

"I would like to believe we are, Professor. But my fear is that if the war situation worsens any further, neither you nor I shall see what we want for our people. You know, I suppose, that Lenin and his Bolsheviks want to sue for peace?"

"Yes, I have heard that."

Kerensky gestured to the young functionary seated behind Masaryk to put down his pen. He leaned forward and spoke more softly.

"I am convinced, Professor, that Lenin and Trotsky are in the pay of the Germans. If they get the chance, the Bolsheviks will betray the Russian people no less than the Romanovs have done. But I swear that my Provisional Government will never surrender to the Germans."

Masaryk sat upright in his chair, slowly removed his pince-nez, and gave Kerensky the same look he once gave to his students at the Charles University when convinced he was revealing an important truth.

"Minister," he said, "up to this point in our conversation I have only asked for your support with the national aspirations of my people. But I have also come here to offer you help."

"I am listening, Professor Masaryk."

"As you know, Minister, all Czech and Slovak men of conscription age living under the Hapsburg yoke have been forced to join the Austrian or Hungarian armies. But as I am sure you realise, our real fight is against the Germans and Austrians, not against our Slav brothers. Czechs living in England, France, Italy and Canada in 1914 signed up with their home armies in their thousands. And nearly 100,000 Czechs and Slovaks who lived in Russia at the outbreak of war now serve in your army. But there are additional Czecho-Slovaks in Russia who would willingly fight with their Russian brothers, Minister, if they were given the chance."

"I take it you mean prisoners of war?"

"Yes, but I wonder if it is justified to speak of these men as prisoners of war, when so many willingly and knowingly surrendered rather than fight against their Russian brothers. Give these men a chance, Minister, and they will fight for you as bravely as any Russian soldier."

"We do have some former Czech prisoners of war already under arms, Professor."

"You have two rifle regiments consisting of 7,300 men. But I am suggesting you allow us to form new units from the prison camps. By the autumn we can have 40,000 under arms. By 1918 it could be 80,000. These are good Czecho-Slovak soldiers, Minister. They will fight for you."

"And why do you offer this, Professor?"

"Because Czechs and Slovaks should be allowed to fight for their own country. Because with a Czecho-Slovak army we can create our own country."

"You want control of such an army on Russian soil?"

"No, Minister, they would fight as directed by Russian High Command under the Supreme War Council of the Allies. But it would be a Czecho-Slovak army with its own officers and its own uniform."

"And what do you think you would gain from this, Professor?"

"A national army. A revived national identity. And at war's end a seat with you at the victors' table."

Kerensky sat back and stared at Masaryk. The two men held one another's gaze as each sought to read the other's thoughts.

"I shall shortly be going to America," said Masaryk. He placed his cup on the table. "There are one-and-a half million Czechs and Slovaks in America, Minister. After Prague the city with the highest population of Czechs in the world is Chicago. There is huge support there for our cause of independence. American troops will soon be arriving to fight in Europe, and then the war will be won. And my Czecho-Slovak Legion might just keep Mother Russia in the war long enough for her to preserve her seat at the victors' table."

"Your argument is very persuasive, Professor. And, of course, in principle I fully support the Czech and Slovak peoples' claim to self-determination. But we Russians must be careful not to encourage similar ideas amongst our own Ukrainian, Polish and Finnish citizens. There is a very difficult balance to be struck here."

"I understand that, Minister. But a German victory in this war will take all those decisions out of our hands. Surely the first priority must be *our* combined victory against the Central Powers."

Kerensky said nothing.

"And, of course, Minister, a Russian victory now would deal a death blow to Lenin and Trotsky and their peace overtures."

Kerensky's eyes had not left Masaryk as he spoke. He stood up and smiled.

"Professor Masaryk. Mr President," he said, offering his hand, "I pride myself on being a man who puts action before protracted analysis. I believe we can help one another."

Chapter Six

May 23rd, 1917

"I think Sedláček's fever is getting worse, Sergeant. Do you think it's the typhus?"

"Has he been complaining about a headache or pain in his legs?"

"He was about an hour ago. The way he was talking I think he took me for his mother."

Pavel lit a match and held it in front of Štefan Sedláček's eyes. The boy moaned and turned his head away as if he found the light painful. Pavel rolled up the boy's trouser legs. His shins and calves were covered in a dull red rash.

"Damn, damn," Pavel said under his breath. He had already nursed Vaněk and Kopeský through the disease, but they were never as bad as this. Štefan had to live. It was the promise Pavel had made to himself as he knelt in the mud with Skála. He would tolerate any death from then on, as long as the boys given into his care lived.

"I keep telling you all not to scratch the bites, Musil. Why in the name of Christ will you not listen to me?"

"They drive you mad, Sergeant. It's so difficult not to."

"Are you crazy, Musil? When you scratch you rub the lice shit into the bite, and it's the shit which brings on the typhus. How many times do I have to tell you?"

"But I haven't had it, Sergeant. I've listened to you. I don't scratch."

Pavel placed his hand on Milan Musil's shoulder.

"I know, son, good for you. Stay with Štefan. Keep bathing his forehead. And try to get him to drink more water."

Pavel left the hut and stepped onto one of the log walkways laid down to stop men sinking into the mud. He stood for a moment and looked out at the network of walkways which criss-crossed the camp; some connecting the forty accommodation huts and others leading to the kitchens and the infirmary. Neither the walkways nor the buildings had existed when they arrived on the train from Brody over a year before.

The train had not taken the men to Moscow as their captain supposed it would. The journey ended instead 480 kilometres to the south-east of the city in the town of Tambov.

"Tambov. That's Old Russian," the captain informed them when they arrived at the station. "I think it means 'wetland'."

Never was a name more appropriately chosen, thought Pavel.

The rain was falling on the day they arrived in April 1916, and it had fallen on most days during the thirteen months since.

The men had been made to wait overnight in their wagons at the station in Tambov. The rain found its way through the roof planking onto the straw, through their clothes and into their flesh. In the morning the Russians had begun to empty the wagons one by one and the men were led under armed guard through the town.

Tambov was a depressing place. The march took the men down street after street of chaotic dwellings, with no sign of people socialising or children playing. At the end of every second or third street they passed a factory alive with movement and noise. Eventually they reached an arched gateway which took them out of the town past a military barracks; a reminder, Pavel learned later, of the days when Tambov had been a fortress town, built as protection against Tartar raids on the state of Moscow.

A further hour's march beyond Tambov brought them to a stockade standing in open countryside next to a wood of fir and silver-birch trees. They entered the stockade through crude wooden gates constructed of logs and barbed wire. The perimeter was formed by more barbed wire strung between high wooden stakes, and at each corner and halfway along each side were watchtowers manned by guards with heavy Maxim Sokolov machine guns.

The Russians had developed a grudging respect for the Czech soldiers after their show of strength and solidarity at the station in Kharkov. They moved only fifty men at a time from Tambov station to the stockade, escorted by at least an equal number of Russian soldiers, walking as always with fixed bayonets. It took nearly 48 hours to herd all 1,800 men of the old 29th Austrian Rifle Regiment from the two trains into their final place of imprisonment, and the initial reaction of each group as they arrived was the same.

How in God's name could they survive on such exposed ground with no food or shelter?

Pavel had asked the same question, and the answer, when it came, further strengthened his confidence in the ingenuity of his people.

Within days of their arrival he watched 1,800 cold, wet and hungry men organised by their officers into a workforce whose skills would have enriched any good-sized town. Beneath the soldiers' uniforms had been concealed carpenters, plumbers, blacksmiths, tailors and coopers. There were foresters who knew how best to forage from the woods, and farmers who could husband animals and coax food from a soil which was used to yielding only coarse, wet grass. And even men who thought they had no skills at all to offer were made to understand that the strength in their bodies, and a willingness to work for the common good, were contribution enough.

The Russians left 80 men to guard the Czechs. The guards were housed in brick-built barracks outside the stockade, and their food arrived three times a week from Tambov in horse-drawn carts. At first the Russians allowed only 30 prisoners at a time into the woods to cut trees and forage, but soon the guards began to covet the food and goods the Czechs were producing, and gradually more and more were allowed out to work. A barter system developed and soon the Czechs were able to obtain proper bedding, better cooking equipment and most other items necessary for a reasonable level of existence.

Then the winter came. The men had prepared for the cold. Food and wood were stockpiled, and shelter was provided for the cattle and sheep they bartered from the Russians. But the cold brought a problem few had foreseen and none had wanted to dwell upon. Prison fever. Typhus.

During the good weather the men were able to stay mostly free of the lice which infected them, through boiling their clothes and keeping themselves clean. But however much they washed, some of the eggs survived, and in the cosy warmth of the cramped huts in winter the nits hatched out. Then the scratching started, followed by the cough, the chill and the fever. By April 1917 nearly 600 of the Czech soldiers who had arrived at the camp 12 months before were dead.

When he reached the infirmary Pavel paused at the door and looked up. It had stopped raining and the sun was burning its way through the thinning cloud. To his left he saw a party of men forming up ready for outside work. The men all looked the same now. Only their different heights set them apart. They were all thin, and all had shaved their heads and faces clean, in order to give the nits as little as possible to cling to.

Pavel opened the door. In front of him twenty beds extended down each side of the hut. All of them were full, but the occupants of the two nearest the door had blankets drawn up over their faces. A medical orderly approached.

"*Dobrý den, Pavel,*" he said.

"*Dobrý den, Erik.* Two more in the night?"

"I'm afraid so, but God willing I think we are coming to the end."

28

"I'm sorry, Erik, but I have one more for you from Hut 8. Štefan Sedláček."

"He's one of your lads, isn't he?"

"He's one of the six of my section I brought out of Galicia with me. He's no older than the kids I used to teach."

"How bad is he?"

"The worst I've seen. He's a music student, you know. From Terezín."

"Try not to worry, Pavel. I'll arrange for him to be brought over now. But wait there a moment, will you? Something very strange has happened. I want your opinion about it."

Within a minute Sergeant Erik Novák was back. Two stretcher bearers acknowledged Pavel as they passed him on their way out.

"Follow me, Pavel, will you?" said Erik. "I want you to see something."

He led him to a storeroom at the far end of the infirmary. The usually empty shelves were now full of cardboard boxes and packages wrapped in brown greaseproof paper.

"Where in God's name did you get all this?" Pavel asked.

"It arrived from Tambov early this morning. Look. There's carbolic soap, iodine, chloroform. There are even bandages, lint and shell dressings. Boxes of the stuff. It's as if we were a front-line regiment again."

"Did you have to barter for any of this?"

"Not a thing. It just arrived out of nowhere."

"I don't understand, Erik."

"But that's not all, Pavel. A second load went to the kitchens. Sugar, flour, powdered eggs and milk, and tins and tins of beef from England. Slavik over there says it was all totally unexpected. What do you make of it?"

"And it all came from the Russians?"

"Who else?"

"I don't know, Erik, but if it did come from them, you can be damned sure they'll want some kind of payment from us in return."

The next morning work was suspended, except for a dozen unlucky carpenters who were busy erecting a raised podium, complete with steps and handrails, on the parade ground. The rest of the men stood outside their huts in small groups, smoking and kicking the drying mud from their boots, and speculating about what such a sudden break in their routine could mean. Was the war over? Were they going home? Who were the victors?

It was a beautiful morning and the men were ordered to assemble on the parade ground in the centre of the compound at a quarter to eleven. As the sun rose higher, it promised to be the hottest day of the year so far, more like mid summer than late May, and there was a feeling of excitement and expectation in the air that no one had experienced since the day of the Easter truce over thirteen months before.

At ten forty-five the men were called to the parade ground. Just before eleven they were stood to attention in lines of ten, six deep, in a crescent formation before the podium. At exactly eleven o'clock a group of six men emerged from the accommodation hut of the regimental commander, Lieutenant-Colonel Navrátil, and made their way along a freshly laid walkway of logs towards the newly built podium. In front of the group a soldier wearing an unfamiliar uniform carried a large flag supported in a leather pouch in a heavy belt around his waist. The top half of the flag was white, the bottom half red, and in the middle was a crown above a crescent of twigs and linden leaves.

Pavel's mouth fell open as he looked upon the old battle flag of the Czech kings. Slowly, as the flag came further into view, he recognised what had been added to it. In the four corners were the emblems of Bohemia, Moravia, Slovakia and Silesia, and in the middle the ancient crown of King Wenceslas.

He looked more closely at the six men making their way to the podium. Five of them were familiar enough. The regimental commander, his adjutant, and the three most senior regimental captains. But the elderly man in civilian clothes walking next to Colonel Navrátil looked familiar too. But it could not be him. Not here, not in Russia, not in this God-forsaken place.

The small group climbed the podium steps. The flag bearer stood in the far corner at the back. The three captains and the adjutant took up position against the back rail behind the civilian who sat in one of the two chairs. He had removed his trilby hat, revealing short white hair which matched his long white moustache and trimmed beard.

Lieutenant-Colonel Navrátil approached the front of the podium and stood erect with his arms at his side. He still wore the field-grey uniform of the Austrian army, but like every soldier he had removed all Austrian insignia from it. He slowly surveyed his men from left to right and back again. Then he spoke in a clear, booming voice.

"*Nazdar!*"

"*Nazdar, plukovniku!*" replied 1,200 men in unison.

"Stand at ease, men. And move in. I want you all to be able to hear what will be said here today.

"But keep silence in the ranks."

The men moved forward without speaking, and without breaking formation. Navrátil turned his gaze slowly to left and right as he spoke.

"Fellow soldiers, this is a good day. And God knows we are due some good days after the hardships we suffered this winter. We have been tested here in this terrible place, men, as severely as in any battle we might have fought together. We have lost many brave comrades. But *you* are still here. And you now know what every soldier must learn. That to get through he must do one thing above all else – endure. And endure we have. And endure we shall! Together! Is that right, men?"

A cheer went up amongst the men. Its intensity surprised even them. Navrátil allowed the cheering to continue for a short time before silencing his men with a slow sweep of his arm.

"I can sense you are ready for a fight. Good! Now I want you to meet someone who will explain why you have all been called together here. And, God willing, you will be one of those amongst us who will live to tell your children and your grandchildren what you learned here today."

Navrátil turned and saluted the elderly gentleman who was already on his feet approaching the front of the podium. He still had on his black overcoat, but he had unbuttoned it, revealing a dark-grey three-piece suit, dark tie and a white shirt with a winged collar.

Although a tall man he was a slighter figure than Navrátil and, when he reached the front of the podium, he placed his left hand on the rail, as if to steady himself. With the other he gripped the lapel of his overcoat. As he spoke, he looked straight ahead.

"Fellow Czechs. Fellow Slovaks. My fellow countrymen. It is an honour to address you here today. My name is Tomáš Masaryk. Like you I find myself in exile, banished from my homeland and separated from the people I love."

There was complete silence. Masaryk hardly seemed to be raising his voice, but his words rang clear and hung in the air.

"But you have suffered an injustice far greater than my own. You have acted through your conscience as honourable Slavs. You have risked everything to fight against the forces which oppress our people, and you have been betrayed. You have been treated as prisoners of war and banished to this dreadful place.

"But, fellow countrymen, there is something you could not know whilst you have languished here, and I can tell you it now, as I have told thousands of other Czech and Slovak soldiers in camps just like this. You were never forgotten or abandoned by your people, and at last the hour of your liberation has arrived."

Hundreds of voices were raised, and immediately suppressed by the protests of men desperate to hear more.

"I am able to tell you that for the first time in three hundred years the Czech and Slovak people now have their own representative body, which is able to negotiate with foreign governments on their behalf. I have the honour to be the President of the Czecho-Slovak National Council, which three weeks ago met with representatives of the Russian Provisional Government to agree the release of all Czech and Slovak prisoners of war, and the immediate creation from their number of a Czecho-Slovak National Army."

This time no protests could stop the shouting and cheering which burst forth. The officers on the parade ground looked anxiously towards the podium for direction, and eventually the Colonel stepped forward to quieten the troops. Masaryk rubbed his eyes, replaced his pince-nez and addressed the men once more.

"It is right that you should celebrate this wonderful news, my fellow countrymen. We Czechs and Slovaks have been offered a great opportunity here to show the world the full extent of the contribution we can make to the Allied cause. Behind me you see the uniform of the new Czecho-Slovak Legion, and the standard of the new Czecho-Slovak Army. And any of you who wish to volunteer to join the Legion and fight the Germans and Austro-Hungarians will be issued with these uniforms very soon."

Another huge cheer went up from the troops and Masaryk turned to Navrátil. Both men smiled broadly. Masaryk raised his arms and then lowered them slowly to signal that he had more to say.

"Yes, we have a great opportunity, men, but I must also advise caution. You and I have everything to win and everything to lose. There can be no compromise. If we Czechs and Slovaks fight in sufficient numbers for the Allied cause and the Allies win, you and I will return one day to an independent Czecho-Slovak nation. The prize for victory will be statehood. Not since 1621, since the Battle of White Mountain, when we lost our sovereignty to the Hapsburgs at the gates of Prague, has there been a more momentous battle than the one we now face. For if we lose, my fellow countrymen, if we lose the battle ahead, none of us will see our homes again."

The men stood in silence. Many bowed their heads.

"I know, my brothers, I know. I have offered you freedom, but only at a price. For how can we be truly free when we remain exiled from our homeland? When we cannot tell our loved ones about our circumstances, about where we are or even that we are still alive? We have much to bear. But we are very fortunate too. Never in history have men been given such a chance to win freedom for those they love, and the chance to create a new nation for them. Never have men been given more to fight for. Lift up your hearts, my fellow countrymen. The choice is to win or fall, and together we shall win. Let us vow, you and I, here and now, to meet again one day in a new Czecho-Slovakia!"

Chapter Seven

August 26th, 1917

Karolína watched Tomáš on the sand, engrossed in his new-found skill. He picked up two stones, using his thumbs and forefingers as pincers, and brought the objects together, fascinated by the sound they made. He looked up at his mother, eager that she should share in his discovery, and when she smiled back at him he held the stones out for her and picked up two more for himself. Now they could both play. "Bang, bang, bang," said his mother, following his lead, and he watched her laugh. He crawled over to her, grasped her leg and levered himself to his feet.

She took him onto her lap and under the shade of her cream, wide-brimmed hat they looked out together over the river. Children played in the shallows off the sandbank, and a few rowing boats, hired from the ferrymen, drifted in the weak current where the River Ohře made its long, lazy turn back on itself at the village of Skalka.

Karolína rested her face gently on Tomáš's head and breathed in the sweet scent of his hair, soft and soothing like his father's. She closed her eyes and concentrated on the pure pleasure of it. It was a perfect summer's day, of the kind that allowed her to forget for brief moments that Pavel was gone.

Karolína let out a deep sigh and Tomáš turned and looked up at her. She kissed his head. "It's alright, my darling. Máma's just a little hungry, that's all. Shall we have something to eat while we wait for our friends?" She lay down a towel and put out the food she and her parents had collected from the forest. "Nature's grocery," her father called it. "Better than any shop." It was just as well, thought Karolina, since the shops in Cheb had nothing in them anyway.

There was a paste of ground hazel and beech nuts, sweetened with a little honey, which she fed to Tomáš on a spoon. And there was bread she had baked using horse-chestnut flour and ground clover meal, and jam made from the fruit of the cherry tree.

"I'm sorry, my precious, that I can't give you better things to eat," she said, as Tomáš drank the blackcurrant juice made by his grandfather from fruit which, under different circumstances, would have found its way into the slivovitz barrel.

Karolína held Tomáš in her lap as he drank, and looked out again over the river. How good it would be to glance casually at all this and imagine everything was normal. But she insisted on facing the truth, and the truth was that contrary to the propaganda coming out of Vienna there was hardly any normality left in Bohemia at all.

Three years of war had affected every part of people's lives. Their obsession with food, or rather the lack of it, the constant fear they felt for their menfolk at the front, and the lack of any information about what the future might hold, had eaten away at people's spirit. Without the resilience of young children and their unstoppable determination to play, Karolína doubted whether there would be any normality left in anyone's life.

She watched the young boys and old men with their fishing poles lined up further along the river bank. That at least appeared normal enough; only there must have been thirty or forty of them standing shoulder to shoulder, each one clearly undernourished, dressed in torn or patched clothes and wearing shoes repaired with wooden soles. And not one man or boy appeared to be having any luck, although she and her father had caught trout and bream easily enough from the same spot when she was a child.

"I think the fish must be angry with us, Tomáš," she said.

Tomáš looked up at her and smiled. Karolína stroked his back, as she continued to watch the old men and boys on the river bank. "No food, my Tomášek, no fish... no young men..."

The absence of young men, and of the hopes invested in them, was the worst shortage of all. Leave from the front had stopped months ago, and the only men below the age of 40 to be seen anywhere now were those in the light-blue uniform with the red collars and cuffs - the uniform of the wounded. It was a man in such a uniform she was waiting for now, and in the moment she turned away from the anglers to look back towards the village she saw him.

"Ernst, Esther, over here," she called out in German.

Esther Neumann waved as she caught sight of her dearest friend, and she steered her large baby carriage down the slipway where the rowing boats were tethered. Ernst Neumann followed a few paces behind. Karolína saw the empty left sleeve of his tunic, pinned back neatly on to his left shoulder and ironed at the fold. In his right hand he held a white handkerchief pressed to his mouth. Halfway down the slipway they stopped.

Karolína stood up slowly with Tomáš in her arms. She was surprised how weary she felt, and how unmoved she was at the sight of Ernst struggling to help his wife manoeuvre the heavy carriage down on to the beach.

A group of young boys rushed over to help the injured hero who wore the Gold Bravery Medal. Karolína saw Ernst nodding at them in thanks, then waving them away. With great effort he pulled the carriage backwards along the sand with his right arm, while little Anna Neumann sat up under her white bonnet, enjoying all the excitement around her. Four-year-old Otto ran ahead to his 'Auntie' Kája and flung his arms around her legs.

"Kája, Tomáš, where have you two been hiding?" said Esther, as she approached. "You haven't been to see me for nearly two weeks."

"Oh, I thought it best to let Ernst have you to himself for a while." The two friends embraced. "Six months is a long time for a man to be away from his family."

Karolína looked past Esther to where Ernst stood. His eyes were fixed on the sand. The handkerchief still hid the fine, gentle features of his handsome face.

"How are you, Ernst?" she said. "It's so wonderful to see you."

Ernst looked up for the first time and removed the handkerchief from the side of his face. Karolína fought not to react.

The flesh of Ernst's left cheek had been ripped away, and in order to avoid infection the field surgeon had pulled the skin of his cheekbone and the skin of his jaw together, and with crude stitching had closed the wound. The corner of his left eye was stretched down his cheek pulling the lid halfway over the eyeball, and the corner of his mouth was pulled up, leaving teeth and gums exposed.

Karolína stepped forward with Tomáš in her arms. Please God, don't let Tomáš flinch or cry, she thought, as she leaned forward to kiss Ernst on his right cheek.

"I'm fine, Kája," Ernst said. His mangled voice came from the right side of his mouth and, as he spoke, he paused to suck back the saliva which threatened to flow over his cruelly misshapen bottom lip. "And what a big boy... you've become... Master Tomáš."

Tomáš stared at this strange man, unsure of what to make of him. He reached out his hand, grabbed Ernst's nose and chuckled, refusing to let go.

"You can't... have that, young Tomášek," said Ernst. "It's the only thing... on my face... that's still where it's meant to be."

The friends sat down on the sand on a large rug Esther had brought with her. All except Otto, who could not wait to run to the water's edge to play.

"Stay close by, where I can see you," his mother called after him.

Tomáš and Anna sat under a large parasol provided by Esther, and were drawn immediately to Anna's toys.

"They play well together.., don't they?" remarked Ernst, pausing every few seconds to suck saliva back through his teeth.

"They're like an old married couple, those two," said Esther, laughing. "Whenever they're together they don't bother with anyone else, do they, Kája?"

"They're certainly very close."

"Tomáš has always been the same with Anna," continued Esther. "As soon as he sees her, he won't leave her side. He's always passing her things, wanting to entertain her. It's true, isn't it, Kája? The only time you see Tomáš cry is when you take him away from Anna."

"Yes, it is true."

"They're... the same age, aren't they?" asked Ernst.

"Tomáš is exactly two weeks older than your Anna," said Karolína.

"I understand Pavel has... never seen little Tomáš."

"Pavel never knew he had a son, Ernst."

"Of course. I'm sorry... Esther tells me you still have... no news."

"Nothing."

"And you have tried... all official channels?"

"Táta and I have been to the Red Cross in Prague. And we wrote to the War Ministry in Vienna. But no one will tell us anything. We don't even know where he was sent or when and how he died."

"I see."

Ernst hesitated for a moment, then placed his right hand on the ground, leaning towards Karolína. He looked around before he spoke.

"You know, Kája, I have wanted to talk to you... about Pavel... for some time. In the military you hear things... rumours, that sort of thing... I shouldn't add to them... but I'm sure I heard the 29th Infantry... were sent north-east... to Galicia."

Karolína turned her head sharply to face him.

"Galicia? Did you say 'Galicia'?" She put her hand to her face and groaned. "Please, no."

"What's the matter, Kája? What have I said?"

"That means Pavel *was* made to fight the Russians. My God, Ernst, you know how he would have hated that."

Ernst quickly sat up again.

"I'm sure he knew he was... protecting... the people he loved, Kája."

"Oh, Ernst, how can you say that? You were Pavel's friend. You know how much he admired Russia. He would have hated having to fight them. He was a Czech."

"I know, and he was right... to be proud of that... but in this war we are all Austrian citizens first, Kája... That is our common bond... In war it's the duty of us all... to stand together... behind our emperor."

Karolína breathed in deeply and let out a long sigh.

"Dear Ernst, I'm sorry to say this, but you are hopelessly out of touch with how Czech people are feeling."

"I understand how tired... people are of the war, Kája... Of course I do."

"It's more than that for us, Ernst. We Czechs are not just tired of the war."

"What then?"

"We are tired of Austria trying to force itself on us. Pavel used to have a word for it..."

"Germanisation?" Ernst offered.

"Yes. 'They're germanising us.' That's what he used to say."

"I remember."

"At least this war has done one thing for us. It has made us remember who we are. It has made us realise, if we're going to sacrifice so much, it should be for something we believe in."

Ernst looked over to the two children playing on the rug. Anna was laughing as Tomáš banged two stones together and put them on his head.

"Surely we're all fighting... for the same thing, aren't we, Kája?" Ernst said, nodding towards the two infants. "For our loved ones... for Otto and Anna, and Tomáš... to keep them safe. Do you want the Russians in Prague... or the Serbs or Italians?"

"No, I don't. But I don't want Germans or Austrians there either, at least not as our rulers. Prague is a Czech city, Ernst. Its history, its culture is Czech."

"Of course it is."

"But our people have to speak German. Our poets have to write in German. And now we have to fight for the Germans, because we are told we must. It's time we Czechs took control of our own lives."

Ernst looked down as she spoke and shook his head slowly. He wiped his mouth.

"My goodness, Kája... how much you sound like Pavel... I've heard this from him... so many times."

"That's the best thing you can say to me, Ernst. I want to speak like Pavel. I want to speak *for* him. I want his voice to be heard."

Karolína turned to Esther.

"Sometimes I panic when I think I can't remember his voice," she said. "When I close my eyes and I can't hear it."

Esther stood up, knelt between her husband and her friend and put her arms around them both.

"Come on, you two. Neither of you should upset yourself. Not on a beautiful day like this. You haven't seen one another for months, and you've both been through so much."

Ernst turned to her and smiled.

"And you mustn't exert yourself too much, Ernst," she said. "You're not fit enough yet."

She took the handkerchief from him and handed him another.

"No, I'm alright, my love... it's because we've all suffered so much... that we should say these things... We must listen to one another... Try to understand one another... Don't you think so, Kája?"

"I suppose I do, Ernst. But Esther is right. You must not upset yourself."

"That's better," said Esther. "You should both try to think of nice things to talk about. I'm going to sit with Anna and Tomáš. At least there's no war in their little world."

Ernst looked at Karolína, who seemed lost in thought as she stared out over the river.

"She's right, you know, Kája... Our time of innocence has passed... Things that seemed so important a short time ago... just do not seem to matter any more."

He held the fresh handkerchief to his mouth.

"Do you remember before the war... how animated Pavel and I used to get... about German and Czech culture?"

"Of course I do."

Ernst laughed gently to himself.

"Pavel used to complain... the only drama I put on at the theatre... was German drama. And that I favoured Mozart and Beethoven... and ignored Dvořák and Smetana... It all seems so meaningless now."

"He didn't object to your preferences, Ernst. Pavel objected because as the director of the theatre you were not allowed to put on performances in Czech."

"Yes, I know. But my point is... at this moment we cannot permit ourselves... the luxury of discussions like that... We have to put our differences behind us for now... fight the common enemy... It matters not whether we are Austrian German, Austrian Czech ... Slovak or Hungarian, does it? The only important thing now... is to stand together."

"I don't want to upset you, Ernst. I know how you have suffered. But you just don't understand."

"I understand, Kája, why we must all fight as one."

"I'm afraid you won't convince me, Ernst."

"Will you let me try... to explain it to you..? Why I was prepared to fight... and why I accept all that's happened to me."

"You can try. Only if you feel up to it."

Ernst wiped his mouth again and breathed deeply and rhythmically.

"I fought on the Isonzo River for one reason only... because the Italians wanted to cross it to invade my country... where my family was. They tried ten times to cross it... and ten times we have pushed them back... It has cost me my arm and part of my face... but my family is safe and that's all that matters to me... And they are safe from the Russians too... because of our soldiers in Galicia."

Karolína continued to look out over the river.

"Don't think the people... who fight the Austrians... are your friends, Kája... Russia is not innocent in all this. Serbia is not innocent... If we let the Italians through at the Isonzo, Serbia will join up with them... and steal Austria's only access to the sea in Dalmatia... All countries are greedy for territory, Kája... We are fighting only to hold on to what is ours... so that our families can live here in peace."

Esther had rejoined them as he spoke. She placed her hand on Ernst's back and gently smoothed his tunic. The three friends sat in silence, and Esther was sure, with her husband's words, some agreement had been found. Until Karolína spoke again.

"Ernst, I know you are a good man and a very brave one, but there is a simple truth you and all other Austrians do not seem able to grasp."

"And what is that?"

"That you are fighting to hold on to land that is not yours. I appreciate what you have been through for your family, Ernst, but you must understand there are millions of people living under the Hapsburgs who regard *you* as the occupiers and oppressors."

"Karolína, that's ridiculous... You are not oppressed... Or Esther or any of the children... They are not oppressed... You all have full rights as Austrian citizens."

"But that's the point, Ernst. I don't want to be an Austrian citizen. This is not Austria. This is Bohemia. Tomáš and I are Czechs. Esther is a Czech. Your children are half Czech. You cannot wish we were from Salzburg or Vienna, in order to make us real Austrians. You have to recognise who we are."

Ernst struggled to suck in more air through the side of his mouth.

"Well, Kája..., you shock me. I never thought... I would hear you say such things... And I would be very careful... if I were you... how loudly you say them."

"So my rights are not that full then?"

"Please stop, you two!" said Esther. "Can we not forget our problems for just one afternoon? Nothing either of you says will make any difference. Do we not already have enough problems in our lives?"

There was a child's cry from the water's edge.

"Oh no. Now it's Otto. This is too much."

"I'm sorry, Esther...," said Karolina.

Esther stood up and hurried across the sand to her son. Ernst and Karolína sat in uncomfortable silence, watching her.

"Poor Esther... She has a lot to put up with," said Ernst. "She never feels at ease... with this type of discussion."

"I'm sorry, Ernst. I know how she feels. You and Pavel used to drive me mad sometimes with your arguments. I think most of us women would prefer to centre our thoughts on our families, rather than all these other things."

"No, it's more than that with Esther, Kája... I think it has a lot to do with her parents... Like many Jewish children... Esther was brought up to avoid controversy... Any talk that's too political... leaves her uneasy."

Karolina saw Tomáš looking at her. He waited for her to smile at him before he went back to his game.

"Believe me, Ernst. I would happily stay out of it too, if Pavel were here. But I want my Tomáš to hear from me the things he would have heard from his father. I have sworn on Pavel's memory that I will fight for the same things he would have fought for. For Tomáš's sake."

"Well, Kája, if it is any comfort to you... it would appear that events... are at last moving in the direction... Pavel always wanted."

"In what way?"

"With our new emperor... Have you not heard... that he has reconvened parliament..? For the first time in three years..."

"Yes, I did."

"And that he has granted an amnesty... for 2,500 political agitators..? Mostly Czechs..."

"No, I know nothing about amnesties. We don't get all the news here."

"So you don't know he has issued a pardon... to that trouble-maker, Masaryk, even though... he has been openly negotiating with our enemies?"

"I've heard nothing about that."

"Masaryk has been stirring up trouble... for us all over Europe... I think Emperor Karl has been badly advised... in pardoning him... It shows weakness. Especially in time of war."

"Pavel studied under Masaryk at Prague University, Ernst. Did you know that? Pavel thought he was a great man."

"He may be in some respects.., but to behave in the way he is now... is nothing less... than traitorous. He has turned on us... when we are at our most vulnerable."

Ernst rested his right hand on the rug and turned to face her.

"Shall I tell you something, Kája?"

"If you like."

"At the Isonzo there were Czech soldiers... fighting with the Italians against us. Masaryk has been encouraging Czechs... to defect to our enemies."

"You mean Austria's enemies?"

"Kája. You must be very careful... what you say... These are dangerous times. What Masaryk is doing... could lose us the war... One Austrian soldier in seven is a Czech... Think what could happen... if they all turned against us... You must understand how serious this is."

Karolína shook her head.

"Kája, I'm going to tell you something now... because you are our friend... I wanted to tell you earlier... but Esther thought I shouldn't... But it's only a rumour. You must promise not to repeat it."

"What?"

"It concerns Pavel."

"It's alright, Ernst. I came to terms with losing Pavel some time ago."

"But that's the point, Kája... The reason no one has heard... anything about the 29th Infantry... is not because they are all dead... Pavel's Regiment defected en masse... to the Russians over a year ago... There is every chance... he is still alive."

Chapter Eight

June, 1917

"The choice is yours, men," said Colonel Navrátil, "and it's a free choice. You can stay here in Tambov and work in the factories or on the farms... or come back to Brody with me and fight the Austrians!"

A cheer erupted from the ranks of men standing on the parade ground.

"Things will be different for you this time, men, I promise you. You will be issued with temporary Russian uniforms for your journey back to Galicia. You will march without escort to the station. Food and water will be provided for your journey. And the wagons will remain unbolted. You will be treated at all times as Russia's free and respected allies. Your days as Austrian prisoners of war are over, men. Your days as Czecho-Slovak Legionnaires are about to begin. *Nazdar*, men. *Nazdar!*"

Choruses of 'nazdar!' rang around the parade ground, before fading away in the woods surrounding the camp. And later that day the smoke from dozens of pyres drifted amongst the silver-birch trees, as the men at last rid themselves of their lice-infested, field-grey uniforms.

One thousand, two hundred and eight men chose to make the journey back to Brody. The only ones who did not were the 48 still suffering from typhus, and the three medical orderlies who volunteered to stay behind to care for them.

Štefan Sedláček belonged to a separate group. He would stay permanently at Tambov Camp, with 587 other Czech and Slovak men and boys, buried together in three mass graves outside the perimeter fence next to the wood.

Štefan fought hard for his life, through three days and nights of raging fever and cramping muscles. Pavel sat with him for hours in the darkened infirmary, talking to him, bathing his face and, with each convulsion, urging him to survive.

During the boy's last night, as the hours passed, Pavel could swear Štefan grew younger and younger, until at the end he seemed to have returned to the child he really was. With pale, smooth skin beneath the dark-red blotches. With fine black hair on his top lip and down his cheeks, where one day he would have needed to shave. Pavel saw the struggle on the young face, the confusion over how much suffering was acceptable for a man, and how much was not. As another day of pain and delirium beckoned, Pavel told him he had done enough.

On the journey back to Brody Pavel sat quietly trying to make sense of what had happened and was about to happen. He looked across at the five boys sitting with their knees up, heads down, staring at the floor as their bodies were shaken this way and that by the jolting progress of the train.

All the men in the wagon chose to spend the first few hours of their journey alone with their thoughts. There was none of the bravado they had demonstrated the previous year. The anger and the sense of injustice at the Russians' betrayal were replaced now by a quiet determination to gain the prize Masaryk had held up before them. They had to win the coming battle. They knew if they failed, there would be no imprisonment and repatriation. They would be shot as deserters. Only if they won could they stay alive and go home. Home to a country that would only exist if they won.

But as the train made its slow progress west, Pavel witnessed scenes which made the prospect of victory seem less and less likely. On the platforms of every small town they passed he saw Russian deserters. Men half-in and half-out of uniform. Some holding weapons, some holding vodka bottles, many holding both. When the train stopped at Kursk, it became clear to the Czechs and Slovaks that the army of their Russian ally was falling apart.

Soldiers stood around in small groups drinking and smoking, while their officers kept their distance. Drunken soldiers shouted at the officers, who either pretended not to hear the abuse or just walked away from it. Six or seven men wearing red armbands were handing out leaflets to the troops and to any civilians brave enough or reckless enough to go near the drunken rabble. One of the men approached the open door of Pavel's wagon and looked inside. When he saw soldiers in new Russian uniforms he threw in some leaflets and shouted,

"*Doloy voyny, tovarishchi! Doloy Kerenskovo!*"

The Czech captain in the wagon stepped forward.

"*Český. Český,*" he said, pointing towards his men, and he fought to close the wagon door. The Russian spat at him, swore, and banged his fist against the wooden planking.

"What was he saying, Captain?" came a voice from a dark corner of the wagon.

"Something about stopping the fighting. And a lot of cursing about his government." He held up one of the leaflets. "According to this, workers should stop fighting one another and fight the '*bourgeoisiya*', whoever they are. And they don't think much of Kerensky."

"Who's Kerensky, Captain?"

"The Russian Minister of War. Professor Masaryk was telling us officers about him last week back at the camp. It's Kerensky who's planning this new offensive. It's him we've got to thank for the Legion."

"It's about time he got this lot in order though, isn't it, sir?" said Jan Vaněk.

"It's what happens when you let discipline go, Vaněk."

"Why don't they just put a stop to it then, sir?"

"I think it's too late. Those Bolsheviks out there have stirred the soldiers up so much, there's no discipline left."

"The officers should just order them to stop, sir."

"I don't think their officers are giving the orders any more, Vaněk. It's done by soldiers' committees taking a vote."

"But that's crazy, sir. Who decides to attack? Do they have a quick vote when the bullets start flying?"

The men in the wagon laughed and cursed.

"I vote I don't get bloody killed," said one.

"I vote we win..."

"But it's serious, men," said the captain. "There are reports of Russian officers being shot by their own soldiers, because someone didn't like an order. Apparently they don't call Kerensky commander-in-chief any more. They call him 'persuader-in-chief'."

"But this is madness, sir. This lot won't be any good to us against the Austrians."

"Maybe not. But remember the Russians need this battle as much as we do. They need to show the French and British they're still in this war, so the Allies keep sending them supplies of arms and food." He stepped towards the middle of the wagon. "But none of that matters to us, men." He screwed up the leaflet and threw it the floor. "Because every one of us knows what we'll be fighting for. And every one of you knows what you have to do."

There was to be a two-pronged attack, in the north against the Germans in occupied Poland, and in the south against the Austrians, where the new Czecho-Slovak Legion would be given a chance to prove itself.

Only 3,500 men of the Legion were to take part in the initial assault. Their objective was the high ground to the south-west of the town of

Zborov. All the men from the Tambov Camp volunteered to fight and 500 were chosen. They included Pavel and the six men of his section who would form a bombing team.

The 500 volunteers were taken to a training camp outside Brody, where they were issued with the new sage-green uniform of Czecho-Slovak legionnaires. Initial training for two weeks improved their physical fitness, while Pavel and the other NCOs received instruction on trench clearance, which they then passed on to the soldiers in their section.

Štefan Sedláček had been replaced by Oskar Vesely, an 18 year-old from a mining town in northern Bohemia. He was small in build but possessed of a wiry strength, ideal for a miner and ideal for close combat in the narrow confines of a trench. Jan Vaněk and Emil Kolár, both farm workers, Karel Kopeský, the shop assistant, and Filip Souček and Milan Musil, both students, completed Pavel's bombing team.

"Our job will be to clear three lines of Austrian trenches. Fifty metres in the first trench, then 100 metres across open ground to the second line of trenches. Clear 50 metres of that and then on to the third. Any questions?"

"We'll be sitting ducks going across open ground, won't we, Sergeant?" asked Vaněk.

"There will be a creeping barrage when we cross, to make sure the Austrians keep their heads down. When we get to the first trench they should still be in their dugouts. And then we clear them out with these.

"This is a fragmentation bomb, supplied by the British. A Mills Bomb they call it. Weighs half a kilo. Has a four second delay on the fuse and a killing radius of five to ten metres. But it's dangerous up to 50 metres, so be damned careful when and where you throw it. The dugouts will have heavy gas curtains in front of them, so you stand to the side of the curtain and throw it in. Any questions?"

"What will we have to defend ourselves with, Sergeant?"

"Good question, Musil."

"Only two of you will be bombers. That's Souček and Musil. Two of you will carry the bombs. That's Vaněk and Kolár. And Vesely and Kopeský, you will have rifles and bayonets and your job will be to protect the rest of the team. And I will fill in when and where I'm needed."

"So why do Souček and Musil get the easy job?" said Vaněk.

Pavel went over to him and grabbed him by the collar. Pavel's face was so close to Vaněk's that the boy was sprayed by spittle as Pavel shouted at him.

"Because I damn well say so, that's why! And don't any of you ever question one of my decisions again. Understood?"

The six all stood in shock at the sudden change in the man who had always shown such concern for them. None of them spoke.

"I asked you if you understood! Now get in line and stand to attention."

They all snapped to and stood to attention.

"Understood?" Pavel shouted.

"Yes, Sergeant!"

"You ask questions when I tell you you can. Otherwise you do everything I say, when I say it. Understood?"

"Yes, Sergeant."

"Now, you will remain at attention while I explain the rest.

"When Souček and Musil have thrown the bombs in the dugout, they stand back. When the bombs have detonated, you Vesely and you Kopeský move forward, and if any poor Austrian bastard comes out, you bayonet them. You save your bullets for any one of theirs in the trench out of bayonet range. Any questions?"

There was no reply.

"Well, now there should be questions! You should be asking when you're going to practise all this. The answer is, all day, every day, for the next two weeks. You will all learn one another's jobs, so if one of you is killed or wounded, I can get any of the others to take over your job. Any questions?"

There was silence.

"Right. Stand at ease. You've got five minutes. Go and take a piss and get back here for bayonet practice. If any one of you is longer than five minutes by my reckoning, you all do two hours extra drill. Now go!"

Pavel watched as they ran towards the latrine block, talking animatedly, no doubt about what a bastard their sergeant had suddenly become. Pavel did not care. As a teacher he had dealt with hundreds of boys like this. He had been strict with them, too, in a much different way. Then it had been to get them through exams, to get them to win their places at university, or just to get a decent school leaver's report. At the time it had all seemed so crucial in determining the course of their lives. Never in his worst nightmare could he have imagined preparing boys for this.

When they came back, well within their five minutes, Pavel explained the subtleties of the use of the bayonet with the same clarity he once employed to explain the use of logarithm tables.

A single thrust to the throat, chest or groin was preferable, but all had their separate disadvantages. The throat was a small target. It could easily be missed and was not instantly fatal. The chest was fatal, but the bayonet could get stuck behind the breastbone, and you would be vulnerable while you struggled to pull it out. The groin was good, but it was so painful the victim often grabbed hold of the rifle to prevent you moving it. All options had their drawbacks. If you were lucky, the bomb had killed everyone in the dugout and no one came out. Or if they did, they were so badly injured they could not resist you wherever you chose to stick your bayonet into them.

By the end of two weeks the first part of Pavel's job was done. His bayonet team were technicians, his bombers could remove the pin and release the strike lever with precise timing, and the carriers were supremely fit and could prime fuses under any conditions. And they were all full of anger. They were ready.

And Pavel was ready too. Ready to do anything to any Austrian who stood between him and getting home. To his parents, to his brothers Teo and Petr, but above all, to his Kája.

Chapter Nine

July 2nd, 1917

"Keep back on the right! Stay behind me! For God's sake..!"

Pavel's words were lost beneath the crump and crack and boom of exploding shells. Sixty a minute for each fifty-metre section of the front. Most of them shrapnel shells exploding forward over the enemy trenches, forcing the Austrian soldiers to stay in their dugouts and bolt holes. Ten out of every sixty high explosive, shaking the ground in front of the Czech Legionnaires and throwing up a curtain of dirt and debris to mask their advance.

Pavel looked again to his left. Souček and Musil were about eight metres from him, crouching instinctively but advancing only at a brisk walk, just as he had ordered. Vaněk and Kolár were crouching too, about four metres to his left, but the weight of the grenade boxes slung between them forced them upright after every ten paces or so, making them a better target for any Austrian who had remained at his post.

"Vesely! Kopeský! Keep back! Stay back, I say!"

But still the two riflemen to his right kept racing ahead. They were now well in front of the rest of the team and beginning to run. Pavel knew if they did not keep at least thirty metres between themselves and the protective barrage being laid down by the Russians, there was a danger they would be killed by their own artillery. But if he went forward to warn them the other four boys would follow him, and they would all be in trouble. He had to let them go and take their chances.

Vesely and Kopeský reached the enemy wire alone and were forced to stop. In their panic they ran first one way and then another looking for the gap the sappers had cut in the night.

"You idiots! Over here! The breach is here!" Pavel shouted at them. They raced towards him.

The whole team stood in front of the enemy trench with ten metres of barbed wire in front of them. It would be less than a minute before the Austrians realised the barrage had crept beyond their position and it was safe to come out to man their guns.

Pavel thanked God the sappers had cut the wire in exactly the spot he had been told to expect. He looked into the six young, sallow faces staring at him and spat his orders at them.

"Now! All of you! You know what to do. It's time. Do it! Do it!"

Pavel charged through the gap in the lead. The two riflemen followed directly behind him, then the bombers and the carriers. They all screamed as they ran.

When he reached the parapet, Pavel jumped down on to the fire step swinging a hardwood club studded with hobnails and weighted at one end with lead, ready to brain the first enemy soldier he saw. But there was no one out yet. In seconds Vesely and Kopeský were next to him.

"Vesely, guard our left flank. Kopeský, to the dugout. Make sure no bastard comes out."

Souček and Musil were the next to drop down into the trench.

"Come with me, both of you. One bomb each at the ready. Now!"

Pavel went to the dugout and lifted back the heavy gas curtain. An Austrian soldier walked through as if someone had politely held the door open for him, and then looked in horror as he realised his mistake.

Souček and Musil threw in their bombs and the six Czechs pressed their backs into the side of the trench on either side of the curtain. Opposite them the Austrian did the same in a pathetic attempt to share their danger and earn a brotherly reprieve. After four seconds the grenades detonated together. The gas curtain billowed and pieces of hot, jagged metal flew through the gap created at the bottom, ripping into the Austrian soldier's shins. He collapsed into a foetal position with his arms wrapped around his legs, screaming with shock. More cries came from within the dugout.

"Souček, one more bomb in there. Stand back!"

Another shower of metal from the dugout flew into the Austrian soldier lying on the floor of the trench, severing his arm and shredding the side of his face. His screams turned into a drone as his mind sought safety. Pavel gestured towards him. "Kopeský, for Christ's sake finish the poor bastard."

Kopeský raised his rifle high in the air and held the bayonet above the man on the ground. To his right Pavel heard German voices.

"For God's sake, boy, do it," he hissed. "They're nearly on us." As Kopeský stood frozen in place Pavel gripped the boy's hands and the rifle beneath them and drove the bayonet into the Austrian's chest.

"Now get the damned thing out yourself. Come on, the rest of you. Follow me. You too, Vesely."

He led them twenty metres to the right where a traverse created a bend preventing bullets and shell fragments sweeping the length of the trench. They paused next to the traverse and crouched down. Pavel strained to hear what was happening two metres away on the other side. He beckoned his team to move in closer to him.

"It's what we expected," he whispered. "The next bit won't be so easy. The Austrians are out. They're on the other side right now listening for us. So all of you keep quiet and do everything I tell you." He looked at his watch.

"Eleven minutes before the next covering barrage. We've got to be quick. Souček, Musil, you crawl over the parapet, outflank them behind this traverse and lob in two bombs each. Now, listen. When you release, you wait two seconds before you throw. I know it's risky, boys, but if those Austrians have any time before those grenades go off, they'll be throwing their own stuff back at us.

"As soon as we hear your bombs we'll be round the corner, so don't throw in any more. Understood?"

The two bombers nodded. Pavel turned and fixed on the others.

"When you get round there, boys, you're not going to think. You're not going to care. You're going to strike terror into those bastards. Remember, if they live, you don't go home." He turned to Karel Kopeský, the linen-shop assistant from Pilsen.

"Kopeský, if you hesitate again and put our lives at risk, I'll kill you first before any Austrian. Do you understand?"

Kopeský looked up at him. He seemed deranged. His skin was clammy and pale and his eyes wide open as if in a state of permanent surprise. He did not blink as he stared at Pavel. Pavel drew back his right hand and hit him hard across his left cheek. The boy's head jolted violently sideways and when he looked back his body tensed and he gripped his rifle. His eyes still stared but the emptiness in them had gone as blood rushed to his face and head.

"Ready, Souček? Musil? Go. Quiet as you can. The rest of you, follow me."

Pavel stood up and crept to the corner of the traverse. The others stood behind him. He turned to look at them, mouthing obscenities as he tapped his club on the palm of his left hand.

There was an explosion followed by the screams and groans of mutilated men.

"Come on, boys," he cried, "Kill the bastards! No mercy!"

He raced around the traverse screaming wildly, "*nazdaaar!*" The bloodied flesh on the floor trying to crawl to safety was not human to him. His only focus the twenty-five metres of trench in front of him and the absolute need to reach the end of it. He kicked and bludgeoned and trampled his way through the mess at his feet until the path ahead was clear.

He paused for breath and looked down the length of the trench. It was so narrow, and the sides so high and dark, he felt he was in a tunnel. At the end he could see more figures in field grey, grouped together with their backs to him, arms flailing. He glimpsed sage-green uniforms amongst them. Souček and Musil.

He hurled his body down the trench. His roar caused everything to stop, as Austrians and Czechs turned to see what could produce such an unholy sound. He crashed into the group, slamming his club into the face of an Austrian who shaped to confront him. The three others fell to the ground. In one fluid movement he brought the club over his left shoulder down onto the steel helmet of one, breaking his neck, and then over his right shoulder shattering the cheekbone of the other.

The last Austrian, paralysed by the overwhelming brutality of the assault, and realising there was nothing he could do physically to prevent it, lay on the ground pleading to be allowed to surrender.

"*Bitte, nein! Ich ergebe mich! Ich bitte dich... Kamerad.*"

Pavel stood over him with his club raised, poised to complete the final swing. The Austrian stretched out his arms, the palms of his hands facing forward, fingers spread as wide as he could make them. He shook his hands frantically, his eyes filled with panic.

"*Bitte, bitte,*" he pleaded. "*Please. Please.*"

Pavel looked down at him and paused, horrified in the brief moment of hesitation to find himself outside the heat of battle. When he looked again at the terrified boy he saw the gap in his front teeth, the small mole on his left cheek...

He dropped the club and turned round. The boy dropped his arms in relief, lay his head back on the earth and closed his eyes. Pavel took Kopeský's rifle, turned, and before the Austrian could look up, fired a bullet into his forehead.

He threw the rifle back at Kopeský.

"It's nearly six o'clock. The guns start again in two minutes. Musil. Souček. Are you ready?"

Pavel looked at his two bombers. Their faces were broken and bloodied.

"We're alright, sergeant. What about you?"

He had not noticed a knife wound to his right arm.

"It's alright. Is everyone else alright?"

He looked at the rest of his team. They stared back at him in awe and unease.

"Take up positions, boys. Four metres apart. The sun will be in their eyes this time. One hundred metres. Stay in line with me. Courage, boys, courage. You're going to come out of this, I promise you. Just do as I say."

All along the line whistles blew and on a five-kilometre front 3,500 Czecho-Slovak Legionnaires rose from the first line of Austrian trenches and advanced at a brisk walk towards the second.

In the centre red and white flags bearing the crown of Saint Wenceslas were held high by a vanguard of a dozen men. From his right Pavel heard the sound of singing drifting towards him across the flat Galician landscape. Legionnaires around him picked up the words of the Hussite war song and passed it along to the men on their left, until even the Russian shells exploding thirty metres in front of them could not drown out their voices. In that moment he felt a part of something no one could ever have tried to create, or ever hope to create again. A single body of men. Alive, invincible, unconstrained.

But the euphoria had caused the confidence of some of the men to rise too high. They were getting too close to the barrage, allowing themselves maximum protection from the Austrians but risking certain death if one of the Russian shells fell short or blew back on them.

"Slow down!" Pavel shouted to Kopeský on his right, as once again the boy's discipline evaporated and he raced ahead. "Stay back, Karel! Stay back!"

Pavel strained to make out the figure of the boy as he disappeared through a curtain of smoke and dirt thrown up in front of them. Pavel continued at the same steady pace hoping to see Kopeský on the other side. As he passed through the smoke he saw a fine pink mist appear on his right. It drifted over him. It smelled sweet and felt sticky, and in a moment it was gone, leaving him with the taste of metal on his tongue. He looked again for Kopeský, but the boy was nowhere.

Chapter Ten

October 31st, 1917

"Kája, you have a visitor."

"Just a moment, Máma. I'll be down in a minute."

Karolína looked at Tomáš lying in his cot. He was fighting to keep his eyes open, sure as always that somewhere nearby something was happening that merited his attention.

Karolína started to sing to him again and stroke his head. It frustrated her that her mother would call out just as he was starting his afternoon nap. Who could it be? She had received so few visitors since moving to her parents' chata at the end of the summer. In two months there had only been Esther and Anna; and Herr Krause, who kept the bookshop where she worked before Pavel left, and who was keen for her to return.

She stepped gently towards the door and coaxed it open. Tomáš did not stir. She made her way down the staircase, which was as finely crafted as all the woodwork and furniture in her parents' otherwise modest cottage. As she paused at the door of the main living area she heard her father speaking, and then the voice of Ernst Neumann.

"Ernst, it's you. You're back from Vienna," she said, as she entered the room.

"Kája, there you are," said Ernst, and he got up from the table where he sat with Michal and Magdaléna.

Karolína held him at arm's length as he went to greet her.

"But let me look at you, Ernst. My, what a wonderful job they're doing."

"I'm very pleased, Kája. I was just telling your parents all about it."

"Well, now you must tell me. I can't believe what a difference it's made."

They sat down facing one another across the large oak table, which for over sixty years had been where family and friends gathered in the Štasný home. It remained one of the few pieces of furniture in the cottage not decorated with hand-painted scenes from the Bohemian Forest.

"Yes, they have the most skilled surgeons in Vienna, Kája," said Ernst.

"I've been so fortunate. I was just saying to your mother and father;

it's a terrible irony, but the war has advanced new medical techniques so much."

"I cannot believe what they have been able to do," said Karolína.

"It's a new idea. The doctors call it a skin graft. It is hard to believe, I know, but Doktor Hofmeyer is taking skin from my back and attaching it to my face. The texture and colour are a bit different, and it will be a bit taut until they have finished. But Doktor Hofmeyer says because it's my own living skin it will stretch naturally in time."

"A miracle. That's what it is. No less. It's a God-given miracle," said Magdaléna.

"Máma's right, Ernst. It is a miracle. I'm so happy for you. And for Esther. She's been so worried about you."

"I know. I know. But at least I can speak more normally now. And I can almost close my left eye. You cannot believe what a relief that is. I'm going back to Vienna before Christmas for a second graft and to have a new arm fitted."

"Not a real one?" exclaimed Magdaléna.

"No, Frau Štasná, not a real one. Even Doktor Hofmeyer cannot work that miracle yet."

Everyone laughed and Magdaléna busied herself pouring more of the coffee she had concocted from ground acorns, beechnuts and roasted barley.

"You all mock," she said, "but you never know what these doctors might manage to do one of these days."

"You are quite right, Frau Štasná. The doctors who treated me are doing amazing things. Even using lightweight metals to recreate parts of soldiers' faces and such. The possibilities seem endless. It intrigues me what use we might make of such things in the theatre one day."

"I think that's a rather trivial consideration next to the suffering this war has created," said Karolína.

"Yes, I'm sorry, Kája. I didn't mean to... to..."

"So, tell us all about Vienna, Herr Neumann," said Michal, casting a stern glance at his daughter. "How are people coping there?"

"Well, Herr Štasný, I can assure you there is no coffee in Vienna as good as this your dear wife has managed to provide for us. Remarkable, Frau Štasná."

"Thankyou, Herr Neumann, it's the coal-tar flavouring makes the difference."

"So the Viennese are suffering shortages too then, Herr Neumann?" asked Michal.

"Yes, at least as bad as here. There's very little in the shops. Mostly thin soup in the restaurants. Reconstituted meat. Very few vegetables. I think they reserve the best for the army."

"Quite right in the circumstances," said Michal.

"Táta! What are you saying?"

"Calm yourself, Kája. I'm only saying all fighting men need to be best cared for. That's all."

"I brought some newspapers back with me from Vienna, Karolína," said Ernst. "There are some articles in them I thought might interest you. I thought if Tomáš is asleep we could walk by the lake and discuss them."

"That's a good idea, Kája," said Magdaléna. "The fresh air will do you the world of good."

Karolína left the table to take her coat from beneath the stairs. When she returned, the others were standing by the front door looking out over the lake. It was the last day of October and already there was a slight chill in the air.

"If you're walking round the lake I advise you not to leave the path, Herr Neumann," said Michal. "Since Graf von Stricker allowed free access to his land for hunting and foraging and the like, there are a lot of traps lying around out there."

"I'll bear it in mind, Herr Štasný. Many thanks for the delicious coffee, Frau Štasná."

"I wish your father wouldn't insist on calling me 'Herr Neumann'", said Ernst to Karolína as they walked together towards the wide path that skirted the lake. "He's known me since I was a child."

"My táta respects the old order, Ernst. You are the German Director of the Municipal Theatre. There are at least three reasons there why he would not want to seem over familiar."

Ernst laughed.

"The formality allows my father some security in an uncertain world, Ernst."

"They are fine people, your parents, Kája. Esther and I have always been so fond of you all."

"As we are of you, Ernst."

"Thankyou for saying that, Kája. I have thought a lot about the conversation we had by the river at the end of the summer. I thought many times of writing to you from Vienna. I was so afraid I might have upset you."

"No more than I might have upset you, Ernst. We disagree, that's all.

We are still friends."

Karolína took his arm as they walked.

"I'm so relieved to hear that, Kája. I have thought so much about you and Pavel recently. I am such a fortunate man. I have survived. I have my family. I'm going back to the work I love. And yet these are the saddest of times for me."

"Why?"

"Because circumstances have aligned you and Pavel and me against one another. It was one thing to discuss and argue before the war, however vehement we were at times. But to take up arms against one another? I cannot reconcile it."

"But it never went further than discussion and argument, Ernst. Remember that Pavel died in an Austrian uniform, just like yours."

"You still think that? Even though I told you about his regiment defecting to the Russians last Easter?"

"But you said it was only a rumour, Ernst. I cannot hold on to rumours. I deal with what I know."

"And all you know is that Pavel left Eger... I'm sorry, Cheb... a year ago last February and you've heard nothing since?"

"I received his last letter six weeks later. Since then there has not been one word about him from anyone. I stopped reading the bulletins at the Town Hall in July, after the Russian offensive in Galicia. The list of dead and missing was in thousands. Seven pages. I cannot go through all that again, Ernst. If Pavel were alive I would know. He would have found a way of telling me."

"I don't think you will ever see Pavel's name on an Austrian list, Kája."

"Why do you keep saying these things?"

"Because there are more than just rumours now about what happened to Pavel's regiment."

Karolína stopped walking and stood motionless with her hands clasped to her forehead.

"Ernst, just tell me quickly whether you have some definite news about Pavel."

"No, Kája. I have nothing definite."

"Then all you are doing is informing me about the progress of the war. Is that right?"

"Yes. I suppose it is."

Karolína breathed out deeply and continued walking.

"You can do that," she said. "But please, Ernst, no more rumours or speculation about Pavel. I cannot live with the uncertainty of it."

"Is there nothing I can say to help you with all of this?"

"Giving me some vague hope is the worst thing you could do. I can live with the thought that Pavel is at peace. But to imagine that he exists somewhere, but he is hurt and needs me and I can do nothing for him... It would paralyse me. And the people here who need me... little Tomáš... would lose me too. Can't you understand that?"

"I think so, Kája. It's not how I would think, but I can try to understand. I do not want to upset you."

"Good. So you can tell me what you learned in Vienna about the war, Ernst, but no more than that. Agreed?"

"Agreed, Kája."

The two friends walked side by side in silence. Ernst looked down, turning over in his mind the words he might best employ to describe to Karolína all he had witnessed in the Austrian capital.

Karolína looked out over the smooth, grey waters of the lake. To her right a carp broke the surface and she watched the ripples it made quickly expand before disappearing slowly, leaving everything as it was.

She found comfort in the lake's permanence in her family's life. Every year it provided the carp for their dinner on Christmas Eve. And whole generations of Štasnýs had relied on the purity of its water, fed by springs from the Ore Mountains in Saxony. And for all the Štasný children and their friends the lake and the woods around it had provided a world of magic. Everyone to the German border and beyond knew this place only as 'Štasný Lake'. There was nowhere in the world now that offered her a greater feeling of security and belonging.

She was relieved that whatever Ernst was about to tell her, he was not going to disturb the fragile peace she had negotiated with herself over the fate of Pavel.

"I told you, didn't I, Kája, that Emperor Karl had recalled parliament?" Ernst said at last.

"Yes, you did."

"Well, that's how I know what happened to the 29th Regiment."

Karolína said nothing.

"There have been terrible scenes in parliament recently. There is a lot of anti-Czech feeling in Vienna, I'm afraid. People there feel betrayed by those Czechs who have defected to the Russians. Questions have been asked in the House of Deputies and it has all been reported in the Viennese papers."

Ernst paused but still Karolína did not speak.

"It has been confirmed now that the 29th Regiment did defect in

April last year. Apparently Masaryk has been in Russia since May forming a Czech army out of these men. And he is still there."

Karolína stopped walking and clasped the sleeve of Ernst's tunic.

"Are you saying there is a Czech army in Russia?"

"Yes, there is. And it was used for the first time during the July offensive in Galicia. Very successfully."

"But we were told the Russians were defeated in Galicia."

"So they were, but not the Czechs. That is why the Austrian deputies have been so outraged. Because the Czechs fought so ferociously against the Austrian troops. The only reason the Czechs eventually withdrew was because after two weeks of fighting the Russians broke and ran. It would have been an even greater Austrian victory if the Czech army had not covered the Russian retreat. Feeling is running so high, Kája, the Czech deputies in parliament dare not walk the streets in Vienna."

"I don't know what to say, Ernst."

"I assumed you would be pleased."

"I am pleased to hear we have a Czech army. But I realise how terrible it must be for you to know we Czechs are actually fighting against your people."

"I have struggled to come to terms with it."

"But you must try to understand what has driven us to it... but I don't want to argue again."

Ernst pulled back his shoulders and with a gesture of his arm invited Karolína to continue their walk.

"Me neither, Kája. I made a decision before I came to see you today," he said. "I am a Bohemian German. A citizen of Austria, loyal to his emperor. But I am also your loyal friend. And although I do not agree with the actions of those Czech soldiers, I am determined to reconcile my two loyalties. I shall not turn my back on either of them. And I shall report to you what I know as fairly and as dispassionately as I can."

"Dear Ernst, if everyone in the world made the same effort as you to be fair-minded, we would need no wars."

"I take my lead from my emperor, Kája. I believe Karl to be a good man, whom we should all trust. He is young, but he's resolute and even-handed. He wants to give all his citizens a voice. Deputies in parliament are now free to speak in their own language about any topic they choose. There's even talk of organising a federal state after the war. If only we could all hold together just for now and give Emperor Karl a chance."

"I'm afraid not everyone is as enlightened as you wish them to be, Ernst. Did you hear that dreadful news from Prostějov?"

"That's Prossnitz, isn't it?"

"Yes, Ernst, to you Austrians I mean Prossnitz. There was a strike there amongst Czech workmen a few weeks ago. All they wanted was food for their families. But twenty-three were shot dead by Austrian troops. There were many more wounded."

"That is terrible, Kája. Of course I condemn such actions. But we must not allow such things to divide us any further."

"I think it is already too late, Ernst. This war is changing everything. It has set too many things in motion."

Karolína stopped and placed her hand gently on the pale skin of Ernst's left cheek. "Let's not talk any more of these things for now," she said. "Let us just be two friends enjoying our walk and our beautiful lake, and what's left of the afternoon sun."

When they returned to the chata Karolína went straight up to Tomáš, while Michal accompanied their visitor to the edge of the clearing where the path led back to Skalka.

"Be sure to visit us again soon, Herr Neumann. It does Kája good to talk to people her own age."

"Herr Štasný..." Ernst hesitated. "I hope you do not think me impertinent, but I am worried about Karolína."

"For what reason, Herr Neumann?"

"Her refusal to talk about Pavel. Her insistence that he is lost to her."

"Oh, don't you worry about our Kája, Herr Neumann. She has come through the worst now."

"But there seems to be an air of resignation about her that I have never seen before. Esther has noticed it too."

Michal turned his face away from Ernst and stared at the black fir trees on the other side of the lake.

"You know, Herr Neumann, for months I listened to my precious girl praying, pleading with God to give her some news about her Pavel. I was afraid she could go out of her mind with it all. But in the end she came to understand she couldn't go on like that. She had to put the little one first. So she's found a place for Pavel now which allows her to carry on with her life."

Michal turned to face Ernst.

"But don't get me wrong, Herr Neumann. I know my Kája. If she didn't have Tomáš to consider she would be scouring the world this very minute looking for her husband. Nothing would stop her."

"And do you think she still believes Pavel died fighting for the

Austrians?"

"I do. I think she has to. I think going back to the not-knowing would unhinge her."

"You know, Herr Štasný, as much as Kája believes Pavel is dead, I am convinced he's still alive and fighting for the Russians."

"You think he defected with the rest of his regiment?"

"You know about that?"

"I must confess to looking at the newspapers you brought for Kája, Herr Neumann. I don't mind admitting some of what I read came as a shock. A Czech army. Who'd ever believe it? There hasn't been a Czech army for 300 years."

"Apparently it's 60,000 strong now, Herr Štasný. It is the only thing preventing a total Austrian breakthrough."

"I'm a simple man, Herr Neumann. I can't pretend to understand all that's going on."

"We live in confused times, Herr Štasný. It's a brave man who says he knows what the final outcome of all this will be."

"Or a foolish one."

"Indeed, Herr Štasný, indeed," said Ernst with a hint of laughter. "Or a foolish one."

"But you know, Herr Neumann, the paper said the defections were made public in September. That may explain something else that's been puzzling me. September was when Kája stopped getting Pavel's pay. No explanation. It just stopped. I suppose once people knew Czech soldiers were changing sides, the authorities saw no more point in pretending it wasn't happening."

"I'm sure that must be it. What did Kája say when the pay stopped?"

"She took it as another sign Pavel was dead."

"I see..."

"But if he is still alive, pray to God, what's going to happen to him if he is in Russia?" asked Michal.

"It does not look very good for him, I'm afraid."

"That's what I thought. The paper seemed to be saying it was all over in the east."

"I think it is. Only Masaryk's Czechs are holding back our troops in the centre, and in the north our German allies are almost in St Petersburg. I should be delighted, of course, but any satisfaction I may feel is tempered by my fears for my friend."

"Do you see any chance of Pavel being able to get back to us, if he is still alive?"

"I see only one hope for him, Herr Štasný. Did you read about the new Russian prime minister, Kerensky?"

"I did. Do you think he'll make a difference?"

"Possibly. If Kerensky's government can remain strong and build morale amongst their troops, they may just hold on long enough."

"Long enough for what, Herr Neumann?"

"For all the warring nations to decide enough is enough; to end the fighting and return to their original frontiers."

"And everyone can come home. I shall pray for that, Herr Neumann."

"But there is one added complication for the Czechs in Russia, I'm afraid. There is a faction of trouble-makers there doing all they can to undermine Kerensky, by weakening the army. Bolsheviks they call themselves. Anarchist rabble most of them. If they manage to turn the Russian soldiers against their own government, they could take power and sue for peace. If that happens Pavel and all the other Czechs will be trapped there."

"May God forbid that," said Michal.

"For the sake of my friend, Herr Štasný, I shall share your prayers."

"Bless you, Herr Neumann."

Ernst extended his hand to Karolína's father and the two men bade one another farewell, and in the fading light Ernst Neumann made his way back through the forest to his home in Skalka.

Eight days later in Petrograd troops of the Bolshevik Red Brigade stormed the Winter Palace. Kerensky fled, and with hardly a shot being fired Vladimir Ilyich Lenin and Leon Trotsky seized power in Russia.

Chapter Eleven

December 23rd, 1917

Through the window of his winter quarters, east of the Ukranian city of Kiev, Tomáš Masaryk looked out on teams of legionnaires in sage-green greatcoats, fur hats and leather boots, working in driving snow to clear the paths between the brick-built accommodation blocks. He imagined the same thing happening at the other barracks just beyond the capital - in Darnica, Brovary and Vyshhorod - where more than 65,000 battle-weary soldiers of the Czecho-Slovak Army in Russia were over-wintering, waiting for their commander-in-chief to decide what their strategy would be in the New Year. He thought of the men and their families, and of his own family, and he voiced a silent apology for the burden his chosen path had placed on them all. He knew the decision he was about to make would determine their fate, and the fate of all his people.

He stood in awe of his legionnaires. He marvelled at their discipline and stoicism and their readiness to always do their best for one another. He did not doubt that those toiling in front of him now had received no order to carry out this work. The men had faith in themselves and each another, and most importantly in their officers, and they needed no persuasion to carry out any task which was for the common good. And he knew they trusted him, and he had resolved that he would not let them down.

"A nation will be built on the backs of these men," he said, as he watched his breath crystallize on the frozen glass.

A knock on the door made him turn round as his adjutant entered. "General Štefanik and General Diterich are here, Mr President."

"Gentlemen, how good to see you. I was afraid this weather might prevent our meeting taking place today." Masaryk shook each man warmly by the hand.

"Out of the question, Mr President," said General Štefanik. "We are far too anxious to learn of your new proposals."

Štefanik shook the snow from his overcoat as he spoke. Although a Slovak by birth and Vice-President of the Czecho-Slovak National Council, he also held French citizenship and still wore the blue uniform of a general in the French army. If this irked Masaryk in any way he was not going to show it. He understood well enough the benefit of his former pupil's hero status amongst the French, who were proving to be a most vital ally.

"Please take General Štefanik's coat," he said to his adjutant, "and help General Diterich with his."

Diterich, a general in the new Czecho-Slovak Army, was struggling to remove his heavy greatcoat. He was no longer a young man and exposure to the raw December weather had thickened his blood and chilled his joints, slowing him almost to a standstill.

"So, gentlemen, take a seat and warm yourselves with some coffee and *buchty* cake," Masaryk said. "We have much to discuss."

The three men each selected one of the grey metal-framed chairs with canvas seats which surrounded a large oval table covered with a cloth of green baize. Apart from a single bed, a wardrobe and a black, wood-burning stove they were the only items of furniture in Masaryk's quarters. Heavy brown curtains hung at the window, and the only decoration on the plain white walls was a large political map showing the world prior to the outbreak of war.

"There are three things I want us to deal with today, gentlemen," Masaryk began. "First, I wish each of us to state what he believes our present position to be. Secondly, I want us to restate our aims in the light of our present position. And finally, once we have restated our aims, I wish to discuss with you how they might best be achieved. Are we agreed to proceed in this way?"

Diterich nodded and muttered his approval. Štefanik nodded too, but with the curt politeness of a young man anxious to get down to business. He sat straight-backed in his chair with his palms pressed firmly on the table in front of him. His piercing green eyes remained fixed on his former teacher and mentor.

"I should like to begin with you, General Diterich," said Masaryk. "I would like to know your opinion of the mood of our men."

"Steadfast, Mr President. Still buoyed by our great victory at Zborov. Still seething at the Russians for running like scared rabbits at Tarnopol. They can't wait to get at the Germans and Austrians again in the spring."

"Good, good," said Masaryk, removing his pince-nez. "I'm delighted to hear it, General. But may I advise some caution concerning any reference you might make to our Russian allies?"

"But their own General Brusilov said it, Mr President. '*The Czecho-Slavs, perfidiously abandoned at Tarnopol by our infantry, fought in such a way that the world ought to fall on its knees before them.*' That's what he said,

Mr President. The words of their own commander. All the men know those words by heart."

"I know, General. I know. And there is no one more proud of our men's achievements than I, but we must consider at all times the delicacy of our position here in Russia."

"I tend to share General Diterich's view on this, Mr President," said Štefanik, still straight-backed, his eyes still on Masaryk. "The Russians are finished. It's three weeks now since they asked the Germans for an armistice. There is not one Russian soldier from the Baltic to the Black Sea still prepared to fight. We should forget them."

"Gentlemen, please," said Masaryk. "I urge you to moderate your opinions when discussing our Russian hosts."

"Perhaps you could update us then, Mr President, regarding the Russian position."

Masaryk took a paper from the small pile in front of him. He hesitated.

"I received this communiqué dated yesterday, 22nd December 1917. It confirms that a Russian delegation led by Trotsky has begun formal peace talks with the Germans at the town of Brest-Litovsk."

"Well, there you are then," said Štefanik, turning to General Diterich, who nodded back his support. "They're going to surrender."

"That may well be the case," said Masaryk, "but that does not make them less important to us. It may even make them more important."

He saw his two generals shaking their heads at one another as he spoke.

"Look, gentlemen, let us be honest with one another. It has been obvious for months that the Russians no longer had the stomach for this fight. And in spite of the bravery of our men, we could not have held the Germans and Austrians back on our own indefinitely. These peace talks might prove to be the best thing for us. They have at least caused the Germans to stop their advance, and that gives us the time we need to regroup and decide what our next move should be."

"I don't understand why the Germans don't just march on Petrograd and finish the Russians off," said Štefanik. "There's nothing to stop them."

"Because, General, they know that if they hold back and allow the Russians to surrender, the Bolsheviks and Tsarists will spend the next few years destroying themselves in a civil war. That way the Germans can transfer 900,000 men to the Western Front rather than use them as an army of occupation here in Russia."

"But if we allow that to happen, Mr President," said Štefanik, "the

Germans will probably win in the west and the war will be over anyway. The situation there is perilous enough as it is. The Romanians are defeated. The Italians are withdrawing so fast the Austrians are boasting they'll be holding a Christmas mass in Venice. The only ones hanging on are the British and the French. And their prospects are not good."

"Problems with the British and French, are there?" asked Diterich.

"In the strictest confidence I can tell you, General, that there were mutinies in the French army this summer, which threatened the collapse of the entire Western Front."

"Good God," said Diterich, hardly able to grasp the magnitude of all he was hearing.

"Then we must put our faith in the Americans," said Masaryk. "And, more importantly, in ourselves. We must retain a positive view of the situation, gentlemen. May I ask us to remember the main reason General Štefanik and I came to Russia in May?"

He looked at Štefanik over his pince-nez. It was a look familiar to Štefanik from his days at the Charles University in Prague.

"To form a Czecho-Slovak Army, Mr President," Štefanik said.

"And that we have achieved. And we did so with the aim of forcing our allies to recognise our right to nationhood. For who but a sovereign independent nation has a right to its own army?"

Before either of his visitors could reply, Masaryk stood up and took another paper from the green baize in front of him.

"Gentlemen, please excuse any theatricality on my part, but I have some very good news amidst the bad. Yesterday I received a second communiqué. It came from Dr Beneš, from our National Council Headquarters in Paris. I have it here. This document, gentlemen, is dated 19th December 1917, and is signed by the French President, Monsieur Poincaré, by Monsieur Clemenceau, the Premier, and Monsieur Pichon, the Foreign Secretary. In it they recognise the formation of a Czecho-Slovak Army on French soil. Furthermore they recognise the status of this army as an autonomous member of the allied forces under the sole political direction of the Czecho-Slovak National Council."

He leaned forward placing both hands on the table and looked first at Diterich and then at Štefanik.

"Gentlemen, we Czecho-Slovaks now have an independent army in France," he said. "At last under our own control. Now we need to give it a country."

Štefanik and Diterich both got to their feet and came around the table to shake Masaryk and one another by the hand.

"So you see, gentlemen," said Masaryk, "the moment of our allies' greatest weakness could prove to be the hour of our greatest strength. The French and British need us now more than ever while they wait for the Americans to arrive. This could be our chance." He smiled. "Please retake your seats, gentlemen."

"But the Russians don't need us at all now, do they, Mr President, if they intend to make peace?" asked Štefanik.

"On the contrary, General. I think every faction in Russia would like us on their side now. The Bolsheviks would like us to help spread their revolution, whilst the Ukrainians would welcome our help too, fighting for their independence from the Russians. They all want to court us. But it is vital, gentlemen, that we maintain absolute neutrality whilst we remain in Russia. We are not an army of mercenaries."

Masaryk turned to General Diterich, who immediately sat forward.

"General, do you get the impression that any of our men have been infected with this Bolshevik nonsense?"

"Some, Mr President. But most of them just want the Germans and Austrians beaten, so they can go home to their own people in their own country. They understand well enough that one depends on the other."

"Good. I will not accept any Bolshevik activity amongst our soldiers, gentlemen. We must come down on it hard. We did not come all this way in order to bring home a Bolshevik revolution to the Czech and Slovak people. We must remain absolutely neutral in Russian affairs. Are we all agreed?"

"Yes, Mr President."

"Of course, Mr President."

"General Štefanik, I shall charge you with the task of seeing that any revolutionary activity amongst our men is quashed. Can I do that?"

"You can, Mr President."

"Good. Well then, gentlemen. We have reviewed our current situation. Now we must decide what our next move should be. General Štefanik, may we hear your views?"

"I believe that our basic aim must not change, Mr President. And that aim remains the creation of a sovereign Czecho-Slovak state."

"Well said. And General Diterich?"

"I am a soldier, Mr President, with 67,000 spirited and disciplined men under my command. We ask only for a chance to fight for what we all believe in."

"Excellent, gentlemen. Then we all agree. Our aim remains the same, and we resolve to fight to attain it. The question now, of course, is how and where do we fight? I have a proposal, gentlemen.

"We agree that Russia is finished, and that we gain nothing by remaining here in Kiev and risking becoming embroiled in her internal politics. The only fight worth anything to us now is taking place in France, where an independent Czecho-Slovak Army already exists. I suggest, gentlemen, that we declare ourselves to be part of that army, and that we resolve today to transfer every one of our men to the Western Front."

For an instant Štefanik lost his formal bearing and jolted back in his chair. Diterich immediately sat up and gripped the edge of the table.

"But... but... how, Mr President? How is that possible?" he asked.

"How would you suggest, General?"

"Well, clearly we cannot take the shortest route to the west. We would have to fight all the way through... no, it's not possible."

"But do you agree with the principle, gentlemen?" asked Masaryk.

"Well, yes, in principle, of course," said Diterich, "but..."

"And you, General Štefanik?"

Štefanik had regained his composure and once again looked Masaryk in the eyes.

"I assume, Mr President, that you have already devised a plan?" he said.

"Yes, a very bold one, but the only one I believe has any chance of success. As General Diterich says, we cannot go west. But neither can we go north and take passage at Archangel. The Germans are too close. South is not possible either. The Germans and Turks control the Crimean and Black Sea routes. There is only one direction which lies open to us, gentlemen. East."

Štefanik laughed nervously.

"East, Mr President? But all that lies to the east are the Ural Mountains and the wastes of Siberia."

"Yes, but at the end of those wastes lie Vladivostok, the Pacific Ocean and ships which will take us to America, and finally, to France."

Štefanik stood and approached the large map which hung on the far wall.

"But it must be the best part of 10,000 kilometres to Vladivostok," he said, sweeping his hand across Siberia. "How in God's name will we transport 67,000 men there?"

"By train," said Masaryk.

Chapter Twelve

May 27th, 1918

"I see Masaryk's in America," said Ernst from the sitting room.

"Who?" Esther called back.

"Tomáš Masaryk, one of Pavel's old professors. He's in Chicago."

"Why?"

"I'll tell you..."

Ernst got up from his armchair and carried his newspaper into the kitchen. Esther was sitting at the far end of the table feeding Anna a brown paste from a teaspoon. Anna in her high-chair pulled a face as she swallowed the strange concoction. She considered the taste for a moment, then opened her mouth hoping for something better. She pulled another face, let the food fall off her tongue and turned her head away.

"Just one more little bit, *Liebling*. Please, just for *Mutti*," Esther pleaded.

"You know once she's made up her mind, she won't change it," laughed Ernst.

"It's not funny, Ernst. She has to eat. I wish Karolína could have brought Tomáš over."

"Why's that?"

"You know why. Because Tomáš will eat anything, and if she sees him have it, she'll have it."

"What are you giving her?"

"It doesn't matter."

"I would like to know."

"It's bread mashed up with a little rabbit and blackberry."

"That sounds nice."

"Yes, my love," said Esther. "I'm sure it's just what she wants."

Ernst kissed Anna on her cheek. "She seems happy enough with her drink."

"She is for now, but she'll be hungry later. Then there'll be trouble. What were you saying in there?"

"Masaryk. He's touring America. He still calls himself 'the President of the Czecho-Slovak National Council'. Pompous so-and-so. He's in Chicago."

"Why ever would he want to go there?"

"Because he obviously believes that's where the political initiative is now. With the Americans. He probably thinks he can persuade all the Czechs and Slovaks there to put pressure on Woodrow Wilson's government."

"Then he sounds like a clever man to me."

"He may be. But I think he's left it all too late. Listen to this from today's paper, Esther. *'Thousands of panic-stricken civilians flee Paris as our glorious armies smash through the French line between Soissons and Reims.'* I think it will all be over in a few weeks. Russia is defeated and we seem to be winning everywhere now. France, Belgium, Italy. At last we're really breaking through."

"I thought you were worried about American troops coming over."

"I was, but they don't seem to be making any difference. It says here they won't be ready in any great numbers until the spring of 1919. I think we shall have won well before then."

Esther took Anna from her high-chair and placed her at her breast.

"I don't care how it ends, Ernst, as long as it ends soon. I don't see how we can carry on much longer with all these shortages."

"But listen to this, Esther. This is the sort of thing that annoys me. According to the paper Emperor Karl met with Emperor Wilhelm on May 12th *'to sign an agreement for the economic exploitation of the Ukraine for the joint benefit of our two empires.'* I don't understand. The Russians have surrendered. We have signed a peace treaty with them. The only honourable thing to do now is withdraw our troops completely. Not stay and help ourselves to their food. We have no right."

Esther continued sitting with her back to Ernst while she fed Anna. She decided against telling him that she and Karolína now found it impossible to find anything nutritious in Eger to give to Otto, Anna and Tomáš. That the bread she fed Anna was probably bulked out with sawdust, and the rabbit from the butcher was almost certainly 'roof rabbit', as the women in the queues now referred to the town's dwindling population of cats. As Esther spoke she looked down at Anna and stroked her head.

"Not everyone in war is prepared to act as honourably as you, Ernst my love. Our taking food from the Russians has nothing to do with rights. It's just the winners taking all they can from the losers. Isn't it normal for the strong to take from the weak?"

"I hear your parents talking when you say things like that, Esther. I find it rather cynical."

"Can you blame me or them? When they only escaped the pogroms in Poland by letting people take everything they owned along the way?

70

And then having to deny their religion and take on the lowest jobs here in Bohemia to get accepted?"

"I know, Esther."

"As far as I can see, people always pick on the weak. And it's always worst when times are hard and people need someone to blame. Look what that mob did to Kája's house last week."

"I know. That is shameful. I can never understand why people do such things."

"For the same reason my parents were treated so badly. They broke Kája's windows because people need someone to blame for their empty hearts and stomachs. So they chose the easiest targets. But instead of Jews this time, they chose the families of Czech deserters."

"Well, it almost makes me ashamed to be an Austrian. As if poor Kája hasn't got enough to worry about."

Esther moved Anna to her other breast.

"Do we know any more about the Czech soldiers in Russia?" she asked.

"Only rumours. Some say Masaryk has sent the whole army to Siberia. God knows what they hope to achieve there."

"But that's a terrible place, isn't it? Mutti always said anyone who criticised the Tsar used to be sent there."

"It is a terrible place. And there are thousands of German and Austrian prisoners of war there, released by the Russians. It's going to be a very dangerous place for everyone."

"Well let's hope Pavel's not there then."

"But he has to be, Esther. If there's any chance he's alive, it has to be with the Czech army in Russia."

Ernst sat down at the opposite end of the table and spread out his newspaper. With his right hand he placed his prosthetic arm on his lap.

"But I don't understand, Ernst. If the Germans and Austrians are going to win like you say, Pavel won't be allowed to come back to Bohemia anyway, will he?"

Ernst stopped reading and looked up.

"I think Emperor Karl might allow it. He is fair-minded and he has granted amnesties in the past."

"I hope you're right, my love."

"And he has been saying for some time now he favours autonomous development for all the minorities in the empire when the war is over. Under a federal government in Vienna, of course."

"They're just words to me, Ernst. I have no idea what you mean."

"Well, take the Czechs and Slovaks. They would have their own assemblies in Prague and Bratislava to decide certain laws for themselves. But bigger matters, such as foreign treaties and the use of the military, would still be decided in Vienna."

"That sounds reasonable."

"It is. That's what I was trying to explain to Karolína yesterday, when she got upset and stormed out. Like so many Czechs, she's so inflexible. But they will have to compromise eventually."

"But what if Austria loses the war? What then?"

"I'm not prepared to consider that possibility at the moment, Esther. It seems so unlikely now. But I suppose if it did happen, the Americans, French and British would be equally fair to us. They are basically decent people."

Esther turned and smiled at him.

"I always loved that about you, Ernst. Your optimism about people. The way you always try to see light through the darkness." She took Anna from her breast and buttoned her blouse. "Come here to us, my love."

Ernst went over and knelt beside her. He kissed Anna's head.

"We all love you, Ernst. Otto, Anna and I," Esther said, stroking his cheek.

"And I love all of you. More than life itself. I am so grateful to Mutti and Vater Lochowitz for allowing you to marry out, Esther. And for not insisting the children be raised too strictly in the faith."

Ernst gripped the edge of the table with his right hand and levered himself to his feet.

"There you are, you see," he said. "Even the intolerance your parents suffered led to some good. They dropped their orthodoxy and allowed us to marry and have our wonderful children."

He placed his hand on Esther's shoulder and kissed the top of her head.

"We, my precious, are a model of cultural co-existence, you and I. It's exactly what all Czechs and Germans should strive for. I have always said it. To Kája... and to Pavel..."

"I know you have, my love. I know you have."

Ernst sat down again at the table. Esther was right, he thought. He was optimistic. He was sure all this would end soon, and the warring factions would reach out the hand of friendship to one another.

He watched the love between his wife and daughter, as Esther rocked Anna, and Anna cooed. Even in the midst of war he believed in a peaceful future for them.

Chapter Thirteen

May 14th, 1918

"Oh, Christ, we've stopped again. Where the hell are we now, Sergeant?"

"I don't know, Vaněk. But keep your damned complaints to yourself. I'll let some fresh air in and take a look."

Pavel slid the door open and a shaft of diagonal light entered the train's last wagon containing forty men. A few got down from their bunks and moved towards the inrush of clean morning air.

"Looks like a big place. Plenty of tracks, so it must be a junction," said Milan Musil, the art student from Karlovy Vary.

"Can you make out the sign on the station?" Pavel asked him. "You've got young eyes."

"Chelya... Chelyabinsk, Sergeant. Is it on the map?"

"Yes, it's here, just east of the Urals. We're in Asia at last, lads. Only the small matter of Siberia to cross now."

The men groaned and cursed.

The men of the rearguard were growing used to waiting. They had waited for months in Kiev whilst General Diterich commandeered the trains to take the 67,000 legionnaires out of Russia, and then they waited until all their fellow legionnaires had left. It was not until March 1918 that the rearguard at last began their journey across Russia to the eastern port of Vladivostok. But progress along the line was so slow that now the journey itself was becoming a trial of every man's patience.

Lenin had promised the legionnaires safe passage to Vladivostok, but not, it seemed, free passage, as at every station along the single-tracked Trans-Siberian railway the local Bolshevik commanders held up the Legion's trains until a ransom, usually of weapons, was handed over.

Pavel knew well that his fellow legionnaires, who had shown they could endure any physical privation, would not tolerate much more humiliation from local commissars, who despised the Czecho-Slovaks as counter-revolutionaries. Nor would they tolerate much more abuse from former German, Austrian and Hungarian prisoners of war, recently released and heading home, who at every junction mocked the legionnaires for travelling 'the wrong way' in a pointless attempt to join a losing cause on the western front.

Pavel climbed down onto the stones by the side of the track. As he looked to his right the brightening morning sun made him turn away, and the large white station building a hundred metres in front of him came slowly into focus. To his left he could make out the grey outline of the mountains they had crossed in the night.

Most of the men had now climbed down to join him and all along the track legionnaires lit cigarettes, stamped their feet and stretched, and urinated against the wheels of the wagons.

"Look, Sergeant, we've caught up with two more of our trains," said Milan Musil, pointing up the track. "God, they're even slower than we are."

"I think you're right, Musil. You stay here, boys," said Pavel to the five young soldiers in his section, who even now, after more than two years in uniform, still stayed close by him whenever they stopped. "I'm going up the line to see who it is."

Pavel walked briskly past the soldiers standing by their wagons. He greeted many personally and nearly all showed him some sign of recognition. They were all members of the rearguard, who had fought like the devil beside him to hold back the Germans in the Ukraine and give their fellow legionnaires the time they needed to board Diterich's trains and escape to the east.

When the Germans were handed the Ukraine as part of their peace treaty with Lenin, they had thrown in thousands of men in early March in an attempt to encircle the Legion at the railhead to the east of Kiev. But against all the odds the 600 soldiers of the Czecho-Slovak rearguard had stood at Bakhmach Junction and held the Germans for five days, allowing more than 66,000 of their fellow legionnaires to escape. But 145 men of the rearguard had been killed there, and the dozens of wounded were now crowded into the front three wagons of Pavel's train.

He stopped at the open door of one of them and greeted his old friend, Erik Novák, the medic from Tambov camp.

"Dobrý den, Erik."

"Dobrý den, Pavel." Novák came over and crouched down by the door.

"How are the men this morning, Erik?"

"Improving slowly. Only forty-two bed patients now. The rest are walking wounded. We're going to move the most serious cases to Colonel Čeček's train later this morning."

"So that's the colonel's train up there, is it?"

"Yes, he's mad as hell apparently. Been held up here for three days while they let more POWs through. The Germans must be desperate to get them back."

"What about the other train?"

"It's one of ours, but I'm not sure who's on it. But the Russians won't be very happy. They don't like too many of us together in one place."

"It makes them nervous, Erik. They're afraid..."

Pavel's words were cut short by the distant whistle of a train approaching from the east.

"That's all we need," he said, "a train full of Germans with our men out on the tracks." He stepped away from the hospital wagon to take a closer look.

He shielded his eyes as he peered towards the east where a column of dense white smoke rose against the morning sky. The shrill of the whistle sounded continuously as the train grew closer. Soon he was able to hear the sound of the engine itself as the train came slowly into view.

"Why the hell is the idiot making so much noise?" Novák shouted down to Pavel.

"I don't know, Erik, but let's hope he goes through on one of the tracks near the station. Well away from here."

The men who had been standing in groups by their wagons were now strung out in a line ready to gesture and hurl abuse at the Germans, Austrians or Hungarians as they sped through. But as the train grew closer it seemed to be slowing down. And as it passed the points a hundred metres down the track, it did not veer to the right towards the station as everyone expected, but came towards the legionnaires on a track parallel to their own, and only a few metres distant.

The men lined up by their wagons fell silent in disbelief as the train appeared directly in front of them. Slowly the brakes of the carriages bit, the metal of wheels and track screeched together and the steam from the brakes was released, briefly obscuring the legionnaires in a white fog. In the quiet that followed, Pavel thought the situation might yet be contained.

But for a reason only the man himself would ever know, the Russian driver of the train decided to vent steam from the engine's whistle one last time. All those by the track covered their ears and turned away until it stopped, but as they looked back at the train they found themselves the objects of laughter and abuse from the men in the light-brown uniforms inside.

"They're bloody Magyars!" shouted a Slovak to Pavel's left. "It's a train full of Hun bastards!"

All the Slovakian legionnaires by the track began to hurl abuse back at the Hungarian soldiers, who responded by standing at the open windows making obscene gestures towards the men below and spitting down on them.

"Come with me at the double, Kovařík!" shouted a figure as he ran past Pavel. It was Captain Krejči, a bull of a man who had led and inspired the rearguard during the defence of Bakhmach Junction.

When Krejči reached his men he stopped running and strode between them and the train full of Hungarians, all the time looking straight ahead and waving the two sides apart with the arm movements of a swimmer doing an extravagant breast stroke. He shouted orders to Pavel behind him.

"I shall stop half way, Kovařík. You carry on and keep the rest of them back. We must contain this at all costs."

"I understand, sir," said Pavel, and when the captain stopped Pavel continued, walking along an imaginary line which the men understood they were not to cross. Any man standing in his way was pulled back by his fellow soldiers. Until he reached the Slovak legionnaire, Drenko.

"Stand back, Rifleman Drenko," he commanded.

"I'm not giving way to those bastards any more," said the Slovak, his teeth gritted and his breathing coming short and sharp through flared nostrils. "We've all had enough."

"You're not giving way to them, Drenko. You're giving way to me and your captain."

Tears of anger and frustration filled Drenko's eyes. "You Czechs don't understand," he snarled. "It's been worse for us."

"I understand, Drenko," said Pavel, placing his hand on his shoulder. "But you and I don't choose the time or place to fight. Do we?"

His hand tightened on the Slovak's shoulder. "Now get back into line."

Drenko stared at Pavel, his eyes bulging with anger. To Pavel's relief he felt the resistance against his hand slacken, and the Slovak took a step back.

Pavel strode on down the line until he reached the men from his own wagon at the end of the train. The five boys in his section stood to attention in front of him and he nodded towards them. He looked back to see the other NCOs had now taken up positions between the men of the rearguard and the train full of Hungarian soldiers.

The legionnaires all stood to attention in front of their wagons, as Captain Krejči walked up and down the line. Behind him Pavel heard the jeers and abuse from the Hungarians, but they had lost their ability to provoke, as the Czech and Slovak soldiers stood to attention in silence, each man with a smile on his face. Pavel looked along the line of 400 men, some still carrying wounds from the fighting at Bakhmach two months earlier, and considered that nothing the legionnaires had done in battle surpassed the strength and discipline they were showing now.

He turned his head to see if there was any sign from the locomotive that they were preparing to leave, but the driver and fireman were looking out from the footplate, clearly enjoying the spectacle.

"For God's sake, captain, get the men back in their wagons," Pavel muttered to himself.

As he turned back to face the men, he glimpsed movement out of the corner of his eye and ducked instinctively as something flew past his right ear. He heard a scream of surprise and pain, and looked up to see Milan Musil slump to the ground.

"Stand fast! Stand fast!" he shouted to the men, who were breaking ranks to see what had happened at the end of their line.

Pavel went to Musil who was lying unconscious on his back, blood pouring from a long, deep wound which exposed the white of his skull. Beside him lay a piece of iron. It was thick and heavy and bent into the shape of the Greek omega. Pavel recognised it as a fixer used all along the track to secure the rails to the sleepers.

"Souček, get me a clean cloth from the wagon," Pavel said calmly.

"But I saw who threw it," protested Souček.

"Just get the damn cloth, boy. Now."

All along the line the NCOs kept the men to attention until Captain Krejčí at last gave the order, "Everyone back in the wagons".

Pavel wrapped the cloth around Musil's head, lifted him up gently, and ran with him to Erik Novák's makeshift hospital. The white cloth turned red as he ran past the men climbing back into their wagons. He kept running, oblivious to their renewed shouts of anger, until he reached the front of the train. Erik Novák was at the open door of the hospital wagon ready to lift Musil inside.

"Help the boy, Erik. For God's sake, help the boy. Some bastard threw this at him."

Pavel held up the piece of bloodstained iron as if examining it might help Novák determine the boy's injuries.

"Leave him with me, Pavel. He'll be alright with me."

Pavel threw the piece of metal to the ground and looked down at Musil's blood on his hands. He bent down and picked up dry dirt to wipe them.

"How is the lad?" asked Captain Krejči, who had followed Pavel up the track.

"I don't know yet, sir. He's unconscious. His eyes were rolling. Lost a lot of blood."

"I can see that. Well done, Kovařík. That could easily have got out of hand back there."

"What the hell were they thinking of, sir? Bringing a train in here."

"Some damned Russian forgot to change the points, I expect. I've told the driver to get those damned Hungarians on their way."

From the other end of the train came a new round of men shouting and jeering, followed by a loud crack.

"Christ! That's a rifle shot," said Krejči. "Come with me, Kovařík."

The two men raced again towards the rear of the train. As legionnaires appeared at the doors of the wagons the captain shouted to them. "Stay where you are, men. Stay where you are. Stay in your quarters, men. Stay in your quarters."

As they came nearer to the end of the train the order changed. "Back in the wagons, men. Get back in now."

At the final wagon Pavel saw five legionnaires standing around a body lying in blood-soaked dust in front of the Hungarians' train. All five held rifles at the shoulder pointed towards the train's empty windows. They were his boys, Vesely, Vaňek, Kolár and Souček. And the Slovak, Drenko.

"Lower your weapons, men," ordered Captain Krejči. "And stand to attention."

All five obeyed.

"Who the hell did this?" he demanded.

"We only... meant... to arrest him," stuttered Filip Souček, turning to Pavel.

"I shot the Hun bastard," said Drenko. "For what he did to the lad."

Krejči went up to him and shouted in his face. "Well, you're a damned idiot, man. You've now put every one of our lives in danger."

No sooner had the words left his mouth than a Russian commissar at the head of a troop of twelve Red Brigade soldiers appeared around the front of the locomotive. He stopped at the footplate and shouted instructions to the driver. Immediately the brakes were released and the train crept forward. Above the din Krejči spoke to the five legionnaires.

"Whatever happens now, men, you will do everything I tell you to do. You put your trust in me and your sergeant here."

He approached the Russian commissar and saluted. The salute was not returned. After a heated exchange it became clear the Russian was telling Krejči exactly what would happen next.

Krejči came back, his face flushed with anger.

"Legionnaires," he ordered, "ground your rifles. Form a line. Right face.

"Now, men," he said, "the Russians are putting you all under arrest and taking you to the station building."

"But it was me..."

"Shut up, Rifleman Drenko."

"They are taking you to the station building for interrogation. I shall send a Russian-speaking officer to accompany you, and I shall come to see you myself in exactly one hour. You've all been bloody fools, and the best you can do now is exactly what the Russians tell you to do."

Captain Krejči went back to the Russian commissar who ordered two of his men forward to pick up the body of the Hungarian. As the others approached to form a guard around the five legionnaires, Pavel stepped forward to Filip Souček .

"Milan is alive," he whispered to him. "Have faith, son. I won't leave you here."

Pavel saw Captain Krejči leave the white station building and stride across the tracks towards Colonel Čeček's train. Pavel left the hospital wagon to intercept him.

"How are they, Captain?" he called out.

"I can't say anything, Kovařík, until I've made my report to the colonel. But I will tell you one thing. I don't trust those bastards one bit. And they don't like being called Bolsheviks any more. We have to refer to them as Communists from now on."

He paused by the steps of Čeček's carriage.

"I know those boys look up to you, Sergeant. I want you to wait here a moment. If the colonel agrees, I would like to hear your opinion on all this."

Within a minute the door to the carriage was opened and Pavel was beckoned inside. He stood to attention in front of the colonel's desk. To his surprise the colonel stood up and leaned forward to shake his hand.

"Good to meet you at last, Kovařík," he said. "I've heard a lot about you. I understand the Russians gave you the Medal of St George after Zborov. First degree."

"It could have gone to a lot of braver men then and since, sir."

"That may be, Sergeant, but I haven't heard of many NCOs going through three lines of Austrian trenches with a handful of raw recruits."

Ček retook his seat.

"They're the lads the Russians have now, aren't they?" he said, turning to Captain Krejči.

"Yes, Colonel. Those four and a Slovak called Drenko. He's a good soldier in a fight, but a bit of a hot-head. He admits killing the Hungarian."

"And he got the right man, did he? It was the same Hungarian who injured one of ours?"

"Without doubt, Colonel. He was seen. Our men boarded the train to get him.

"And how is the lad who was hurt?"

Krejči looked towards Pavel. "Musil is still unconscious, sir. His skull may be fractured. He's one of my section too, sir. I think the four lads were just trying to get him some justice. I've taught them to stick together."

"And how are the Russians reacting, Captain Krejči?" asked Ček.

"They haven't mistreated our men yet, Colonel. But there's no doubt their sympathy is not with us. The Germans are putting them under a lot of pressure, as we know. I think if it had been a German soldier killed out there, our five men would already be dead."

"I tend to agree with you, Captain," said Ček.

"And there's something else, Colonel," continued Krejči. "I am certain I heard German voices in the offices of that station. They could just be returning POWs, but I think it's more than that. I think there are Germans out there influencing the way the Russians are treating us."

"And what do the Russians want to do with our five men?" asked the colonel.

"Take them into the town to appear before a People's Tribunal, sir. But I think if they do that we'll not see them again. Chelyabinsk is a big place. Over half a million people. They'll just disappear."

"I see," said Ček. He stood up and walked slowly behind his chair with his hands on the small of his back. He turned, placed his hands on the back of his chair and looked towards Pavel.

"And what do you think about all this, Sergeant Kovařík?" he said.

"May I speak freely, sir?"

"Of course."

"I agree with Captain Krejči. I think the Russian guarantee of safe passage to Vladivostok has become worthless. They have not openly declared it, but I think the Russians now have a policy of separating our forces along this railway and slowly disarming us, until they can target us in small groups."

"In what way do you think we'll be targeted?"

"I don't know, sir. Imprison us again perhaps. Or maybe they already have an agreement to turn us over to the Germans and Austrians. And we all know what they would like to do with us. And the Slovaks know too well what the Hungarians will do to them. The men sense it, sir. They feel trapped. With no way of fighting back. In two months we are less than one-sixth of the way to the Pacific. At this pace the war could be lost before we get back to the fighting. And the men know it. They know if it goes on like this they have little or no chance of seeing their families again."

"Are you married, Kovařík?" the colonel asked.

"Yes, sir. But it's not so bad for me. We have no children."

"How about you, Captain Krejči?"

"I have two daughters I haven't seen for two and a half years. I agree with Sergeant Kovařík, Colonel. The men are showing the strain. They see no progress. And they haven't even been able to get word to their families that they're still alive out here."

"There is some communication along the line," said Čeček. "We know Professor Masaryk and General Diterich both reached Vladivostok in April. We know the professor is in America. And I'm sure people at home know something about us out here. But I understand what you're both saying. It's hard on the men."

There was silence as Čeček looked down at his desk. Pavel knew the colonel had a reputation as a man of action, that he had gained his promotions through personal bravery and leadership in battle. The silence continued and Pavel waited. He felt his heart racing.

The colonel looked up. "Gentlemen," he said, "I have come to a decision. It is time for the Legion to become master of its own fate. This is what I propose. We shall send a delegation to the Russians demanding that our men be returned. But I don't expect that demand to be met.

"Captain Krejči, how many men on your train are fit enough to fight?"

"Without the five prisoners I have 397, sir."

"Good. With the men on my train and Captain Kudela's train we have a force of over 1,200 men. What weapons do you still have, Captain?"

"A Mosin-Nagant for every second man. And about ten rounds per rifle."

"Anything heavier?"

"Our Maxims were taken off us at Samara, sir."

"We still have two Maxims and enough rifles for about half the men on our train," said Čeček. "What do you think, Kovařík? Is it enough?"

"It's more than enough, Colonel. The Russians are an ill-disciplined rabble. Everywhere we have stopped I've not seen one sign of any central command."

"So you think our men could take the town?"

"I think we could take the whole railway, sir."

"Do you agree with that, Captain Krejči?"

"Yes, sir. Kovařík's right. If we act together, the Legion is the strongest force east of the Ural Mountains."

"Maybe the Russians have done us a favour," said the colonel, "stringing our forces out in trains along the whole length of the railway. They have put us in a position to secure every station and major junction.

"Before we act I have to consider, of course, the warning President Masaryk has given us about getting involved in Russia's internal politics. But the safety of our men must come first, and I know the President recognises the need for his commanders in the field to take decisions as circumstances dictate."

Čeček took his hands from the back of his chair and placed them firmly on his hips.

"Gentlemen," he said, "this is what we shall do. When the Russians refuse to release our men today, as I expect them to, we shall take the town.

"Word will then be sent up the line to all our forces that no more weapons are to be surrendered under any circumstances. And any future attempts to delay our trains will be met on every occasion with force.

"Gentlemen, from now on whenever or wherever the Legion is attacked, we shall fight back. We shall take control of the whole Trans-Siberian railway, if necessary. All the way to Vladivostok."

Chapter Fourteen

June 19th, 1918

"Thankyou, Robert, as always, for a very interesting briefing. So you think this Masaryk is a wily old fox, do you?"

"Well, Mr President, he's got the French and British on his side, and he was well in with the Russian Kerensky before those damned Communists took over."

"And you don't expect much will come from this Dr Beneš during the meeting?"

"No, Mr President. Professor Masaryk will do all the talking. Dr Beneš runs their headquarters in Paris, and he's well in there with President Poincaré. But it's definitely Masaryk who runs the show."

"Okay, Robert, have them shown through."

President Woodrow Wilson stood by the door of the Oval Office ready to receive his visitors. "Professor Masaryk, Dr Beneš, it's a great pleasure and a privilege to welcome you personally to the United States of America. I believe you both know Secretary of State Lansing."

Masaryk nodded towards Robert Lansing and smiled. It was Lansing who had advised him against the 'presumption' of expecting the title 'Mr President' when he was addressed during the meeting.

Masaryk and Beneš were offered seats on a low, white couch, while Lansing sat on an identical couch opposite them. President Wilson, a tall, stocky man in his early sixties, took his place on a straight-backed chair with striped blue and white upholstery, positioned so all three men had to turn their heads and look up in order to address him. An identical chair next to Wilson, reserved for visiting heads of state, remained empty.

"I believe, Professor," began Wilson, "that you have won the hearts of the American people during your tour of our cities, especially in Chicago."

"It's very good of you to say so, Mr President," said Masaryk, "but, of course, America won my heart first. My wife, Charlotte, is American. We were married here 40 years ago."

"My, my. I should have remembered that," said Wilson, looking over at Lansing. "And is your family well, Professor?"

"I regret that my family has had to suffer like so many Czech and Slovak families, Mr President. The Austrian secret police keep my wife under constant surveillance, and she has had to suffer the imprisonment of our daughter, Alice, for her open support of our cause. And, of course, there has been the death of our son, Herbert."

"Your son died in the war?"

"Indirectly, Mr President. He died of typhus."

"I am so sorry to hear these things, Professor Masaryk. I guess there's hardly a family in Europe that's been spared similar tragedies. And now we Americans had better get used to it. The first American troops entered the front line in France yesterday, ready for the allied counter-offensive."

"I am amazed, Mr President, how quickly the situation has changed on the western front," said Masaryk. "At the end of May the Germans seemed unstoppable."

"Everything's changed in the last three weeks, Professor. The Germans have blown themselves out, just as the French did last year. I'm told by our General Pershing that it's only been the British holding on over there."

"And I like to think we Czecho-Slovaks have also played our small part, Mr President. In France, in Italy, in Serbia, and in Russia."

"Of course, of course. And it's your role in Russia that really occupies me at the moment, Professor. I have been receiving reports that your men over there have started taking on the Germans *and* the Bolsheviks."

"It is a very complicated situation in Russia, Mr President. To explain our actions there it is necessary to understand how our people must view the world."

"I'm listening, Professor."

"We Czecho-Slovaks know that we shall always be at the mercy of the major powers, Mr President. In Europe we have always sat uncomfortably between the Teutons and our fellow Slavs. Between Germany, Austria and Hungary on the one hand and Russia and the Balkan Slavs on the other. In the past we always looked to Russia to deliver us one day from our Teutonic masters, but now the world has changed. Now, Mr President, we look to France and Britain, but above all to America, to help us become once again a sovereign people."

"I'd like to know how your policy in Russia fits in with that, Professor."

"Our policy in Russia was initially to fight *with* the Russians against Germany and Austro-Hungary, Mr President. But since the Communists made peace with Germany and the Hapsburgs in March, our only aim has been to get our men out of Russia to join the Czecho-Slovak Army in France, in order to fight alongside our remaining allies. That is still our only aim."

"So why does our State Department keep getting reports of your

Czecho-Slovak Legion fighting the Communists, and taking over large areas of Siberia?"

"Our men have tried very hard to stay neutral in Russia, Mr President, but it became clear that under pressure from Germany Lenin was withdrawing his promise of safe passage and ships. He intended to turn our men over to the Germans and Austrians. We could not allow that."

"So let's get this straight, Professor Masaryk. Are your men now in control in Siberia?"

"No, Mr President. We do not seek control of Siberia. Only the railway. In order to get our men out."

Wilson paused and with the palm of his right hand he massaged the left side of his chest to quell the angina. He breathed out deeply and sat forward.

"Professor Masaryk. Can you tell me," he said slowly, "why you went to so much trouble through our mutual acquaintances to get this meeting with me here today?"

Masaryk showed no surprise at the question. He leaned further back so that he could look Wilson in the eyes.

"I shall tell you with the greatest of pleasure, Mr President. I came here today to secure your support for the creation of an independent Czecho-Slovak state at the war's end. The whole world knows that you are the greatest advocate of oppressed peoples' right to self-determination, Mr President, and I would like you to state publicly that the Czecho-Slovaks have that right."

"Have I not already done so before Congress in January, in my fourteen-point plan for peace?"

"With respect, sir, no. You said then that the Czechs and Slovaks would have a right to 'autonomous development'. That is not enough for us, Mr President. We want no less than you promised the Poles. We want an independent, sovereign state for our people."

Wilson looked over at Robert Lansing who stared impassively back at him. Then he looked again at Masaryk.

"I have to say, Professor, that your request here today comes as no surprise to me."

"I had hoped it would not, Mr President."

"Could you tell me, Professor Masaryk, what structure your new state would have and which alignments it would seek?"

"The Czecho-Slovak state would be a federal state of Czechs and Slovaks as outlined in the recent agreement between our two peoples in Pittsburgh."

Wilson took a paper from a side table and looked down at it as he spoke.

"You say in this agreement that there is to be an autonomous administration for the Slovaks with their own assembly in Bratislava and their own law courts. And Slovakian is to be recognised as their language of education and administration. Is that right?"

"We are flattered, Mr President, that you are so well informed about our agreement in Pittsburgh."

"But the Czechs do intend to allow the Slovaks all of this, do they? Because, besides the Czechs, we have a strong Slovak lobby in this country."

"Mr President, I am surprised by the suggestion of any doubt on your part. My own father was a Slovak. And General Štefanik is a stalwart of our cause. Such a partnership is not new to us Czechs and Slovaks. One thousand years ago we were united in the Great Moravian Kingdom. We shall be equal partners in our new country, and we shall follow the traditions of Britain, France and the United States as blueprints for our democracy."

"Please don't be offended, Professor. If we do come to some kind of an agreement on all this today, we must know what we're signing up to."

"Of course, Mr President. Please ask as many questions as you find necessary."

"I have only one more, Professor. How important is it to you to get your men out of Russia?"

"Vital, Mr President. We want to strengthen the Czecho-Slovak Army in France and play our full part in the allied victory."

"What if I told you that you could play an even more important part by keeping your men in Russia?"

"I don't understand, Mr President."

"Let me be very honest with you, Professor Masaryk. We don't need more men in France. By next spring, if the war lasts that long, we plan to have three million American troops over there. General Pershing is one hundred per cent certain we will win then, if not before. But what we don't have is men in Russia."

"But what good can my men do there?"

"Two things. They can start a new front against the Germans in southern Russia and the Caucasus to stop the Germans transferring their men to the west..."

"But, President Wilson, that means asking my men to stop fighting their way to Vladivostok and to return to the Volga."

"No, Professor. It means they return to the Volga *and* keep the whole railroad open right up to Vladivostok. When we've finished with the Germans we intend to land allied troops in Vladivostok, make it an allied protectorate, and take on the Reds. We want your men to hold the area until we get there."

Masaryk turned to Dr Beneš. All colour had drained from his colleague's face. He thought of the men he had left behind in Russia, his army without a country, who would not be allowed to return home even when the war was won.

"I knew there would be a price to pay for our statehood, President Wilson," he said, "but not one as high as this."

He removed his pince-nez and stared at the floor, rubbing the bridge of his nose. When he looked up to speak his voice was firm.

"I know our men in Russia will do whatever their people ask of them," he said. "I just pray they will understand, and forgive us."

Chapter Fifteen

November 21st, 1918

"...happy birthday, dear Tomáš, happy birthday to y-o-u."

Everyone around the table clapped and cheered.

"*Jetzt muss er seine Kerzen ausblasen,*" said Otto, a veteran of five birthdays, two of which he remembered very well.

"We speak Czech when we are in Tomáš's house," his father corrected him.

"He has to blow out his candles," shouted Otto once more, this time with words sometimes used by his mother and a few of his friends.

Tomáš, raised up by the three cushions placed beneath him on a kitchen chair, looked inquiringly at Karolína.

"Go on, my darling, blow them out," she said, "and make a wish."

Tomáš blew out the two candles on his cake and wished that Anna had sung too.

"However did you find the ingredients for such a wonderful cake, pani Štasná?" asked Ernst.

"Oh, my word. Don't ask, Herr Neumann," said Magdaléna, as she cut through the icing into the fruit cake. "You could buy a horse and cart before the war for the price of what this cost."

"Nothing's too good for my Tomášek," said Michal, pouring more of his cherry slivovitz.

"Excellent kirsch, pan Štasný," said Ernst. "My, that's enough, sir. Many thanks."

"I propose a toast," said Michal, rising with some difficulty to his feet. "To our wonderful, precious grandson and to our very good friends. And to a world at peace at last. To Tomáš, to friends and to peace."

"Tomáš, friends and peace," chorused the adults, while the three children busied themselves with their cake.

"We're so sorry your dear wife could not join us today, Herr Neumann," said Michal, showing some surprise as he sat down that his chair was much lower than he had remembered.

"Esther's very disappointed and sends her love to you all," Ernst replied.

"Tell Esther I'll look by and see how she is in the morning."

"I'm sorry, Kája, but I think it's probably best to leave it for a day or two."

"Why? It's nothing serious, is it?"

"No, just a touch of fever, I think. I'll let you know when she's feeling better."

"Give her my love then, won't you?"

"Yes, of course."

"And mine," said Magdaléna. "So unfair, isn't it? Poor Esther keeps going right through that terrible war and then, just when it's all over, the poor dear's too ill to come over and celebrate. It doesn't seem right."

"No one says life has to be fair, Máma," said Karolína.

She stood up and removed the picture of Pavel she had placed on the table next to the birthday cake.

Ernst noticed the look Michal and Magdaléna exchanged as Karolína returned the photo to the large dresser behind them. Pavel's picture now had a strip of fine black ribbon running diagonally across its top left hand corner; an addition Karolína had made ten days before, when the end of the war was officially announced.

Ernst watched her as she went to the sink to fetch a cloth to clean up the children. She tried to wipe Tomáš's hands, but he took the cloth from her.

"I do it myself, Máma," he said.

She lifted him down from the chair and he waited by the table next to Anna while his mother cleaned her hands and face and lifted her down too. Tomáš took Anna's hand and led her to the corner where his presents were.

"Can I play with the train?" asked Otto, looking over to his father.

"You must ask Tomáš. It's his present."

"Tomáš won't mind," said Karolína. "He and Anna seem happy enough playing together with the other toys."

"That's a very fine train you've made for your grandson, pan Štasný," Ernst said. "I wonder if people might start spending their money on such beautiful things once more, now the war is over."

"I don't think I'll ever make a living as a toy-maker, Herr Neumann. But I am hoping people will want new houses and furniture now the fighting has stopped."

"But the fighting hasn't stopped, Táta" said Karolína, as she joined Ernst and her parents at the table. She passed her empty glass to her father, who filled only half of it with slivovitz.

"What about our men in Russia? Our army without a country, as

Professor Masaryk always called them. They are still having to fight."

"Wonderful men they are," said Magdaléna. "Famous the world over now."

"Yes, Máma, they are wonderful men. Brave men. But I think it's time we brought them home. The Hapsburgs and the German Kaiser are gone. We have our own country at last. Our soldiers have done enough."

"But they are doing an important job over there, Kája," said Ernst. "Fighting against the Reds who murdered the Tsar."

"I'm sorry, Ernst, but I cannot shed tears for the Tsar. He was just as bad as the Hapsburgs and the German Kaiser. I accept that your Emperor Karl may have been one of the few decent men amongst them, but we ordinary people are well rid of royal families in my opinion."

"But I still think your men in Russia are fighting for a good cause, Kája. If the Communists get the chance, I believe they will prove to be far worse than any of the old royal houses. And there are already Communist uprisings in Germany, you know. Just over the border in Bavaria. It needs to be stopped."

"I notice you say 'your' men in Russia, Ernst, not 'our' men. So you do not regard yourself yet as a fellow citizen of Czecho-Slovakia then? Not one of us?"

"Please, Kája," said Michal. "Herr Neumann is our guest. Please show some respect. I do apologise, Herr..."

"No, no, pan Štasný. As long as you and your dear wife do not object, I appreciate the chance to discuss such matters. I have learned over the last year and a half to appreciate Karolína's views. We are all friends. I like to hear them."

He turned to Karolína and smiled. "However, I cannot promise to always agree with everything she says."

"She was always headstrong, our Kája," said Magdaléna. "From a little girl she always let you have the benefit of her opinion. Like it or not."

"I am voicing what I believe, Máma."

"That may be, Kája. But it's true. You were always headstrong. I'm only telling what's true."

"But I wasn't giving an opinion anyway. I was just asking Ernst a simple question." She turned back to him. "Are you going to become a citizen of the new Czecho-Slovakia, Ernst, or not?"

Ernst looked over at the children. The light was dim and he rested in the secure warmth radiating from Magda's tiled stove and the inner glow from Michal's slivovitz. He saw Otto in his smart sailor suit, lost in his own world of trains and adventure. Tomáš and Anna, dressed identically in white smocks and long white socks, were in their own world too. Tomáš rebuilt a tower from the blocks of wood his grandfather had crafted for him and Anna knocked it down again, and they laughed together as the blocks scattered once more over the floor.

"If only we could stay like the children," Ernst said. "They don't mind what language they use, as long as they understand one another. And if they are happy they don't seek to spoil the happiness of others. But unfortunately they will not stay like that. They will learn soon that language sets them apart. And that although people may look the same as they do, they are different in this way or that. And they will be taught to be suspicious of those differences."

He looked back at Karolína. There was a weariness in his voice.

"My answer to your question is simple, Kája. I always shared your nationality. Previously we were all Austrian. Now we are all Czecho-Slovakian. I no longer care what I am, as long as my dear wife and children can live in peace. It is the only thing I would still fight for."

"The only thing?" said Karolína. "What about the German-speakers here who want to stay as part of Austria? Wouldn't you fight with them?"

"Kája, Kája...," tutted Magdaléna and she pushed her chair away from the table. Ernst waited until she had collected the plates and disappeared into the kitchen.

"No, Kája," he said quietly. "I would not fight with them. But I think Masaryk would do well to listen to them. He expects three and a half million German Austrians to become Czecho-Slovakian citizens overnight. He needs to tread gently with them, to respect prior allegiances."

"But you just said you wouldn't mind becoming a Czecho-Slovak."

"I know, Kája, but I think I am the exception. I have a Czech wife and Czech friends. But I still understand how my fellow German-speakers feel."

"But this is Bohemia, Ernst. It's always been Czech."

"I respect that. But the fact remains that most people in Egerland and the rest of the Sudetenland still see themselves as German."

"Then they will just have to be Czecho-Slovaks who happen to speak German."

"Just as you were expected to be an Austrian who happened to speak Czech?"

"That was different, Ernst."

"How?"

"Because we were *forbidden* to speak our own language and because the Austrians claimed our land as theirs. The Sudeten Germans, as you call them, may be a majority here, but this was always Czech land."

"You may be right, Kája, but I am afraid your new country may be born with the same malady that crippled Austro-Hungary."

"What malady?"

"Too many minorities who do not feel they owe it any allegiance."

"I have faith in our leaders."

"My God, Kája, do you realise that in a few short months you and I have completely swapped our positions?"

"No. How?"

"I had such faith in Emperor Karl to reconcile the different nationalities he ruled over, and you have the same faith in Masaryk and Beneš and Štefanik."

"But this is different. We have right on our side."

Ernst started to laugh, but then stopped himself and apologised.

"I'm sorry, Kája. I'm not laughing at you. I'm just thinking of the millions who have just died thinking they had right on their side."

Magdaléna reappeared from the kitchen. "Well, I think you've all had too much of your father's slivovitz. That's what I think," she said. "Look. Your father's fast asleep in his chair."

"I hadn't even noticed," said Karolína, and she and Ernst laughed gently at the sound of Michal's snoring.

"We must be going," said Ernst. "Come on children, it's getting dark."

Karolína fetched hats and coats and kissed Otto. She reached up to kiss Anna, half asleep against Ernst's shoulder, and at the last moment she kissed him too.

"Thankyou for talking to me, Ernst. Give Esther my love and tell her I shall visit her soon," she said.

"I will, Kája."

Michal came drowsily to the door and called after them. "Goodnight, Herr Neumann. Bye, bye, little ones."

As their visitors disappeared into the dusk at the edge of the clearing, Karolína closed the door with Tomáš in her arms and, realising Anna had gone, Tomáš began to cry.

Chapter Sixteen

November 22nd, 1918 – 25th May, 1919

The day after Tomáš's birthday party Esther died. She was one of the first victims in Bohemia of an influenza virus which arrived in France in the final summer of the war and grew in strength as it crept slowly eastwards. When the influenza arrived in Cheb at the end of November, almost half the population fell ill with it.

Tomáš and Magdaléna were both stricken by the virus but both recovered within a week, and for the same reason. Neither was in their prime. Tomáš because he had not yet reached his, and Magdaléna because hers was long passed. The virus reserved its most deadly effects for the fit and vigorous, turning their bodies' own defence system against them, so that the strongest adults enjoying their healthiest years became the most vulnerable.

Esther, still a nursing mother, suffered its worst effects. On the night of Tomáš's party she simply felt weak and feverish and took to her bed, insisting that Ernst should leave her and not disappoint the children. During the next three hours the virus slowly denied her control of her mind and body. When Ernst returned home with the children he found her in a delirium, her face tinted blue and blood trickling from her nose, mouth and ears.

The doctor who was summoned from Cheb sat with Ernst all night by Esther's bedside. Only the needs of the children in the morning tore Ernst away from her. And when Esther died in the early afternoon, only the thought of Otto and Anna stopped him from ending his life too.

By the 21st December 1918, the day President Masaryk returned in triumph to the new state of Czecho-Slovakia, the influenza virus left Cheb as abruptly as it had arrived. On its two-year journey around the world it paused at a prisoner-of-war camp for Austrian soldiers in Serbia. Here it claimed the life of Petr Kovařík, one of Pavel's younger brothers, who survived three and a half years of fighting unscathed, only to die when the war was over, still wearing the uniform of the old Hapsburg Empire.

During the months that followed his wife's death Ernst strove to maintain as much normality as possible in the lives of his children.

It was a perversely fortunate consequence of the war that children had become accustomed to death, and were not marked out by it. So when Otto returned to his primary school in Skalka after his mother's funeral, he was only one of many in his class struggling to come to terms with the loss of someone precious to them.

Ernst felt the greatest need of his children was for reassurance they would be cared for, and he did all he could to fill the void that had appeared so suddenly in their lives. But the lack of an extended family for Otto and Anna in Cheb was a great worry to him. His own parents had returned to their birthplace in Austria years before, and Esther's parents, Jakub and Hannah, were crippled by the death of their only child. In it they saw the judgement of a God stirred to anger by their 'neglect' of strict religious observance in their own lives, and in the life of their daughter and grandchildren, and they withdrew into the secure world they could find only in one another.

Without the help of Karolína and Michal and Magdaléna, Ernst did not know how he and the children would have coped in the six months after Esther's death. In the immediate aftermath little Anna understood only that her mother was not there, and she asked continually after her. But every morning throughout the winter months Karolína walked to Skalka to be at the Neumann house to coax the little girl awake, to love and reassure her, and dress and feed her.

And when Otto left for school she and Ernst made their way to the Štasný chata where they left Anna to spend the day with Tomáš, Magdaléna and Michal. Then they turned on their heels and walked together to their work in Cheb; Ernst to his post of director of the Municipal Theatre, and Karolína to the colonnade opposite the New Town Hall, where she now worked once more in the bookshop of Herr Alois Krause.

In this way a reassuring routine developed which gradually and steadily allowed comfort and then happiness back into all their lives; quite quickly for the children but far more slowly for the adults.

"I feel blessed to have your friendship, Kája," said Ernst, as they sat together one day in late spring by the River Ohře. "And that of your parents. And dear little Tomáš, of course. I don't know what my Anna would do without him."

"Or Tomáš without her," said Karolína. "I think those two just love one another."

They watched Anna and Tomáš playing in the sand a short distance from the rug where they sat with their picnic hamper. Both children wore smocks and sun bonnets and were busy running barefoot into the shallows to collect water for the moat which protected the castle they were building together. Further along Otto played alone, seeing how far he could skim a stone across the lazy current of the river.

The people of Skalka and Cheb had been made to wait until the end of May for a Sunday warm enough for them to parade in the park or sit by the river, and they had come out in their hundreds. Some were wearing fine, colourful fashions which had been kept packed away during the harsh years of war, but these were not the majority. Most still opted for modest wear and muted colours, as if to show that their suffering was not yet over and their future still uncertain.

"Have you noticed that Anna and Tomáš never argue?" Karolína remarked to Ernst.

"Only because Tomáš gives her whatever she wants," he replied, smiling at her.

"I taught him that." Karolína imitated a man's low voice. "To keep a woman happy, Tomáš, you must allow her to have her own way at all times."

Ernst looked at her as they laughed together.

"It's good to hear you laugh again, Kája. I know it has been hard for you."

"Hard for me? Surely it's you who have suffered most?"

"I'm not sure, Kája. Losing my darling Esther has made me understand how much more you have endured than I."

"I don't understand."

"I have been allowed to grieve for my Esther. I have her grave to visit. I have the certainty of it."

"I admit I have found it difficult. Her death seemed so unfair. The war was over. The danger past. The same with Petr."

"I'm sorry, Kája. I meant you have had more to endure than me because of Pavel."

"Oh, I see. Why have I had more?"

"Because you had to persuade foolish people like me to allow you to grieve. Because I see now you had to move forward for Tomáš's sake, just as I must for Otto and Anna. And I tried to persuade you that you should not. I apologise for that, Kája."

"Dear, dear Ernst," said Karolína, placing her hand on his right arm, "you do not need to apologise to me for anything. When I think of how you deny yourself all self-pity. How nothing stops you reaching out to the world. I have learned so much from you."

"Esther always said I was an optimist."

"You are. Your new play. The way you have accepted all the changes around you. I was afraid you might leave us and go back to Austria with the children."

"No, I would never do that. I am still very proud of my Austrian heritage, but the mother of my children was born in Bohemia of Polish Jews. I want Otto and Anna to always be a part of that."

Karolína turned towards Ernst, who kept his eyes on the children by the river as she spoke.

"I was worried in March," she said. "When Prague sent our troops to put down the uprising. That's when I was sure you would leave."

"I must admit, Kája, I did consider it then. Seeing people shot down simply because they wanted to remain a part of Austria. It was a terrible thing."

Ernst looked around towards the riverside park. "Do you notice something about all these people by the river today?" he said. "Some have dressed up for a special occasion, but most still remain drab and sullen. It's my guess that the ones who are smiling are Czech, and the rest are German."

"You're probably right. But Czecho-Slovakia is a young country, Ernst. It must be allowed to make mistakes."

"I understand that."

"The government could not simply sit back and allow this whole area to become the German Province of... What did they want to call it?"

"The Province of German Bohemia."

"Masaryk could not allow that. Our wonderful new country needs to fight every day to survive. We have our German-speakers here wanting to separate from us. And in Slovakia we have the Hungarians trying to invade us."

"It will take time for the world to adjust to peace, Kája. People have to become accustomed to the new realities in their lives."

"I am still struggling to believe the Hungarians have killed General Štefanik."

"I don't think anyone knows with any certainty who killed Štefanik, Kája."

"Well, I only know the poor man died before he ever had a chance to set foot in his own country. I think we should bring our Legion home from Russia. They would sort the Hungarians out right away."

"I think Masaryk understands the importance of the Legion remaining where it is, Kája. 'The men who created a country they have yet to see'. It's making Czecho-Slovakia famous throughout the world. Everyone wants to hear stories about them."

"Well, I think it's wicked. Asking those poor men to stay and fight thousands of miles away from their homes. Seven months after the war has ended. It's inhuman."

"Most things a soldier is asked to do are inhuman, Kája. Your men... *our* men in Russia understand that."

Karolína waved towards Tomáš who waved excitedly back to her and pointed to the castle he and Anna had created on the sand.

"Wonderful, *miláček*," she called out to him. "It's wonderful, darling."

Ernst looked at Karolína and they both smiled as they recognised the pleasure they shared in their children's happiness.

"Kája, may I ask you something? I am so anxious not to upset you."

"Of course, Ernst. What is it?"

"It's about our men in Russia. I know there is a lot of anger amongst families here because no lists have been made of the men still out there."

"Yes."

"I wondered if you still remain convinced that Pavel is not with the Legion in Russia?"

"Oh, Ernst. Three and a half years. Three and a half years and not one word. Not one report. What do you think?"

"But he couldn't contact you, Kája. There has been no way."

"I've heard of people receiving letters."

"Yes, from America. A lucky few in Vladivostok with relatives in Chicago have managed to get letters through. But Pavel could not do that."

"I know my Pavel. He would have found a way."

"But that's not fair on him, Kája. With the hardships those men must have faced, and are still facing, their only preoccupation is survival, and for officers the care of their men. I know what it's like. There is no room for anything else."

"Why are you saying all these things again, Ernst? What is the sense in it?"

"I want to try to explain something to you, Kája. But please be patient with me."

"Of course."

"When people look at my face and see my false arm, I sometimes see pity in their eyes. But they are wrong. I was lucky. The shrapnel shell that exploded over our trench and did this to me killed every man to my left and right. Nine in total."

"Dear Ernst..."

"No, Kája, let me explain. I saw whole lines of men, theirs and ours, cut down by machine gun fire. Dozens at a time. But often one or two men would remain standing right in the middle of it all. Completely untouched. And then my darling Esther. So happy. So healthy. Why was she cut down and so many others older and weaker were not?"

Ernst took Karolína's hand, as she dabbed her eyes with a handkerchief.

"No, don't cry, darling Kája. I do not want to upset you. I just want to say there is no reason why some are taken and some are spared. But we have been spared, Kája, you and I. And our children are spared, thank God. I simply ask myself whether this gives us some special responsibility."

"What responsibility?"

"To carry on. To be happy, and to make our children happy and secure. Give them a mother and a father. We already spend so much time together with them, Kája."

Karolína stopped wiping her eyes and looked at Ernst. He saw the shock on her face.

"Ernst, are you suggesting we...you and I..?"

"One day. Not for a time. Perhaps a long time. Only when the pain we both feel has lessened. And only if you are sure of your feelings about Pavel."

"I know my feelings towards Pavel, Ernst. I shall always love Pavel."

"Of course, and I shall always love my Esther. What I really meant was... if you are convinced that Pavel is not going to come back..."

Karolína started to get to her feet and Ernst quickly stood up to help her.

"I just need to walk, Ernst. On my own is best, I think."

"Kája, I have upset you. I am so sorry. It's the last thing..."

"No, Ernst, you have not upset me. But I do need to walk for a while. On my own. I won't be long."

Ernst watched her as she walked briskly along the narrow strip of sand by the river and climbed the steps leading up the bank into the park.

He sat down again on the rug and waved half-heartedly to the children, who studied him briefly before resuming their play. For five, ten, twenty minutes he sat there cursing himself for being so forward and so clumsy. Then he caught sight of Karolína coming back along the sand and he stood up. To his great relief he saw she was smiling at him as she approached.

"My dear Kája, please forgive me for being so thoughtless. I should have realised..."

"No, Ernst, no. You must not say that."

"Come and sit down, Kája. Tell me I have not spoiled everything."

"You have not spoiled anything, Ernst. Not at all."

She took his right hand in both of hers and they turned towards one another.

"You are a wonderful man, Ernst. I am so flattered that you should ask me such a thing. And I do see the perfect sense of it. For our children and for us."

She looked away from him.

"But, without meaning to, you have challenged me. You see, I would need to register Pavel's death, and..."

She bowed her head and her words were lost.

"I'm sorry, Kája. I should not have said anything. It was the wrong thing. The wrong time. I'm such a fool. "

"No. It really is alright," said Karolína, looking up at him again. "You have done the best thing for me, dearest Ernst. You force me to confront myself. To see if I am still clinging to the slightest piece of hope. But I need time to think."

"Of course, Kája, of course."

"Tomorrow, Ernst. I shall have an answer for you tomorrow."

Chapter Seventeen

October 28th, 1919

Pavel wanted to close his eyes and surrender to his emotions. He knew he dare not. Emotion was an unvoiced taboo amongst battle-hardened men. But the beauty of the music disarmed him and rendered him powerless. The notes tiptoed, trotted and stomped around him before grabbing him and threatening to give his emotions flight. Who would have imagined that the rough, scarred hands of a Slovakian legionnaire could produce such a sound?

Pavel sat motionless and tight-lipped, as the Heroic passage from Chopin's Polonaise took him on a journey he could not resist. As with all those seated in the drawing room the music's power filled his head with thoughts of those he loved most. Of his parents, of his brothers, but overwhelmingly of Kája, who seemed further away now than ever before.

The men were desperate to get home.

When the final punishing notes faded, the pianist held his hands in his lap and paused as silence filled the room. Then, as he stood and bowed in front of the grand piano, the sixty men in his audience rose as one and clapped and cheered and stamped their feet, at last able to release their feelings in disguised bravado. The men only retook their seats after several minutes, when invited to do so by Colonel Čeček.

"A bravura performance, Rifleman Gavalya," he declared. "Appreciated even more coming from such an unexpected source."

Gavalya bowed again and to renewed cheers and applause he took his seat in the front row.

"Now, fellow legionnaires," continued Čeček, "I want to congratulate you again for being those chosen by your fellow soldiers to attend this celebration. Unfortunately it has not been possible to assemble all 1,200 men of the Irkutsk garrison, but you will be charged with the duty of passing on to your units what you are told here today.

"But first, men, we must leave the Volkonskys' splendid drawing room and assemble in the reception room next door, where vodka is available for our toasts. Please make your way through, gentlemen."

Pavel filed through the high, narrow doorway with his friend Erik Novák. They entered the large reception room, which still boasted its original burgundy wallpaper and burgundy carpet, and each took a large glass of vodka from a trestle table to their left. The high windows were shuttered, and the room lit by candles in holders on the walls and in the single chandelier hanging low from an ornate rose in the centre of the ceiling.

"Move forward, men," called out Colonel Ček, who was not a tall man and had taken up position on a raised platform at the far end of the room.

"Move forward. That's right. Now, men, so that we do not have to stand here all day without taking a drink, I shall propose a toast. A toast which reminds us why we all find ourselves here, on the crossroads between China and Mongolia, so far from our loved ones. I give you a toast to our homeland, which today, the 28th October 1919, celebrates its first birthday.

"Gentlemen. Raise your glasses. The toast is 'our blessed Czecho-Slovakia'."

"Our blessed Czecho-Slovakia," chorused the men in one baritone voice. All emptied their glasses in a single draught.

"Fill your glasses, men," Ček encouraged them. "Those of you at the back, pass some bottles forward.

"Now, men...," the colonel paused amidst the noise. He raised his hand and the legionnaires standing shoulder to shoulder fell silent. "Our maestro Gavalya..."

The men cheered.

"Our maestro Gavalya..." Ček bowed in the Slovak's direction. "... chose a most appropriate piece of music to play for us today. Because, when Chopin wrote that piece, he had in mind that one day his Polish homeland would become a free and independent nation again, just as so many of our forebears dreamed of a free and independent country for our people.

"Men, President Masaryk has asked for the following message to be passed on to all his soldiers in Russia on this special day."

The colonel took a piece of paper from the breast pocket of his tunic and held it at arm's length in his right hand. He paused and cleared his throat.

"The message reads, '*On the occasion of the first anniversary of the rebirth of our nation, its people acknowledge a simple truth. Without our Legion in Russia there would be no Czecho-Slovakia*'. It is signed, '*T. G. Masaryk*.'"

The men stood in silence. No one moved.

"Copies of that message have been made for you to show to your fellow legionnaires," said Čeček softly. "You can take them from the far table when you leave."

"But now, men," he commanded, "I propose another toast. To the two men who fought more than any others to create our new nation. And for which one has been asked to lay down his life. To Masaryk, and to Štefanik, may he rest in peace. Gentlemen, I give you 'President Masaryk and General Štefanik'."

The soldiers raised their glasses and stood to attention. "President Masaryk and General Štefanik," they said, in one rich, firm voice.

Bottles and glasses clinked together, as the vodka warmed the men to their task, and they prepared for the next toast.

"I have only one more toast to propose, gentlemen," said Colonel Čeček, "and I think it is appropriate that it is made in this house.

"As you will know by now, this was once the home of Prince Volkonsky. Volkonsky was a brave man. One hundred years ago he called for the freedom of the Russian serfs, and for his trouble Tsar Nicolas the First sent him into exile, here in Irkutsk. Once he was here they had no need to build a prison for him. The isolation of this place meant he had no way out.

"We legionnaires have one thing in common with Volkonsky. For we are suffering our own exile here. We dared to ask for the freedom of our people, and for our trouble we were sent here to Siberia to fight the Reds. But that is the only thing we do have in common with Volkonsky, men, because I promise you, we *shall* get out."

If Čeček was expecting a cheer, he was disappointed. As his words hung in the air many men looked down and shuffled their feet. Some took a drink. All were silent.

"I can see from your faces you have had enough of fine words, men," he said, looking down at his full glass. "I cannot blame you. You have already achieved the impossible. Taking the whole line. Fighting the Reds off for almost a year. I salute you, men, and wish I could tell you that you are all going home soon. But I cannot. Not yet.

"But there is some good news, for the most unfortunate amongst us. I can tell you that next month all our wounded will be evacuated from Vladivostok. They will sail from there to America, then on to Europe and home. It's a start, men. It is a start."

Encouraged by the animated talk that now spread amongst the men, Čeček took his chance to propose a final toast.

"One last toast, men," he called out above their noise. "The toast is,

'The Legion. Nazdar.'"

"The Legion. Nazdar," shouted the men, as once more they faced him and stood to attention.

Pavel was talking with Erik Novák when Colonel Čeček approached them.

"I trust that was the news you wanted to hear, Captain Novák," said the colonel.

"It's excellent news, sir. Have our people at home arranged it?"

"Indirectly. Czechs and Slovaks in America have provided funds for a Red Cross ship."

"How many wounded can it take, Colonel?" asked Pavel.

"About 8,000. Will that be enough, Captain Novák?"

"It should be, sir. But we're taking fresh casualties every day as the Reds push us further up the line."

"I know. It's a mess," said Čeček. "But what can we do against three and a half million of them? It's an impossible task."

"I don't understand why we're getting no help from the Allies in Vladivostok, Colonel," said Pavel. "I heard the Japanese have 70,000 men there now. They call it the Allied Intervention, but they're not intervening at all to help us."

"It's because they want the Legion to do their dirty work," said Čeček. "It's not just the Japanese," he continued. "The British have 16,000 men warming their arses in Vladivostok. The French have 12,000, the Americans 13,000. The Japanese are here to grab eastern Siberia, Kovařík, have no doubt. And the rest have come to make sure they don't grab too much. I understand only too well why our men have had enough of it."

"It's not just the lack of help from the Allies that's affecting the men, sir," said Pavel. He paused as Erik filled his glass.

"Go on. What else is it, Kovařík?" asked Čeček.

"It's the behaviour of the people fighting with us, Colonel. Admiral Kolchak's White Russians and the Cossacks."

"But they're good fighting men, Kovařík. Especially the Cossacks."

"I know, sir, but they have no discipline. Our men see what they do to the women and the children. Kolchak's people are not soldiers. They are murdering thugs. We don't want to be a part of that."

"I know, Kovařík, it's a terrible thing. But it happens on both sides."

"Not by our men, it doesn't. It's a civil war, Colonel. The worst kind of war. Our men should not be part of it."

"I'm not like you, Kovařík. I've been a professional soldier all my life.

I have grown used to these things."

"But most of our men aren't used to it, Colonel. No one can doubt their bravery when they're fighting for what they believe in, but they're sick of this. Can I tell you what my boys witnessed recently, sir?"

"Go on."

Erik excused himself and left the two men alone.

"Admiral Kolchak appointed a new commander at Omsk," continued Pavel.

"Semenov," said Ček. "The Japanese appointed him. A hard man."

"A sadistic man. Before Omsk fell, Semenov took 800 Red prisoners. The next day he ordered 200 to be shot. The day after 200 were gassed. Then he drowned 200 in the Om River, and the last 200 were buried alive. And do you know what the bastard's excuse was? He did not want his soldiers to get bored. I do not see, Colonel, how fighting alongside a man like that helps Czecho-Slovakia."

Ček stared at Pavel. He was clearly agitated but said nothing. He took Pavel's arm. "Come with me, Kovařík," he said, and led him towards the narrow door into the drawing room.

Ček took two chairs used earlier for the concert and placed them in a corner facing one another.

"Sit down, Pavel, I want to tell you something. But you must not repeat it."

The colonel looked around to check no one could overhear their conversation.

"You have been in my command for a year and a half now, Pavel. Since Chelyabinsk. I'm going to tell you something because I know you are a good man and I can trust you. And I think you need to know it.

"When we captured that armoured train back at the Volga the summer before last, do you remember where we went next?"

"We made a detour to Kazan. To the armoury. To rearm."

"That's right. And do you remember how many wagons we filled?"

"Fifteen."

"Right again. But I can tell you those wagons were not all filled with armaments."

"I'm sorry, Colonel. I don't follow you."

"You really don't know what else was at Kazan?"

"No, sir. I don't."

"Well, I shall tell you. Kazan was not just an armoury; it was also where the Tsar's gold bullion was stored. Eight of those wagons we took away from Kazan were loaded full of it. They still are."

Pavel looked hard at his colonel. He knew Čeček had been drinking but he seemed sober enough, and his eyes were clear.

"Where are these wagons now, Colonel?" Pavel asked.

"Here, in Irkutsk."

"And who knows about this?"

"Everyone senior to me in rank. Certain people in Prague. And, I am pleased to say, Lenin and Trotsky."

Pavel was no longer so sure of Čeček's sobriety.

"How can it be good that they know?"

"Because if they were not absolutely sure we had the Kazan gold, they might not deal with us."

"Deal? To do what?"

"To let us get out of this mess."

Čeček rested his left forearm on his knee and leaned forward.

"You are right, Pavel. We can all see the men have had enough. They no longer believe in the fight, and why should they? The Allies have abandoned us. They have no intention of involving their own troops in all this. And most important, Masaryk wants us home. He needs us against the Hungarians in Slovakia and against the possibility of trouble on the German border."

"The German border, sir? That's where my family is. In Cheb."

"Well, don't worry. I believe most of the trouble there is over now. But things in Germany and Hungary are very unsettled. There's a lot of Communist agitation."

"How do you get all this information from home, sir, if I may ask?"

"There are plenty of telegraph links at the higher levels, Pavel. Just not for the lower ranks, I'm afraid."

"So what is the plan, Colonel?"

"We give Lenin the gold, and we give him Admiral Kolchak. In return Lenin will allow Red Cross ships in. Keep everything to yourself, Sergeant, but in the New Year we are all going home."

As the late afternoon turned into evening and the legionnaires drifted back to their billets, Pavel sought out Erik. He found him sitting at the grand piano in the drawing room, his head bowed and shoulders slumped as he picked out random notes with his forefingers.

"This is a Lichtenthal," Erik said without looking up. "It belonged to Prince Volkonsky's wife. The wives were given a choice, you know. They could go with their husbands into exile or stay with their children. Husband or children. Not both."

He looked at Pavel through reddened eyes.

"Strange, isn't it, the cruelties we devise to add to the misery of others?"

"It is, Erik."

"We've got a grand piano at home, you know. Both my children play."

"Maybe you will hear them again soon."

"They'd have to play damned loud."

"No. I mean you'll see them soon. You will be going back with the wounded, won't you?"

"No. The Red Cross will have their own people on the ship. I'm stuck here with you, Pavel, my friend. Indefinitely. Or maybe longer."

Pavel put his hand on his friend's shoulder. "No, Erik, I think you'll see your family soon. I sense it."

He pulled up a chair and sat by the side of the piano facing his friend.

"Erik, can you tell me if you are planning to send Milan Musil home on that ship?"

"I think I must, Pavel. I know you want to keep your boys together. I know they do all they can for him, but Musil needs specialist help."

"I realise."

"Brain injuries are very hard to treat. Musil has grand mal. Any one of those seizures could kill him."

"I know."

"Are they still coming once a day?"

"More sometimes. You don't understand what I'm saying, Erik. I *want* Milan to go. I can see he's getting worse. He needs constant supervision. He has no idea of risk or danger. I am desperate to get him on that boat."

"Good. Then I shall see that he does."

"Thankyou, Erik. That's a great relief to me. Shall we go now, old friend? Come on, I'll give you a hand."

Pavel found their greatcoats and fur hats, and helped Erik on with his. He put his right arm around Erik's back and placed his hand under his right armpit to steady him. When they reached the wooden steps outside the front door he helped him down to the street. The sky was clear and starful. Their breath condensed in front of them and the mud, frozen into ruts beneath their feet, made walking treacherous.

The crisp air multiplied the effect of the vodka on Erik, and Pavel found it difficult to steer him on a safe path. As they walked, Pavel talked to him to keep him alert.

"I have something to confess, Erik," he said. "There is another reason I'm pleased Musil will be on that ship."

"Oh?"

"He comes from Karlovy Vary. That's not too far from Cheb, where I live. Are you listening, Erik?"

"I think I am."

"Musil will be home before any of us. I'm going to ask him to carry a letter for me. Are you still listening?"

"Yes. Musil... Karlovy Vary."

"He can take my letter with him. Do you see, Erik? At last I can get word to my Kája that I'm still alive. Isn't that good?"

"Yes, Pavel. That's really good..."

Chapter Eighteen

May 26th, 1919 – February 10th, 1920

Karolína slept very little during the night following Ernst's proposal. In the early hours she grew concerned that her restless state might disturb Tomáš, who still shared her room in her parents' chata. She went over to look at her boy asleep in his cot by the window.

It was a warm night and the shutters were left open, allowing the blue light of the full moon into the bedroom. Tomáš had kicked the blanket from his body and lay on his back with both arms above his head. Karolína smiled at the pure joy she felt looking at him. He was exactly two and a half years old now and already she could see the man her little boy would one day become. Loving and giving, intelligent and inquisitive, physical and strong. Just like his father.

Karolína put on her shawl and slippers. She took Pavel's picture from her dresser and, clutching it to her breast, crept down the stairs and out of the cottage. She went over to the cherry tree at the edge of the wood, brushed the white blossom from the bench beneath it, and sat down.

It was the first time for nearly two years she had sought to be alone with Pavel. She looked down at the photograph on her lap. The young man in his best suit was sitting face on to the camera, staring straight at her. He had a serious expression on his face, but Karolína recognised the crease at the corner of his eyes and mouth which betrayed the beginning of a self-conscious smile. "I cannot take this photograph seriously, Kája," he seemed to be saying.

She smiled at him. "You fool," she said softly.

Her right hand touched a piece of paper tucked in the top of the frame. She had not allowed herself to look at it for a long time. She unfolded it. '6th April, 1916,' it said at the top. And at the bottom was the last communication Pavel had sent to her. *I shall live and come home to you.*

"Oh Pavel, why have you left me so long? What shall I do?"

At the front door of the chata Michal heard his daughter's sobs drifting into the trees and over the water of the lake. He stayed out of sight and said a silent prayer of thanks, before tiptoeing up the stairs back to bed.

In the morning Karolína went as usual to Ernst's house to help him with the children. At seven thirty they saw Otto off to his school in Skalka and then walked the two kilometres to the Štasný chata. They said little to one another as they walked, but they indulged Anna in every question she asked about the flowers, rabbits and butterflies which constantly drew her attention.

When they arrived at the cottage, Tomáš was sitting at the far end of the table dipping pieces of his grandmother's *rohliky* bread in his hot chocolate. Michal, in his carpenter's apron with shirt sleeves rolled up to his elbows as always, sat at the corner of the table, watching his grandson and chatting to him.

"Anna's here," shouted Tomáš, "And Máma too!"

Michal looked over at Karolína and held her gaze, nodding and smiling reassuringly.

"Would you like some coffee, Herr Neumann?" asked Magdaléna. "We have real beans."

"Very kind of you, pani Štasná, but I really must be going." He took his pocket watch from his waistcoat. "I must open the theatre for rehearsals at eight o' clock."

"I have to go too, Máma," said Karolína. "Herr Krause is stocktaking."

"We'll see you both this evening then," said Magdaléna.

Ernst opened the front door and stepped back to allow Karolína through. He turned and looked towards Magdaléna.

"Pani Štasná, I want to say... I cannot thank you enough for all you have done for my darling Anna. I know Esther would want to thank you too..."

Magdaléna took a handkerchief from her apron pocket and held it to her chest.

"Oh, my dear Herr Neumann," she said, "you must understand. We love Anna like one of our own. Don't we, Děda?"

Michal got to his feet and picked up the little girl. "Of course we do," he said, and he kissed her.

"Just as we loved dear Esther like one of our own," said Magdaléna.

"Thankyou," said Ernst. "You are such kind people." He turned to leave. "Thankyou," he said again.

Karolína was waiting for him outside. "What were you talking about?" she asked.

"I wanted to tell your parents how grateful I am to them."

"I am sure they know that."

"Perhaps. But of all the things Esther's death has taught me, the most important is to declare your feelings when you have the chance. Leave nothing good unsaid."

"Did you not do that with Esther?"

"Yes, I did, thank God. She knew how much I loved her. She could have had no doubt."

They walked in silence and Ernst glanced again at his pocket watch. "We must hurry, Kája. We shall be late."

"No, Ernst. Let's not hurry at all. We can both afford to be a little late for once. Let us walk slowly and take our time. What you said just then is very true. We need to say the things that should be said. We need to be very honest with one another and trust one another."

"Trust one another? In what way?"

"Trust that neither of us would ever say or do anything with the purpose of hurting the other."

"That sounds ominous. Should I prepare myself to be hurt?"

"I hope not, Ernst. I spent much of last night awake. I sat for hours back there under the tree."

"In the middle of the night?"

"Yes. I was with Pavel again. For the first time for years I allowed him back into my life. I've tried so hard to keep him alive in Tomáš's life, but I realised I had shut him out of mine. For a long time it was just too painful. But I do not want to be without him any more. I want to embrace him and have him with me all the time."

"Does that mean you think he is alive after all?"

"No. I don't mean that. I'm not a little girl, Ernst. I don't believe a miracle will happen after three years and Pavel will simply walk through the door. I'm not going to torture myself with that thought again."

"So what do you believe?"

"I believe Pavel must be dead, but I see now that does not mean he is lost to me. Even without him I am still his wife. I want to keep him with me. I want to stay married to him."

"I see."

"Does that hurt you terribly?"

"It hurts only if you think I do not have the same feelings for my Esther. The way you describe your need for Pavel's presence is the same need I have for her. But I have never denied myself those feelings, Kája, as you have for so long. They are part of how I live. How I shall always live. But they are new for you. I think it is wonderful if you have found such a place for Pavel in your life. If thoughts of him make you happy again."

"I have you to thank for making it so clear to me, Ernst."

They had reached the point where the path from Skalka joined the road to Františkovy Lázně. They turned right and continued on their way over the bridge to Cheb. Early on a Monday morning the road was quiet and they were able to walk undisturbed in the middle of it.

"I also slept very little last night," said Ernst.

"Were you sitting under a tree too?"

Ernst did not laugh or smile.

"No. I was in my kitchen. Worrying."

"About what?"

"About upsetting you. About whether I was being disloyal to my wife and my best friend by my proposal."

"Can you see that you have not upset me at all, Ernst? You cannot be blamed for searching for happiness for yourself and your children. It shows the optimism and courage in you that Esther loved so much. Don't turn it against yourself."

"Thankyou for saying such things."

"I am sorry I cannot help you find happiness by being your wife, Ernst. You must know, I do have feelings for you."

"Do you?"

"Of course, and I am sorry it must be like this. I feel so ungrateful. I hope we can still carry on the way we are. I would still like to help with Otto and Anna."

"I think it's best not, Kája. Above all, it's not fair to subject you to any more of the gossip. When people see us leaving together in the morning."

"I don't care a jot about gossip, Ernst. You know that. You and the children will always come before that."

Ernst placed his hand lightly on her back.

"Bless you for such generous thoughts, Kája. But I think the three of us can manage quite well now in the mornings. Otto is growing up and you have seen how much he can help now. Tying Anna's laces and ribbons and such. Getting his own food. He's a good boy. A brave boy."

"If you're sure it's better for them."

"We can manage now in the mornings, Kája. But it would help so much if we could keep the arrangements with Anna during the day."

"Of course. My mother and Tomáš would be heartbroken without her. You must let her come."

"I will, of course. Thankyou."

"And will you be alright, Ernst?"

"Yes, Kája. I am a practical man. I shall move forward, and so will my children. But they need a mother. It is not good for them to be without a loving woman in their home. And one day, not yet, but one day, I shall need companionship."

"I can see what a good match our two little families would have made, Ernst. Maybe, one day... No, I'm sorry. That's not fair of me."

"Kája, I hope I did not make my proposal yesterday sound too much a matter of practicality."

"No. I understood."

"Perhaps you didn't, Kája. I should not like you to think I regarded you only as a replacement homemaker. After what you have explained to me this morning it may seem indelicate of me to say this, but I admire you greatly, Kája. And I feel the deepest affection for you."

Karolína linked his arm and moved closer to him.

"Dearest Ernst, I could not have found better words to describe my feelings for you. I place you alongside Pavel and my father as the most wonderful of men. I can see so clearly why Esther loved you so much. Whatever happens in our lives, I know we shall always remain close to one another."

Over the following months Michal noticed a change in his elder daughter. She took to spending hours alone in the house she had once shared with Pavel. And two or three times every week she would pack some bread and cheese and beer into a bag and take off on her own on the long walk around the lake.

At the meal table she showed interest in the smallest detail of his and Magdaléna's day. And she was more relaxed with Tomáš, worrying less about the things she felt she ought to be teaching him, and allowing the little boy to follow his own path.

"She's found some peace at last, Máma," concluded Michal to his wife. "God be praised."

And then one day in early February a letter arrived for Karolína from Karlovy Vary. The address was written in a hand neither Michal nor Magdaléna recognised. On the back of the envelope was the address of the sender embossed in black lettering.

Pan a paní Eduard Musil
Villa Musil
Taborska ulici
Karlovy Vary

When Karolína arrived home she too did not recognise the name

'Musil', and she made little of the letter. Only when she had been upstairs to wash and change did she sit down at the kitchen table to open it. Michal watched, as first a red flush appeared on her face and then all colour drained from it.

"My God. What does it mean?" she said.

Karolína stood up. Tomáš forgot the important journey he was taking with his train and looked up anxiously at his mother.

"She wants me to go to see them. In Karlovy Vary."

Karolina took the letter to her father. "Look, Táta. "What does it all mean?"

Michal held the letter, and Karolína read it again over her father's shoulder.

Sunday, 8 February, 1920

Vážení paní Kovaříková,

Please excuse my writing to you when I am unknown to you and we remain without the benefit of mutual acquaintance. I assure you I would not do so if I were not pressed by the most wonderful, yet most tragic, of circumstances.

I write, you see, on behalf of my dear son, Milan, who has recently been delivered to his family after four long years during which his father and I supposed he had been killed in action, as have so many of his friends.

Our darling Milan has been grievously injured and it has taken us long, painful hours to learn of all that has befallen him. Suffice to say that having left his home as an infantryman in the Imperial Army he has been made to endure the most terrible privations. He has now been returned to us in the uniform of the Czech Legion in Russia.

The nature of Milan's injury makes it very difficult for him to communicate with others. He very easily becomes agitated and this will often cause my dear child to suffer the most dreadful seizures. The greatest source of his agitation would appear to be a letter which he bore with him on his return. It was from the envelope of that letter, pani Kovaříková, that I have managed to secure your name and address.

Milan refuses all entreaties we might make to post the letter to you. Indeed he is insistent that he will only allow the letter out of his possession by delivering it personally into your hand. We know nothing of the contents of this letter, but we assume that it must have been entrusted to Milan by someone known to you.

Pani Kovaříková, it is with humility that I ask you to bring an end to my son's anxiety. For I fear that it is only you who can do so by coming in person to our home in Karlovy Vary to take delivery of your letter from Milan's own hand. I know it is much to ask of you, but you can be assured that by coming here you will bring much needed peace into the life of my dear troubled boy.

Madame, I remain your humble servant as I await your urgent reply,

Nataša Musilová

Chapter Nineteen

February 16th, 1920

"Here we are, Ernst. A compartment all to ourselves. Do you mind if we sit by the window?"

Ernst waited for Karolína to take her seat. He considered sitting beside her and taking her hand, but thought better of it. He took the seat opposite.

"It's not a very nice day, is it?" she said. "I prefer snow to all this rain."

"It's because it's so mild. It's not cold enough to snow."

"How long will it take us?"

"Less than an hour. It's only 40 kilometres, and we don't have to change."

"That's good."

Ernst removed his Homburg and gently brushed away the droplets of rain.

"Are you very nervous, Kája?"

"No, not really. I've been to Karlovy Vary before."

"That's not what I meant."

"I know you didn't." Karolína looked out at the platform.

A whistle blew and the carriage lurched forward. Ernst saw Karolína close her eyes as the train slowly pulled out of Cheb station.

"I'm so grateful you are coming with me, Ernst."

"I'm very pleased you asked me, Kája. I wondered whether your parents would really like to have accompanied you."

"No, it's too much for them, Ernst. Karlovy Vary. The Villa Musil. And that poor boy. It would have overawed them."

"I understand."

"No one knows what we shall find out, do they?"

"No, Kája. And I think it's best not to speculate too much."

"It could be a letter from Pavel. Or it could be from someone who knows him... or knew him. I don't know."

Ernst leaned forward and took her hand.

"Whatever we learn, Kája, we shall deal with it together. You as Pavel's wife, and I as his friend."

The train was soon in open countryside, following as closely as it could the valley of the River Ohře as it, too, made its way northeast to the old imperial spa town of Karlovy Vary. Ernst sat back and searched for the outline of the Ore Mountains to the north, but everything beyond the middle distance was obscured by the rain.

He drew his gaze back to the foreground and glimpsed Karolína's reflection in the window. Her eyes were cast down and fixed on the side of the track. She was so lost in thought she had not noticed that the wide brim of her hat was creased against the glass.

"Don't spoil your nice hat, Kája."

She looked up, but showed no sign she had taken in what he had said to her.

"Can I tell you something, Ernst? You won't think I'm too silly?"

"You can tell me whatever you like, Kája. You know I won't think that."

"I was thinking about all the years I spent convinced that Pavel was dead. I was so certain of it. And then last spring when you honoured me with your proposal... It was then..."

"It's alright, Kája. You can tell me."

"It was then that Pavel came back to me. And he has been with me ever since. We go for walks together around the lake. I talk to him. And I started to go to church again. Did you know that?"

"No, I didn't."

"Every morning for months. It has given me peace and brought him closer to me. And then the letter came. And now we are going to Karlovy Vary. I wonder... is it possible..?"

"Is what possible, Kája?"

"That I have somehow brought him back? That without faith it could not have happened? And with faith anything can happen?"

"Oh, Kája, what a question you ask me. You know I'm not a religious man. Religion caused so many problems for Esther and me. But I can say this. I do believe that good and bad exist in our world, and it is our duty to add only to the good. That is your way, Kája, and I believe that your goodness invites good into your life. You can call it faith of a sort, if you like."

"I am so nervous, Ernst. I feel now that if I stop believing for a second the letter is from Pavel... if I lose faith... I can make it all go wrong..."

Ernst got up and sat next to her. He took her hand and kissed it.

"My dear Kája," he said. "Whatever we learn today, Pavel has already come back to you. Nothing you do or think can change that."

The train pulled in to Karlovy Vary. Karolina and Ernst walked in silence past the ticket collector and through the station's elegant concourse. At the main entrance they paused at the top of the steps and looked down onto the winding, wooded valley containing the main part of the town. Below the station the Tepla River emerged from the valley and flowed into the larger Ohře as it edged past Karlovy Vary on its way north.

At the foot of the station steps a dozen or so motorised and horse-drawn taxis were lined up, waiting to take new arrivals into the town's sanatoria and fine spa hotels.

"Pani Musilová definitely wrote that she would send someone to meet us here, did she, Kája?" asked Ernst.

"Yes. Eleven o'clock at the front entrance."

Ernst glanced over Karolína's shoulder. "This could be our man," he said.

A tall figure in a light-grey chauffeur's uniform walked towards them up the steps, carrying a large umbrella. As he drew nearer he removed his peaked hat and bowed his head gently to Karolina.

"*Entschuldigen Sie, bitte, gnädige Frau. Sind Sie vielleicht Frau Kovařík?*"

"I am most certainly *paní Kovaříková*," replied Karolína.

"Of course, madam. I have been sent to collect you. Would you care to follow me?" He nodded towards Ernst. "Sir, if you would please follow me."

The chauffeur led them under the cover of the umbrella to a large red Mercedes with a black hood. He opened the door for Karolína, and Ernst helped her up the step into the passenger compartment. Ernst took his place next to her on the black leather seat. As they crossed the bridge over the Ohře and drove along the main street of Karlovy Vary beside the Tepla River, he felt Karolína's grip on his hand grow tighter.

By the Grand Hotel-Pupp, the most opulent in Karlovy Vary, the chauffeur turned right over one of the many bridges which crossed the Tepla River. Slowly the car wound its way up the side of the steep, wooded valley until at the top they arrived at the entrance to a long driveway guarded by two stone pillars. As they passed between the pillars, Ernst glimpsed a brass shield bearing the inscription, 'Villa Musil'.

The car pulled up in front of a grand house built of white sandstone. Immediately a butler approached with an umbrella.

"Please follow me, madam and sir," he instructed in German.

He led Ernst and Karolína into a tiled entrance hall, where two maids took their coats and Ernst's hat. The butler seemed surprised when Karolína removed her hat-pin and hat and handed them both to him.

117

"Madam may retain her headwear, if she wishes," he said, passing the items to a maid.

Karolína did not hear him.

"Madam does not choose to retain it," said Ernst. "Please announce us to your mistress."

"As you wish, sir," said the butler. He ushered them towards a large mahogany door.

"One moment," Ernst ordered. "You will please announce us in Czech. We are pani Kovaříková and Captain Ernst Neumann."

When they entered the large drawing room it was not immediately apparent that the lady of the house was there. Ernst saw only the fine antique furniture, the damask curtains beside the tall windows, and on the walls a dozen or more abstract oil paintings, all in striking colours.

As soon as the butler announced them, Ernst glimpsed movement at the far end of the room, where glass-paned double doors led into a conservatory. A lady emerged from behind a screen and walked towards them holding both arms outstretched in greeting. Ernst thought she must be in her early fifties. Her hair was waved and she wore an elegant day dress of grey silk. She went straight to Karolína.

"My dear pani Kovaříková, how good of you to come all this way," she said. "I am Nataša Musilová. My husband is unfortunately detained on business in France this week, but he also wishes to thank you. We are both so relieved that you agreed to come."

"I'm very relieved to be here, paní Musilová," said Karolína. "I can scarcely wait to speak to your son." She looked around. "Where is Milan?"

"Be patient, my dear. Milan is in the conservatory. Before you see him there are some things I must explain to you. But please come and sit down." Milan's mother turned to Ernst and held out her hand. "Please excuse my poor manners, Captain Neumann. There are times when we mothers have thoughts solely for our children."

Only now did Ernst notice the hollowness around Natasa Musilová's liquid eyes, and the pallor of her face, which was marked by the war as surely as his own.

"I do understand, madam. My only wish is for you and pani Kovaříková to give all your attention to one another, and to Milan."

Ernst sat down in an armchair looking towards the conservatory. The two women sat together on a sofa facing the fire. Natasa held both of Karolína's hands in hers.

"Before you see Milan," she said, "I must warn you that the injuries he suffered are severe. So severe that our doctors tell us he was very fortunate to survive. They say that soon after he received the blow, someone performed surgery on him to release the pressure on his brain. Whoever did that saved my boy's life."

"Do you know who it was?" Karolína asked.

"No, we have no information. Only what may be contained in the letter. But as I explained when I wrote to you, pani Kovaříková, he refuses to give it up to anyone but you."

"I am very anxious to see it," said Karolína.

"I do understand your impatience, pani Kovaříková, but it is vital that you know what to expect when you meet my dear boy. You see, the injury is to the front part of the brain. His doctors call it the frontal lobe. This has left Milan hardly able to follow a conversation. You will find that he focuses on single thoughts. Mainly the letter and some people of whom he talks constantly. Jan, Štefan, Emil. And then there is a Karel and a Filip. And someone he refers to only as 'the sergeant'. Do you know who these people could be?"

"I'm sorry. I don't. The closest person to me who went to war was my husband. His name was Pavel. But he never returned. And he was a rifleman, not a sergeant."

"But of course you hope the letter is from him."

"Desperately. But my fear is that it could be from someone giving me news of him... news I won't want to hear."

"I understand, my dear. I do not wish to delay you any more, and I appreciate you have come here at my behest. But please allow me to explain one last thing to you before you see Milan."

Natasa again took Karolína's hands in hers and both women looked down.

"It is very important when you speak to my son that he does not become agitated. You will find him in a bath chair surrounded by cushions. These are to protect him. Because if my boy becomes too agitated he can fit, and he can easily injure himself. And it is so important for him not to suffer too many seizures, because..."

Natasa brought her head up quickly and fixed her eyes on the painting over the fireplace. Karolína looked into her face.

"I am very sorry. I still find this very difficult to say. Milan must not have fits because they can cause further damage to his brain. And further shorten his life."

She tightened her lips. "I am so sorry," she said. "I don't know what is happening to me today."

"Please don't be sorry," said Karolína. "I understand how you feel."

"Do you, pani Kovaříková? Do you have children?"

"I have a son."

"How old is he?"

"Three years and three months."

"Milan is my only child. I waited so long for him. I was almost thirty when he was born."

"I was twenty-eight when my Tomáš was born. I had already lost two before him. No one knows more than I how precious your Milan is to you, pani Musilová. I shall be very patient and very gentle. I shall treat him as my own child."

Natasa stood up, still holding Karolína's hands. "Come, my dear," she said, helping Karolína to her feet. "It's time for you to meet Milan. I have asked his nurse to leave the two of you alone. He will probably be drawing when you go in. It is what he likes to do most. He always has."

"Are any of these his paintings?" said Karolína as they walked arm in arm, hand in hand, towards the conservatory.

"They all are. Milan was studying at the academy in Prague when his call-up papers came. Painting was his life."

"A very talented young man," said Ernst, who stood in front of the painting over the fireplace. "A disciple of Kupka and Kandinsky, I see."

"That's right, Captain Neumann." Natasa stopped and looked back at him. "How clever of you. Milan would have been delighted to hear you say that. They were his heroes."

"And still are, I'm sure, pani Musilová. We should never underestimate the healing power of creative activity."

"Do you really think so?"

"I know it to be true. I suspect that the spiritual power we see in these paintings is still very strong in Milan."

"Thankyou so much for saying that, Captain. It is a great comfort." Natasa opened the doors to the conservatory. Ernst continued to study the painting.

"Milan, my darling, you have a visitor," he heard pani Musilová say.

Karolína did not move away from the doors when they were closed behind her. The room was so silent she immediately became aware of the sound of her own quickened breathing. She stood for a moment and opened her mouth wide in an attempt to quieten the sound and control the pace of her heart.

The room was full of plants Karolína did not recognise. Through some type of palm she noticed the back of a wicker bath chair. She walked slowly towards it, but stopped when she realised she might startle Milan if she appeared suddenly from behind him.

She walked around to the side of the room and approached him from his right. When she was only a few steps away she stood and looked at him, but he showed no sign he knew she was there. She sat down on a chair and continued to watch him as he transferred the view of the Tepla valley in front of him onto a sketch pad with chalk pastels.

Milan's legs were covered by a red blanket and his upper body was dressed immaculately in a cream jacket, white shirt and striped tie. His pale handsome face was clean shaven, and his brown hair parted neatly at the side and held in place across his forehead with what smelled like coconut oil. To all outward appearances, thought Karolína, he looked every bit like a normal young man of his age and class.

She sat watching Milan for a long time, fighting to think only of him and not of the letter which now surely lay so close. Every now and again the young man rolled his head to look at her, but still he made no indication he had registered her presence there.

"May I please come over and look at your drawing?" Karolína asked him.

When there was no reply she stood up and went to look over his shoulder. As she brought her eyes down to view the drawing, she saw a thick raised scar running from above his hairline to the middle of his forehead. Either side of the scar she was puzzled to see two round indentations, each roughly the size of a five-kroner piece. They were the marks left by Erik Novák when he trepanned Milan's skull in a desperate effort to save his life, while Pavel fought for two hours to hold the boy's head steady against the jolting movement of the train.

Karolína went back to fetch her chair and placed it beside Milan, facing him.

"Milan," she said softly. "Can you hear me?"

He turned his head towards her and she kept her eyes fixed on his as she spoke. "Milan, my name is Karolína. Can I please look at your drawing?"

She saw a small movement in his eyes, and for the first time felt Milan was aware of her.

"Your drawing. May I see it?" she asked again. He relaxed his grip on the pad and allowed her to turn it slowly towards her.

Karolína recognised nothing in the drawing resembling the splendid view beyond the windows. But what was clear to her was the intricacy and delicacy of the shading which, she thought, could only be the product of a focused, rational mind.

"It's wonderful, Milan. Beautiful."

Milan turned his head to the left and tried to reach down to a side table.

"Are there more?" asked Karolína. She stood up and went round to the other side of his bath chair. On the table she found more drawings. The first half dozen were very similar in content. Views of the woods, the town and the river.

"They are all wonderful, Milan." Then she came to a drawing similar in style but with a quite different content. In it she could make out a human face, but there was no attempt at perspective, and each part of the face was disconnected from the rest. Everything was exquisitely drawn.

"Jan. Jan Vaňek," said Milan.

"I see. That's Jan. Your friend Jan?"

Milan smiled, and she looked through the others. There were more faces, each drawn in the same style but each evoking the individual characteristics of the subject. The drawings changed again. There was a face with hollow staring eyes, bared teeth beneath taut lips and skin stretched across the cheeks. The disconnected, flat images magnified the horror of the picture. There was no character in the face. Only the sameness of death.

"Štefan," said Milan.

She found similar drawings of young faces, beautifully drawn, but each one terrified and torn apart. After each drawing Milan provided a name. "Kopeský," he said. "Skála. Martinek..."

She came to one last drawing. It had a face distorted like the rest. But it was a full figure, broken into disconnected parts yet harmonious in representing the person. It was a living, uniformed figure. The body showed power and violence, and the face, distorted once by the artist, was distorted again by hate and rage.

"My God," said Karolína. "My God."

She went back to her chair and eased herself into it. Tears ran down her face.

"Sergeant," said Milan. "Sergeant."

"I know," she said. "I know who it is. Milan, I am the sergeant's wife. I am Karolína Kovaříková. Please may I have my letter?"

Chapter Twenty

February 16th, 1920

> *Irkutsk Garrison*
> *Wednesday, 12 November, 1919*

My darling Kája,

I can hardly believe that at last I may have found a way of contacting you, and that one day soon you may touch the very paper which I am touching now. My darling Kája, I have been able to bear without complaint every hardship since we parted, but not being able to have some contact with you has been the worst. Not to see your face, or talk to you, or read your words has been close to unbearable. The thought that this letter might soon lie in your precious hands fills my heart with a joy I cannot describe.

Darling Kája, I must reassure you at once that I am well. I find myself in Siberia with the Legion, as I hope you will know by now. My health is good and I have escaped serious injury. I vow to you that I shall stay out of trouble during the remaining months that I must spend in this unholy place. I know how much my Kája will have worried about me, and I must confess that the thought of her torment has weighed very heavily with me over these years. Please believe me that I would have done anything to get word to you to end your suffering, but I believe that in this place we are as far from civilisation as it is possible to be.

I have worried too about my dear parents. Please tell them as soon as you can that I am safe and that I embrace them both. I cannot imagine the trials they have been through with all three of us at the front. I pray to God now the war is over, that Teo and Petr have returned home safe and well to them in Pilsen. Remember me also to your parents and to Zuzana. And of course to Esther and Ernst and dear little Otto. He must be a big boy now. I pray that everyone has come through this terrible time unscathed.

My darling Kája, I know that we have been robbed of precious years together, but we must remain optimistic about what lies ahead. There may still be time for us to be blessed with a family of our own, but if not I want you to know that sharing my life with you is all I need to be the happiest of men. My love for you endures everything and increases with every day I live.

We men out here do get some news from home. We know, of course, of our wonderful, brave, young country and we know that our countrymen have not forgotten us. Two and a half years ago when I was in a Russian prisoner-of-war camp we were visited by Masaryk himself. He freed us and restored our honour. He is a great man, Kája. Everyone at home should know that the Legion willingly does his bidding. Please be sure that everyone understands that. Even so, I have to say that we are all ready to come home now and help make our country strong from within.

Kája, this war has been an evil thing. I have discovered how cruel any man can be, however civilised he may once have thought himself to be. But I have also learned about the greatness of our people. I do not think that any one of us here could have survived these years relying on his own talents alone, regardless of his intelligence or education or innate qualities. But together anything, everything, has been possible. We turned our trains into communities; we tamed a wilderness and created an independent state here in Siberia. Our people have a great future, Kája. Czecho-Slovakia has a wonderful future.

I hope you will meet the boy who will carry this letter. His name is Milan Musil. He comes from Karlovy Vary. There are so many boys like him here. Boys just like those I used to teach. Each one is talented and special, and so many have been lost. I have found we do not lose many men in war, Kája. We lose mostly boys, who never get the chance to grow into men. But they are all heroes. Milan is a hero. He has a special place in the birth of our country. Without his sacrifice the revolt of the legion and all that followed from it would never have happened. Tell his parents that, Kája, if you get the chance.

I must go now, my darling sweet Kája. Milan is leaving in the morning for Vladivostok and I must entrust this letter to him tonight. His journey will take about three months and then you will read my words. I cannot say with certainty when I shall be home, my darling, but I shall come home, maybe before the summer, in time for the cherry blossom. Very soon we shall walk together again around our lake.

No words I can write can express my love for you. You are

with me always.

Your devoted husband,

Pavel

Karolína sat in the corner of the conservatory with the letter and wept. She could not separate her feelings of relief and joy and sadness and shame. Each time one emotion rose alone to the surface it was swept away by the others. Every attempt to hold on to a rational thought proved hopeless.

At last she became aware that Milan was watching her. She went over to him and sat down next to him. She took his right hand in both of hers and kissed it and held it to her cheek.

"I am so sorry, Milan," she sobbed. "I am so sorry for what we have done to you. For what we have done to all of you. Please forgive us."

She felt Milan draw his hand away from hers and rest it on her head. She bowed her head under the gentle weight of it and at last felt calmed. They stayed together like this for a long time.

Chapter Twenty-One

July 2nd, 1920

Karolína's reply to Pavel's letter arrived at the Headquarters of the American Red Cross in Vladivostok in early May 1920, two weeks after Pavel left Russia on his long journey home.

With Masaryk's approval the Czecho-Slovak Legion in Siberia had agreed a truce with Lenin and the Red Army in February, ending nearly two years of fighting for control of the Trans-Siberian railway. In return for safe passage to Vladivostok and embarkation to Japan, the Legion agreed to hand over the White Russian leader, Admiral Kolchak, and all the Tsar's gold seized by the Legion from the imperial reserve in Kazan in 1918.

By March 1920 over 67,000 legionnaires were gathered in Vladivostok waiting for passage back to the country they had never seen; a country united by Masaryk and its new constitution into one nation under its new, unified name – Czechoslovakia.

Forty-two ships carried the legionnaires back to Europe by many different routes, and by the end of September 1920 every Czech and Slovak had at last quit Russia, leaving the Tsarist Whites and Communist Reds to continue their bloody civil war.

Pavel and the last four of his section, Jan Vaněk, Filip Souček, Oskar Vesely and Emil Kolár, sailed in the Japanese steamer, *Takamatsu*, on 18th April. After three days at sea they arrived in Yokohama, and after a week in port they spent a further month and a half crossing the 16,000 kilometres of the Pacific Ocean to San Diego, stopping only to refuel in the Hawaiian Islands.

In San Diego Pavel was at last able to send further word to Karolína that he was on his way home. In a week he had crossed America by train and boarded the French steamer, *Narbonne*, sailing from Norfolk, Virginia, to Marseilles.

Pavel had seen no signs of the war on his journey home, except amongst the exhausted men with whom he travelled. America seemed unaffected by it, and only Czech and Slovak émigrés showed interest in what the Legion had achieved. In Kansas the men discarded their uniforms and changed into civilian clothes.

Making his way along the south coast of France, it appeared to Pavel that life there had also returned to normal. Tourists crowded the stations in Cannes and Nice, and in Italy too the towns of San Remo and Savona teemed with people determined, it seemed, to leave the hardships of the war behind them.

It was only when he left Verona and headed north-east towards Austria that Pavel saw for the first time evidence the war had really happened, and that great changes had taken place in Europe during his four years away.

As the train reached the mountains of the South Tyrol the customs posts of the old Hapsburg Empire were no longer where they once had been. The names of former Austrian towns were now written in Italian. Trient had become Trento, Bozen was Bolzano, and Freienfeld was now the Italian resort of Campo di Treno. The train was a mere 40 kilometres from Innsbruck before it finally stopped at a sign announcing 'Die Republik Österreich'.

Austrian customs officers boarded the train. There was not a smile to be seen amongst them. They looked in disgust at the letters of transit which Pavel offered them. Pavel pointed out the official stamps of the eleven foreign legations in Vladivostok, including Czechoslovakia, guaranteeing the bearers safe passage.

"We are Czechoslovakian citizens," he said.

One of the officials muttered an obscenity and thrust the documents back at him.

"Be careful with those, won't you?" said Jan Vaněk with a smile. "We Czechs have waited three hundred years to give you those."

In Innsbruck Pavel changed trains for the final time. The express to Berlin would stop first in Munich and then briefly in Cheb. There were no border controls between Austria and Germany, symbolic of the German people's wish to unite as one country after the war; a wish denied them by the Allied Powers. All that Austrians and Germans were left to share, thought Pavel, was the same haunted look of their citizens and the hatred of all their European neighbours.

On the 76th day of his journey from Vladivostok Pavel arrived at the border of Czechoslovakia and Germany, only eight kilometres from Cheb. The red, white and sky-blue flag of his new country flew from both sides of the track above signs proclaiming, 'Československe Republiky'. All five legionnaires stood to look out of the window, hardly able to believe what they were seeing.

"Well, boys, this is what we were fighting for," said Pavel.

"*Pasy, prosím,*" demanded the customs official behind them.

Pavel held out their papers as he continued to stare out of the window at his new national flag flying high from a white flagstaff.

"But you are legionnaires," said the customs officer, half in exclamation, half questioning. "You have come from Russia?"

"Yes, from Vladivostok," said Pavel.

"But you are heroes. Please let me shake you by the hand. All of you. This is wonderful. Legionnaires."

He went out into the corridor.

"We have men from the Legion," he shouted. "On this train."

"Bless you. Bless you all," he said, when he returned to their compartment. "But I must go. The train must leave. Good luck, *legionáři*."

He hurried down the corridor and reappeared on the track outside their window as the train pulled away.

"You have chosen a good day to return," he shouted running alongside them. "It is National Army Day. The second of July. Today we celebrate your glorious victory at Zborov."

He waved to them with both arms in the air as the train picked up speed. When he could no longer keep up he stopped by the track, pulled back his shoulders, and saluted.

Minutes later the train stopped again and the five legionnaires stepped down on to the platform in Cheb. Together they crossed the tracks to the opposite platform where the four remaining boys of Pavel's section would take the train to Prague.

"You don't have to wait with us, Sergeant," said Jan Vaněk.

"No, boys. I would like to see you off. We've come this far together. You all have my address here in Cheb, don't you? Remember you are all welcome to come and see me at any time."

"If you see Milan before I do, Sergeant, you will tell him I'll visit him soon, won't you?" said Souček.

"Yes, Filip. I will. You were a good team, you and Milan."

When the Prague train arrived, Pavel stood at the door and shook each man's hand as they boarded. No one spoke. A whistle blew and the train started to move. Pavel picked up his bag and walked alongside the train towards the exit. A face appeared at one of the windows. It was Jan Vaněk.

"Thankyou, Sergeant," he shouted, "for getting us home."

Pavel watched the train disappear into the distance. It was four years and five months since Karolína had stood on this same spot and watched him go off to war.

The station in Cheb lay to the east of the town and it took Pavel ten minutes to walk to the main square. Nothing had changed there. The cobbles, the fountain, the old merchants' houses, brightly painted, were just as he remembered. He had closed his eyes and seen this place so often during the past four and a half years, but in his imaginings Kája had always been there strolling beside him. Now there was not a soul to be seen.

He quickened his pace across the square, down Krámařská Street to their house by the bridge. He approached the door and realised that within a minute he might see his Kája again. He knocked and waited, but there was no answer. He knocked again. Nothing. He stepped back and looked up at the windows. All the curtains were drawn.

He hurried across the bridge and turned down the path to the village of Skalka. Then he understood why the town was deserted and his house empty. It was a public holiday, a glorious July day, and everyone had gone to the park by the river or to the lake.

He came to the track leading to the chata of Kája's parents and paused at the top to catch his breath and smell the dried undergrowth of the forest. He started down the track to the lake. In the distance he heard the sound of adult laughter and children playing. Then he saw them. Ernst and Michal and Magdaléna. And little Otto with two younger children he did not recognise. And sitting under the cherry tree, talking to her sister Zuzana was his Kája in a long white dress. He stopped and watched them, listening to their happy voices.

The little boy with Otto noticed him. He stopped playing and stood quite still, staring at him. The little boy waved. Pavel hesitated, then waved back. Seeing her son distracted by something on the track, Karolína turned. She brought her hand up to shield her eyes from the sun, and then clasped the hand to her mouth and scrambled to her feet.

"Pavel," she cried. "Pavel, Pavel."

She tried to run towards him but found herself stumbling. Her legs refused to carry her fast enough over the last piece of ground separating them. Tears ran down her cheeks as each step brought her closer to him. "Pavel, Pavel. You're safe. You're safe."

Pavel dropped his bag and strode towards her. His eyes took in everything about her as she came nearer. It was real. His beautiful Kája coming closer and closer, reaching out to him.

"Kája, my Kája," he cried as he held her at last. Her smell, her softness and her warmth were instantly familiar to him and filled him with pleasure.

"You're safe, my darling. You're safe," said Karolína. She leaned back and looked into his face. Pavel's face. Lined and weary. But his face. His wonderful face.

"It's you," she said. "It's really you."

"I said I would come back to you, Kája."

"I know you did, my darling. I know you did. I should never have doubted you."

They kissed and cried and held one another, and when they turned to walk to the chata they saw that everyone had gone.

"Did you receive my letters, Kája? Did you know I was on my way?"

"I received one from Milan Musil. That was all. Did my reply reach you at the Red Cross in Vladivostok?"

"No. I checked but there was nothing there."

"Oh, Pavel, if you haven't had my letter, there is so much you don't know."

"I don't need to know anything, Kája, now I see you are safe and well."

They stood on the edge of the clearing, embracing, holding on to one another. Karolína looked down to take a handkerchief from her sleeve. She wiped her eyes.

"Let's sit down under the tree, Pavel. Do you want anything? Some food or a drink?"

"No, I'm fine, Kája. Tell me what you need to."

"Most news can wait, darling, but there are some things you must know before you see the others."

"Go on."

"Your brothers, Pavel..."

"Don't cry, my darling. I've grown used to these things." He held her hand. "I always realised it would take a miracle for all three of us to live through this."

"Teo was reported missing in Italy three years ago. We have heard nothing."

"And Petr?"

"My poor darling. Your brother Petr survived the war, but he died of influenza in March last year."

Pavel stood up. "Dear God, my poor parents. What they must have been through. How are they?"

"They were very bad. But they are much better now, since they learned you were alive."

"I must go to see them."

"Soon, darling. We'll go together soon. Sit down. I have more to tell you. About Esther and Ernst."

"I didn't see Esther with the others."

"No, my darling... I'm afraid Esther was lost too... to the influenza..."

"My God, Kája. When will it end? We have made such a mess of the world. We have so much to put right."

"But there is also wonderful news to tell you, Pavel, my darling. News that will make everything alright."

She took both his hands in hers and smiled as she looked into his eyes.

"Ernst and Esther had a little girl three years ago. You saw her playing with Otto. They called her Anna. And do you remember the little boy who waved to you."

"Yes. He looked a lovely little boy."

"He is. His name is Tomáš. He is three years and seven months old. He is the most wonderful child. Kind, intelligent, always happy. The most loving child you will ever meet. Pavel, my darling husband, these are the most precious words I shall ever say to you.

"Tomáš is your son."

Chapter Twenty-Two

July 2nd, 1920

Pavel wanted to meet Tomáš alone, before being reunited with the others. He waited as Karolína went over to the chata, and a few minutes later Tomáš appeared at the door. Pavel beckoned the little boy to join him by the tree, and watched him as he walked across the clearing. He was dressed in a light-blue smock and white socks and was marching like a soldier, swinging his arms and looking around him with all the confidence of a well-loved child.

When he was a few paces from the bench, Pavel raised himself up, stood to attention and saluted. "Nazdar, Tomášek," he said.

"*Hallo,*" replied Tomáš, holding his right hand hesitantly to the side of his head.

"Put your fingers together, Tomáš, and touch the side of your head with just your middle finger. Like this.

"Yes, that's right. That is a perfect salute. Well done, *důstojník.*"

Tomáš smiled broadly and practised a few more times on his own.

"Perfect, Tomášek. Come and sit down on the bench next to me. Do you know who I am?"

"You're a legionnaire. You're my *Tatka.*"

"Yes, I am your tatka. Do you think you could call me that from now on? I would like it very much."

"I say it anyway at bedtime. Máma tells me too."

"Does she? What does she tell you to say?"

"Night, night, Tatka. And we kiss your picture."

"That's funny. Because every time I went to sleep whilst I was away, I'm sure I felt those kisses."

Tomáš thought for a moment. "The kisses must have flown like a bird – like this - and plopped on your cheek," he said, as he swept his hand in front of him. He put his hand over his mouth to stifle a laugh.

Pavel looked down at his son's happy, flawless face and laughed with him.

"You're a little joker, Tomášek. I can see that."

"I'm going to be a legionnaire too when I'm older. Děda says legionnaires are the bravest men in the world, and that's why today is a holiday." He looked up at Pavel. "Are you really a legionnaire, Tatka?" he asked.

"Yes, I am, Tomáš. But there are even better things to be than a legionnaire, you know."

"Děda doesn't think so."

"I'm sure he does really. Do you know that the greatest man in the world is not a legionnaire, Tomáš? And that Máma gave you the same name as him?"

"Tomáš Kovařík?"

"His name is Tomáš, like yours. But he is called Tomáš Masaryk. He is a teacher and the leader of our country. He has made sure that all the land you see around you here belongs to us Czechs. And that is the greatest thing you can be, Tomáš. A Czech. A Czech teacher, or a Czech doctor, or an engineer. Someone who builds things and makes things better for people."

Tomáš sat swinging his legs, considering this new information.

"Like Děda. He makes me toys," he offered.

"Yes, my clever boy. Just like Děda."

"And he makes Uncle Ernst's arm go better."

"Does he? How?"

"Uncle Ernst takes off his arm and Děda mends it for him."

"Oh, I see. I think I understand."

"And Uncle Ernst says it's alright having a bad arm and a hurt face, because he has all of us. And that makes everything much better."

"Uncle Ernst is quite right, Tomáš. You children do make everything better. Come on, my brave legionnaire, will you take me to meet all the others?"

Pavel stood up, and Tomáš jumped down from the bench and took his father's hand as they walked across the clearing. Pavel looked down at Tomáš as the little boy continued to chat away.

"But Uncle Ernst gets sad sometimes and then Anna gets sad."

"And Anna is your friend, is she?"

"She's my best friend out of everyone."

"And you make her happy again, I expect."

"I try."

"I think everyone has been a bit unhappy recently, Tomáš, but things are going to be much better from now on."

Half way across the clearing Pavel stopped and knelt down to look into his son's face.

"Tomáš, I can see what a big boy you are, and how grown up you are, but would you mind if I carried you a little way? I've never had the chance before."

Tomáš did not answer, but held up his arms to his father. Pavel lifted him into the air and felt his boy's arms tighten around his neck. He stroked Tomáš's back as he walked very slowly to the chata.

He breathed in his son's scent and the world seemed in an instant to be a perfect place. Everything that was bad was behind him, and all that was good lay ahead.

For a reason he could not explain, Pavel knocked and waited when he reached the front door of the chata. The door was opened immediately by Magdaléna, who had clearly been crying.

"There you are. There you are. My dear, dear boy," she said. She reached up and cupped Pavel's face in her hands. "We are so happy you are home," she cried, and kissed him several times on both cheeks. "Come in, come in. But you are so thin. Come in. Everyone is waiting for you."

As soon as Pavel entered the room Tomáš wriggled to be put down and ran over to the corner where Anna was playing happily by herself. The four adults and seven-year-old Otto sitting at the table stood up and, to their own surprise and amusement, started to applaud. Still applauding, Michal stepped forward, smiling broadly.

"Welcome home, my boy," he said, shaking Pavel's hand. "What a wonderful day you have chosen. I can't tell you what this means to me... to all of us... to have you back. I have a special bottle ready..."

"Hello, Pavel," said Zuzana, stepping between them. "It's nice to see you again." She kissed him lightly on both cheeks.

"Thankyou, Zuzana."

Pavel noticed Ernst Neumann standing by the table. Ernst walked towards him offering his hand.

"Pavel, my dear friend, it's so very good to see you."

"And you, Ernst."

The two friends clasped hands and stood square on facing one another.

"I see you had your fair share of it, Ernst," said Pavel.

"I think we both know I'm one of the lucky ones."

"It's true, Ernst. But Kája told me about Esther. I'm very sorry. That was a cruel thing to happen."

"Thankyou, Pavel. It has been the worst.

"But we are still a happy little family, aren't we, Otto?" he said, releasing Pavel's hand and placing his arm around his son standing next to him. "We still keep Mutti with us, don't we? We know she is happy when we are happy."

"Of course," said Pavel cheerfully. He held out his hand to Otto. "I cannot believe what a grown-up young man you have become, Otto. I don't expect you remember me."

"I think I do," replied Otto. "I think I remember you and Vati and Uncle Michal dancing in the snow."

"That was outside here in February 1916, when Pavel had his last leave," exclaimed Michal from the other side of the room. "The boy's got a good memory. My, we did have some fun that night."

"You all had too much of your slivovitz, Děda," said Magdaléna, as she brought even more food to the table. "That's what you had. All three of you."

Everyone laughed and Karolína came over to put her arms around Pavel. He kissed her and they held on to one another.

"I have put out a bowl and a nice fresh towel for you in Kája's old room, if you want, Pavel," said Magdaléna. "It will help put the journey behind you."

"Thankyou, you're very kind, Magda. I would like that. I won't be long. But I think I left my bag out on the path."

"Don't worry, my boy. I'll get it," said Michal, as he headed for the door. "You just take your time."

When they heard Pavel coming back down the stairs, everyone took their seats at the table.

"There he is, bless him. Now sit down here, Pavel, next to Kája, and have something to eat and drink," said Magdaléna. "Děda, put the little ones in their high chairs and then fetch Pavel a glass of beer. The boy needs looking after."

"I've got something better than that," said Michal. "I've got the Becherovka Kája and Herr Neumann brought back from Karlovy Vary."

"We bought it when we went to see Milan," said Karolína. "Dear Milan refused to give up your letter to anyone but me in person."

"Really?" said Pavel. He reached for Karolína's hand. "Did he take my instructions that seriously?"

"He took them very seriously. I had to convince him I really was your wife."

"And how is he now?"

"He's still very poorly, but I think he is a wonderful young man. He has gifts I can't describe."

"Did you see him, Ernst?"

"I only met his mother, Pavel. A very elegant lady, but crushed by what has happened to her son. There are so many like her."

"I know. I must get to Pilsen to see my mother as soon as possible."

"I'm sorry, Pavel," said Ernst. "That was clumsy of me."

"No, there is no need to apologise, Ernst. You are right. There is hardly a family anywhere which has escaped the misery. But we must put the past where it belongs. It is all about the future now. I look at my beautiful son sitting there, and your Otto and dear little Anna. It's all about them and the world we build for them. It is so good to be back with you all."

"Then let's have a toast," said Michal. "You all have a glass of Becherovka. Let us all drink to the most important thing in life. The children and their future."

"The children and their future," said everyone in unison, and the golden liqueur disappeared from every glass.

"Well, I have made a decision concerning my children," said Ernst. "I have decided Otto and Anna will be brought up in the Jewish faith. I want their mother's heritage to be part of their lives, and it is the best way I know to reconcile them to Esther's family."

"I think that's a wonderful idea, Ernst," said Karolína. "I think we should make use of all the freedom and tolerance that our brave new country allows us."

Pavel looked at her. She smiled back at him. "There is no one anywhere in Czechoslovakia more proud of their country than I," she said. "And that includes even you, Pavel Kovařík."

"You can be very proud of your Kája, my old friend," said Ernst. "In your absence she has argued and fought every battle with me that you would have fought."

"But more successfully, I think," said Karolína and everyone laughed again.

"From what I hear, you seem able to persuade Ernst to agree with you on just about anything you choose," said Zuzana.

"I don't know what..."

"Now, come on, all of you. All this talking going on and no one is eating any of this food I've put out," said Magdaléna.

Michal poured everyone more Becherovka to fill the silence. "Zuzana might be a colleague of yours in the autumn, Pavel," he said. "If you're planning to go back to your teaching."

"I can't wait to get back to it, sir. But I'm surprised to hear that about you, Zuzana. I always thought you intended to stay in Prague."

"I would like to, of course, but the government is offering so much money to Czechs to settle in these border areas, it would be silly to turn it down."

"I don't understand."

"There are posters all over Prague offering Czechs priority in getting jobs in areas like this. Where the majority of the population is German."

"We had a lot of trouble here right after the war, you see, Pavel," said Ernst. "The German majority wanted to be part of a united Austria and Germany. Masaryk sent in troops to put down the protests. It got quite bloody. I think he wants to encourage more Czechs to settle here to dilute the threat."

"Yes, I heard about the protests. From one of our officers."

"To be fair on Masaryk he did grant an amnesty to the Germans who led the revolt," said Karolína.

"For goodness sake, give the poor boy a rest from all this talk," said Magdaléna. "I want to see you eat, Pavel, after all you've been through. All this talking and you already look worn out."

"No, it's alright, Magda. Believe me, I've never felt better in my whole life than I do at this moment. I really need to know about all that has been happening here."

Pavel turned again to Ernst.

"So tell me," he said. "What are things like around Cheb now?"

"To be honest, Pavel, I think most Germans here look at the chaos there has been in Austria and Germany since the war, and are only too happy now to live in a settled country."

"But they still refused to take part in the elections in May, didn't they?" said Karolína. "When Masaryk was re-elected."

"Yes, it's true. They did."

"And so where do you stand on all this, Ernst?" Pavel asked.

"Pavel, my old friend, I live for three things. My darling children, my dear friends, and my work at the theatre. If those three things can flourish in the state of Czechoslovakia, then I shall support that state with all my heart and with what is left of my body."

"Here, here, Herr Neumann. Well said, well said," enthused Michal, who was well into his self-imposed task of leaving none of the Becherovka for another day.

Pavel put down his knife and fork and sat upright in his chair with the palms of his hands pressed down on the table.

"Czechoslovakia won't let you down, Ernst," he said, looking directly at his friend.

"I hope it doesn't let any of us down, Pavel."

"It won't. We have a wonderful chance here now to start afresh. To build new alliances and a better society."

"What alliances do you have in mind?"

"Not the Russians, that's for sure," said Pavel. "I was wrong about the Russians. I have seen them now at first hand, and I have learned that we Czechs must never trust them again. Never, ever again."

He relaxed the tension in his shoulders and leaned forward with his forearms on the table.

"No. I believe we must continue what Masaryk and Beneš have started. We must look west and put our faith in the democracies, France and Britain and America. If we do that, I know we shall build a strong, prosperous country here where all our children can flourish, safe from anything."

"Well, at last I think we can agree on something, my old friend," said Ernst. "You're right. Czechoslovakia needs to face west, not east. That's where her future lies."

"Here, here," said Zuzana.

Karolína, whose eyes had not strayed from her husband as he spoke, placed her arm around his shoulders and kissed him.

"And we have our legionnaires back now," proclaimed Michal. "They will keep us safe, sure enough."

"Wonderful boys, all of them," said Magdaléna. "Everyone's so proud of you, Pavel, for what you've done. The whole world will never forget."

"I propose another toast," said Michal, "with this blessed elixir from Karlovy Vary's thirteenth spring. To our Pavel, and to the Legion. Welcome home, my boy. May God bless you."

In the early evening Pavel and Karolína made their way back to Cheb with Tomáš, and installed themselves once more in their former home by the bridge.

While Karolína washed and dressed Tomáš ready for bed, Pavel went into the back parlour and was soon fast asleep in his old chair by the fireplace. Karolína came in to find him. His face was grey with exhaustion. She kissed him and coaxed him awake.

"Come on, my darling. Tomáš is asleep. Up you go and see him. I'll be along in a minute."

Without a word Pavel climbed the narrow stairs to their room. He knelt down and kissed Tomáš, asleep on a makeshift bed Karolína had made next to theirs. The window was open and the night air was warm and still. As he undressed, he looked out over the river. Karolína had left soap, water and a towel on the washstand by the window. The familiarity of it all comforted him. When he climbed into bed, the sheets felt cool and refreshing on his weary body.

Karolína came in and placed an infusion for him on the bedside table. He drank it as he watched her undress in the half light. Soon he felt her next to him and he lay on his back with his arm around her. She rested her head on his chest and he stroked her hair. They lay there saying little, listening to the river and the gentle 'quok', 'quok', 'quok' of the night herons.

Outside their window the noise from a group of revellers returning from Skalka grew louder as they passed over the bridge, and faded again as they made their way up Krámařská Street towards the main square. Karolína looked up at Pavel's worn face. His eyes were open.

"Did they disturb you, darling?" she asked.

"No, my love."

"Try to sleep. I'm worried about you."

"It's alright, Kája. I am tired, but so much has happened today, I'm just not ready for sleep."

He looked down at Tomáš on the cushions by their bed. As if he knew he was being watched, Tomáš smiled in his sleep, turned onto his side and placed his thumb in his mouth.

"Do you know, Kája, this has been the strangest day. Leaving those boys at the station this morning seems like a different lifetime. Then learning about my brothers and about Esther... It should be the worst day of my life."

"Please, darling..."

"It's alright, Kája. The thing is, none of the death and misery seems to be able to reach me. All I know is, I have come back to my country, I have found you safe and well, and I discover we have our Tomášek. I feel joyous."

Karolína looked up at him again and smiled, and he leaned forward to kiss her.

"Whatever happens during the rest of my life, Kája, this will always be the best day."

"And for me, my darling. At long last I feel truly happy again."

She rested her head once more on his chest and Pavel stroked her.

"Did you ever think I would not come back?" he asked her.

"Oh, my love. That is not a fair question."

"Why not?"

"Because if I say 'yes' it will seem that I abandoned you, and I never did."

"I always knew you never would."

"I want you to know that I searched everywhere for news of you."

"I know. Don't upset yourself."

"Táta and I went to Prague and Vienna but no one would tell us anything. But when the pain of missing you became too much for me, I had to let you go, my darling. For Tomáš's sake. Can you understand that? Can you forgive me?"

Pavel lay on his side and put both his arms around her and kissed her.

"You never need to ask me that," he said. "We have had to survive, Kája, you and I. We have both had to do and feel things that make no sense to another person."

"I have prayed you would understand why I stopped searching."

"I do understand, my precious. Let me tell you something. Today I could not keep my eyes off Tomášek."

"I know. I watched you at the meal table. It was lovely to see."

"All day I have wanted to hold him and never let go of him. I wanted to tell him over and over how wonderful I think he is. And yet..."

"What, darling?"

"And yet I am so glad I knew nothing of him whilst I was away. Because I would have become too anxious, too impatient, too scared. Can you understand that?"

"I think I can."

"But you see, Kája, that's the point. It does not matter."

"What doesn't?"

"It does not matter whether we understand everything or not. Because neither of us has to explain anything about what we have thought or felt or done, whilst we were apart. All we have to do now is love one another and Tomášek, and do all we can to put the last four years behind us."

He kissed her and laid her head gently on the pillow. She put her arms around his neck and pulled him towards her.

"My darling Kája, I shall not allow anything ever again to stand in the way of our happiness."

"I know, my darling. I know." She tightened her arms around him. "I thank God you have come back to me."

Chapter Twenty-Three

September 16th, 1920

Tomáš Masaryk read the communiqué from Vladivostok for a third time. He smoothed the paper and held on to it, knowing he would want to read it again.

He walked to the fireplace and studied his portrait hanging above it. He was proud of the painting, but wondered why it made him feel ill at ease. And at last he understood why. It held the worst associations. Sitting erect on a magnificent stallion, gazing into the distance, he looked almost imperial.

He was pleased he had heeded his own counsel and worn only the cap of a legionnaire, and not allowed himself to be portrayed in full military uniform, breaching the first principle of the new constitution. That Czechoslovakia would be a democratic state, in which only a civilian president, elected by the people and responsible to parliament, would control the armed forces.

He looked again at the inscription on the frame. *'Presented to T.G. Masaryk, our President Liberator, on the occasion of his seventieth birthday, by the Senate and National Assembly, on behalf of a grateful nation. 7th March, 1920.'*

He went over to the window on the south side of his office. It was less than three years since he had stood in a cold barrack in Kiev and looked out at his legionnaires clearing the snow that trapped them in their winter quarters. "Those men were the real liberators," he said.

He looked down at the Charles Bridge, the River Vltava, and as far as the eye could see, his beloved Prague. "It was they who made this possible." He read the communiqué again. Now, thank God, the very last of them were on their way home.

The phone rang.

"Prime Minister Černý and Foreign Minister Beneš are waiting in the conference room, Mr President," said a secretary.

"Thank you. I am going through now. Please ensure we are not disturbed."

Masaryk opened the door to the right of the fireplace and entered a large room dominated by an oval table of fine Bohemian oak, large enough to seat the full cabinet. At the far end Černý and Beneš stood up.

"Good morning, gentlemen," said Masaryk, as he walked over to them and took his seat. "Please sit down.

"I have asked you to meet me today for two reasons, gentlemen. Firstly, I wish to once again congratulate Prime Minister Černý on forming his government, and welcome him to his offices in the castle." He nodded towards Jan Černý, a socialist who had been the only party leader prepared to head an unstable coalition. "You are settling in well, I hope?"

"Yes, Mr President. Dr Minister Beneš and his staff have been helpful."

"Good, good. And the second reason we are here is for Minister Beneš to update us on matters of foreign policy and internal security, prior to my speech before parliament on our second Independence Day.

"However, you will notice that I have not asked for a stenographer to be present at this meeting," he continued, "and I want no notes taken. I want a frank and open discussion between us, gentlemen, starting with any lingering problems we might have with our five less than friendly neighbours..."

Eduard Beneš smiled at him and nodded.

"... and then moving on to our relations with the major powers, before we finally decide whether any matters under discussion pose a threat to our external or internal security. Minister Beneš may I ask you to begin? With the Polish problem in Silesia, perhaps."

"Thank you, Mr President. I am pleased to say that matters with the Poles over the disputed territory seem near to resolution. All fighting has stopped, and the Poles have agreed to accept arbitration through the League of Nations."

"Excellent news," said Masaryk. "Let us thank God for the League. Far better to cooperate for peace than to prepare for war."

"I'm not so sure the Czech miners on the Karvina coalfields would agree with you, Mr President," said Černý. "There are well over 100,000 workers up there relying on those fields. With Poland tied up with her war with Russia, I don't see why we don't just walk in and take the whole area."

Beneš leant forward and looked Černý in the eyes.

"Because, Prime Minister, it is not in our interests to force a quarter of a million Poles to become reluctant citizens of Czechoslovakia," he said. "We have enough of those already. I remain confident that we shall retain the coalfields, most of the iron and steel works, and all of our Czech citizens through negotiation."

"Minister Beneš is right, Prime Minister," said Masaryk, ignoring Černý's agitation. "We are a fledgling nation, surrounded by five hostile neighbours. How we conduct ourselves in these formative years and the level of support we can gain from the major powers through the League will be crucial to our survival."

He turned to Beneš.

"And what is the situation with Hungary in southern Slovakia, Minister?"

"You know the Hungarians, Mr President. They simply refuse to accept that Slovakia is no longer their territory. The Austrians are finally resigned to the loss of Bohemia and Moravia, but the Hungarian attitude to Slovakia is quite another matter."

"But there have been no more border incidents?"

"No. We have troops stationed in large numbers in southern Slovakia. Mostly legionnaires. Hotha knows his Hungarian army would stand no chance against them."

"And what about the rumours of Karl Hapsburg trying to regain power in Budapest?"

Černý shifted in his seat, tutting loudly.

"There is a strong possibility he will try," continued Beneš, "especially with the monarchists in power. But I think the League would act if he did."

"I'm sorry, Beneš," said Černý, "but all this faith you put in the League of Nations baffles me. They have no teeth. They have no army. Wilson couldn't even get the Americans to join. If that Hapsburg bastard Karl shows his face around here again, I suggest we send in those legionnaires and string him up by his royal neck."

"Prime Minister Černý," said Masaryk slowly, "Czechoslovakia is the only democracy to be found east of the River Rhine, and whilst I am its president we shall always behave like one, and not like a smaller version of the tyranny your comrades have created in Russia. I hope that is clear to you."

He turned to Eduard Beneš, who had heard the tone many times before from his former professor.

"What do you propose we do about the Hungarian situation, Foreign Minister?" he asked him.

"I think if Karl Hapsburg did try to return, it would throw Hungary into such internal chaos that it would cease to pose any real threat to us. However, the Magyars continue to make territorial claims on all their neighbours, and for this reason, as you know, Mr President, we are seeking an alliance with Romania and Yugoslavia, guaranteeing concerted action against Hungary if it takes military action against any one of us."

Masaryk turned back to Černý. "There you are, you see, Prime Minister," he said. "We call it diplomacy."

"That may well be, President Masaryk," replied Černý, "but I know the Slovaks want our troops to move against Hungary. I've heard more than one Slovakian deputy say the troops are there to keep the Slovaks down, more than keep the Hungarians out."

"What? Have you taken leave of your senses, man?" said Beneš. "Why would any Slovak think that?"

"Maybe because you promised them their own assembly and they still haven't got it. Or maybe because when the Hungarians left Bratislava, the Czechs moved in and filled all the government posts and most other top jobs."

"That is a preposterous remark," said Beneš.

"But the Slovaks aren't the equal partners you promised, are they, Minister Beneš?" said Černý.

As Beneš leant forward, Masaryk placed a gentle hand on his arm.

"We are aware of the contradictions between our present actions and our earlier promises, Prime Minister Černý," he said. "But I can assure you that Minister Beneš and I regard the Czechs and Slovaks as sharing a common ethnicity, and as complete equals within the Czechoslovakian state."

"For God's sake," Beneš said to Černý, "our own President is a living symbol of our country's common Czech and Slovak heritage. I do not know how you can say such things."

"I can say them, because wherever I see peasants or workers exploited by anyone, be they Czechs, Slovaks, Germans or Magyars, I have a duty to speak out."

"Prime Minister Černý, let me please try to explain to you our policy towards our Slovakian brothers," said Masaryk, "in order that you can convey that message to any disgruntled deputies in the National Assembly. It is true that there is a disproportionate number of Czechs in senior posts in Bratislava; in the judiciary, the civil service and in education. That is simply because the Hungarians barred Slovaks from these posts, and when our country was formed we did not have sufficient Slovaks trained to fill them. But that training is now under way, and when it is completed, Slovak representation will naturally increase."

"And the assembly they were promised?"

"I am aware that I promised that in the Pittsburgh Agreement, and also to President Wilson in person in the White House. But please reassure our Slovakian deputies that at this early stage of our country's development, when we are still fighting to maintain our borders and establish ourselves on the world stage, we must have a strong central government in Prague."

"And how would you like me to explain the death of Štefanik to them, Mr President?" asked Černý.

"Good God, now this really is too much," said Beneš.

"No, Eduard, it is alright," said Masaryk. "I invited open and honest discussion, and I thank the Prime Minister for his candour. How else can we know of the mood amongst certain of our citizens?"

He turned to Černý.

"No one will ever know who shot down the plane carrying my dear friend and pupil, Milan Štefanik. I have spent many long hours considering it, and I fear that a decision I once made in the Ukraine may hold the key.

"Three years ago at a meeting in Kiev, I gave General Štefanik the task of suppressing all Bolshevik activity amongst our legionnaires in Russia. This he did most successfully, but it left him with few friends amongst socialists anywhere. And since his plane was shot down over Bratislava, which at the time was under the control of the Hungarian and Slovakian Soviet, I think you might look for his slayers amongst people inclined to stay closer to you, Prime Minister Černý, than they ever would be to me."

Černý chose not to fill the silence that followed.

"So, Foreign Minister Beneš," continued Masaryk, "could you please now bring us up to date with our German and Austrian neighbours?"

Beneš shuffled the papers on the table in front of him and cleared his throat.

"Well, Mr President, little has changed since you and I were last in conference. The situation in both countries remains chaotic. It is hard to keep up with the most recent attempts at a putsch in Berlin and Munich. And Austria remains paralysed with inflation and social unrest. But the allied nations are monitoring both countries so closely, I believe neither Austria nor Germany poses an external threat to us."

"Does that mean they might pose an internal one?"

"As you know, Mr President, I have long held the view that the position regarding our three and a half million citizens of German origin in the so-called Sudetenland is most problematic. On the one hand we need the border areas because of the industry and lignite there. But on the other hand I share your opinion that it would have been better for us to have ceded some of the territory to Germany at Versailles, if it also meant ridding ourselves of some of our most reluctant citizens."

"But we always knew the French would not stand for that."

"Precisely, Mr President. As you say, France's fear of Germany will not allow them to sanction any increase in German territory, even if in the long term it might bring more stability for us."

"So why bother listening to the French at all then?" said Černý. "Why not give the Germans just a bit of their precious Sudetenland and kick out all their people with it?"

"Because, Prime Minister," said Beneš, "we shall always be dependent on French support. As our President says, a small country like ours is only as secure as the alliances it makes with major powers. Whilst America and Britain pursue isolationist policies, we are wholly dependent on our French ally. We cannot afford to upset them in any way. That must remain the cornerstone of our diplomacy."

"It makes no damn sense to me..." Černý muttered to himself.

"So this brings us to the final point on our agenda, gentlemen," said Masaryk. "What internal threat do our citizens of German origin pose to us? Dr Beneš, if you could please now speak in your capacity as Interior Minister."

"Certainly, Mr President. The biggest problem still remains in western Bohemia along the German border. Our Land Control Act last year split up the big estates there, which were almost exclusively in German hands. The building of defences along the border is progressing well, and we have begun to station more troops in the area."

"And the resettlement policy?"

"There has been a good take-up of Czechs moving into the area. As we discussed in cabinet, they are being given either requisitioned land to farm, or in urban areas preferential employment and housing. But in some areas it is very difficult to dilute the overwhelming percentage of ethnic Germans in the population."

"Where is the biggest concentration?"

"As you are aware, there are small pockets everywhere along the borders in western and southern Bohemia, and northern Moravia. But the biggest problem is around the town of Cheb. That is the area our German population refer to as the 'Egerland triangle'. Nearly ninety percent of citizens there are ethnic German. That is not in itself so unusual, but that particular area is known for its strong nationalist tendencies."

"I know Cheb," said Masaryk, "I went on a walking holiday there once before the war. A beautiful area."

"It is, Mr President, but there is an unhealthy political tradition there amongst a minority of the German population."

"I am familiar with it, Eduard. Anti-Slav, anti-Semitic, anti-clerical. Always harking back to the *volkisch* idea of pure German stock. I heard it often enough at the university. As you did too, I am sure. The idea has been around for centuries."

"Yes, it has, Mr President, but in Egerland it has become politicised into the belief that all Germans must unite in one German state."

"But that's why we sent troops there in 1918, isn't it?" said Černý. "To put a stop to all that pan-German nonsense. We have the power. Let's send them in again."

Masaryk looked at Černý, the embodiment of one of his greatest fears; that many of his country's elected leaders failed to understand the responsibilities that came with democracy.

"When we used troops before it was to suppress an insurrection, Prime Minister," he said. "Now we are a sovereign democratic state we do not use military force against our citizens simply because we disagree with their political views."

"Quite right, Mr President," said Beneš. "However, it does concern me that some of our German-speaking citizens have formed themselves into a political party with links to right-wing parties in Munich and Vienna."

"And the names of these parties?"

"In their so-called 'Egerland' they are the German Workers' Party. It is run by a few activists through bookshops. They distribute propaganda through the shops and arrange meetings with their opposite numbers in Vienna and Munich. In Munich they call themselves the German National Socialist Workers' Party."

"I know some of those people," said Černý. "A lot of them were trade unionists, the same as me. Anton Drexler, Hans Knirsch, Franko Stein. I remember them, Mr President. A lot of hot-heads and windbags. I wouldn't waste a minute of your time worrying about any of them."

"I think, Prime Minister Černý, we may at last have found something on which we all agree," said Masaryk. "But get some of our people to keep an eye on the situation in this 'Egerland triangle'," he added, turning to Beneš. "Just as a precaution."

Chapter Twenty-Four

October 28th, 1920

"Come along, Kája, we're going to be late."

"It's only six thirty. It doesn't start until seven."

"But it's a fifteen-minute walk to the theatre. And we have to find Zuzana in the foyer. We can't be late on Ernst's first night."

Pavel heard Karolína's footsteps on the stairs leading from their bedroom, and the sound of her sighing.

"I don't know whether this is good enough."

She appeared in the doorway of the front sitting-room wearing a white, lace-collared blouse, buttoned at the front and tucked into the waistband of a lightly gathered dark-brown skirt. The skirt extended to just above her ankles, showing her black and beige ankle boots, laced tightly at the side. Her hair was waved at the front and fastened in a bun at the back. Pavel thought she looked beautiful.

"I wish now I had gone to Františkovy Lázně to get something special," she said. "This is embarrassing. I look terrible."

Pavel came over and smoothed the hair on her forehead with the back of his fingers. "We shall go to Karlovy Vary soon," he said, "to see Milan again. You can buy whatever you like there. But trust me, darling. You look wonderful." He kissed her gently on the lips.

"And what about your escort for this evening's performance, madam? Is he dressed fit for the occasion?" he asked, as he attempted a pirouette in the middle of the room and collided with the low coffee table.

"Pavel, no. That's your wedding suit. It's more than ten years old. And that winged collar. No one is wearing those now."

Pavel bowed and rubbed his shin. He passed Karolína her wide-brimmed hat, and helped her on with her matching three-quarter-length coat with fur cuffs.

"I don't care what I wear," he said, "as long as we get there on time."

They walked arm in arm along Krámařská Street through the old Jewish quarter and into the main square, talking and laughing. They passed the Krause bookshop in the colonnade where Karolína still worked on Mondays and Fridays, mostly due to Tomáš's insistence that he be allowed to spend at least those days with Anna at his grandparents' chata.

"It's a strange choice of play Ernst has made to celebrate Independence Day, don't you think?" said Pavel.

"I'm not sure. I suppose he couldn't really choose anything in Czech. He would be lucky to get a dozen people through the door, if he had."

"He could have put on a concert. Dvořák, Smetana, maybe some Mozart. That sort of thing. It would have pulled in the crowds."

"I don't know, Pavel. I'm sure Ernst has good reasons for his choice."

"The whole *Wallenstein* trilogy lasts ten hours, Kája. You do realise we won't be home until six in the morning?"

"No?"

Pavel smiled at her. "It's alright, I had a word with Ernst and as a special favour to you he has reduced it to two."

Karolína slapped him lightly on his hand and held on tightly to his arm as they continued across the square.

"To be fair on Ernst, Kája, he has made a very clever choice of play for tonight, if you think about it. A Bohemian nobleman fights for the Hapsburgs before changing sides and suing for peace for the sake of his homeland. It's a story to please all sides."

"Yes, I suppose it is."

"And Wallenstein was killed here in Cheb. And Schiller wrote the play here. A famous German dramatist adopted by a Czech town. It all fits. He can be a clever man, our Ernst."

"Yes, I know he can, but I still don't think we shall find many Czechs there."

Within minutes they had arrived at Cheb's theatre, built in French renaissance style and fronted by four Doric columns. Uplights illuminated the façade against the October night sky. Pavel and Karolína climbed the steps, still arm in arm, and entered a large foyer filled with the town's cultural elite and their excited chatter.

"I can't see Zuzana. Can you?" said Karolína.

"Yes, over there on the stairs."

"Oh, my goodness, look at that dress." Karolina's heart sank.

Zuzana spotted them by the door. She waved, excused herself from the small group she was obliging with her company and started across the foyer towards them. They both watched her as she weaved her way through the crowd, smiling confidently at everyone and stopping only briefly to exchange pleasantries with a select few.

Zuzana was seven years younger than Karolína. 'God's choice' was how Magdaléna described her second child, who was much wanted but wholly unexpected so long after the first.

"*Guten Abend*, Kája. *Guten Abend*, Pavel," said Zuzana, as she kissed them both on the cheek.

"Please, Zuzana. Can't we speak Czech amongst ourselves? At least until we're outnumbered and have no choice," said Karolína.

"Oh, don't make such a fuss," her sister laughed.

"You are very well presented tonight, Zuzana," said Pavel.

"Thank you, kind sir."

Zuzana bowed her head and curtsied. Karolína studied the pale-blue silk dress, which she assumed must be the latest Prague or even Viennese fashion. The dress had a dropped waist, a sash tied at the back and it stopped at mid calf. A dress such as that was certainly not available in Cheb, and neither was the matching cloche hat. Karolina felt her face redden.

"Ernst has got us the best seats together in the dress circle," said Zuzana. "He apologises for not being able to see you until after the play finishes. He says I must bring you backstage when everyone has left."

"Oh, you've spoken to Ernst already?" asked Karolína.

"Yes, he asked some time ago if he could escort me after tonight's performance. He is such a gentleman." Zuzana, acknowledged someone making their way into the auditorium. "Come on, you two. We must take our seats."

"Bravo, Neumann."

"Well done, Ernst."

"Excellent adaptation, Herr Neumann."

"Thank you... very kind...very gracious of you... so pleased you enjoyed it... thank you..."

Ernst at last came over to Pavel, Karolína and Zuzana, who were standing at the side of the stage holding their glasses of sekt. He was wearing a tuxedo of the latest fashion with a white cotton shirt and black bowtie, He was smiling broadly.

"My dear friends, I am so sorry to keep you waiting so long," he said. "Please forgive me."

"Nothing to forgive," said Pavel, shaking his hand. "You deserve all the plaudits, Ernst. I never thought *Wallenstein* could be so enjoyable."

"Thank you, Pavel. That means a lot to me."

Ernst offered his hand to Karolína but she ignored it and embraced him and kissed him on both cheeks.

"It was wonderful, Ernst. You never cease to amaze us."

"Thank you, Kája. I am very touched."

He turned to Zuzana and hesitated before offering his hand. She took it and then hesitated too before leaning forward to kiss him. As she did so Ernst turned his head to offer his right cheek.

"I thought it was wonderful too," Zuzana said. "I am certainly going to bring my students to see it."

"That's a marvellous idea, Zuzana. Perhaps I could come to your school and talk to them about it beforehand."

"Oh, yes please, Ernst. Would you?"

"Of course, it would be a pleasure. But could you please excuse me a moment? There is someone over there I must speak to. Perhaps you wouldn't mind if they joined us."

Ernst approached a middle-aged couple who had been standing at a respectful distance, apparently waiting for him to come over to them. As they shook hands, Pavel noticed his friend afforded them the slightest bow of the head. After a few minutes Ernst escorted the couple over to join him and Karolína and Zuzana.

"My dear friends," he said, "may I have the honour of introducing to you the Graf and Gräfin von Stricker?

"Graf, Gräfin, please meet my dear friend, Pavel Kovařík, his wife, Karolína Kovaříková, and Frau Kovaříková's sister, Fräulein Zuzana Štasná."

"You have come a long way to see Herr Neumann's play, Graf," said Pavel after much nodding and shaking of hands. "I believe your home is near Bayreuth."

"It was, Herr Kovařík, it was. But I'm afraid certain events since the war made it necessary to sell the family seat in Bavaria. We now live at our property a few kilometres from Eger. In Reissig."

"Yes, we know Reissig. My wife and I have often admired your residence there."

"You seem to be very familiar with my family's affairs, Herr Kovařík."

"Perhaps I should explain, Graf. My wife's family owns a small freehold on your estate here. Next to Štasný Lake."

"I thought I recognised the name 'Štasná' when Herr Neumann introduced your sister-in-law. Well I never. So you two ladies are from the Štasný family. It was my great-grandfather who gave your people the title to that land, you know."

"Our father still speaks of your family with great affection, Graf," said Zuzana. "Your ancestor's generosity has afforded great security for our family."

"Well, that's as it may be, Fräulein Štasná. But what my great-grandfather didn't choose to give away to his tenants in the 1850s has been stolen from us now anyway. The farms, the forests. The whole lot has been confiscated."

"Is that why you have sold your home in Bavaria, Graf?" asked Pavel.

"No other choice. That damned government in Prague has left us with nothing except 250 hectares around Reissig. So the family seat in Bavaria had to go. Couldn't afford it without the income from Bohemia. It's legalised theft. Nothing less."

"Everyone has to make sacrifices, Graf," said Pavel, "if we are to build a fairer society."

"Well, what may seem fair to some seems very unfair to others, Kovařík. That's all I can say."

"You don't…"

"Did you know, Gräfin, that Fräulein Štasná is a teacher at your son's new school?" Ernst interrupted.

"No, I did not. What do you teach at the *Gymnasium,* Fräulein?"

"German literature, Gräfin. It was my degree subject at the Charles University in Prague."

"Isn't that rather unusual for a Czech to study German literature and teach in a German school?"

"Not at all, Gräfin. There are many Czech writers in Prague who choose to write in German. They reach a wider audience that way."

"Quite, quite. So have you met my Heinrich in your school, Fräulein? He started in September."

"No, I haven't had the pleasure as yet. But I shall certainly keep an eye open for him."

"Very kind, Fräulein. Very kind."

"I'm a teacher too, Gräfin," said Pavel. "I teach mathematics in Czech to Czechoslovak students in a Czechoslovakian school. But, of course, all schools in Cheb are Czechoslovakian now, whatever the language of instruction they use. Aren't they, Zuzana?"

"Yes, Pavel. Please don't make a thing of it."

"Zuzana has been very kind in helping me with a translation of *Wallenstein* from German to Czech," said Ernst.

"Is there a call for that sort of thing then?" asked von Stricker.

"Yes, Graf. We put on one performance a week in Czech."

Von Stricker laughed. "Schiller in Czech, eh? What next, I wonder. Goethe in Romanian? Bach on the tin whistle?"

"It's the law, Graf," said Pavel. "Herr Neumann is obliged by our government's Minority Law to put on one performance a week in the language of the minority population. And here the minority happens to be Czech for now. Isn't that so, Ernst?"

"Yes, but..."

"Just put up with it, Neumann," said von Stricker. "That's what we all have to do with that rabble in Prague." He held out his hand to Ernst. "Well done tonight. Excellent job. Thoroughly enjoyable."

He turned to Pavel, Karolína and Zuzana. "My wife and I bid you *Gute Nacht.*" He stood erect and nodded at each of them in turn. "Frau Kovařík, Fräulein Štasný. Kovařík."

"Slow down, Pavel. For goodness sake, slow down. I can't keep up with you."

"Did you hear the cheek of the man? Referring to our president and Dr Beneš as 'that rabble in Prague'."

"Of course I did."

"And his wife was no better. 'Rather unusual for a Czech to teach in a German school'. Who the hell does she think she is?"

"Pavel Kovařík, if you don't slow down and stop shouting, I shall ship you off to Siberia again. Now come here."

Pavel turned and walked over to where Karolína had stopped on the square. When he stood in front of her she reached up and cupped his face in her hands and kissed him.

"It's wonderful to have you back," she said. And they continued walking arm in arm to the chata by the lake, where the three children were sleeping.

When Magdaléna heard they had met the Graf and Gräfin von Stricker she could hardly contain her excitement, and Michal regarded the meeting as such an honour that Pavel and Karolína could not bring themselves to reveal the true nature of the encounter.

An hour later Ernst and Zuzana arrived in high spirits, and supper was served for everyone at the table. The talk was of the play and of Ernst's achievement, and there seemed to be an unspoken understanding between the two couples that during the meal none of the issues raised in the conversation with the von Strickers would be revisited.

Only later when the light in the room had dimmed, and Michal's cherry slivovitz had been taken by everyone in its usual generous quantities, did Ernst begin to muse on the events of the evening. Michal and Magdaléna had long retired to their easy chairs by the fire, while Pavel, Karolína and Zuzana sat at the table listening to their friend.

"I feel very reassured by the reaction I received to tonight's play," he said. "I think Friedrich Schiller must be my favourite dramatist. Even more than Goethe or Shakespeare. Because above all he was a poet of freedom. The idea of political freedom and the rights of the individual are at the heart of all his plays. Yes, I think Schiller was the right choice for Independence Day."

"It was a clever choice," said Pavel. "I'm just sorry most of the audience were probably like the von Strickers."

"In what way?"

"People like the von Strickers wouldn't see your play as a celebration of Czechoslovakia's independence, Ernst. They are more likely to see it as a call for their own independence *from* Czechoslovakia."

"Do you think so?"

"Yes, I do. Perhaps when you put on the required performance in Czech, you will reach the audience you were hoping to reach."

"I'm not staging a performance in Czech just because the law demands it of me, Pavel. I would do it anyway."

"I'm pleased to hear it."

"Could you ever doubt it? Let me tell you something about Schiller, Pavel. He saw the theatre as a moral institution. He believed in moral beauty. And he believed we achieve moral beauty when our duty and inclination are in harmony."

Ernst looked down at the empty glass in his hand. "I have been very fortunate in my life," he said, "because I have never had to do anything out of duty that I did not feel inclined to do anyway. And when with Zuzana's help I stage the performance of tonight's work in Czech, it will not be because the law demands that I do so. It will be because I am inclined anyway to use the language of my friends, and of the mother of my children, and of our country. I hope you can all see that."

"I do, Ernst."

"Thank you, Zuzana."

"Of course we see it," said Karolína. "All of us."

"Ernst, there is not one person in this room, or in the whole of Cheb, who does not trust absolutely your integrity," said Pavel. "But most of our German citizens are not like you. What I said is true. There are far more like the von Strickers, who still regard themselves as our superiors and have no loyalty to the Czechoslovakian state."

"Then I think the best thing the Prague government can do now to impress its German citizens is to treat them fairly," said Ernst. "This land grab and the tax on savings will not get their loyalty. It has hit them hardest of all."

"Only because they owned most of the land and held most of the money in the first place," said Pavel.

"That lot in Prague took one fifth of my money too," said Michal from his chair by the fire. "I agree with Herr Neumann. It's plain robbery."

"I've told you before, Táta," said Karolína. "Everyone has had to pay that. It was to get our country on its feet at the very beginning."

"But not everyone had been saving all their lives like your mother and me, had they? Those who hadn't bothered lost nothing. I'm a simple man, but even I know that's not right. And the von Strickers shouldn't lose their land either. They've always been good people. They gave your great-grandfather this freehold, you know."

"Yes, we know, Táta. We know."

"You see, Ernst, the government has been very fair," said Pavel, sitting back and shrugging his shoulders. "They have applied the same rules to everyone, even to a hardworking Czech like pan Štasný."

"If you say so," said Ernst.

Pavel leaned forward again with his forearms on the table.

"I exclude you when I say this, Ernst, but we Czechs and Slovaks have had enough of being regarded as a lower order, simply because we are Slavs. Of being made to feel that German language and culture is superior to our own. As far as I am concerned people like the von Strickers need to be put in their place."

"Please do not include me in your opinions, Pavel."

"No, Zuzana, I know better than to include you in any of my opinions."

"You know, Pavel, you always worry me, when you speak like that," said Ernst. "I have always tried to understand your grievances, and I have always respected your convictions. But you Czechs have a wonderful opportunity now to show that you are not going to replace German arrogance with an arrogance of your own. God knows you have fought hard enough for the power you now hold. But I hope you realise that choosing not to use that power may prove a surer way of increasing your authority with some people."

"Wise words, Herr Neumann. Wise words," said Michal.

"They are wise words, sir," said Pavel to Michal, "for certain situations. But my worry for our country is not our use of too much power, but whether we shall ever have enough of it."

"Well," said Magdaléna, easing herself up from her chair, "the only question I'm interested in just now is having enough energy for those children in the morning. Thank goodness those dear little mites don't have to worry about any of all this. That's all I've got to say."

Chapter Twenty-Five

August 1921

The time approached for Tomáš to start school in September 1921, and the question arose of the language he would use in his education. There was no doubt at all in his father's mind, and there was no doubt at all in Tomáš's.

Cheb had two primary schools offering teaching in Czech, and Pavel approved of them both. It had many more offering instruction in German which, in spite of the efforts of the Prague government, stubbornly remained the first language for eight out of ten of the town's population. Pavel disapproved of them all.

The village of Skalka, where the Neumann family lived, had only one primary school and it employed German in all its teaching. It was the local school already attended by Otto, and for Ernst it was the natural choice for Anna. And once that decision was made, it was the only school Tomáš would consider for himself.

It came as a shock to Pavel to find his young son prepared to stand in open opposition to his wishes, whereas to everyone else it came as no surprise at all that he had a son as strong-willed as himself.

Magdaléna and Michal could not see what difference the choice of either language made. Zuzana was sure it would be to her nephew's great advantage to attend a German-speaking school, and Ernst sought a compromise.

"Since Esther's passing," he told Pavel and Karolina, "I have encouraged Otto and Anna to speak Czech at home and at the chata, and German when they are outside. They need reminding sometimes, but not often."

"And they don't mind?" asked Pavel.

"Why should they mind? They are children. We often make a game of it. Someone speaks in one language right up to the threshold and then has to swap over in mid-sentence. It's fun. It's good for them."

"We only ever speak Czech to Tomáš, and so do all his grandparents," said Karolína. "I suppose it must confuse him when he hears us using words with strangers that we never use with him."

"Tomáš would not be confused, Kája," Ernst insisted. "A boy as young and intelligent as he is does not consciously discriminate between languages. He simply uses the words which produce the desired result from the person he is speaking to. He has spoken to me in German often enough without even thinking about it."

"He never uses German with me," said Pavel.

"Does that surprise you, dear friend? Look, how about this for a solution? Let Tomáš attend primary school in Skalka with Anna, and then if the two of them are still as close in five years time, I shall suggest to Anna that they both go to your secondary school, Pavel, and be taught in Czech."

"You would do that?"

"Of course. They are two children, devoted to one another since each became aware the other existed. I couldn't believe it when I first saw it, but now I recognise the truth of it. And that's what is important to their happiness, not something we impose on them because of some political principle or prejudice."

"Ernst is right, Pavel. Tomáš will never be happy if you separate him from Anna," said Karolína.

Pavel looked at her, groaned, and it was agreed.

Tomáš did not like doing anything which displeased his father. His tatka became his hero from the moment he first met him on his return from the war. And ever since that moment his father's stature grew with every story he read in his adventure books about legionnaires.

Often, when his parents were downstairs, Tomáš would tiptoe into their room and open the drawer containing his father's medals. There were four of them, and his favourite was the silver one with four overlapping circles which together formed a cross. On one of the circles was a lion with two tails, which he thought very odd. On the other three were pictures of eagles and mountains and strange shapes. Attached to the ribbon of his favourite were some leaves whose purpose he did not understand at all. Máma said the medal was so important that the President himself had sent it to his tatka from Prague.

Tomáš was disappointed that his tatka never wore his medals. Not even on National Army Day, when the other legionnaires wore theirs and marched down the street wearing them. Tatka did not even want to watch the parade. Instead he packed a bag and disappeared into the forest all day, and not even Máma could say why.

Tomáš loved the routine at the end of every day when his máma kissed him goodnight and his tatka came in to tell him a story. His father never *read* stories; he always told stories of his own and promised they were all true.

"So, Tomášek, what would you like to hear about tonight," said his tatka, as he sat on the bed facing him.

"A legionnaire story. The one about the magic train that ruled all the railway line in Siberia."

"It wasn't a magic train, Tomáš. It was a real one. But it had armour and guns and was so powerful that it could go wherever it wanted to."

"And the legionnaires drove it."

"We did. We lived on it for more than a year. Do you remember what it was called?"

"*Orlik*, because it could fly like an eagle."

"It couldn't actually fly. But it was fast like an eagle and very strong, and no one could stop it."

"Tell me about it again, Tatka."

"Why don't I tell you another type of story for a change, about the woods and a very clever bear?"

"Are there bears in the woods?"

"Yes, there are. There are brown bears, and wolves and big cats called lynx."

"And boars."

"Yes, and wild boars, and they are all very fierce, so we have to be very careful when we go into those woods."

"Or they might eat you."

"They might, Tomášek, if you didn't have a gun. One day I shall show you how to hunt wild boars with a gun. Would you like that?"

"Yes, please, Tatka. Yes, please. Can we go tomorrow?"

"Well, not tomorrow, but soon, Tomášek. Very soon. Would you like to hear about a very clever man who pretended to hunt bears?"

"Pretend? How can he pretend?"

"Well, this man... he was a clever Czech called Hašek... had a pet bear."

"A brown bear?"

"Yes."

"But you said brown bears were dangerous."

"They are normally, but Hašek had reared this bear since it was a baby bear cub. He fed it and looked after it, and the bear cub thought Hašek was his tatka, so he always did what he was told. And as the bear grew up, Hašek taught him to do clever things."

"What was the bear cub's name?"

"Bruno."

"What clever things did he do?"

"All sorts of tricks. Dancing on his hind legs, balancing a ball on his nose, and even riding a bicycle... So many tricks that when a circus owner heard about Hašek and Bruno he offered them a job in the circus ring, performing in front of hundreds of people. Bruno and Hašek loved doing all their tricks, but as the years passed and Bruno got older, Hašek decided that his friend needed a quieter life. So he brought him here to Cheb."

"Here? Can I see him?"

"Probably not. All this happened a long time ago when I was a little boy, and Bruno and Hašek may have gone by now. But when they were here, Hašek thought up a very clever way of making lots of money."

"How?"

"Well, he knew there were German people here who liked to shoot bears, but they were very lazy people and did not want the trouble of finding the bears themselves. They liked someone else to do it for them. So Hašek thought up a plan. He told the lazy Germans that he knew where bears liked to go in the forest and, if they paid him lots of money, he would find them a bear to shoot."

"But that's not fair on Bruno."

"Ah, you see, Hašek said the money was only for finding a bear. It was up to the Germans whether they managed to shoot it or not."

"So did they shoot Bruno?"

"You must let me tell you, Tomášek. Hašek was a very clever Czech, you see. He showed Bruno where to come to in the forest and exactly where to stand. Hašek and the lazy German would be waiting out of sight, and when Bruno was in place the German would raise his gun, ready to fire. But Hašek taught Bruno that as soon as he heard a certain sound he had to run away as fast as he could. And it worked. Every time a German started to raise his rifle, Hašek cocked the trigger on his own gun, and the click it made was the signal for Bruno to run away."

"And did he always run away?"

"Yes, it worked perfectly. And Hašek made lots of money from the stupid Germans who all thought it was just bad luck that the bear ran off, just as they were ready to shoot. But one day it all went wrong."

Tomáš clasped his hands to his chest. "Bruno got shot."

"Don't worry, Tomášek. It's alright. Just let me tell you what happened. One day Bruno was in the woods making his way as usual to the spot where Hašek and a German hunter were waiting. But as he crossed the forest path just a little way from Děda's chata, the postman from Cheb happened to be cycling along bringing Děda his letters. Now you can imagine what the postman thought when he saw a big brown bear on the path in front of him."

"He was scared."

"Yes, he was. So scared that he fell off his bicycle and ran back to Cheb as fast as his legs would carry him. Bruno stopped and watched the postman running away, and scratched his head wondering what he should do. He still had a long way to go to get to his usual spot in the forest and he was feeling very tired. So what do you think he did?"

"He picked up Děda's letters."

"Well, perhaps he should have done, but that's not what he did. Remember he knew Hašek was waiting for him, and by now he was very late. So instead of picking up the letters he picked up the postman's bicycle and, being a circus bear, he got on it. And happy as you like he pedalled off into the wood."

Tomáš started to giggle.

"So there was Hašek waiting with the stupid German when he heard Bruno approaching. 'I think I can hear a bear coming,' he said to the German. 'Get ready.' And the German raised his rifle waiting for a bear to walk into view, when out of the trees came Bruno, sitting up on his bicycle, looking about, grinning and pedalling along without a care in the world."

Tomáš started to laugh.

"The German could not believe his eyes. His mouth fell open and he dropped his rifle with the shock of it all. The rifle hit the ground, went off and shot the stupid German in the foot. Whilst the silly German hopped around shouting and screaming, Hašek ran after Bruno calling to him, 'Keep pedalling, Bruno. Don't stop, keep pedalling.' Bruno leaned over the handlebars and pedalled as fast as he could and the two of them disappeared into the wood. And were never seen again."

Tomáš laughed more loudly, and the sight of him made his tatka laugh too. Karolína came into the room and stood watching them.

"Come on, you two rascals. Pavel, you're meant to be settling Tomáš down with a bedtime story, not getting him all excited."

"The stupid German shot himself in the foot..," said Tomáš, as he rolled around on the bed.

"Go on, Pavel. Get downstairs and leave this to me," said Karolína.

At the bedroom door Pavel paused and turned round to Tomáš, who fell silent.

"And some people do say that Hašek and Bruno are still out there somewhere in those woods," he whispered.

"He's such a wonderful little boy, Kája," said Pavel, as he and Karolína sat later in the front parlour. "You did a marvellous job with him all on your own. He's a proper little Czech boy. Bright and clever, and with such a sense of fun. But he's down to earth. He speaks his mind. I like that about our Tomášek."

Karolína smiled at him and carried on with her mending. Pavel went back to his newspaper.

Beyond the open windows, just across the street, the waters of the River Ohře flowed gently beneath the bridge leading out of town to the north. Like most Czechs Pavel and Karolína loved being on, in or by the water. From the sound the river made, as it was channelled by the bridge's stone pillars, they could tell how much rain had fallen in recent days over the Ore Mountains in Saxony. Sometimes the water rushed; tonight it glided. It had been another long, hot summer.

"I hope we have made the right decision about him starting at that school next week," said Pavel.

"We've discussed it so much, my love. The decision's made. He'll be fine."

"I know Tomáš will cope. He would cope anywhere. I just feel I am betraying a principle, that's all. As if I am sending him into the enemy camp. It's ridiculous a Czech boy in his own country being taught in a foreign tongue."

"But you admitted it yourself. It's just not realistic to think a child can grow up here without a knowledge of German."

"It is for now, but it will have to change. I just wish he could be learning French or English instead. At least I would feel then he was learning a language spoken by honourable people. People with decent principles of democracy and humanity. People with a culture we can admire."

"I thought you had nothing against German culture."

"I have nothing against Leibniz or Kant, or Beethoven and Schiller. I just dislike the people who think they're superior, simply because they happen to share their language. The snobs with their noses in the air. And hangers-on like your sister, I'm sorry to say."

"Don't apologise to me for saying anything about Zuzana. You know how I feel about her."

"She even speaks German with a *Hochdeutsch* upper-class accent. Even Ernst sounds like a Bavarian farmer next to her."

"She always thought she was grand, even as a child. Perhaps it's because she's so pretty."

"She's no more pretty than you."

"Thank you for saying so, my darling, but..."

"I mean it. She may be pretty, but she behaves too often like a silly, spoilt girl. Whereas you are a beautiful woman, Kája. There's a big difference."

Karolína looked at Pavel and smiled broadly. "I think Zuzana went to Prague because Cheb wasn't grand enough for her," she said, "and then studied German as a way of becoming even more sophisticated. I suppose it has worked."

"Well, Ernst seems very impressed."

Karolína put down the skirt she was stitching.

"Why? What has he said?"

"Nothing in particular. He just seems very taken with her."

"I know they get on well, my love, but that's only because they share the same interest in the theatre."

"Yes, there is that. And the fact I saw Ernst in Zuckermann's last week. Looking at rings."

Pavel looked over at Karolína.

"Are you being serious?" she said.

"Yes. I saw Ernst in Zuckermann's."

"Why didn't you say anything before?"

"It's none of our business."

"Well, it is our business if he intends to... No, it's not possible. She's too young. How would she manage with the children?"

"Surely that's up to them. It's not our concern, is it?"

"But she's my sister. Ernst is our closest friend. And what about Esther?"

"Look, Kája. Whatever Zuzana and Ernst decide between themselves has nothing to do with us. What difference does it make?"

"I don't know," said Karolina. "None, I suppose." She put down her half-mended skirt, folded it slowly, and sat with it on her lap.

Chapter Twenty-Six

December 24th, 1921 – January, 1922

When Zuzana lived in Prague she rarely visited Cheb, but since her return her parents treated her as if she had never been away. She occupied her old room in the chata, and came home from school with the same expectations she had as a child, assuming her mother would cook her favourite food, and her father would perform any task she asked of him. The attention Zuzana regarded as a right annoyed Karolina more than she cared to admit.

But nothing Zuzana did annoyed Karolina more than the way she behaved in the company of Ernst. And nothing confused Karolina more than the way the intelligent and level-headed Ernst could be manipulated by Zuzana so easily.

It was agreed by the Štasnýs, the Kovaříks and the Neumanns that the main festivity of Christmas 1921 would be spent at the Štasný chata by the lake. On Christmas Eve the six adults and three children gathered there around the large oak table which had been set for ten.

"It's bad luck to lay for an odd number at Christmas dinner," Magdaléna explained to the children. "And no one must eat a morsel until the first star appears in the sky," she warned, "or bad things can happen."

Michal had taken it upon himself to ignore the old superstition that no alcohol should be served on Christmas Eve, and had fetched two large jugs of beer from Skalka village to add to the Moravian wine provided by Ernst. The room was decorated with holly, and with twigs cut from the cherry tree on Saint Barbora's Day and placed in bowls of water inside the cottage. Twenty days later, according to Magdaléna, if the twigs blossomed, as they had, it was a sign there would be a wedding in the family within twelve months.

The previous weekend Michal, Pavel and Tomáš had taken a boat out onto the lake and caught one of the largest carp Michal had ever seen. The carp spent its last days in the Štasnýs' tin bath, enduring regular visits from the children, who were fascinated by it. Now it sizzled in two large frying pans on the range.

Magdaléna's table was, as always, crowded with food: with bowls of beef soup with potato dumplings, with potato salad to accompany the carp, and dishes full of vegetables and bread dumplings. When everyone was seated Michal began to pour the beer.

"Please, Táta, do not forget what I told you."

"Oh, yes. Sorry, Zuzana. Excuse me everyone. Could I please ask you all to bow your heads whilst I say grace?" said Michal. "Thank you, Lord, for this bountiful table and for the company of our dear family and friends. Amen."

"Amen."

"Now, would anyone like some beer?"

"Just a moment, Táta. Ernst would like to ask you something."

"Yes. Excuse me, pan Štasný, but would it be acceptable to you if my Otto said a grace? He asked me if he might."

"Of course, Herr Neumann. Of course..."

Otto took a bowl his father had left on a side table and poured water into it from a pitcher by the sink. Anna went with him and collected a towel.

"You all have to rinse the water over your hands?" said Otto. "Bring the towel, Anna."

Anna followed her brother round the table as he repeated a prayer. "Blessed are you, Hashem, our God, who brings forth bread from the earth. Bless this food to our use."

"Now you all have to eat some bread," said Anna, as she returned to her place. And everyone did as they were asked.

"That was lovely, my children," said Ernst. "Well done." And everyone applauded.

"Oh dear, Herr Neumann," said Magdaléna. "I never thought about any of the food being kosher or anything of that sort."

"That's alright, Máma," said Zuzana. "As long as the food is blessed, the children can eat it. And Otto asked for it to be blessed in his prayer."

"Zuzana is quite right, pani Štasná," said Ernst. "And besides we do not intend to be too strict about these things."

Karolína was about to say something when Tomáš spoke up.

"I know a grace I learned at school."

"Do you really, my love?" said Karolína "I am sure everyone would like to hear it."

Everyone fell silent again as Tomáš began. "*Alles das wir haben, alles ist gegaben. Es kommt, O Gott von dir. Wir danken dir dafür.*"

The adults looked towards Pavel, who sighed gently and turned to Tomáš and smiled. "That is a very interesting prayer, Tomášek," he said. "Clever boy for remembering it." And everyone applauded again.

"Now can I pour some beer?" asked Michal.

"Yes, come on, all of you," added Magdaléna. "Now you've pleased the Lord, it's time for you all to please me. Start eating this food."

Conversation during the meal was unusually muted for a gathering around the Štasný table. Magdaléna took this as a sign that everyone was hungry and too busy enjoying her food to talk, while Michal put it down to a lack of beer and Moravian wine, and kept trying unsuccessfully to fill Ernst's glass. Ernst seemed distracted during the meal and turned down Michal's beer and every opening Pavel offered him to engage in some verbal sparring.

Sensing the lack of natural conversation around the table everyone enthused more than ever about the food, until even Magdaléna thought she had heard enough about it. It came as a relief when Ernst finally stood up and confirmed to everyone that there was, after all, something special about the evening.

"My dear friends," he said. "I hope you do not mind my commandeering the evening... as it were. Only I wish to inform you all of some very important... some very wonderful news. Well, really, I suppose it is only Karolína and Pavel... and of course, Tomáš... I have to inform, because everyone else knows something about it already...

"But the thing is... I recently asked pan Štasný's permission... which he graciously gave... for me to... to ask his daughter, Zuzana, if she would do me the greatest honour... and become my wife. And I am delighted to say that she has consented."

Michal, Magdaléna and Pavel immediately stood up and went around the table to congratulate the couple. As Zuzana turned to receive a kiss of congratulation from her father, she glimpsed her sister sitting impassively on her chair opposite. It was only the sound of Ernst popping open a bottle of sekt which brought Karolína to her feet. She stood watching the excited exchanges on the other side of the table.

"Have you set a date?"

"We thought the summer. Perhaps July."

"Please call me Ernst, pan Štasný. It's about time."

"I'm very pleased for you both, Ernst."

"Thank you."

"There's the ring. I wondered where you were hiding it."

"I think we should..."

Amidst the laughter and excited voices Karolína felt a tug on her sleeve. Tomáš gestured to her to bend down closer to him. "It doesn't mean Anna will be going away, does it?" he whispered. "I don't think so, my darling," said Karolína and, seeing his anxious face, she took his hand and led him over to join in the celebration.

At the end of the evening Pavel, Karolína and Tomáš were the first to leave. The air was so cold and the ground so hard that it reminded Pavel of Siberia, and he shivered. He felt his son's arms around his neck and the touch of his wife's hand on his sleeve, and immediately felt soothed.

"Look, Tatka," said Tomáš. "There are no stars in the sky. Babička said that was bad luck."

They both looked up and Pavel kissed Tomáš on his cold, round cheek.

"That's because there is so much cloud up there that we cannot see them, Tomášek. It means only that tomorrow we shall have lots of snow."

In the New Year, a few days after the start of the new school term, Zuzana answered her sister's invitation to call at the house by the bridge on her way home from work.

"Come in, Zuzana," said Karolína as she hurried to close the door. "Let me shake out your coat for you. Go into the front room and warm yourself by the fire."

"It's one of the worst winters I can remember, Kája. So much snow."

"I know, it's terrible. Would you like coffee or tea or..."

"Do you have any hot chocolate? I love hot chocolate after a long day."

"I expect so."

"How is your work?" asked Karolína from the kitchen.

"It's hard. I like some of my classes, but I am surprised how horrible some of the children can be. Especially in a Gymnasium."

"Weren't they like that in Prague?"

"I was lucky in Prague. We had the very best there, and the Austrian system was much stricter. The children did as they were told, or else."

Karolína came in carrying a tray. She put it down on a small table between the two armchairs in front of the fire.

"Thank you, Kája. Ooh, that's perfect."

"Do you think you will carry on working after you're married?" Karolína asked.

"I think Ernst would prefer it if I didn't. His first wife didn't work apparently."

"But Esther had two small children to look after."

"And so shall I."

"But surely Otto and Anna will both be at school?"

167

"Not in the holidays. And I shall have the house to run, of course. And Ernst is very keen to have my help in the theatre."

"Oh, I see."

"Even in these enlightened times, it's still not regarded as quite the right thing for a woman to continue in teaching after she's married."

"I thought the war had changed all that."

"No, not at all. Not in certain circles."

"And do you think you will manage looking after two small children?"

"I expect I shall. Otto is a very well-behaved little boy. Anna is rather demanding, but I expect she will grow out of it."

"Anna is a lovely child. How can you say she's demanding?"

"I'm not sure, Kája. I don't know her very well yet. I must be allowed time."

"I'm sorry, Zuzana. It's just that Esther was such a good friend, and the children have been through so much."

"I know they've suffered. But things will be better for them now, because they have their father who loves them, and they will also have me, who makes their father happy."

"But you don't talk about loving them."

"They're not my children, Kája. I shall probably come to love them. Ernst even talks about us having children of our own one day."

"Do you think you might?"

"I'm not sure. It's not as important to me as it always was to you."

"Oh, I don't know," said Karolína and she put down her cup and saucer heavily on the table and sat back in the chair.

"What don't you know?"

"Why you are doing this. Why you want to marry Ernst."

"That's very presumptuous of you. What would you say if I asked why you wanted to marry Pavel?"

"I could tell you without a moment's hesitation. Because I love him and could not imagine a life without him."

"Well, I would probably give the same answer about Ernst."

"Oh, be honest with yourself, Zuzana. Ernst is ten years older than you. He's a widower with two children, and..."

"And what?"

"And he carries scars from the war."

Zuzana unclipped her bag, took out a cigarette and held it, unlit, between her fingers. She sat forward with her legs crossed.

"Kája, let me tell you something. There's not one man left out there who doesn't carry scars from the war. Try to tell me that your Pavel has no scars. That he doesn't turn and shout in his sleep. That there aren't times when you wake up in the middle of the night and find him down here sitting in the dark. I am 26, Kája. I have experienced enough of those men. Believe me, Ernst is one of the least scarred of any I've met."

Karolina looked up at her. "But you still don't talk of love," she said.

"I don't see how anything Ernst and I say or do can be any business of yours."

"Well, you *should* see. Ernst is our dear friend. And we love the children."

"And you obviously don't think I'll be good for them."

"I want you to be, Zuzana. But it worries me that this has never been what you wanted. You always hated Cheb. Be honest, you hated the chata. It was never good enough for you. I worry about the damage you will do if you just decide one day that Cheb isn't what you want. If you decide you miss Prague and the nightlife, and the intellectuals you're always going on about."

"Well, yes, it's true. I do like all that. But I first went to Prague in 1913, Kája. A lot has changed there since then. And here in Cheb I have Ernst now. And he's one of the most intellectual men I've ever met. That's what I find so exciting about him. He's such a talented director. And he writes for the theatre also. I keep telling him he should stage his own work."

"I know. He should."

"Oh, has he shown you his work then?"

"I've seen some of it."

"I didn't know that. Then perhaps you agree that he should be encouraged to move to Prague one day. Perhaps Prague is where he belongs."

"No, Zuzana. That's not what I am saying. It wouldn't be fair."

"On whom?"

"On the children. On Tomáš and Anna. It would break their hearts if they were separated. On all of us. We love Ernst and the children."

Zuzana lit her cigarette and sat back in the chair.

"I think it is time for you to be honest, Kája. You keep telling me I should be. You're simply jealous. You just want to keep Ernst for yourself."

Karolína got to her feet and walked to the door. She stood with her back to her sister. "I don't know what you're talking about," she said.

"Yes, you do," said Zuzana. "You're just jealous of me."

"Don't be ridiculous. Why should I be jealous?"

"It seems obvious enough to me. Because you think in Ernst you have your own refined German intellectual to call your friend, and you're afraid I'm going to take him away from you."

Karolína said nothing but started to laugh. She turned around.

"My God, Zuzana, you don't understand anything, do you?"

"Yes, I do. You with your sensible clothes and your sensible job with a sensible husband. You're jealous of me because I went to university in Prague. I have experience. I have lived. I have met important people, and now you're afraid I'm going to steal the only bit of your life which is refined and cultured."

"You silly girl."

"You like to think of me like that, don't you, Karolína? But I'm the one Ernst has fallen in love with. I'm the one he regards as sophisticated."

"I've heard enough."

Zuzana stood up and faced her sister.

"Well, hear this. You and Pavel think you're so liberal and tolerant in your new Czechoslovakia, don't you? But you're narrow-minded and prejudiced and jealous. And you hate the Germans because they're everything you would like to be. Well, I don't hate them. I admire them."

"You don't know what you're talking about, Zuzana."

"Yes, I do. You just don't like the truth. How many times did we hear Pavel talk about how wonderful the Russians were? Those ignorant, uncouth, anti-Semitic Slavs who would put Otto and Anna in a ghetto if they lived in Russia. But ask him about the Germans, who are sophisticated and cultured and live decently, and he spouts hatred. 'Please don't take our Ernst away,' you're saying, 'because he's the one German we like.'"

"Have you finished?"

"Yes, except to wonder if you would ever have bothered to know Ernst if he hadn't been married to your friend, Esther Lochowitz."

Zuzana went into the hall and put on her coat. At the door she turned and faced Karolína. "And I thought you had asked me here today to give me an engagement present, dear sister," she said. "You know, Kája, I will be honest with you. I have had my doubts about whether I should marry Ernst. But not any more. Now I'm determined I shall."

Chapter Twenty-Seven

February 20th, 1922

The snowfall which began on Christmas Eve 1921 continued to fall on most days during the early months of the new year. Ice floes appeared in the River Ohře and became trapped under the bridge outside Pavel and Karolína's house. Men were employed to stand along the parapet and break up the ice with long iron rods to keep the water flowing and prevent the river from bursting its banks.

On many mornings, after heavy falls of snow in the night, Michal hitched a plough behind two donkeys and kept open a path from the Františkovy Lázně road to the village of Skalka, in order that Karolína could walk with Tomáš to the primary school there.

As the harsh winter dragged on, Karolína saw it as a blessing that visits between families and friends became more difficult and more infrequent. It was true that it meant there was less opportunity to heal her rift with Zuzana, but it also meant the rift was less noticeable to others.

For Tomáš the fun of playing in the snow with his tatka was initially some consolation for the time he lost with Anna at his grandparents' chata. But by the middle of February the short winter days had turned into long weeks, during which people could hardly venture out of their houses at all. It was then that the visits to the chata and to the Neumann house stopped completely.

Throughout this time, in spite of the weather, Tomáš remained more determined than ever to reach his school in Skalka every day. Karolina was surprised at his unwillingness to miss a single day during the blizzards of early 1922. Sometimes the pride and admiration she felt for Tomáš's determination threatened to turn into less positive feelings, as she battled with him against the snow which swept across the lake from the north.

Each afternoon Tomáš came home full of excitement and fun with stories which, for him, made every day momentous and unforgettable. Around the dinner table he would chat with his parents about his day and theirs, and Pavel and Karolína would marvel anew at their son's inquisitiveness and insights.

Which made it a surprise and a worry to them on the first day back after the February holiday, when Tomáš returned home from school silent and morose, and unwilling to explain why. After a long evening unlike any before, Karolína put Tomáš to bed and returned to the front room. "He wants to speak to you," she said to Pavel.

Pavel made his way slowly up the stairs to Tomáš's room. He sat on the bed and looked into his son's face. Tomáš pulled the top of his blanket over his chin, and gripped the edge of the blanket with clenched fists.

"What is it, Tomášek? Are you going to tell me?"

"You promised me all your legionnaire stories were true, Tatka."

"They are, Tomáš. Every one I told you is true."

"That's not what Fräulein Steiner says."

"What does Fräulein Steiner say?"

"She says you must be lying, because Czechoslovakia hasn't got any sea. So it can't have a navy."

"Oh, I understand. You told her about the guns on the steamer and the rafts. Was that today in school?"

"Someone always tells a story on Mondays. And today was my turn. So I told them your story. In front of the whole class. And now they all think I'm stupid."

"Well, I can tell you that you're not the tiniest bit stupid, Tomáš. The people who don't listen carefully, and make no effort to understand are the stupid ones. And I don't think your teacher and your class could have been listening properly."

"I told them everything. They should understand."

"What did you tell them?"

"I told them you're a legionnaire, but I've told them that before. Lots of times. And I told them you were in Russia on the train. And you came to a lake."

"Did you remember the name of the lake?"

"Baikal."

"That's right, Lake Baikal. Good boy."

Tomáš pushed his blanket down from his chin.

"And you couldn't go past the lake because the Russians had guns and might blow up your train."

"Did you say where the Russian guns were?"

"On ships on the lake."

"On gunboats. That's right."

"And they were going to smash up your train with their guns, and smash up the tunnels and smash up the railway line."

"It seems to me you got everything right, Tomáš. Which bit didn't they believe?"

172

"When you built boats..."

"Rafts."

"When you built rafts and put guns on them and made a navy for Czechoslovakia."

"Well, we did. We put big artillery guns on those rafts. And we captured a passenger steamer and put some guns on that too."

"I told them you did, but they still didn't believe me. And I said you sailed into the lake and smashed the Russian ships."

"How many? Do you remember?"

"Six."

"Good boy. We attacked six Russian boats and put them all out of action. Then we could carry on our journey in the train, you see."

"Fräulein Steiner says that wasn't a navy, and it wasn't a real battle."

"Well, I suppose it was a very small navy, but I promise you and Fräulein Steiner that it was a very real battle. Czechoslovakia's only naval engagement. I was there."

"I told her it was the Battle of Lake Baikal, and people got killed."

"And you're right, Tomáš. And your teacher is wrong."

"But they still laughed at me."

"Does that matter, now you know you were right?"

"It's still not very nice."

"I know, Tomáš. I had a lot of people laughing at me once. And shouting things. It's not nice at all."

"Did you cry?"

"No. I wanted to, but I decided not to."

"I wanted to, but I didn't."

"Good boy, Tomášek."

"I didn't want Anna to see me cry."

"Of course, you didn't. I don't expect she laughed, did she?"

"She did a little bit, but not as much as the others."

"I expect it was the German children who laughed, was it?"

"Mostly. Why do they want to laugh at me?"

"It's hard to explain, Tomáš, but German children don't like legionnaire stories as much as Czech children."

Tomáš looked up at the ceiling as he considered this new information from his father.

"Is Anna Czech or German, Tatka?" he asked.

"That's hard to explain too, Tomáš."

"I don't want her to be German. I asked her if she was, but she didn't know."

"I think Anna is half Czech and half German. Her mother was Czech and her father is German."

"I wish I was half Czech and half German. Then everyone would like me. And we would be the same."

"You really like Anna, don't you?"

"Of course."

"Why do you like her so much, do you think?"

Tomáš looked up at the ceiling again as he answered. "Because everything is nicer when Anna is there."

Pavel smiled and looked down at his boy.

"You know, Tomáš, you and Anna are the same. Because you are both Czechoslovakian. And all the children in your class are Czechoslovakian too. Even Fräulein Steiner. And that is a real privilege for all of you. Although sometimes I wonder if some of them deserve it."

"What's a 'privilege'?"

"It's when you are allowed to do something, or allowed to belong to something, which is very special. And being Czechoslovakian is very special. It's the best thing in the world. So if anyone in your class laughs at you again, Tomáš, tell them how lucky they are."

"I will, Tatka."

"And I promise you, Tomáš, all my stories are true."

Pavel kissed him and pulled the blanket over his shoulders.

"Do you still want to go to that school?" he asked.

"I always want to go to school, Tatka."

"*Dobrou noc*, Tomášek."

"*Dobrou noc*, Tatka."

Pavel closed the door of the front room behind him. Karolína looked towards him from her chair by the fire.

"Those damned Germans," he said. He took the book he had been reading from his chair and sat down. "I knew it was a bad idea to send Tomáš to that damned school."

"What's happened, for goodness sake?" said Karolína, dropping her needles into her lap.

Pavel told her about Tomáš's day and she immediately wanted to go up to see him.

"He's fine about it now, Kája. Just leave him in peace."

She sighed and looked into the fire, and tried not to mind that Tomáš did not need her to go to him. "I don't know where all this German and Czech nonsense is going to end," she said. "I remember Ernst warning us once that it would affect the children one day."

"They have to know about the world they live in, Kája. You can't keep these things from them."

"But Tomáš is so young. I was hoping everything would be settled by the time he grew up. I don't understand why people can't just enjoy being happy and normal. It's as if they find life more exciting when there are problems."

"Blame it on the way Germans think, Kája. They always want things their way. They cannot stand it when they're not in charge. Well, they'll just have to damn well learn. It's us who are in charge now."

"But that's just being like them, Pavel. Don't we all need to work together?"

"We've tried, haven't we? But the damned fools just refuse to take part. They don't vote in elections. They complain about everything Prague does to improve things."

"But you must admit, my love, some of the things we're doing are a bit harsh."

"No, Kája. I don't admit it. What do you mean?"

"Well, most of the top people in the Town Hall are Czech now. And most of the police. It's not very fair, is it?"

Pavel closed his book and looked over at Karolína.

"I cannot believe I'm hearing this from you, Kája. How are we going to enforce the rules and laws from Prague if the Germans refuse to do it? We have to have Czechs in those jobs."

"I suppose so. But look at all that business with the land..."

"But the land *should* be Czech. What's better? Having a handful of rich Germans in Saxony or Bavaria owning all our farming land, or sharing it out to ordinary farmers, so they can raise their families and maybe have a bit of money left over sometimes? I don't see how anyone can be against that. Especially you."

"I'm not against it, my love. It's just..."

"It's just nothing..."

"You can at least let me speak, Pavel. I do have my own opinions."

Pavel lowered his head and gripped the arms of his chair.

"Yes, of course. I'm sorry."

"It's just that Táta was saying the other day that even part of the forest is fenced off now. It was von Stricker land, but now it belongs to no one. The army have taken it over. That doesn't seem right."

Pavel leaned forward and dropped his book down on the rug in front of the fire.

"Of course it's right. It's obvious why the army wants that land. Why they must have that land. They have to strengthen the border with Germany. I have no doubt that when this weather lets up, we shall be building all sorts of strong points in those forests."

"But Pavel, is that what we went through all that hardship for? So we could prepare for another war?"

"But that's the point, Kája. If we make ourselves strong from within, and build the right sort of defences, we can avoid another war. But we have to protect ourselves so well that no Germans or Magyars would ever dare make war against us again. It's a precaution, darling."

"I suppose so."

"I've seen what our men can do, Kája. The war was a terrible time, but, my God, how our men can fight. And they can build. You wouldn't believe how resourceful Czechs can be."

Karolína watched her husband as he stared into the fire. His elbows rested on his knees and his hands were clasped tightly together. The reflection of the flames from a fresh log showed the lines and hollows on his face.

"I see the same talents in the boys in school," he said. "We must be strong, so they get a chance to use those talents. They must never have to fight."

"Why do you never talk to me about the war, my love?" asked Karolína. "Only your stories to Tomáš."

"There's no need, Kája. It's over. And I want it to be over for good."

He picked up his book and sat back in his chair. "It's time now to build," he said. "Roads. Cars. We shouldn't be sitting here in gaslight, Kája. We should have electricity. Lights. Radios. You would not believe what I saw in America. They have everything there. They even have picture houses where you can sit down and watch films. 'Flickers' they call them. Every town has one. Cheb should have one."

"That's more my old Pavel," said Karolína and she smiled at him and laughed gently through closed lips. "I like it when you talk like that."

"I want to talk like that. I want us all to go forward. Don't think for a minute I'm anti-German, Kája, although, God knows, I have reason to be."

"I know you're not. I know how fair you are."

"It's just that they need to show us more respect for what we're trying to do in our country. They need to join in with us. That business today with Tomáš just makes me wonder if they're bringing up their children with the same damned arrogance as before."

"Oh, I hope you're wrong, Pavel."

"I hope I'm wrong."

Pavel opened his book and started reading. Karolína took up her knitting again, at an ever quickening pace.

"I've fallen out with Zuzana over all this, you know," she said.

"How have you fallen out?"

"Over the wedding. She seems convinced I believe she's not good enough for Ernst."

"She isn't."

"She is my sister, Pavel."

Pavel looked at Karolína over his book.

"Yes, but I'm afraid she is scheming, insincere and superficial. The exact opposite of you, fortunately."

"She thinks you and I want to keep Ernst with us here in Cheb, because we need his German sophistication in our lives."

"What? Is the girl completely mad?"

"I told her she was being silly."

"Ernst can go wherever he likes as far as I am concerned. He's a good friend. I enjoy his company, but we don't need him to be here."

"I think I might. A little. He was a great support whilst you were away. He let me talk to him about my feelings and my worries. And I like to think I helped him too."

"That's good, my love, but that's all in the past."

"I know. But Tomáš would certainly miss Anna if they left Cheb."

"I expect he would, but not for long, Kája. I can see Tomáš is very fond of Anna, but they're just children. He will grow out of it. He'll have another friend in a few months time."

"I don't think so, Pavel. Some friends develop a bond that's just too painful to break."

When there was no reply, Karolína looked across at Pavel, who did not look up.

Chapter Twenty-Eight

June 24th, 1922 – October 13th, 1923

Ernst and Zuzana were married in Cheb on June 24th 1922. It was a Saturday. On the same day in Berlin Walther Rathenau, the German Foreign Minister, was shot dead in the street by right-wing nationalists. His assassins objected to Rathenau agreeing to honour the full terms of the Treaty of Versailles. They also objected to him being a Jew.

Ernst and Zuzana's wedding took place at the beginning of the school summer holidays. Tomáš and Otto were page boys, and Anna was Zuzana's bridesmaid. At Zuzana's insistence the marriage ceremony was conducted in the Church of Saint Nicholas which, as she pointed out to everyone, was designed by one of Ernst's famous ancestors, the baroque architect Balthasar Neumann.

Karolína, at her own insistence, was wearing a dress of the latest fashion. She had purchased it in Karlovy Vary in May, while Pavel was making his monthly visit to the Villa Musil. The dress, made from silk with a dropped waist and a hemline at mid-calf, was a delicate shade of lemon and drew glances of admiration from all the guests at the wedding breakfast.

Michal and Magdaléna hid their disappointment that Zuzana chose not to hold the celebration at the chata, but nothing could lessen the pride and joy they felt as their younger daughter, dressed in a splendid white gown, became the wife of Ernst Neumann.

The couple left Cheb in the late afternoon, and were waved off on the train to Munich by more than fifty well-wishers. After spending their wedding night at the Hotel Bayerischer Hof in Munich, they left the next day in a chauffeur-driven Mercedes for a two-week tour of the Bavarian Alps. And in mid July they returned to the house in Skalka, which Zuzana then began to run, while helping Ernst from time to time with his work at the theatre.

The next twelve months in the theatre were some of Ernst's happiest, and some of his most successful. He chose to stage a whole season of Mozart's operas, because, as he explained to Pavel and Karolína, 'in troubled times music is the least political of all the arts'.

In the summer of 1923 Ernst and Zuzana returned to Munich and the Bavarian Alps to celebrate the first anniversary of their marriage. Otto and Anna spent those weeks, and most of the rest of the summer, with their cousin Tomáš at the chata by the lake, and on fine evenings and at weekends the whole family gathered there to swim and fish and play during the day, and eat and talk late into the evening.

Karolína convinced herself that the many happy hours she and Zuzana were spending together with their extended family were smoothing over their rift, and turning the feelings between them from animosity into no more than irritation.

But all of that changed one Saturday morning in October, when Zuzana knocked at the front door of the house by the bridge. As soon as Pavel opened the door she stepped inside and pushed her way past him into the front room. In her hand she held a buff-coloured envelope, which she thrust at Karolína as she emerged from the kitchen.

"There you are, Karolína. Read that," she said. "There's your precious Czechoslovakia for you."

Karolína took the envelope and unfolded the letter it contained. As she read it, Pavel led Tomáš by the hand out into the hallway.

"Be a good boy," he whispered, "and play in your room until I call you down."

When Pavel went back into the front room Zuzana was sitting at the dining table, rubbing her forehead with her fingertips. Her breathing was short and fast.

"So what do you make of *that*?" she snapped.

"I don't know, Zuzana. I don't understand why they would do this," said Karolína.

"May I take a look?" asked Pavel, and Karolína handed him the letter.

Pavel scanned it quickly. It was from the Ministry of Culture in Prague, and addressed to Ernst Neumann, Director of the Municipal Theatre of Cheb. '...*inform you that your replacement as director of the theatre... deep gratitude for the many years... will terminate on 31st December, 1923... regret no alternative positions exist at this time... well for the future...*'

"Dear, dear, dear," muttered Pavel. "Poor old Ernst..."

"Is that all you can say? 'Poor old Ernst'," said Zuzana. "They throw your friend out into the street and that's all you can say."

"How is Ernst?" asked Karolína. She dabbed her eyes with a handkerchief.

Zuzana pulled herself upright in the chair, folded her arms and raised her head.

"He is as he always is. Acting like a gentleman and thinking only of others."

Then she stood up. "But I am as mad as hell on his behalf," she shouted. "Those people in Prague. They are nothing but small-minded, bigoted upstarts. I told you, Kája, you're all just jealous of what a talented man like Ernst can achieve."

"Oh, calm yourself and sit down, Zuzana, and stop all your theatrics," said Pavel. "That's not going to help anyone."

Zuzana sat down and looked straight ahead with her arms once again folded tightly across her chest.

"This isn't directed at Ernst personally," said Pavel. "They're just trying to make room for more Czechs in areas where there's still a German majority. That's all. You took advantage of that yourself, Zuzana."

"But I didn't take anyone else's job, did I? Mine was a new post."

"You don't know that."

Zuzana turned towards Karolína.

"There you are, Kája. I told you. Your husband's best friend is sacked because he's not a Czech, and neither of you say one word in support of him. A man who has tried so hard to be fair in his work, and you stand back as he is sacrificed simply because he's German. I said you were both provincial and narrow-minded."

"Now you stop that, Zuzana," said Pavel. "You are in your sister's house and my house and you will show us due respect. Don't come in here acting like a spoilt child. If you want us to discuss this with you, you will act in a reasonable way."

"So you think that letter is reasonable, do you, Pavel?"

"I think it seems very unreasonable when it affects an honourable man like our friend Ernst, but you need to look at the bigger picture, Zuzana. The Germans were our masters for centuries. They took our land, our wealth, even our language..."

"Oh, don't start that again. I know all that."

"Do you, Zuzana? Do you really know? Do you know how many Czechs and Slovaks fought and died against the Germans to make this country's existence possible? Do you know what we had to do? Do you even care?"

Zuzana looked up at Pavel out of the corner of her eye.

"No, of course you don't care, because you've never valued being a Czech woman in the first place. And you take no pride in being Czechoslovakian. It means nothing to you that so many men suffered and died to give you this country."

Pavel looked down at Zuzana but still she did not move or speak.

"I lost two brothers and countless friends in that war caused by German aggression and arrogance. So please do not expect me to get too upset about one German losing his job."

"Well, that one German just happens to be your friend," said Zuzana. "And doing this to him won't bring back your brothers or any of the others. As far as I see, you're just being petty and mean, and picking on people who can't fight back. And you had just better hope they never can."

"That's enough of your nonsense," said Pavel. "I want you out of my house. Go on."

Zuzana stood up.

"Please tell Ernst we are sorry, and if there is anything we can do…" Karolína said, wiping her eyes.

"I'll tell him, Kája, but I doubt he'll believe it any more than I do."

She turned to Pavel.

"And you're right, Pavel. I am ashamed to be Czech, if this is how you treat men like my husband. But we shall survive. Ernst and I both have connections on the Prague literary scene where, you will be very annoyed to hear, most Czechs with any talent still choose to write in German."

"Oh, get out, you silly child."

Zuzana walked slowly from the room. "You're not half the man my Ernst is, Pavel Kovařík," she said without turning. "You're nothing but a bully and a bore."

They heard the front door slam and Karolína immediately slumped into an armchair and sobbed.

"Don't upset yourself, Kája," said Pavel. He went over to her and put his arm around her shoulder. "She'll be back."

"I'm not worried about Zuzana. It's Ernst. We must do something. He's such a good man. Zuzana is right for once. This is so unfair on him."

"But Ernst understands. He always had plenty of reasons before the war to excuse the injustices we suffered under the Austrians."

"I don't care about that, Pavel," shouted Karolína, and her sobs grew louder. "If we drive decent people like Ernst away, what is the point of it all?"

"I don't understand, Kája."

"You told me once we don't need to understand everything about one another," said Karolína, as she buried her head into his chest. "Just do something, Pavel. Please, please, do something. Just find a way to stop it."

Chapter Twenty-Nine

28th – 29th October, 1923

Tomáš was worried but did not want to tell his mother why. He went into the kitchen and stood by the table where she was preparing dumplings for their dinner. She looked at him and smiled.

"Máma," he said, "Tatka's medals have gone. But I didn't take them."

"How do you know they are gone?"

"Because I look at them in your drawer sometimes. And they're not there any more."

"Did tatka give you permission to go into our room and look at his medals?"

"No, but I never touch them."

"You should not even look in the drawer if no one has given you permission, Tomáš. You know that, don't you?"

"Sorry, Máma."

Karolína looked down and saw the furrows on his forehead and the disappointment in his face.

"Don't worry, Tomáš. I expect tatka took his medals to Prague with him. For today's parade."

"But I thought he didn't like parades."

"He doesn't usually, but this one is special. You know why, don't you?"

"Because it's Independence Day, and our country is five years old."

"That's right."

"I wish tatka had taken me with him to the parade."

"I'm sure he will one day, Tomášek. When you are older."

Pavel stood in Wenceslas Square watching veterans of the Legion marching behind regular soldiers of the Czechoslovakian Army. On a podium to their left the head of the army, General Čeček, took the salute. Many of the veterans could only be in their mid twenties, thought Pavel, but not one had a young man's face.

His medals remained in the inside pocket of his overcoat. He stood three rows back amongst the cheering crowd, seeking anonymity and scanning the faces for his boys. He couldn't see them. He looked down at the cobbles. The sound of marching feet and the military band brought everything back to him. He saw Martinek and Skála, Sedláček and Kopeský. He saw the pink mist again, the Austrian boy pleading with him, and the faces of the Russian sailor cadets calling out to him as they breathed in the dark, choppy water of Lake Baikal.

He turned and walked away, along *Na můstku*, a narrow street leading to the old town, still familiar to him from his years as a student at the Charles University. Soon he came to the Old Town Square and saw something he had not seen before: a large statue of Jan Hus erected to celebrate the five-hundredth anniversary of the death of the Czech reformer. The Marian Column, which stood for nearly three centuries celebrating Hapsburg rule, had been demolished. Pavel sat down at the foot of the Jan Hus statue in the autumn sunshine and watched the people of Prague, as they went peacefully about their lives.

The next day he got up early at the small hotel. He pinned his four medals onto his suit jacket, put on his overcoat and walked once more into the Old Town Square. He made his way across the Charles Bridge and climbed the steep narrow streets leading to Prague Castle. When he reached the large square at the top, he paused outside the castle entrance to compose himself. He took the letter from the pocket of his overcoat and checked the instructions again. This was Matthias Gate. The right gate. He entered beneath the ornate ironwork bridging two large pillars, and crossed first one courtyard, then another, and found himself in front of the Cathedral of Saint Vitus.

He walked into the shade along the north side of the cathedral and there on his right he saw the entrance to the Royal Palace, where his path was blocked. In front of two large wooden gates stood two guards in ceremonial uniform holding M98 Mauser rifles. A policeman appeared from a side office and asked Pavel his business. He took the letter Pavel offered him and went back inside. A few moments later he reappeared with a smile on his face and saluted.

"When you go through these gates, sir," he said, "cross the courtyard and go into the office on your left. Wait there. I have just telephoned through. Someone will come down to meet you."

Pavel followed the policeman's directions and entered a small waiting room. On one wall hung a shield bearing the crest of the Republic and on another a full-length portrait of the President. Pavel had barely sat down when a door opened to his left and a young man in a dark suit appeared. The young man came towards him, holding out his hand and smiling broadly.

"Sergeant Kovařík, what a pleasure it is to see you again," he said.

"My goodness." Pavel got to his feet. "Filip Souček. What are you doing here?"

The two men stood shaking hands and smiling at one other as they spoke.

"I work here in the Office of the President."

"But this explains everything."

"I couldn't believe it when I saw your name. I thought, 'it must be him. Pavel Kovařík from Cheb.' It had to be you."

"So did you arrange this?"

"I helped a little, but the President would doubtless have seen you anyway. Being a legionnaire, especially in Russia, opens a lot of doors barred to most people."

"Well, well. Filip Souček. What a wonderful surprise."

Each released his grip on the other's hand and they sat down.

"Milan's mother told me you had been to see him, Filip. But she didn't tell me you worked here."

"I finished my degree when I got back. Then I applied for this job and got it. I think my Legion background helped."

"So tell me what you do here."

"I work in the President's private office. I'm one of many who sift through his mail, reply to most on his behalf, and occasionally pass something on to one of his private secretaries for his personal attention. That's what happened to your letter."

"I have a lot to thank you for, Filip."

"You have nothing to thank me for, Sergeant. It is a privilege to help you in any way I can."

"Thank you anyway."

"Would you like to come with me now?"

"Yes, Filip, of course."

As they stood up, Pavel put his hand on Souček's sleeve. "Tell me, Filip," he said, "has everything been alright for you since you got back?"

"Yes, Sergeant. Better than many, I think."

"I am very pleased to hear it, Filip. Very pleased indeed."

Souček led Pavel up some stairs to the first floor. They walked down a long, wide corridor. The windows on one side looked out onto a courtyard. Those opposite offered a splendid view over the city.

"You are very privileged actually, Sergeant. Yours is the only appointment President Masaryk has today. But I must tell you, you may find him rather tired after all the celebrations yesterday. And he only got back from a state visit to England last Friday."

"I see. It's extremely good of him to see me."

At the end of the corridor Souček paused in front of two tall, highly polished doors. In alcoves on either side of the doors two soldiers in ceremonial uniform stood to attention.

"I shall introduce you first to the President's private secretary, who will take you into the President's office," said Souček.

He opened the doors and made way for Pavel to enter before him. A man in a morning suit looked up from behind his desk and stood up.

"Pan Hájek, this is Sergeant Kovařík. He has an appointment with the President at ten o'clock," said Souček.

"Good morning, Sergeant Kovařík. May I take your coat?"

"Thank you."

Pavel wished a hundred times over that he had not put on his medals that morning. As he passed his overcoat to Hájek they felt like a boastful sign hanging across his chest. He watched Pan Hájek approach two double doors leading into another room. Hájek opened one of them without knocking, and Pavel heard him speaking softly to someone as he closed the door behind him.

"I'll see you again later downstairs, Sergeant," whispered Souček, and before Pavel could respond, the young man was gone.

"President Masaryk will see you now, Sergeant Kovařík."

Masaryk was standing in front of the fireplace beneath a large portrait of himself on horseback. He looked exactly as Pavel remembered him, and exactly as he appeared in the newspapers every day. Tall and upright, with a slim frame, wearing a dark suit with his usual winged collar and pince-nez spectacles. His white hair was thinning now, but his white moustache was as full as ever and merged into his short trimmed beard.

Pavel took a few steps towards him and Masaryk approached across a rug bearing the crest of the Republic.

"It is a pleasure to meet you, Sergeant Kovařík," said the President, as they shook hands.

"Thank you very much for inviting me here, Mr President. It is more than I could ever have hoped for."

"The honour is all mine, Sergeant Kovařík. It is always a pleasure to meet old comrades who were with me in Russia. Please come and sit by the fire. I have asked for coffee to be served in fifteen minutes."

"Thank you, sir."

"I like to see a soldier who is proud to wear his medals, Sergeant, especially the War Cross with linden leaves. There are not many entitled to wear that. You won it at Zborov, I believe."

"Yes, sir, that is correct."

"I have read your army file, Sergeant. And young Souček talks of you with much pride and enthusiasm. General Čeček remembers you too."

"Souček was in my section for four years, Mr President. And I met Colonel Čeček, as he was then, for the first time at Chelyabinsk. My section served under him for eighteen months after that. Mostly on the Orlik."

"Men such as you have done so much for our country, Sergeant Kovařík. We all owe you a great debt."

"Thank you, sir."

"Tell me how I can be of service to you."

"When I sit here and I imagine the issues you have to deal with, President Masaryk, the problem that brought me here seems so trivial now."

"Nothing that concerns a legionnaire is trivial to me, Sergeant Kovařík. None of our country's citizens has a greater right to sit in this office and ask something of me than the men I left behind in Russia. Please ask."

"It concerns a friend of mine in Cheb, sir. But the fact that this man is my friend is irrelevant. He is a good man. A loyal citizen of Czechoslovakia. And I believe we may be about to do him a great injustice."

"You are talking about Ernst Neumann."

"Yes, sir."

"I have read your letter, Sergeant Kovařík, but I would like us both to be clear about the facts of this case. Neumann is an Austrian German by birth. Is that right?"

"Yes, sir, but he is married to a Czech and is the father of two Czech children."

"And he has fallen foul in some way of our Minority Laws."

"Yes, Mr President. He has been the director of our municipal theatre in Cheb since before the war, and he is much respected in the town. But he has just been informed by the Ministry of Culture that he is to lose his job in the New Year. I imagine so that a Czech can be appointed in his place."

"That is more than likely. Tell me, did Neumann serve in the war?"

"Yes, sir. He fought for the Austrians in Italy. But then so did one of my own brothers."

"I understand, Sergeant. And did Neumann take part in the insurrection around Cheb at the end of the war?"

"No, sir. I know he did not. He is a man of great honour and integrity, and loyal to the state."

"And you think he should be protected in his present post?"

"I do, sir."

The door opened and Hájek entered, accompanied by a young woman carrying a tray, which she placed on a small table between the two men. Masaryk thanked her and asked her to leave the tray there. Pavel watched as the President of the Republic poured his morning coffee.

"I would like to try to explain something to you, Sergeant Kovařík," said Masaryk as he sat back stirring his drink.

"The area where you and Neumann live, which the Germans still insist on calling the Sudetenland, is of great concern to us here in Prague. There are three and a half million ethnic-German citizens of our country living there, most of whom refuse to participate in our democratic processes."

"I do understand that, sir."

"These citizens present a great dilemma to us, I am afraid. Because the more we try to correct the social injustices inflicted on our people by the Hapsburgs, the more we seem to upset our citizens of German extraction. Our land reforms, the redistribution of wealth, and the need for more Czech representation in towns like yours, are not endearing us to the very people whose support we need."

"Does that not make the case for supporting men like Ernst Neumann even stronger, Mr President? He is just the sort of German we need to encourage."

"I do see logic in that argument, Sergeant Kovařík, but I must ask you to view the larger picture, as we must view it from Prague. The imperative for us is to dilute the threat posed by so many Germans living in our border areas. There are several ways we can do this. We can forcibly resettle people, a morally questionable step which would contravene our own laws; we can encourage more Czechs to move into the area, which we have tried with only limited success; or we can replace Germans in influential posts with Czechs, in the hope of encouraging our citizens of a German background to move to other areas of the Republic. All these options pass the test of logic, but whatever we do will at times seem crude and cruel when applied to individuals."

"But the ordinary citizen only sees what happens to individuals, Mr President. To friends and members of their family."

"I do realise that, Sergeant Kovařík. But there are times in government when we are obliged to demote the needs of the individual in the interests of what we consider to be the greater good. I am sure in the war you, like me, often had to do that. Am I right?"

"I'm afraid you are, sir."

"You know then that such decisions are never easy. But in war people accept the need to make such decisions more readily than they do in times of peace. With the bravery and effort of men like you, Sergeant, we succeeded in creating a state from that war. What we need from you now is your understanding and patience as we try to build a nation."

"You have my understanding, sir, and my unconditional support. But it is not always easy to explain such things to people who view government policy only through the prism of their own lives."

"I realise that, Sergeant. The war is over and people expect life to return to normal immediately. They do not realise that even though the fighting is over, the struggle and the danger remain as great as ever. They do not understand that we still live in perilous times."

He removed his pince-nez and rubbed his eyes. When he replaced them he fixed Pavel with his gaze.

"I shall share something with you, Sergeant Kovařík," he said, folding his arms. "It is my opinion that if the democracies do not act with great wisdom now, we could one day see a Fascist dictatorship in Germany to equal the one Mussolini has created in Italy."

"Is that possible, Mr President?"

"I am afraid it is. The Reichsmark is now worthless. Since Germany defaulted on their reparation payments and the French occupied the Ruhr, there has been armed resistance and an upsurge of support for right-wing groups. Only two weeks ago the government in Berlin suspended the Reichstag and took on dictatorial powers."

"I read about that."

"But there are some things you will not read about, Sergeant Kovařík. Did you know that in the state of Bavaria, only 15 kilometres from your town, there are right-wing groups which threaten to march on Berlin, in the same way that Mussolini marched on Rome?"

"No, sir, I did not."

"We are receiving reports from Munich that General Ludendorff himself has lent his name to a party of extremists who intend to stage a coup, first in Bavaria, and then in Berlin. And these are the same people who insist that all Germans, no matter what their present citizenship may be, should one day be part of a single German nation."

"Including our three and a half million."

"Especially our three and a half million, Sergeant. As I say, we live in perilous times."

"But what can we do to stop it, sir?"

"Encourage our German citizens to move away from the borders.

Move more Czechs in. But above all we must make our country so strong and prosperous that all our citizens wish to play a full part in its democratic life. People do not seek conflict when their stomachs are full and they have money in the bank. That is the key. But until that time we must take steps to protect ourselves."

"Is that why we're fortifying our borders near Cheb?"

"That is one precaution. We are a small country, Sergeant, but our soldiers enjoy a reputation like no others in the world, thanks to men like you. But what we need most vitally is the support of other, bigger nations."

"France."

"Yes, primarily France. Once the French grant us their protection and guarantee our borders in a formal treaty, I think we shall all be able to sleep more peacefully in our beds. Dr Beneš works on very little else."

"I suppose we should be pleased the French are occupying the Ruhr and the Rhineland. At least the Germans cannot start anything whilst they are there."

"The French occupation can only be a short-term solution, Sergeant. The irony of our situation is that we, more than any country in Europe, need Germany's economy to recover. Much of our industry is still German owned, and it is still the biggest market for our goods. What our country needs is a Germany that is economically and democratically strong, but militarily weak. Our greatest hope for that lies with France and the League of Nations."

Pavel leaned forward in his chair and looked across at Masaryk, now in his seventy-fourth year, but showing no signs that his powers were diminishing.

"I feel honoured, Mr President, that you take so much time to talk to me about such important matters as these," he said.

"You are mistaken, Sergeant Kovařík. I can assure you again that the honour is mine. Talking to a citizen of your background and experience can often be more valuable to a man in my position than a hundred briefings by civil servants, or a month of cabinet meetings. I just hope I have been able to explain to you the wider implications of the case concerning your friend."

"Yes, Mr President, you have, sir. I do understand completely the reasons behind our policy in the border areas, and I do not wish to seem ungrateful or ungracious after all the time you have afforded me this morning. But I am surprised, sir, that you have not agreed to make an exception in the case of Ernst Neumann."

"Really, Sergeant Kovařík? Why does that surprise you?"

Pavel remained sitting forward. He felt his hands shaking. When he spoke his voice trembled.

"Because, sir, I feel that I know you. I know that you are above all a defender of the truth. As a lawyer you stood up for the truth when people scorned you for it. When I was a student I attended your lectures on ethics at Charles University. On our country's crest you have placed the words of Jan Hus, 'Truth Prevails'. I agree with you, sir, that there are times when responsibility carries with it the need to carry through an order or policy, which we know will sacrifice individuals for the greater good. And we have to do that, sir, and perhaps live for the rest of our lives with the burden of it. But when it concerns an individual we know... when we are made aware of an individual case of injustice... we may still keep hold fast to the principle, but we must right the individual wrong."

"The difference is knowing. That is what you are saying, isn't it, Sergeant? Once we know, it becomes a truth, and we must not ignore it."

"That is what I am saying, sir. 'Pravda vítězí.' The words on the rug."

Masaryk stood up. Pavel stood up too, and together they walked to the double doors.

"That was well said, Sergeant Kovařík. I have enjoyed our talk this morning immensely."

"So have I, sir. I thank you again."

Masaryk opened the door and shook Pavel's hand. "Please be sure to speak to Filip Souček before you leave us, won't you, Sergeant Kovařík?" he said.

When Pavel returned to the small waiting room on the ground floor, he was pleased to find Filip standing at the foot of the stairs waiting for him.

"Thank you, Filip, for making that possible for me. I shall always be grateful to you."

"Was the President able to help you with your friend's case?" asked Souček.

"He explained to me why he is not able to help, and I understand."

"I think the President would like to help you, Sergeant."

"Yes, I know that, Filip. But I have been reminded today that intelligence and wisdom are not enough in themselves to be a great leader. Our President also needs to be resolute in these troubled times, and by choosing not to help me he has shown his strength. I see that now. There can be no exceptions."

"I expect he explained the problems we have with extremists in the border areas, did he?"

"Yes. He did."

"I wonder. Did the President mention the name Karl Hermann Wolf to you?"

"No."

"Do you know who he is?"

"Yes, of course. He was the Austrian deputy in the National Assembly who said Czechs were wild animals who should be controlled by the whip."

"That's the man. Wolf was born in Cheb. He founded the German Workers' Party before the war."

"Is that relevant to any of this, Filip?"

"Have you heard of Franko Stein?"

"No, never."

"He was born in Cheb too. He's an associate of Wolf's."

"What is the point of your question?"

"Bear with me, Sergeant, please. The party Wolf and Stein founded is now known as the German National Socialist Workers' Party. Have you heard of that?"

"No, I haven't."

"The Austrian branch of this party is now centred in Vienna. But it began in Cheb and still has strong links and strong support there. Do you recognise the name Karl Hermann Frank, by any chance?"

"No, I don't, Filip. Should I?"

"Frank is also a member of the German National Socialist Workers' Party. He was born in Karlovy Vary and still lives there. He runs a bookshop by the railway station. The Party use it as a centre for the distribution of propaganda, and for meetings."

"I've never heard of him."

"Frank has strong ties with an off-shoot of the Austrian party in Munich. The leader there is called Adolf Hitler. Have you heard of him perhaps?"

"No, Filip, I haven't heard of any of these people, and I don't wish to appear ungrateful, but your questions are beginning to vex me. Will you please explain what this is all about?"

"Let me give you just one more name, Sergeant. Alois Krause. Do you know him?"

"Yes, of course I know Herr Krause. He owns the bookshop in the colonnade back in Cheb."

"Do you know what sort of books he sells?"

"School textbooks mostly. That's how I met my wife. She still works there every Friday."

"We know that."

"You know that? What the devil is going on here, Filip? What do you really do here at the castle?"

"I work in the Office of the President, Sergeant, as I said. On the communications side."

"Oh, 'on the communications side'. I see. You could have just asked me, Filip. You didn't need this charade."

"It's no charade, Sergeant. I thought the President was going to ask you himself to help us; but he clearly did not feel comfortable about it. He really did want to meet you this morning. There was no need for him to do so. But President Masaryk admires you. As I do."

"I shall choose to believe you, Filip. Come on. Let's sit down somewhere. Explain what it is you need from me."

Chapter Thirty

November 7th, 1923 – October 28th, 1928

The letter reinstating Ernst arrived in early November. Zuzana went immediately to Karolína's house to tell her.

"I'm delighted, Zuzana. It's wonderful news. Ernst must be thrilled."

"He doesn't know yet. I shall tell him when he gets back from the theatre. I hope you realise it is the German patrons of the theatre we have to thank for this, Kája. They all wrote to Prague, you know."

"I'm just delighted you're all staying, Zuzana. I don't care why."

"Well, I care why. Those fools in Prague were obviously made to realise there are certain positions which can only be filled by someone with a sound background and knowledge of German culture."

Karolína handed the letter back to Zuzana.

"Please, Zuzana, don't let Pavel hear you say that."

"Your husband needs to understand, Kája, that German culture isn't a threat. It's a civilising influence on his country."

"Pavel will be home for lunch soon. I think it would be for the best if he didn't hear about this from you."

"It's alright. I'm going. You tell him in your own way. But I hope he feels ashamed for not supporting such a good friend."

"Goodbye, Zuzana."

Karolína stood by the window and watched her sister, head held high, striding back across the bridge. She wished she could have shown Zuzana the other letter; the one she found only a few days before in Pavel's drawer, when she checked to see if his medals were back in their usual place. Beneath the medals she had found an envelope. She knew she should not open it and, once she did, she knew she would never be able to ask Pavel what it meant. The letter was dated 15th October 1923, and it invited him to an interview with the President himself, the day after Independence Day.

At the end of his meeting with Filip Souček Pavel agreed to act as the President's 'eyes and ears' in Cheb and await specific instructions from the castle. Pavel refused to make Ernst's reinstatement a condition of the agreement, and insisted he only wanted the decision to be reversed if the

President was persuaded by his arguments, and for no other reason. When he heard of Ernst's reinstatement from Karolína he took it as further proof of the President's humanity and of his constant search for the truth.

Over the weeks and months following his visit Pavel's confidence in Masaryk reached new heights, as events predicted by the President during their meeting were reported in the national press, and policies pursued by him and Beneš gradually came to fruition.

In mid November came news of an attempt by right-wing extremists in Munich to overthrow the government of Bavaria, just as the President had warned they would. It involved the leader of the nationalist party in which Filip Souček had shown so much interest, and one of Germany's greatest war heroes, General Ludendorff. The coup failed, and the party leader imprisoned.

In early 1924 Pavel read of an event he knew would be celebrated more than any other at Prague Castle. On January 25th Beneš signed a treaty in Paris with Poincaré, the French Foreign Minister, in which they agreed that, if the security of either country were threatened, the other would come to their aid.

And later in 1924 came more good news, as the United States instigated a plan to save the wrecked German economy. Inflation was brought under control, reparation payments resumed, and in July 1925 France withdrew its occupying troops from the Ruhr. With increased political security and Germany's economic revival the economy of Czechoslovakia improved dramatically too. And, as Masaryk had predicted, once the Sudeten Germans became more prosperous within Czechoslovakia they became more willing to take part in its democratic processes.

In 1927 Sudeten Germans at last voted in the elections to the National Assembly, and some of their chosen representatives accepted Masaryk's offer of posts in his new cabinet. When Masaryk was re-elected President, even Zuzana seemed genuinely pleased as the family celebrated at the chata on the day the results were announced.

Pavel and Karolína had never been happier. Neither they nor Ernst and Zuzana were blessed with more children, as they all hoped they would, but Otto, Anna and Tomáš were happy and flourished. Anna and Tomáš started at secondary school at the end of August, 1927, and Otto moved into his third year of the Gymnasium. Anna and Tomáš were now taught in different classes at Pavel's school, where all instruction was in Czech, but whenever they could they sought each other out and remained devoted to one another.

At Cheb's municipal theatre Ernst's reputation grew from strength to strength, and although he was invited to be guest director in Karlovy Vary, and even in Prague and Vienna, he always returned to his permanent post in Cheb. He never heard from the Ministry of Culture again.

Pavel did not hear from Filip Souček again either. When he first returned from his meeting with Masaryk, he expected a letter from Filip at any time, detailing the information Prague wanted him to gather in Cheb. Pavel decided he would take Karolína into his confidence and enlist her help, as soon as word arrived. But when no letter came after weeks, months and then years, he decided instead that any threats must have passed, until finally he thought nothing more about it at all.

In October, 1928, Pavel went back to Prague to celebrate the tenth anniversary of the founding of the Republic.

Since Independence Day fell on a Sunday, the Kovařík, Štasný and Neumann families decided over long discussions at the chata that they would spend the three days of the national holiday in the capital. And so, early on the Saturday morning, after weeks of preparation, they made their way together across the main square in Cheb on their way to the railway station.

In front of the New Town Hall a bandstand had been erected, and the members of a brass band in traditional Egerland costumes were gathered in front of it. The men wore black leather breeches, tied below the knee over white socks, and red velvet jackets over white shirts. The women dancers to the side were dressed in a similar style with black skirts over white stockings and colourful aprons and bodices. The men raised their hunting hats in greeting as the family passed.

"*Grüsst euch,*" they called out. "*Habt Spass. Have fun.*"

The women dancers smiled and waved.

"*Grüss Gott,*" said Ernst in reply. "*Recht vielen Dank.*"

"*Servus, Männer,*" called out Pavel. "*Und gnädige Frauen.*" He raised his trilby hat and nodded.

"That was decent of you, Pavel," said Ernst as they walked on.

"If they are willing to turn out to celebrate Independence Day with the rest of us, I am only too happy to greet my fellow countrymen in German," replied Pavel. "I'm delighted to see them joining in at last."

He felt Karolína squeeze his arm and returned her smile.

The luggage had been sent on ahead, not, as Magdaléna first suggested, in a donkey cart but, as Zuzana and Michal insisted, in one of Cheb's new motorised taxis.

"Have no worry, my dear," Michal reassured his wife. "We can afford such things now our savings are doing so well."

Michal had even tried to persuade Magdaléna to buy new clothes for the trip, but she refused such extravagance and insisted on wearing the same dress and coat she had bought six years earlier for her daughter's summer wedding.

"The more the wear I get out of them, the cheaper they were in the first place," she reasoned.

In the early afternoon they arrived at the modest hotel, which Pavel had booked by letter, close to Prague's main station. It was only a quarter of the price of the Hotel Grand Bohemia where Ernst and Zuzana usually stayed, and Ernst only managed to calm his wife's objections to the 'degrading facilities' by agreeing that Otto and Anna would have a room of their own and not share with their father and stepmother.

Tomáš was happy enough to share with his parents although, given the chance, he would have preferred to be with Otto and Anna, or rather just with Anna. But something, he was not sure what, told him such an arrangement might not be quite right, and he decided not to ask.

Michal and Magdaléna had never known such luxury. They had stayed once in a *pension* in Karlovy Vary before the girls came along, but nothing as grand as this. And in Prague, of all places. Magdaléna went back and forth to admire the bathroom they shared with the other guests on their floor. And she examined the telephone in the hallway outside their room, and even touched it, but did not dare to pick up the earpiece.

She stood at the window with Michal, watching the crowds, the cars and the trams in the street below their room. She took a handkerchief from her sleeve and wiped her eyes.

"I can't believe what I'm seeing, Michal. Everything's so perfect. All together here with the girls and the little ones. Thank you for persuading me."

Michal felt for her hand as they stood side by side.

"Well, you've waited long enough and you deserve it, my dear. And I'm taking you somewhere special this afternoon. I'm not saying what."

"Nowhere expensive, Michal. Please."

"I keep telling you, Magda, the money's alright now. I've asked Ernst to suggest somewhere nice."

"But, Michal..."

"No, Magda, my love. We're going. Now let's have an end to it."

In the afternoon they all gathered in the small foyer of the hotel for a walk into the Old Town, and waited while Ernst stood at the front desk giving

Michal directions.

"I don't know what your father has in mind, I'm sure," said Magdaléna, and she continued to brush unseen specks from the sleeves of her coat.

"Don't worry, Máma. You're going to have a nice time whatever it is," said Karolína.

"Doesn't your Babička look lovely?" she asked Tomáš, looking for some support.

"You do, Babička," agreed Tomáš, but he had never seen his grandmother wearing make-up, lavishly applied by Zuzana, and suspected he was lying.

"Come on, Magda. We're off," announced Michal, transformed in his new black suit.

Magdaléna began kissing everyone as if there was a chance she might not see them again, and they all went out onto the pavement. The couple were waved off as they crossed the busy road, with Magdaléna hanging on to Michal as if her life depended on it.

"It's so wonderful to see Máma and Táta so excited," said Karolína, as the rest of the family made their way along Krizikova Street towards the Old Town. "Are you going to tell us now where you sent them, Ernst?"

"To the Hotel Pariz for cocktails," he said over his shoulder.

"And then *Kaffee und Kuchen* at four o'clock in the lounge," added Zuzana.

"My God, those waiters will scare Magdaléna half to death," said Pavel.

"Not our máma. Give her two cocktails and they'll be the ones who are scared. She'll have them running everywhere, won't she, Zuzana?"

"She'll be in the kitchens telling them how to cook..."

"And in the restaurant insisting no one leaves anything. 'Now come on, all of you. This food needs eating.' I can hear her now."

Everyone laughed as they walked along, even Otto, who usually joined in so little.

For the children Prague was a different world. They had never seen such crowds, and there was no end to the streets which ran off in every direction, making it impossible to remember which one they had taken last.

"Don't go off on your own," Pavel warned them, but they really needed no telling.

Even Karolína was overawed by the noise and pace of the city, but she was not going to let it be known to anyone. And Pavel was amazed by the changes that had taken place since his visit to see President Masaryk five

197

years before. Everything seemed so prosperous and modern. The horses had disappeared from the streets, and there were cars everywhere. And there were so many new buildings - shops and offices and hotels - built in the most modern style which, Zuzana informed him, the French called 'Art Déco'.

All the streets were lit by electricity, and there were notices throughout the city reminding locals and visitors that later that day at five o'clock the castle, the *Pražský Hrad,* would be illuminated for the very first time by electric lights in honour of President Masaryk and the tenth anniversary of the founding of the Republic.

"Can we go and see it, Tatka?" asked Tomáš and, when told he could, he ran back to tell Anna and Otto, who were looking in wonder at the latest 'radiogram' in the window of a shop. From the shop's open door the sound of a jazz recording drifted across the street.

Pavel and Karolína stood watching Anna, Tomáš and Otto talking and laughing excitedly. Tomáš put his arm casually around Anna's shoulders as they looked in the window, and she automatically put her arm around his waist. They were like a young modern couple in miniature, he with his knee-length flannel trousers, flannel jacket, long socks and cap, and Anna with her serge skirt and hand-knitted jumper with woollen stockings and beret.

"So, do you still think they will grow out of it?" Karolína asked Pavel, as they too put their arms around one another.

"I expect so."

"You have been saying that since you first came home, and yet they're still as close as the day they were born."

"Yes, but they're still only children, Kája."

"They're nearly twelve."

"But they're still just playing together. In a few years' time they will be in and out of love with someone different every week. You know how it is."

"Oh, I do, do I? I only ever remember being in love with you."

Pavel pulled Karolína close and kissed her forehead.

"You and I are the exception, my Kája. Come on, let's find Ernst and Zuzana and take the children to the Old Square."

At four o'clock the small family group gathered in front of the Astronomical Clock in the Old Square to listen to it strike, and to watch the Procession of the Apostles through the doors which opened at the top.

Karolína and Zuzana announced they were spending the next hour looking at the garment shops in Pařížská Street and, although Pavel and

Ernst made a show of protesting, they were both quietly relieved to see their wives so happy together and taking pleasure at long last in one another's company.

Just before five they met up again in front of the clock and made their way to the Charles Bridge, which offered the best view of the castle as it was lit up for the first time in its history. It was getting colder since the sun went down, and the seven of them put their arms around one another as they lined up along the parapet and waited.

Finally the crowds around them started to count down. *Pět...čtyři... tři...dva...jeden...Hura!* And everyone in the crowd clapped and cheered and embraced the people nearest to them as the Pražský Hrad, symbol of their country's solidity and security, suddenly appeared on the hill across the Vltava, lifted by uplights into the dark autumn sky.

Karolína in her happiness turned to embrace yet another person in the crowd. It was Ernst. They looked at one another, and then looked at Tomáš and Anna jumping up and down and cheering next to them. They embraced and laughed. Their cheeks touched.

"Everything has worked out for the best, dear Kája," Ernst whispered.

"It has for me, Ernst. I hope it has for you."

"As long as the children are happy, and you are my friend, dear Kája, I am content."

"And Babička fell asleep during the film," exclaimed Tomáš at breakfast the next day.

"I wasn't asleep," protested Magdaléna. "I closed my eyes to enjoy the music, that's all."

"During a Charlie Chaplin film, Máma?" said Zuzana. "That doesn't seem very likely."

"It isn't," said Karolína, "the pianist was so dreadful, she would have woken the dead. Admit it, Máma, it was the cocktails in the afternoon."

"Well, I thought I was ordering tea. Your táta should have warned me."

"Don't blame me, Magda. I didn't know what Long Island Tea had in it."

"What is in it, Děda?" asked Anna.

"I still don't know, my darling," said Michal. "All I know is, I couldn't stop your Babička from drinking it."

Everyone around the table laughed.

"It has gin, tequila, vodka and rum in it," confirmed Zuzana. "And a little bit of Coca Cola. It's quite the thing to serve it in cups and teapots in America, in order to fool the police."

"I did like the Coca Cola," said Magdaléna, and everyone laughed again.

"Did you enjoy the concert last night, Ernst?" Pavel asked.

"It was splendid," said Zuzana, clapping her hands. "I adore Mozart. I think Don Giovanni must be my favourite. But, I dare to say it, I do not think it was as well directed as Ernst's production in Karlovy Vary in '26."

"Please, Zuzana, I think you may be exaggerating."

"I am not, Ernst. You really must not allow your achievements to pass so unrecognised."

"I don't think I do, do I?"

"And what was the reception like beforehand?" asked Karolína.

"Oh, I forgot to tell you," said Zuzana. "The Austrian ambassador was there. To celebrate Mozart's association with Prague, you know. I said to Ernst he should ask to be presented, but he never..."

"Please, Zuzana, I think it was honour enough that we were invited, don't you? Let us talk about today instead. What time is the parade, Pavel?"

"Ten o'clock. In just over an hour. And the President speaks at twelve. Does everyone want to come?"

"Yes, of course," they all agreed.

"And then this afternoon I am going to take my son somewhere special," said Pavel. "If the rest of you can do without us for an hour or so."

"Really, Tatka? Where?"

"I am not saying until we get there. But there is something here in Prague I have always wanted to tell you about."

Pavel felt uncomfortable marching with his medals in front of Ernst. He knew his friend held the Austro-Hungary Military Merit Cross, First Class, for an act of bravery equal to anything he or anyone else might have done. But he also knew Ernst would never get the chance to wear his medals in any parade.

"I know there are no parades for those on the losing side, Ernst," he said, as they walked together towards Wenceslas Square, "but I promised the boy I would bring him here one day, and wear my medals for him. Just once. I hope you understand."

Ernst smiled at his friend and placed his hand lightly on his back.

"I would only feel I were on the losing side, Pavel, if what we did in that war had not led to some improvement in the world. And I believe it has."

"It's a good way to look at it, Ernst. I was lucky, I suppose, that I was given such a clear purpose to fight for."

"I had a clear purpose, Pavel. I fought to hold on to what I had, and I still have it. I have my children, and I believe you and I are both doing our best for them. When you parade, my friend, you can parade for me too."

It was the veterans of the Legion who received the loudest cheers from the crowds packed into Wenceslas Square, as they did every year. And no one cheered louder than Tomáš.

"Tatka, Tatka," he cried when he spotted his father in the midst of a group of men, all in black civilian suits and each wearing the cap of the Legion. They all had medals pinned to their chest but Tomáš saw no one wearing the War Cross with linden leaves other than his father. The men marched in step to the sound of a military band which went before them, and Tomáš kept his eyes fixed on just one legionnaire who seemed taller than the rest and who, to him, was everything a man should be.

When the parade was over they all made their way to the Old Town side of Charles Bridge to meet up again with Pavel. Karolína and Magdaléna both greeted him with kisses and tears, as if he had just returned anew from the war, and Zuzana hovered behind them waiting for an opening to step forward and peck him on the cheek. Ernst and Michal both offered Pavel strong handshakes, while the Neumann children stood back unsure what to do. Tomáš stood with them, until he realised he had left it too late to approach his father and show him how proud he was of him.

"Come on then," said Pavel, "let's go and hear what our President has to say. Are you alright, Magdaléna? It's quite a steep climb."

"Yes, I'm alright. A little walk like that is no problem for us, is it, Táta? Not after what we've been through over the years."

"Tell her there's a waiter with Long Island Tea at the top," Karolína called out. "That will get her up there fast enough."

Thousands had gathered in the square at the top of the hill to hear President Masaryk give his speech, the first to be broadcast over a loudspeaker system. Many crowded forward, still under the impression they would hear nothing unless they were near the podium. But Ernst found a raised area further back, which afforded a clear view and was within easy earshot of a loudspeaker.

When Masaryk appeared at twelve o'clock the whole crowd roared their approval and applauded. Pavel experienced the same feelings of privilege and anticipation he always felt in the great man's presence.

Masaryk looked unchanged, but when he raised his hat to acknowledge the cheering crowd, he revealed that the last five of his 78 years had claimed the remainder of his thin white hair. When he spoke, his voice carried the same clarity and authority it always had.

For twenty minutes he held the crowd, silencing them with his reasoning and reflections and then stirring them with his passion for his vision of the Czechoslovakia he needed them to create. At the end he lowered his head and spoke softly to the crowd, as if he were taking each person into his confidence. Pavel and Karolína gripped each other's hand.

"There were times, I do admit, when I was exiled in the vastness of Russia, when I asked myself if our people at home were really aware of that moment in their history. I asked myself, 'Are they ripe for freedom? Are they ready for democracy, and for the responsibility it carries for the ordinary citizen?'

"And yes, I must admit, there have been times since October 28th 1918 when I have even asked, 'Are we, whom our citizens have entrusted with power, ready to maintain and administer an independent state?'

"And today on the tenth birthday of our brave young country I have the answer to all those questions. Our country stands here now on the crossroads of Europe as a model of democracy. Our citizens of every background and prior allegiance have at last joined together and created not just a country, but a nation, strong and united in purpose. The answer to all my questions is 'yes, yes'.

"The answer is our one united nation. Our Czechoslovakia."

"When are you going to tell me where we're going, Tatka?"

"I am not saying anything until we get there, Tomáš."

"But this is the way back to the hotel, isn't it?"

"What I want to show you is just around the corner from there. When we get there I shall tell you one more story about the Legion. It will be the last."

"The last, Tatka?"

Soon after leaving the Old Town they walked past the Municipal House and into Na Poříčí Street. Halfway down Pavel stopped and pointed to a building across the road. It was a new building, very solid-looking, built of heavy stone and standing alone, seven storeys tall.

Each storey was supported by six columns of reddish-brown marble, except the ground to the first floor, where only four much larger columns supported the whole edifice. Each of these four columns of brown and white marble was topped by a large carved stone, and above them was a frieze relief, also carved in stone.

"Come with me," said Pavel, and he ushered Tomáš across the street, where they stood on the pavement in front of the main doors.

Tomáš read the name spelt out in bold letters above the two large windows, which fronted the building. *Banka Legií.*

"It's a bank," he said.

"It is the Bank of the Legions, Tomáš. Can you read the names on those four carvings above the columns?"

Tomáš walked with his father from right to left along the front of the building. The first said *'Vouzier'*, and the carving showed three faces. One was fierce and determined, one twisted by pain or fear, and a third covered with a gas mask.

"The Legion in France," said Pavel.

The second, next to the main door, read *'Magistrale'* and showed two men wearing makeshift scarves around their heads against the cold. One was holding a gloved hand to shield his eyes and was staring into the distance. In front of them was the head of a bear.

"What's 'Magistrale', Tatka?"

"It's a Russian word for railway, Tomáš."

And on the other side of the door the third carving read 'Zborov' and showed two soldiers looking across to their comrades, as they supported a third who seemed either dead or dying.

And the final carving in the left-hand corner of the building read *'Doss Alto'* and showed three more soldiers defiantly holding the Legion's battle standard.

"The Legion in Italy," said Pavel.

"Does the Legion have its own bank?" asked Tomáš.

"I am going to tell you something that only a few men in the world know, Tomáš. It's a secret, and I have been waiting until you were old enough to share the secret with you."

Tomáš looked at his father and nodded in agreement.

"Everybody thinks the money to finance this bank came from the pay the legionnaires were owed when they came back from the war, Tomáš. And to a certain point it did, but not enough to build a beautiful new building like this and have its vaults full of money.

"Do you remember me telling you about the gold we found in Russia at a place called Kazan?"

"Yes, the Tsar's gold."

"And do you remember how much there was?"

"Eight wagons full," said Tomáš, who knew every detail of every story his father had ever told him. "You gave it to the Russians in return for ships to get home."

A big smile spread across Pavel's face.

"Ah, but there you are mistaken, my son. The whole world thinks we gave those eight wagons of gold back to the Russians. But we didn't. We gave them only seven. The gold from the eighth wagon is in there."

"Wow! Really? How much is that?"

"You must never tell."

"No, never."

"More than one hundred million dollars. Forty thousand million kroner."

"In there?"

"Yes, in that very building."

"Wow, Tatka. That's the best Legion story ever."

"And I promise you it is true. And that will be my last story, Tomáš, because I can see you are getting too old for them. But there is one more thing."

Pavel unclipped his medals from his jacket.

"I want you to have these, Tomáš, because I think you are old enough now to take care of them, and to understand their real worth."

"But, Tatka, I could never take your medals."

"Yes, you must. Giving them to you is important to me. Not because of any glory contained in them, but because they belong in the past. In my past. In our country's past. And one day, Tomáš, you can show them to your children and grandchildren and, God willing, you will have to explain to them what war means, because they will have no knowledge of it."

"Thank you, Tatka. I'll always look after them."

And Tomáš did not care how old he was or where he was. He wrapped his arms around his father and hugged him, as he had always done as a child.

Chapter Thirty-One

May 24th, 1929

In his house in Skalka Ernst was worried about his son.

It was a fine spring day and the sports club to which Otto belonged had organised a trip to the Fichtelberg, one of the highest peaks in the Ore Mountains across the border in Saxony.

Otto had been preparing for the trip for some weeks. The previous weekend he had camped out in his tent with a friend down by the river to make sure he had everything he needed for his five days away. But now it was time to leave, Otto was in his room complaining of feeling unwell, while his rucksack, which had been packed for days, stood ready by the front door.

Ernst had been pleased when his son initially showed such enthusiasm for the trip. Otto was a quiet boy and often chose his own company over the company of others. Zuzana called him sullen. But the one thing Otto did enjoy was physical activity, especially swimming and hiking, and so Ernst did all he could to encourage his membership of the Eger *Turnverband*, the gymnastics club.

There were certain things about the Turnverband Ernst did not like. The idea of super-fit young men reconnecting with the ancient soil of their ancestors seemed absurd to him, but any reservations he had were outweighed by the opportunity he saw for Otto to forge friendships with youths of his own age. And gymnastics was not the only activity offered by the club; Otto loved all the other sports too, as well as the hiking and camping and fieldcraft. Ernst had been a member of the *Wandervogel* when he was a boy, and he was sure that a similar experience would do Otto nothing but good.

Ernst knew that some leaders of sports clubs in the Egerland had even stranger ideas than those of the Turnverband; that as well as physical exercise some used nationalistic pride and strict discipline to encourage bonding amongst youths who were anxious to belong and to conform. Such methods reminded him far too much of his own military training and he disapproved of all such groups, especially the *Volkssport*, who strutted around Cheb in ridiculous uniforms and openly professed allegiance to political parties in Munich and Berlin.

Ernst had reassured himself that Otto's Turnverband had nothing in common with such people. He knew Konrad Henlein, their leader, and had talked with him on many occasions. He was a mild-mannered man of 31, a bank clerk. It was true that only young men with a German background chose to join the Turnverband, but Henlein was non-political, eschewed all contact with extremists and openly stated his allegiance to the state of Czechoslovakia. Ernst considered his group suitable enough for his son.

"Otto," Ernst asked, as he paused at his son's bedroom door, "are you feeling any better?"

"*Nein, Vater*, please leave me alone."

"Do you not think you will be well enough to go with the others?"

"I don't want to go, Vater. Please."

"May I come in and talk to you about it?"

When there was no reply Ernst opened the door to the attic room and peeked inside. Otto was sitting against the headrest of his bed with his knees up and his arms tightly folded. He had combed his dark-brown hair into a parting on one side, and was wearing the new *Lederhosen*, short-sleeved shirt and long white socks he had bought with the pocket money he earned painting props in the theatre. He did not look round as Ernst stepped into the room.

"May I come in and join you, Otto?"

Otto moved his legs slightly to the side and Ernst sat down at the foot of the bed. Otto looked out of the window away from his father. He was a big boy for 15 and not given to self-pity, but Ernst could see that something had hurt him badly.

"You don't have to go if you don't want to," he said.

Otto continued to look out of the window and did not turn his head as he spoke.

"Why did you make me Jewish, Vater?"

"Why? Because your dear mother was Jewish."

"But you are Roman Catholic. You could just as easily have made Anna and me the same as you."

"I could, but I wanted you both to have something of your mother."

Otto at last turned towards his father.

"So you chose her Jewishness?"

"Yes. I wanted to reach out to your Opa and Oma Lochowitz. To try to heal the wounds. Was I wrong?"

"Do you know how difficult it is to be a Jew in Eger, Vater?"

"I know there are some idiots around, but there always have been,

Otto. You should not take notice of people like that."

Otto smiled at him and looked down.

"Your sister does not seem to mind," said Ernst.

"Anna is in a Czech school. It makes a big difference. And she's only 12 and has cousin Tomáš to protect her. Wait until she's older and wants to mix with German boys."

"Do you think she will have problems?"

"Oh, *Vati*, you have no idea." Otto shook his head. He turned and looked once more out of the window. "And it would have been so easy to hide it with a name like Neumann," he sighed.

"You wish you could hide your faith, Otto? Is that what you are saying?"

Otto sat forward and wrapped his arms around his knees.

"But what makes it my faith, Vater? I had no Bar Mitzvah. I don't go to the synagogue."

"But you did not want a Bar Mitzvah."

"Of course, I didn't. I didn't want to stand out in school. If you hadn't registered me as Jewish, no one would ever have known about it."

Ernst stood up and looked down at his son.

"I don't know whether to feel sympathy for you, Otto, or to feel anger. Of course I don't want anything to hurt you, but this is your heritage. You should be proud of it. Of your mother..."

"But I can hardly remember my mother."

Ernst turned away and looked into the corner of the room. "When I look at you, Otto, I see her," he said. "You have the same hair colour, the same eyes. The same gentle nature. It's in your face. She would be very proud of you."

"Am I letting her down, Vater?"

Ernst turned and sat down next to his son.

"No, dear Otto, never think that. You are learning how difficult the world can be, that's all. And I'm sorry if I have made it more difficult for you and Anna in any way."

"It's alright, Vater."

"I can never regret making your mother's heritage a part of you both."

"No."

"So do you think you can go on your trip after all?"

"No, Vater."

"But I expect it's only a bit of name-calling, isn't it? That's not too bad."

"It was at first at school. 'Dirty Jew.' 'Christ killer.' Stupid stuff."

"You can put up with that, can't you?"

"I always have. But it's more than that now in the Turnverband. They just don't want you in there."

"Who doesn't?"

"Everyone. Especially the group leaders. They're the worst. They give you the worst jobs. Latrine duty every day."

"But that sort of thing went on in the army."

"They put things in your food. And they order the others to do it. Disgusting things."

"That's why you don't want to go today?"

"I'm not a coward, Vater. I've put up with all that for months. But now it's different."

"How?"

"You don't have to know."

"I do. You must tell me."

Otto closed his eyes and bowed his head.

"I've been told that if I go today I won't come back. They've planned an accident for the 'dirty Yid'."

"Who said that to you?"

"My group leader."

"What's his name?"

"It doesn't matter."

"I want to know, Otto."

"Heinrich von Stricker."

Under different circumstances Ernst would have enjoyed the short drive to the von Stricker residence in Reissig along deserted country roads in his new Adler Standard Six.

It was his first car, chosen with Zuzana's help from the dealership in Karlovy Vary, and supplied with a special attachment which allowed him to steady the steering wheel with his left hand. The admiring glances the car often drew in Cheb gave great pleasure to Zuzana, but Ernst was always discomfited by them, and by the not-so-gentle teasing he regularly received from his brother-in-law.

A few hundred metres beyond Reissig Ernst turned off the road and waited by a single-storey, circular lodge while a man dressed in leather breeches and jacket opened tall iron gates for him. The man bowed his head as Ernst drove past along a driveway bordered by fir trees. In front of him Ernst saw a white castle, small in scale but with all the features of something much grander. Its vaulted windows were covered by red and yellow striped shutters; a round turret at each corner was topped with a slate roof rising to a point; and in the centre at the front were five steps leading up to two heavy oak doors. As Ernst climbed the steps one of the doors was opened.

"Hauptmann Neumann, the Graf is expecting you," said a man dressed in similar style to the lodge keeper, but with clothes of much finer quality.

Ernst was led across the flagstone floor to another vaulted oak door. He entered a large room open to the roof, its walls covered with portraits, antique swords and guns, and the heads of boar, deer, bears and wolves.

In front of an unlit fireplace stood the Graf von Stricker. He was wearing a loden green hunting suit. Somehow he had managed to button the jacket across his ample stomach. He made no attempt to approach Ernst. He clearly felt his visitor should come over to greet him where he stood. Ernst walked to the centre of the room and stopped.

"*Guten Morgen*, Graf," he said. "I am pleased to find you at home at such short notice."

"*Morgen*, Neumann. It's always a pleasure to see you."

"Perhaps not on this occasion, Graf."

"I see. Won't you sit down?"

"I would rather stand if it's all the same to you. I have come to see you about your son."

"Really? Heino isn't here. He left this morning on some trip."

"I know he did. That's what I want to talk to you about."

"Whatever the trip is, Neumann, it's Heino's business. You'll have to talk to him about it. He's 19 now. He's his own man."

"You're right. I shall talk to Heinrich when he returns, but I think you ought to know what he's been doing."

"Reporting a man behind his back, Hauptmann Neumann. Not a very honourable thing to do."

"That rule does not apply in this case, Graf. Your Heinrich has threatened to kill my son."

"He's what? Nonsense, man. I doubt Heino even knows your son. He's still a boy, isn't he?"

"Otto is 15. Heinrich is his group leader in the Turnverband and has been persecuting him for months. He doesn't want my son in the group and told him if he went on the camp today he would be killed."

"Neumann, I really think you've lost your mind. I've never heard such nonsense. Why would Heino say that to your boy?"

"Because my son is Jewish."

Von Stricker bent forward, slapped his thighs and laughed.

"Now I know you're mad, Neumann. Jewish? You're not Jewish."

"My first wife, Otto's mother, was Jewish."

"She was? I didn't know that. But that pretty wife of yours now isn't an Israelite, is she?"

"No."

"Then why in God's name are you telling the world about it, man?"

"My children had a Jewish Czech mother. I see no reason to keep that from anyone."

"Then you are a fool, Neumann. You are German, your children could be German. They could even be Czech, if you must. But you have registered them officially as Jewish?"

"I have."

"Well, don't blame my Heinrich, Neumann. You've done it to them yourself."

"I have done nothing."

"Don't you understand how much the Yids are hated, man? Those Christ killers lost the war for us, for God's sake."

"I thought the Romans killed Christ."

"Don't get clever with me, Neumann."

"I'm not. And I can tell you another thing, Graf. I fought alongside many brave Germans of the Jewish faith in the war. They may have died for Germany and Austria, but they certainly did not lose the war for them."

"Learn your facts before you speak, Neumann. Everyone knows the Zionists dragged America into the war because they wanted Palestine at the end of it. It was the Jews who agreed to the Versailles Diktat."

"They weren't all Jews."

"Of course they were. And the so-called 'Weimar Constitution' was scribbled down by that Jew Pruess, so all his banker friends could get rich off our backs."

"You cannot possibly believe that."

"Of course I do, because it's true. And then we had that bastard Rathenau trying to sell us out to his Communist friends in Russia. All Yids. Trotsky and Lenin and the rest of them."

"So we blame the Jews for capitalism and Communism at the same time, do we? That's convenient."

Von Stricker took a pipe from his pocket and tapped it against the fireplace.

"All these years and I never took you for a fool, Neumann. Have you never heard of Rothschild and Karl Marx, man? They're all part of the same world conspiracy. The Jews are everywhere. They owe allegiance to no country. But the one country they want to destroy most is Germany."

"Why would you think that?"

"Do you really have to ask why? Because if Germany was allowed to unite its people, and to have all the territory that belongs to it by rights, it would be too strong for the Jews to have any influence over it."

"And is this what you teach your son?"

"I teach him the facts, Neumann. That his family's wealth was lost by inflation manufactured by Yiddish bankers. That his family's land, his inheritance, was stolen by those Slav bastards in Prague. I teach Heino this is not Slav land. This is sacred German land, owned for centuries by his ancestors. And the people on it should be Germans, not Slavs or Jews."

"My God, Graf, I knew people with your views existed, but I never imagined that someone of my own acquaintance would be one of them. I think I shall accept your offer to sit down."

Von Stricker smiled and opened his arms as if to offer Ernst any seat of his choice.

"That's better. Don't take it personally, Neumann. I'm sure my Heino has nothing personal against your boy. It's just unfortunate he's a Jew."

Ernst sat in an armchair shaking his head.

"The thing is, Neumann..." said von Stricker. He put the pipe in his mouth, gripped his lapels with both hands and planted his feet firmly apart before he continued. "This wretched little Czechoslovakia is based on nothing but a lie. Masaryk only asked the Slavs and Jews in America what they wanted. But he didn't ask the Germans here, did he? And they don't want to be part of this hybrid mess. No. A nation is strongest when it is pure, and shaped on its ethnic roots."

"I always thought it should be shaped by its ideals and intentions."

Von Stricker laughed.

"That's your trouble, Neumann. You're an idealist. You Austrians tried to hold a hybrid empire together but it wasn't possible. Now the Czechs have the same problem, and they won't succeed any more than you did."

"I thought they were doing rather well."

"No, Neumann, no. Believe me, each race has its own destiny, and the German destiny is to tidy up Central Europe. At the moment our German race has lost its pride. We have lost our identity, but trust us, Neumann, we shall get it back. But without the Yids and the Slavs and the Communists, I'm telling you."

Ernst got to his feet and walked over to where von Stricker was standing. He came so close to him that von Stricker was forced to step back until his shoulders were pressed against the fireplace. Ernst leaned his face into his.

"You said earlier, Graf, that neither Otto nor I should take the views of you or your son personally. But I have been listening to your filth, and I have decided that I shall take it personally. Tell your Heino that whatever he does to my boy in the future, I shall do to him, and then I shall come here and do the same to you."

When Ernst returned home, Otto's rucksack was no longer standing in the hallway. When he called out to him, there was no answer. Ernst quickly climbed the two flights of stairs to Otto's attic room and found the rucksack there, lying next to the bed with a note attached .

Vater
Please do not worry about me. I have gone for a walk by the lake. Anna
and Zuzana are at the cottage with Tante Kája and Tomáš. I shall meet
them there later.
Thank you, Vati,
Otto.

Ernst did not want to stay alone in the house, but neither did he want all the company offered at the chata. He was pleased when he found Pavel at home and only too happy to join him for lunch at the *Gasthof zum Alten Schloss.*

As they walked along the cobbled street beside the River Ohře, Ernst explained to his friend the events of the morning. They entered the *Gasthof* and made their way to a table in the corner. The man behind the bar welcomed them.

"*Grüss Gott, meine Herren. Grosse oder kleine? Large or small?*"

Pavel looked at Ernst, smiled and shrugged his shoulders. The choice would be his.

"*Grosse, bitte,*" called out Ernst. "*Und zwei Schnapps dazu.*"

A waitress in Egerland costume served them their drinks, acknowledging them both by name.

"*Bitte schön, Herr Neumann. Zum Wohl, Herr Kovařík.*"

"*Prosit,*" said Ernst as he raised his schnapps. "*Na zdravi,*" replied Pavel, and they touched glasses and drank their *Jägermeister* in one draught, followed by generous mouthfuls of *Pilsner Uralt.*

"I remember a time when you would refuse to come into a Gasthof where the only language offered was German," said Ernst.

"Ah, but you'll notice it's Czech beer we're drinking."

Ernst nodded and looked down at his glass.

"We have come a long way in ten years, haven't we?" he said.

"Yes, we have. A long way."

"But if you heard that oaf this morning, Pavel, you would think we had gone backwards. I know you warned me about von Stricker years ago. But I had no idea..."

"There are always going to be extremists like him, Ernst, however much progress we make."

"But it's the irrationality of the prejudice which angers me, Pavel. He blames Jews for being greedy capitalists, and then for being Bolsheviks. There's no logic. If the Jews try to assimilate they're devious for wanting to hide, and if they live together they're accused of only looking out for one another."

"Don't look for logic in prejudice, Ernst. There cannot be any."

"What harm have I done to my children, Pavel? My darling Esther would be so angry with me for being so naive."

"How is Otto?"

"He's the bravest boy. I'm so proud of him. He's gone for a walk by the lake. I'll meet him at the chata later."

"So he won't be going back to the Turnverband?"

"No. Absolutely not. I'm inclined to report those thugs to the authorities."

"Have you thought about him joining the *Sokol*? They do the same things, and Tomáš loves it. There's no anti-Semitism there."

"I know. But it's only Czechs who join the Sokol. They don't include Germans, do they?"

"It's for Czechoslovaks, Ernst. We are all Czechoslovaks."

"Be realistic, my old friend. The Sokol is for Slavs."

"Only because Czechoslovak youths from German families choose not to join."

"Let's not argue, Pavel. I want at least to feel I have the support of my friends and family in this."

"You always have that, Ernst."

"I'm afraid I have put Otto in an impossible position. Not Anna so much. But certainly Otto."

"How?"

"He has a German name in a German school. But I have registered him as a Jew, so he remains an outsider. Perhaps if I had put him in the

Czech school with Anna he could have belonged as a Czech. She is happy enough."

"Ernst, your thinking is all wrong. Otto is a Czechoslovak citizen."

"Just as you were once an Austrian citizen, I suppose?"

"You should not say that, Ernst."

"I know, Pavel. I'm sorry. But I find it difficult to think clearly at the moment. My whole life I have put one principle before all others; to protect my family and provide a good life for them. But at times like this I wonder if it's possible to live a peaceful life anywhere."

"There is no better place than Czechoslovakia to raise your children, Ernst. We have peace and prosperity, and things are improving all the time."

"But I worry about the harm people like von Stricker can do."

"They can do nothing to us, Ernst. Masaryk has founded our country on ideals which form the natural state of man. Democracy, humanity, freedom. Extremism will never find nourishment in a country like ours."

"I have developed a great respect for Masaryk over the years, Pavel, but if you could have heard the vile filth coming from von Stricker this morning..."

"You know, Ernst, I was once privileged to hear Masaryk speak about people like von Stricker. He said the greatest defence against them was the creation of a nation which was free and prosperous. People do not look for revolution if they have food on the table and money in the bank."

"But von Stricker has both."

"There will always be some like him nurturing their grievances and looking for scapegoats. Germany still has plenty of those. But most Germans in Czechoslovakia realise now they are in the best place."

"Do you really think so?"

"Yes, of course. We are one of the top industrialised countries in the world. We have one of the strongest economies in Europe. Look how prosperous we all are."

"You're not going to mention my car again, are you?" said Ernst, looking up from his glass and smiling at last.

"No, I won't. I'll share a secret with you, Ernst. Kája and I are thinking of getting one ourselves. Not quite as grand as yours, of course."

"You old hypocrite."

"Well, everyone else seems to be able to afford one. Even Michal was talking about it."

"Has he done that well?"

"He must have. He and Magda are always buying some new luxury or other."

"And you think prosperity is the answer against the von Strickers of this world, do you?"

"I do, Ernst. Most people here are doing well and living happily enough together. All we must do is confront the odd extremist like von Stricker when they crawl out of their holes; and reassure our children that the whole world is not full of people like them."

"But is it enough?"

"Yes, it will be enough."

Pavel took a long drink from his glass and placed it carefully on his beer mat.

"But Masaryk did suggest an additional strategy when I heard him speak," he said. "A sort of insurance policy."

"What was that?"

"To dig in as many Škoda guns as we can along our borders."

Chapter Thirty-Two

October 28th, 1929

It was a treat for the whole family. Everyone had been invited to the house by the bridge for seven-thirty. Karolína had prepared food in the back parlour, and even though they had school the next day, the children were to be allowed to stay up late.

Pavel had borrowed nine chairs from his classroom and set them out in the front room facing the corner where the wireless radiogram stood. Michal, dressed in his best suit, was bent over it, running his fingers over the walnut and examining the grain. Eventually he was able to confirm that although, as was to be expected, it was only veneer, it was veneer cut from wood of the finest quality.

"This is a day that will go down in history," he announced, encouraged by the excellent Moravian wine Pavel was offering with Karolína's canapés. "October 28th 1929, the day the President's actual voice will be heard in this actual room. And thousands of other rooms, I dare say, throughout the land. Who would ever have thought it possible?"

"Oh, sit down, Děda," protested Magdaléna. "No one can see it lit up with you in the way."

Tomáš and Anna looked at one another and laughed silently together.

"I don't know how they do it, I don't," continued Magdaléna. "I heard one in Fischer's in the colonnade. It's like someone is actually inside the box."

"It's not a box, Magda," corrected Michal. "I keep telling you, it's a cabinet."

"Oh, I don't know. But there was a whole orchestra in the one in Fischer's the other day."

"It's like the wind-up phonograph Děda bought you, Babička," explained Tomáš. "The people aren't inside playing the music."

"I know that, silly boy. I can see the black thing and the needle."

"Well, the wire on top of our house is like the needle. It picks up the sound waves coming from Prague."

"Now stop it, just stop it. I don't want to hear any more of your nonsense. I know you're only teasing me. Sound waves indeed. I'm off to help your mother with the food."

"It's all done, Máma," said Karolína from the doorway. "We all need to stay in our seats now. It's nearly eight o'clock."

At eight the pips sounded and the national anthem played. Pavel was the first to stand as the opening bars of *'Kde domov můj?* strained through the small oval speaker.

"Where is my home?" sang Pavel and Tomáš together, until the others, one by one, caught up with them. "*...spring blossoms glitter in the orchards, paradise on earth to see ...this is my beautiful country, the Czech country, my homeland..."*

They stood and sang through the second verse, dedicated to Slovakia, and then sat down to hear their President.

Pavel took Karolína's hand as they listened to the voice of Masaryk in their home. As Masaryk spoke, Pavel's grip grew tighter until Karolina had to take hold of his arm and pull her hand away.

"...and so, fellow citizens, I address you tonight in a mood of great optimism, as we welcome Ludwig Czech into our government as Minister for Social Care; our first minister representing our citizens of German heritage in the German Social Democratic Labour Party.

May we enter the new decade in a spirit of friendship and cooperation for the sake of all we hold dear. For our families, our freedoms and all that our proud, democratic country has come to stand for amongst the brotherhood of nations. May God bless our Czechoslovakia and all its people."

Everyone stood as one, as the national anthem played again, and all applauded when the singing was over.

"Now, if you would all like to come into the dining room, and all bring a chair," announced Karolína, "you will see from the mountain of food I've prepared that I really am my mother's daughter." And everyone laughed and applauded again.

On the way home to Skalka later that evening Michal carried a storm lamp to light the way for Magda, Zuzana and Anna. Otto and Ernst were already several paces behind them by the time they reached the bridge, and father and son turned to wave to the Kovaříks, who were still standing at their front door.

"They are good people, aren't they, Vater?" said Otto.

"Yes, they are. And they are the best kind of friends. The kind who may not always agree with you, but stand by you anyway."

"It's nice that we are related to them."

"I am so pleased to hear you say that, Otto. I know you find it difficult with Zuzana sometimes."

"No, Vater. Zuzana is alright. It's just sometimes she can be... oh, I don't know."

"I understand, Otto. You don't have to say."

"It's different for Anna. Zuzana is the only mother she remembers. She calls her 'Mutti', and they enjoy talking about girls' things. It's just different."

"It has been very important for me, Otto, to have Zuzana."

"I know, Vater."

"I'm pleased you understand."

"Vater, when I had that trouble a few months ago, I remember saying something to you that wasn't really true."

"What was that?"

"I said I couldn't remember my mother very much, and perhaps it was more true then. But since I've been going to the synagogue on the Sabbath, I have started to remember her very well. Rabbi Nathan says it is my faith bringing her closer to me."

"Is that what you feel?"

"Yes, I do. I share her religion and I feel what she must have felt. The deeper my faith becomes, the more I know her and feel her with me."

"I cannot tell you how happy that makes me, Otto."

"Rabbi Nathan told me there are 491 Jews in Eger and only 75 are registered. You did the right thing, Vater."

"Thank you, dear Otto."

"I suppose I should thank Heinrich von Stricker too," said Otto.

"Now there's a thought.. Do you ever get any trouble from people like him now?"

"No, not much. I never see von Stricker and, if I did, it wouldn't worry me. The Rabbi has explained how irrational the hatred of people towards us is. We must remain above it and concentrate on other issues."

"What issues?"

"Our faith. He says what other people say about us should not distract us."

"He's right."

"Rabbi Nathan wants me to read from the Torah in the synagogue next March during the festival of Purim."

"And do you want to?"

"I do. Very much. But first I must be a Bar Mitzvah, so that I can read from the scriptures. I want you and all the others to come to the festival of Purim, Vater. And Opa and Oma Lochowitz too. Purim is great fun. People dress up and make lots of noise. It's not like a normal service in the synagogue."

"What does it celebrate?"

"A young Jewish heroine who saved the Jews of Persia from slaughter. Her name was Esther. I shall read from the Megillah, the Book of Esther."

"I think that's wonderful, Otto. I shall be honoured to be there."

The next morning Karolína kissed Pavel goodbye as he left for work, and she went back into the house to clear everything away from the night before. It had been such a successful party.

During the four years when she thought Pavel was gone, she had craved only some peace of mind and a sense of normality. Now she had both of those things. And she had contentment and times of great joy. She was happy.

She smoothed her hand over the new radiogram and, although she knew it was an indulgence, switched it on. Slowly the light behind the dial glowed brighter and she smelled the heat of the valves as they grew warmer. Then the faint sound of music came closer, until the room was filled with a female voice singing Gershwin's 'Someone to Watch over Me'.

She was surprised how loud the radio must have been when they listened to Masaryk's speech the night before, and she turned down the volume. She went into the kitchen and sang along as best she could, while washing up the dishes from the previous evening. When the music stopped, her happiness continued and she sang to herself, improvising where she was unsure of the words. Her joy drowned out the news coming over the radio.

"...reports from New York that there were further large falls yesterday on the Wall Street Stock Exchange. Brokers are already calling the 28th October 'Black Monday' after shares plunged a further 13%, following a 15% fall the previous Thursday. Already investors are nervous about the fate of shares when Wall Street opens again in seven hours' time.

Stocks in Prague and Vienna have already fallen heavily on the news from New York, and brokers here are fearing today could become a 'Black Tuesday'."

Chapter Thirty-Three

24th December, 1929 – May 14th, 1931

Tomáš had been looking forward to Christmas. He knew how lucky he was that the people who loved him most were also those with whom he had the most fun.

His grandparents were so generous in the way they made everyone welcome, and their funny ways always made him and Anna laugh. And he looked forward too to his father's stories, and to the lively discussions that usually took place between the adults around the table.

There had been a time when their talking bored him, but recently he found himself wanting to listen more, and trying to work out who had the best arguments. He thought his father was best, always sure about everything. Then probably Máma, who seemed to agree with him but then for some reason always tried to stop him. Uncle Ernst was good too, but he stood up for Germans too much. Děda didn't say much at all, and it was usually about how things were better a long time ago. And Auntie Zuzana's comments were always about how she felt, and how upset she was about something, and they never seemed to lead anywhere. He often thought about trying to join in, but he never dared, just in case he had not really understood everything and might be saying something stupid.

He wondered why Otto didn't join in. He was sure when he was 16 there would be plenty of things he would be able to talk about. He felt sorry for Otto. He was a lot older than he and Anna, but still not old enough to be one of the adults. He was so quiet and seemed to live in a world of his own. Even when they went swimming in the lake in the summer, Otto would swim up and down on his own, rather than join in the games he and Anna played.

It was hard to believe sometimes that Anna was Otto's sister. She was so friendly towards everyone and so funny. More than anything he was looking forward to spending time with her this Christmas. Since September they hadn't seen so much of one another, because he was more involved in the Sokol and she spent more time with her girlfriends. But that didn't matter, because although they never said anything, he knew they would always come back to one another and be as close as they had always been.

Babička had gone to her usual trouble to load the table with soup, a large carp, and plates full of potato salad, dumplings, and all sorts of different vegetables. He was pleased when Anna pulled her chair close to his, and every now and then, even when she was concentrating on something else, she rested her hand against his without thinking. Everything was as it should be, as it had always been. Except, that is, for Děda.

Děda was drinking his cherry slivovitz, as he always did, but he didn't seem to be enjoying it. He was not standing up proposing toasts and making speeches in his usual way, making Babička complain and Anna laugh. Instead he was sitting silently in his chair at the head of the table, his eyes moving back and forth from his glass to his bottle.

The conversation seemed unnatural too, as if the adults were taking turns to think of something to say, and then laughing too much at things which didn't seem funny. The only person around the table more lively than normal was Otto, who was examining every bowl of food with Uncle Ernst before explaining whether he was allowed to eat it or not. Christmas Eve 1929 was the only time Tomáš could remember being pleased to leave his grandparents' chata.

"What's the matter with Děda, Táta?" he asked, as soon as his Babička closed the door behind them all.

"Děda is very unhappy and very worried, Tomáš."

"Why?"

"Because he's been a damned fool, that's why," said Zuzana.

"Zuzana, that's very unfair of you," snapped Karolína. "And don't speak about our táta like that in front of the children."

"Come on now, my love," said Ernst, "let us go on ahead, and leave Pavel and Kája to talk to Tomáš, if they want to."

Ernst offered Zuzana his arm, which she did not take, and they walked off together across the clearing along a path Michal had dug through the snow. Otto chose to walk alongside his father, while Anna remained with Tomáš.

"I'll catch up with you later, Vati," she called out, and she took Tomáš's hand as they walked a few paces behind Pavel and Karolína.

"So what is the matter with Děda?" Tomáš asked again.

"Your Děda has lost a lot of money and is feeling very bad about it," said Pavel.

"How did he lose it?"

"Have you heard of the stock exchange?"

"Yes, but I'm not sure what it is."

"It's where people buy shares in different companies. If the company does well, like Škoda, the value of your shares go up. If it does badly, the shares go down."

"And Děda's went down?"

"Yes. A lot."

"Is that what they mean by the 'crash'?"

"That's right, Tomáš. The shares didn't just fall. They crashed."

"So has Děda lost all his money?" asked Anna.

"No, Anna, not all of it. But nearly half of it. And he won't be getting his dividend this year either."

Tomáš was pleased when Anna admitted she did not know what a dividend was. He felt privileged that his father was talking to them as members of his adult world and wished now he had taken more trouble to inform himself about such things.

"A dividend is the money shareholders get every year from a company's profits, Anna. But if the company makes no profit, there is no dividend."

"So Děda and Babička won't have any money then?" she asked.

"They won't have as much as they've had over the past few years, that's for sure. Děda will probably have to go back to his furniture making."

"Poor Táta," said Karolína, "he was so enjoying being retired. Starting up again at his time of life will be so hard..."

"Don't worry, Kája," said Pavel. "We can always help out."

"You know my father would never allow that, Pavel. He's far too proud to accept help from us or anyone else."

"Yes, of course. You're right, my love."

Pavel turned to look over his shoulder towards Tomáš and Anna.

"In fact, it's probably best if you don't mention any of this to your Děda, Tomáš and Anna. He worked and saved all his life for that money. He's very upset about it."

"We won't say anything," said Tomáš.

"But Děda will get all his money back when his shares go up again, won't he, Uncle Pavel?" asked Anna.

"It's too late, Anna. Your Děda has sold them all now and put his money in the bank."

"Where we all thought it was in the first place," said Karolína.

"But Anna's right, isn't she, Táta? If shares go up now, Děda would have got his money back."

"He might have, but it was too much of a risk. He could have lost the lot if he'd left it in shares. At least now, what he has left is safe."

From that day on Tomáš read every newspaper delivered to his home.

It seemed his Děda had done the right thing taking his money from the stock market and putting it in the bank. Over the first few months of 1930 the value of shares fell 60 percent from the high they reached before the crash in October. By April they had recovered a bit, but by then the damage to the world economy had begun.

Tomáš understood for the first time how much Czechoslovakia depended on the countries around it, especially Germany, and even on countries thousands of kilometres away, like Britain and America.

"Is it right what it says, Táta?" he asked one day after dinner. "Czechoslovakia doesn't really own all its factories and mines and everything?"

"We own a lot of them, Tomáš. But there are still some in the hands of people who owned them before we became independent."

"In this paper it says we only own about a quarter of our industry. I don't understand how so much can belong to somebody else if it's in our country."

Pavel put down his book and turned to look at his son, who was still sitting at the dining table studying the newspaper.

"Well, you know I told you about shares, Tomáš. Anyone can buy shares in any company anywhere. A lot of German banks and businesses own shares in our glassworks and textile factories, and such. They may even own some in Škoda."

"Is it just Germans?"

"No, the British and the French own a lot of the shares in our mines. Most of the bicycle factories in Cheb are owned by the British."

"So most of Bohemia where we live doesn't belong to us?"

"Yes, it belongs to us. It's all part of Czechoslovakia. There is a difference you see, Tomáš, between what is politically part of our territory, and what people from other countries are allowed to own through investment."

Tomáš looked puzzled.

"It's like this, Tomáš," said his father, turning in his chair to face him. "Take your Děda. He bought shares to invest money in different companies. Some may have been in France or Germany or even America. It didn't mean he owned any part of those countries. He just invested there."

"How did Děda know which ones to buy?" asked Tomáš, impressed by a skill he never dreamed his Děda possessed.

"He let someone do it for him. He bought shares in what's called an investment trust. The trusts then buy shares all over the world. That's how industry gets the money to invent things and produce things."

"But Děda took all his money out."

"He's allowed to. He could see their value going down."

"But what if everyone took their money out?"

"That is a very good question, Tomáš," said Pavel, turning back to his book. "If everyone did it at the same time, the world would get into one big mess."

Tomáš continued to read the papers every day, keen to understand the adult world his father and grandfather inhabited, but which stubbornly remained a mystery to him. Throughout 1930 it seemed the fear which had gripped his Děda was affecting people everywhere, including investors large and small, and even whole governments. Gradually he began to understand the process of recession as week by week he watched one development lead to another.

First, America withdrew the loans it promised to Germany to help it pay back money it owed because of the war. Then German banks wanted back the money they had loaned to German industry. And finally the banks decided they wanted the money owed to them by German-owned industries in Bohemia. And without that money, Tomáš realised, factories produced less, people lost their jobs and bought less, demand fell further and the whole process started again.

It seemed like bad luck to Tomáš that the area of Czechoslovakia affected most by all this economics was where he lived in Bohemia, where most of the country's industry was. Apparently it was not so bad for Czech businesses, because they were usually smaller than the German firms and sold most of the things they made inside Czechoslovakia. But the larger, German-owned industries, which employed mostly 'German-Czechoslovaks', as the papers called them, relied on exports, mainly to Germany; and that market had almost ceased to exist.

He watched Cheb's famous old glassworks go on short time in the spring of 1930, and in late summer two of the bicycle factories closed completely. Five times as many people were unemployed in Western Bohemia than in the rest of the country, his táta's paper said, and most of them were German-Czechoslovaks.

Tomáš was able to see with his own eyes the evidence of it. Men sitting silently on the wall around the fountain when he and Anna crossed the main square on their way back from school; and others standing round in small groups by the colonnade smoking and spitting and kicking their boots on the cobbles.

In the colonnade Fischer's music shop, where his máma and táta had bought their new radiogram only eighteen months before, was now closed down. And in front of its boarded-up windows there were women who set up stalls selling home-grown vegetables and second-hand clothes, until the police came by one day and closed them down too.

Pavel found his son's passion for learning, and the shared interest it created for them, some compensation for the bad news delivered to his door every day. But even the pleasure of discussing events with Tomáš could not soften the headline which greeted him on the morning of Tuesday 16th September.

'Huge Gains For Extremists in German Poll'.

Just across the border one of Masaryk's greatest fears was becoming a reality. With German industry crippled, unemployment rising by the week, and government assistance halved because there was so little tax revenue to pay for it, twelve million desperate voters had turned their backs on democratic parties in the elections to the Reichstag.

Pavel folded back the paper to study the details. The Communists had taken 13 percent of the vote, and a right-wing party once on the lunatic fringe had taken more than 18 percent. With 107 seats in the Reichstag the National Socialist Workers' Party was now the second largest party in Germany.

Pavel thanked God for Masaryk and Beneš, and for the healthy democracy they had created in Czechoslovakia. He put the paper down in his lap. He had complete faith in them. He knew they would never allow the economic crisis to create political problems for their country, however bad things got elsewhere.

And things did get bad elsewhere, throughout 1930 and into the new year, until, in the second week of May 1931, the economic crisis struck once again deep into his own family.

"I can't face it, Pavel," said Karolína, "and I'm not sure you should be taking Tomáš with you."

"Our son is not a child any more, Kája. Your father recognises that. Tomáš understands more about what is going on than most adults do."

Pavel and Tomáš walked slowly to the chata, neither in any great hurry to give Michal the news.

"You know, Táta," said Tomáš, "I have studied everything so much, but there's still something about all this I don't understand."

"What's that?"

225

"Why the crisis can't be reversed. Everything in the world is still the same, isn't it? The factories are still there. All the raw materials are still there. People still want to work and make things. And people still want to buy things. So why is everything stopping?"

"If you could answer that, Tomáš, you would be the greatest economist in the world. There is no real reason, except for people's lack of confidence."

"Confidence?"

"Yes. People buy shares because they are confident they will make money. Others put money in the bank, because they are confident it will be safe. And banks lend money because they are confident they will get it back. But when the confidence goes, everything stops."

"And that's all it is? All these problems everywhere and it's all because of that? People's confidence? Poor Děda."

"I know, Tomáš. Be strong for him."

When they reached the chata Magda was surprised and delighted to see them.

"Just the two of you, is it? No Kája?"

"We have come to see Michal, Magda. Do you know if he has seen the paper today?"

"No, he hasn't been out. He's got some work at last. A nice new bedroom set for the Zelenka family. Some people can still afford things, thank the Lord. And they haven't forgotten your dear old Děda yet, Tomášek. Come on, you both sit at the table and I'll fetch him."

Moments later Michal came in wiping his hands on a rag. "Hello, you two," he said, smiling. "This is a nice surprise. Magda, fetch us men a jug of beer, will you? And three glasses."

Magda brought in the beer and poured two and a half glasses.

"Fill up your grandson's glass, my love. We're all men together now. So, my friends, *na zdraví.*"

"Na zdraví, sir."

"Na zdraví, Děda."

Under different circumstances this moment with his father and grandfather would have been one of the best of Tomáš's life but, as he sipped the beer, his stomach turned and he felt wretched.

"So, what can I do for you both?" said Michal. He looked with approval at the foam finding its way to the bottom of his empty glass.

"Well, sir," said Pavel, "I know this may seem rude of me, but can I ask you which bank you put your savings in after the crash 18 months ago?"

"Yes, you can ask. The *Kreditanstalt*."

"All of it?"

"Yes, a Rothschild bank. I wasn't going to take any chances this time."

"Then I have some bad news for you, sir, I'm afraid. It's in today's paper, and I have checked the news on the radio. The Kreditanstalt has closed its doors."

"Closed its doors?" Michal sat bolt upright and his cheeks and forehead turned bright red. "Don't talk nonsense, Pavel. That's the biggest bank in Austria. What are you talking about?"

"The bank has collapsed, sir. Everyone who is not an Austrian national has lost their money. I'm so sorry."

Tomáš saw his Děda's big, kind face drain of colour. He watched as this wonderful, powerful man turned towards his wife with a look of shock and fear, as his mind refused to accept the meaning of what he had heard.

"What's happening, Magda? What have I done?" he cried out to her, and Tomáš realised for the first time that the world was not the secure and certain place he had believed it to be.

Chapter Thirty-Four

June 20th, 1931

The chants changed as the slogans on the banners changed. *'Gebt uns Arbeit,'* was the first. 'Give us work.' The banner was carried aloft by men normally found loitering around the fountain and under the colonnade.

There must have been four or five thousand people crammed into the main square in Cheb, but for all their noise and anger, they managed to preserve a thoroughfare through the middle, allowing the marchers to pass in good order.

The marchers, who must themselves have numbered nearly a thousand, were strung out on a circular route which took them from the square to the theatre, then on a right turn below the castle ruins, and along the river bank past the Kovařík house, before turning right again up Krámařská Street and back to their starting point.

'Land für Sudetendeutsche.' *'Land for Sudeten Germans,'* read the next banner, and thousands of voices chanted their support.

'Kontrakte für deutsche Firmen... Kontrakte für deutsche Firmen...'

'Prag soll uns helfen... Prag soll uns helfen...' *'Prague should help us...'*

The sound of a band could be heard approaching from Krámařská Street, accompanied by a military drumbeat and the staccato rhythm of marching feet. As the band came into the main square, Pavel could see its members were all young and dressed in the same uniform: brown shirts and shorts with white socks, heavy black boots and a black leather belt.

Behind them followed a rectangle of one hundred more men dressed in identical fashion and marching as one. At their head was a tall young man of about twenty, wearing a second leather belt diagonally across his chest.

"That's Heinrich von Stricker," Pavel said to Tomáš. "So now he's in charge of the Volkssport."

Behind von Stricker two of his lieutenants held a banner demanding, *'Heim ins Reich.'* *'Home to the Reich.'* The only chant supporting it came from a small group of youths who had climbed onto the fountain and were making as much noise as they could. Most of the crowd fell silent at the sight of the Volkssport uniforms and their banners, and merely applauded, mostly, it seemed to Pavel, in appreciation of the music.

"Come on, Tomáš I think we've seen enough."

"Can I stay, please, Táta? I've never seen anything like this before."

"I don't think your mother would be very pleased if I left you here on your own."

"That's alright, Sergeant. I'll keep an eye on him for you if you like," came a voice from behind them.

Pavel turned to see Filip Souček.

"Filip, whatever are you doing here?" Pavel's handshake was so enthusiastic that Souček had to use both hands to slow it down. "It must be five years."

"Nearly seven, Sergeant."

"This is my son Tomáš, Filip. Tomáš, this is a very good friend of mine from my army days. Filip Souček."

"I am pleased to meet you, sir," said Tomáš offering his hand.

"And it's a great pleasure to meet you, Tomáš."

"We were just leaving, Filip. We only live around the corner. Do you have time to come and meet my wife?"

"I would be honoured, Sergeant."

"Just follow us, Filip, as best you can."

It was not easy keeping one another in view as they made their way against the oncoming marchers in Krámařská Street. By the time Pavel and Tomáš reached their front door there was no sign of Souček. Pavel was so disappointed to have lost him that he was about to head back to search, when Souček appeared at the bottom of the steps.

"Here I am, Sergeant," he said. He turned towards the marchers who were passing behind him in the road. "You would have thought they'd had enough by now, wouldn't you?"

"I know, Filip, it's pathetic. I don't know what they hope to achieve with their nonsense. Come in and meet Karolína."

Tomáš had gone into the house to warn his mother they had a visitor, and when his father and fellow legionnaire entered the front living room, she was standing ready to greet them.

"Karolína my love, I would like very much for you to meet a good friend of mine from the old days. Filip Souček. Filip works in the President's office at Prague Castle. Or at least he did."

"I still do, Sergeant. I am honoured to meet you, pani Kovaříková."

"How do you do, pan Souček. I wonder, is it possible we have met before?"

"I don't think so, pani Kovaříková. I must say, what a charming house you have here. Does the river ever give you any trouble?"

"We have had one or two floods in the cellar over the years, but nothing really serious."

"That's good."

"Now, come on," said Pavel. "What would you like to drink, Filip? Coffee or chocolate, or a beer perhaps, or something even stronger?"

"A beer would be perfect, Sergeant. It was hot out there. I think it's going to be another long summer."

"I'll get them for you," said Karolína.

She went into the kitchen and the two men sat down at the table.

"Tomáš, I thought you were going over to Skalka to see Anna this afternoon," Pavel said.

"I was, but I wouldn't mind staying here now."

"A young man shouldn't keep a lady waiting, Tomáš," said Filip Souček.

"That's right," agreed Pavel.

"But I don't mind staying."

His mother came in with a tray and placed it on the table. As she was returning to the kitchen, their visitor asked her if she was going to join them. She came back and sat down. Tomáš waited, and when he was not invited, he turned abruptly and walked out.

Moments later the three adults heard him coming down the stairs and the front door slam shut. Pavel looked at Karolína with raised eyebrows. She frowned and looked down.

"So tell me, Filip," said Pavel. "What have you heard from the others? I believe Milan is doing well."

"Yes, I was with him only yesterday. His concentration is much better now, and his speech is much clearer. His last exhibition in Prague was a great success."

"I hear the President has two of his paintings."

"Yes, indeed. President Masaryk is a great patron of the arts."

"We must go and see Milan again soon, Pavel," said Karolína.

"Milan speaks of both you and the sergeant with great affection, pani Kovaříková."

"Thankyou. We are both very fond of him."

"And what about the others, Filip? How are they getting along?" asked Pavel

"Jan Vaněk and Emil Kolár both own their own farms now. They have done well."

"Good. I still get cards from them at Christmas. Every year there are more children. But I haven't heard from Vesely for a long time."

"Oskar is still working in the mines. He's a deputy manager now."

"Wonderful. So he hasn't been affected by all the lay-offs and closures then?"

"No, Sergeant. Not Oskar. We like to look after our own, as I'm sure you appreciate."

"Yes, of course."

"But there are so many who are suffering from the economic crisis," said Karolína. "Even my own father."

"In what way, pani Kovaříková?"

"He lost his life savings in May, when the Kreditanstalt collapsed."

"But your family isn't Austrian."

"No, Filip," said Pavel, who knew how difficult Karolína found it to talk about what had happened to her father. "But he's a product of the old empire in believing anything from Vienna was the best."

"I'm sorry to hear that. We are very proud at the castle that there has not been one default amongst Czechoslovakian banks since the collapse began."

"But so many German and Austrian banks have gone," said Karolína.

"Almost the entire European credit structure has gone, pani Kovaříková. I am truly sorry about what happened to your father, but I have little sympathy with the Sudeten Germans, I'm afraid. They've all been so keen on economic union with Germany and insisted on using German banks. They're singing a different tune now."

"I noticed the 'Heim ins Reich' banner wasn't well received in the square," said Pavel.

"Yes, that was very encouraging. But as I say, if our citizens who looked so much to Germany had used the National Bank of Czechoslovakia over the years, they wouldn't be in such a mess now."

"But that doesn't stop the hardship these people are suffering, pan Souček," said Karolína.

"We know. And we are extending credit to some German firms. But the Germans in this area have had a much higher standard of living than Czechs for many, many years, pani Kovaříková. It won't hurt to redress the balance a little."

"But it can't be good to make them so resentful, can it? Look at all this going on today."

"We monitor the situation very closely. We keep a very careful eye on any extremists."

"I'm relieved to hear it. Look how that dreadful Nazi Party has suddenly come from nowhere."

"Oh, that's not such a surprise to us, pani Kovaříková. We know exactly where National Socialism came from, and it wasn't from Munich or Berlin."

"Really? From where then?"

"From here in Cheb. Or Eger, as they like to call it."

"Surely that can't be right."

"I'm afraid it is, pani Kovaříková. Nazism began with Franko Stein 40 years ago, when he founded the German National Workers' League here. The 25-point plan he put forward then is in many respects the same one Hitler has now. Stein was born in Cheb."

"I remember you telling me about Stein when we last met, Filip," said Pavel.

"I did. And I believe I mentioned another son of Cheb, Karl Hermann Wolf. His German Workers' Party took over from Stein's League here 30 years ago."

"I've heard of him," said Karolína. "He was our deputy in Vienna. I remember my father talking about him."

"That's the man, pani Kovaříková." Souček took a drink of beer. "There were three branches of Wolf's party. In Cheb, Asch and Vienna. And just after the war a man named Anton Drexler founded a branch in Munich. And we all know who party member number six was in Drexler's Party."

"I don't," said Karolína.

"Are you talking about Adolf Hitler?" said Pavel.

"Yes, I am, Sergeant. In 1920 Hitler took over Drexler's party and renamed it the National Socialist German Workers' Party. But he was only copying Wolf's Austrian Party. Hitler got his entire blueprint from what was started here in Cheb."

"Is this all true, Pavel?" asked Karolína.

"It must be, if Prague says so."

"I had no idea."

"Few people have, pani Kovaříková, but it is true, I'm afraid. In Prague we have known for a long time that if we want to monitor our own German extremists the best place to do it is here in Cheb and Karlovy Vary."

"You shock me, pan Souček. I knew we had some hotheads here but I never imagined..."

"Which hotheads do you mean?"

"I think my wife means people like Heinrich von Stricker, Filip. You saw him today. He's a thug."

"You both know him then?"

"We know of him. Our niece and nephew had a Jewish mother. Von Stricker made threats to the boy because of that."

"Well, the one thing that unites all these people is their anti-Semitism. But this Volkssport really concerns us. They claim to be a sports organisation, but really they're nothing but a paramilitary group trying to stir up trouble. They've been seen in the woods near here mapping out our fortifications near the border. May I share a confidence with you both?"

"Of course, Filip."

"Yes, of course."

"This is why I encouraged your son to leave us. I hope I didn't upset the lad, but it wouldn't be fair on him to know these things. We intend to clamp down on these people."

"How, Filip?"

"By banning the entire Volkssport organisation for a start, and the wearing of Nazi Party uniforms. We might even make an example of a few of them."

"How?"

"Any of our citizens in the Volkssport could be charged with all sorts of things. Plotting armed rebellion in league with a foreign power would seem appropriate for von Stricker and Haider."

"Who's Haider?" asked Karolína.

Souček reached into his inside pocket and placed a photo on the table in front of Pavel.

"This is Alois Haider. He's the real leader of the Volkssport. Von Stricker is only a follower, albeit a nasty one. Have either of you ever seen Haider?"

"No."

"How about you, pani Kovaříková?"

"No, never."

"How about this man?"

"That's Herr Frank," said Karolína. "I've met him lots of times."

"When you worked for Alois Krause?"

"Yes, Herr Frank owns a bookshop in Karlovy Vary. He was always coming to see Herr Krause... but yes... of course... I have seen you before, pan Souček. You used to come into the shop too. Some years ago. That's where I've seen you."

"I'm sorry, pani Kovaříková. You're quite right. You may have seen me before in Cheb."

"You didn't just happen to bump into me today, did you, Filip?"

"No, Sergeant, I'm afraid not."

"Don't you think it is time you explained what you're really doing here?"

"Yes, Sergeant. I'm sorry. I should have explained earlier, but..."

"I waited to hear from you once before, if you remember. I thought the time had passed."

"The time did pass, Sergeant. Back in '23 we thought there might be trouble here on the border. But the situation in Germany improved and we've had seven years with hardly a problem."

"And now?"

"Now, since the latest economic crisis the threat has become very real again. The extremists on the left and the right see it as a chance to blame 'bourgeois democracy' and to bring it down. So the Communists and Fascists have all started to crawl out of the woodwork again."

"And you want my help again?"

"If possible, sergeant. We need reliable people to monitor the situation for us in hotspots like this. We need to know about the mood of people. For example, the crowd's reaction to the Volkssport today tells us a lot."

"Because they want help, but don't want to be part of the Reich."

"Exactly, that is invaluable information we can only obtain from people like you here on the spot. We also need to know of any more activity near the border. So if you happen to be out walking, or on a hunting trip, and you happen to see..."

"I understand, Filip."

"Good. And it would also help a great deal if we could get any more information on certain individuals. Von Stricker, for example, or Karl Hermann Frank, who you recognised, pani Kovaříková. It's a shame you don't still work in the bookshop."

"I don't want my wife involved in any of this, Filip."

"Yes, Sergeant, of course. I underdstand."

"Why is Herr Frank so important?" asked Karolína.

"People like Frank are the real danger, much more than loud-mouth thugs like von Stricker. Frank is outwardly respectable, low-key. Just a bookseller from Karlovy Vary. But he's a member of the German National Socialist Workers' Party, and some of the material that comes out of his shop, out of the back door, as it were, is racist, seditious propaganda. Alois Krause helps him distribute it."

"Oh, my Lord. But I never saw anything like that."

"That's alright, pani Kovaříková. We realise you knew nothing about it. Frank and Krause keep what they do well hidden."

"I can't believe it."

"Frank is also a member of the *Kameradschaftsbund*. Are either of you familiar with them?"

"They're just another sports group, aren't they?" said Pavel.

"So they say. But in lots of these groups people like Frank hide behind sport and culture, when their real aims are political. They say they just want cultural links with Germany, when really they're pan-Germanists who want the whole *Volk* reunited in one Greater Germany, dominating Central Europe."

"Leaving no room for Czechoslovakia, I take it."

"Exactly, Sergeant. And they say 'Volk' is only a term to describe people who share a common language, but really they exclude anyone who is not racially pure, as they put it, such as Jews and Slavs. It's a tradition that goes right back through Wolf to Franko Stein and many others."

"I hope the Sokol isn't a Slav version of that," said Karolína.

"Don't be silly, Kája."

"Don't call me silly, Pavel. I'm just as concerned as you are. What if Tomáš is getting propaganda like that?"

"Don't worry, pani Kovaříková. I know it's a shock to learn of these things happening around you here in Cheb, but the Sokol has been investigated too. It really is only a sports club."

"I'm relieved to hear it."

"Groups like the Kameradschaftsbund engage in sport too, of course, but they use it to indoctrinate their youth and instil obedience. It finds its extreme form in the Volkssport, who mould themselves on Hitler's SA."

"SA?" asked Karolína.

"*Sturmabteilung*. Hitler's paramilitary. But they're really no more than street fighters."

"And you are saying we have all this here now in our lovely town?"

"I'm afraid so, pani Kovaříková. But as I said, the Volkssport are so easy to spot they're not the real threat. Here's a far greater danger."

Souček took out another photo and laid it on the table.

"But that's Herr Henlein," said Karolína. "He organises the Turnverband. You're surely not going to tell us he's a risk."

"Well, it's hard to say, pani Kovaříková, and that's what could make Henlein as dangerous as Haider. We think he infiltrated the Turnverband for his own ends. He's had the sense to throw von Stricker out, but the Turnverband is still *volkisch* and anti-Semitic."

"We know that from our nephew."

"But Henlein swears he's a loyal citizen of Czechoslovakia, which makes it very difficult to get anything on him. But one has to ask how he can be a democrat when he refers to himself as the *'Führer'* and insists on absolute obedience from his followers."

"The Germans have been waiting since Charlemagne for another Führer to rule central Europe," said Pavel. "It's part of their pathetic mythology."

"Well, let's hope it remains a myth and Henlein's not their new messiah," said Souček, as he rose from his chair.

"Please excuse my abrupt departure but I have to get back to Prague before this evening. Pani Kovaříková, many thanks for your hospitality this afternoon. Please apologise to your son for me, and pardon any intrusion on my part and any undue concern I may have caused you."

"Any former comrade of my husband is always welcome in my house, pan Souček."

"That reminds me of something, Filip," said Pavel. "Please wait a minute while I fetch it for you."

Pavel left the room and went up to his bedroom.

"Do you mind me asking you, pan Souček," asked Karolína while they waited, "why you still address my husband as 'sergeant' after all these years?"

"Your husband will always be the Sergeant to those of us who served with him, pani Kovaříková. You know, I suppose, he twice turned down a commission after Zborov?"

"No, he never talks about anything like that."

"He insisted on remaining an NCO so that he could stay with me and Milan and the others. Calling him 'sergeant' is the greatest respect we can show him."

"I see."

"If it were not for your husband, pani Kovaříková, none of us would be alive today, nor our children, of course. He is the bravest and best man I have ever known."

"Here we are," said Pavel as he came down the stairs. He came into the room holding a photograph. "This is for you, Filip. You have shown us so many photos this afternoon; I have one for you to keep. It's the six of us in Irkutsk. I want you to have it."

"Thank you, Sergeant, I shall treasure it. And here is my card. Please contact me there if you ever feel there is anything we need to know."

"I will, Filip. And you can always reach me here."

"We are very grateful for your help in all this, Sergeant."

"I'll help in any way I can." Pavel held out his hand. "Goodbye, Filip. It's been very good to see you again."

"Goodbye, Sergeant, and thankyou. Thankyou, pani Kovaříková."

When Pavel came back into the room after closing the front door, Karolína walked towards him and stood in front of him.

"What's the matter, Kája?"

She placed her hands on his cheeks, looked into his face and kissed him gently on the lips. "Nothing," she said. "As long as you are here, nothing at all."

Chapter Thirty-Five

July 27th, 1931 – November 18th, 1933

In the weeks following Souček's visit Pavel received two pieces of news, one expected, the other not.

The news he was expecting appeared in a headline on the front page of his newspaper in late July. It announced that the government in Prague had banned the entire Volkssport organisation within the borders of Czechoslovakia, and prohibited the wearing of all Nazi uniforms.

The unexpected news was delivered one day by Karolína when she returned from visiting the Neumann house in Skalka. Ernst told her that Otto, who was now 18, had decided to go to Prague that September to study Hebrew at Charles University. He had realised he could no longer live his life as an 'outsider' and needed to 'belong'. After graduation he intended to continue his studies at a yeshiva, in order to become a rabbi.

Ernst was relieved in September to see his son leave for the safety of Prague, as the economic situation in the border area worsened and the usual search for scapegoats intensified.

Regular worshippers at Cheb's synagogue, which Otto had so recently attended, were subjected to more and more abuse as anger amongst Cheb's majority German population mounted, and their support for extremist politicians on the right grew. In the municipal elections of March 1932 the German National Socialist Workers' Party won most of the seats on the town's council, and their Party leader, Josef Knirsch, was installed as Cheb's new mayor. In the early evening of election day Knirsch stood on the steps of the New Town Hall, struggling to deliver his acceptance speech through blasts of late winter snow and the constant heckling coming from Pavel and Tomáš Kovarik, who stood at the front of the crowd.

Across the border in Germany, too, it was politicians on the extreme right who were gaining most from the economic crisis. One month after the elections in Cheb Adolf Hitler stood against President Paul von Hindenburg, hero of the Great War, for Germany's presidency, and instead of the humiliating defeat most people expected for 'the Austrian corporal', Hitler came a close second to von Hindenburg with over 13 million votes.

By early summer Masaryk and Beneš decided enough was enough and they acted again against the extremists in Cheb, as Filip Souček promised they would. Seven 'students', members of the outlawed Volkssport, were arrested for plotting armed rebellion in league with a foreign power, and put on trial. Amongst those tried were their leader, Alois Haider, and his most willing henchman, Heinrich von Stricker.

When Haider and von Stricker were each jailed for three years, Ernst and Pavel met in a local hostelry to celebrate. Otto had heard about the verdict in Prague and written to his father to tell him he felt no animosity towards Heinrich von Stricker. Quite the opposite. He sought only reconciliation with the person he saw as God's agent, since he had compelled Otto to confront himself and choose the right path. He prayed that Ernst would see the good von Stricker had unwittingly done him, and feel no bitterness.

"Your son is a better man than I can ever be," Pavel admitted to Ernst. "If I had my way, von Stricker and all the other thugs around here would be locked up for good."

Bitterness deepened on both sides as a result of the Volkssport trial. Many Sudeten Germans openly blamed Prague for a miscarriage of justice, and such was the number of protest marches organised in Cheb and other towns near the border, that Tomáš became used to people with banners marching outside his house, and he often weaved his way between them to cross the bridge to Skalka without giving them a second thought.

Towards the end of 1932 attitudes amongst Sudeten Germans hardened even further, as parts of Czechoslovakia's economy began to recover, while the industrialised areas in western and northern Bohemian, where they lived, stubbornly remained in a slump, dragged down by their dependence on exports to Germany.

In Prague Masaryk and Beneš understood that little could be done to ease the hardships in the Sudetenland, until the economy of Germany recovered. But that seemed a long way off. By the beginning of 1933 two thirds of international trade, so vital to Germany, had disappeared. Forty percent of the German workforce was unemployed, and across the border in Czechoslovakia the rate amongst Sudeten Germans was even higher.

Finally, with no signs of recovery, the people of Germany clamoured for a change of leadership and direction. In the November elections of 1932 they demonstrated their loss of faith in democratic parties of the centre, when nearly 50 percent of Germans voted either for the Nazis or the Communists. With the popularity of the Communists rising, the power brokers in Berlin took fright and decided a less unpalatable option would be the National Socialists. At least their leader was so inexperienced, argued President Hindenburg, that it should not be too difficult to manipulate and control him.

And so on 30th January 1933 Adolf Hitler was invited by the president to become Germany's new chancellor. Three weeks later the Reichstag in Berlin burnt down, and within a month its members, meeting in the Kroll Opera House, voted themselves out of existence. The new chancellor-dictator, free now to act decisively in tackling the economic crisis threatening Germany, announced that his first priority would be the introduction of a series of racial laws.

In April he decreed that anyone with one Jewish grandparent was a non-Aryan and no longer entitled to the full rights of a German citizen. Immediately a boycott of Jewish shops and businesses began and beatings were handed out on the streets, usually to the indifference of passers-by. Soon Jews were excluded from participating in the arts, from editing newspapers, or from owning land.

In Czechoslovakia the government responded. From October 1st the German Nazi Party and Wolf's DNSAP were outlawed, and all municipal councillors and mayors belonging to these parties, including Josef Knirsch, were removed and replaced by appointments made from Prague.

On the same day a new party emerged in Western Bohemia, claiming to represent all of Czechoslovakia's German population. It called itself the *Sudetendeutsche Heimatsfront. The Sudeten-German Home Front.* To the surprise of neither Filip Souček in Prague nor Pavel Kovařík in Cheb, the self-proclaimed leader of this new party was Konrad Henlein, the gymnastics teacher. And his deputy was Karl Hermann Frank, the owner of a bookshop by the railway station in Karlovy Vary.

Ernst threw his newspaper to the floor.

"I cannot bear the shame of it, Zuzana. Can you believe they are flogging people in the street, purely because of their religion? I swear some of those thugs would murder my own children, if they got the chance. How dare they say they are doing it in my name?"

"But you are Austrian, Ernst. The people doing those things are German."

"It's strange you make the distinction now, Zuzana. You have always referred to me in the past as German."

"I saw no need to distinguish before."

"Hitler makes no distinction. He's an Austrian like me, but he insists all German-speakers are part of one German Volk."

"Well, if you're determined to upset yourself about it, Ernst, it's up to you. It's probably all exaggerated anyway."

"How can you say that? You've seen all the Jewish refugees passing through here over the past twelve months. They arrive with nothing, as if they are running for their lives."

"Perhaps they didn't have much in the first place."

Ernst looked at Zuzana as she took a cigarette from the silver box on the tall oak mantelpiece. She put the cigarette to her bright red lips and held it there between two extended fingers while she lit it. Her hair was immaculate, and even on a Sunday she had chosen to wear a black silk cocktail dress with flesh coloured stockings and shoes with a heel, accentuating the perfect line of her legs. Ernst felt rising annoyance and frustration, as he recognised his all too familiar desire for her.

"Do you think Jakob at the theatre only possessed one suit and one shirt when he worked at the State Opera in Munich?" he said. "He was an important man there, but they threw him out of his job and his apartment. He was in fear of his life when he got here."

"Alright, Ernst. You've made your point."

"I know now how Otto felt. I don't know what I'm supposed to be any more. I was an Austrian German. Now I am a German Czechoslovak. My parents live in Salzburg and are Austrian. But I was born here so I cannot be Austrian…"

"Oh, be quiet about it, Ernst. What does it matter?"

She tapped the ash from her cigarette into an ashtray balanced on the palm of her hand.

"It matters, Zuzana, because the government in Berlin now considers Jews to be the ultimate enemy of the German people. Even if my own children were not Jewish, I would still feel abandoned by the culture I love. I have always felt a part of German culture. It was my culture. These people have stolen it. They have stolen my feeling of self."

"I don't know why you fuss so. I've always loved German culture as much as you. I don't feel abandoned by it. It's still there. Goethe and Schiller and Beethoven."

"That may be, but you won't hear any Mendelssohn or read any Heine in Germany any more, will you? And what about the people I worked with? Fritz Busch in Dresden and poor Arnold Schönburg in Berlin, dismissed without a thought."

"Yes, it is a shame about dear Fritz. I liked him. But he's so talented, there are bound to be opera houses that still want him."

"But that's not the point, Zuzana. It's the principle of it. The injustice of victimising people on the basis of their religion."

"I thought Hitler was saying it's more a question of their race."

"Jews are not a race. They're simply followers of Judaism."

"I thought Hitler was saying a Jew is anyone with a Jewish parent, like Otto and Anna. Even if they don't go to the synagogue."

"But I could convert and become a Jew if I wanted to. Anyone can. This race argument is just nonsense."

"Oh, I don't know, Ernst. All I do know is, you can't blame the Germans for all of this. Everyone knows they have been treated really shabbily."

"That may be true to an extent, but it does not excuse all they're doing now."

"I remember when the French sent in all those negro soldiers to occupy the Rhineland. That was done just to annoy people."

"But that was years ago. What has it got to do with anything now?"

"I don't know. It's just that a lot of the Germans I know here feel they are victimised as much as the Jews."

"But that's nonsense."

"Everything I say is nonsense to you, Ernst. But everyone knows government contracts around here only go to Czech firms. And look how the Germans were all kicked off the council last year. It's no wonder so many of them support Hitler. I can understand it."

"You can?"

"Absolutely. He stands up for them. He tells them how strong they can be. It's an exciting, young movement. I would probably vote for him if I were German."

"You could ignore his anti-Semitism?"

"If all it means is giving jobs to Germans instead of Jews. It's only the same kind of thing that happens here."

"But the Jews who live in Germany *are* Germans. They are the same nationality."

"Oh, I don't know Ernst. Germans and Czechs here are supposed to be the same nationality, aren't they? But they're not treated the same."

Zuzana took another cigarette and lit it without ceremony. "I find this all so boring anyway."

Ernst got up from his chair and stretched, before walking to the picture window and gazing out over the river.

"You're not a very loyal Czech, are you, Zuzana?"

"Why should I be? I can't help it if I don't find Czech people interesting.

They're so... oh, I don't know... unrefined."

"What about Karolína and Pavel? And Tomáš?"

"Tomáš is a nice boy..."

"He's 17. He's a young man."

"He's a nice young man then. Very handsome, I must say. But you wouldn't want Anna to marry him, would you? Be honest."

Ernst turned to face Zuzana, who was leaning with her right elbow on the mantelpiece and her right foot raised on the brass rail of the fender. "If Anna wanted to, I would be delighted," he said.

"You don't find him a bit like Pavel? A bit unsophisticated?"

"If you mean honest and forthright, I would agree with you. But they are both highly intelligent and very well educated."

"But rather like Karolína. Not very cultured."

"She may not wear the latest fashion or know a Hock from an Auslese, but I think your sister is a woman of great character, Zuzana."

"Really? Is that all you think of her?"

"What do you mean by that remark?"

"Oh, come on, Ernst. Everyone can see you and my sister share some pathetic little secret. Do you think I am the only one who notices?"

"I don't know what you're talking about. Karolina gave the children and me invaluable support when they lost their mother. That's all. I have never made a secret of that."

"If you say so, Ernst. It makes no difference to me anyway how the two of you try to embellish your dreary lives."

"My only remark to you, Zuzana, was that I find Karolina to be a person of great character."

"Alright, Ernst, if you say so. But my sister is hardly a person of refinement and culture, is she? And neither is her son. Like most Czechs, they just don't have refinement in their nature."

"Well, I think they do. Anna tells me Tomáš writes poetry for her. Very good poetry."

"Perhaps he does. But I just can't think of Czechs as poets. Or playwrights. There may be one or two, but not on the same level as the Germans or the French, or even the English. Czech is such a coarse language."

"Why must you always be so narrow-minded, Zuzana? Surely we can appreciate the beauty of one country's culture without needing to denigrate another, can't we? German culture may seem exceptional to you and me, but it is no more worthy than any other."

"I think it is. Look at this town. Look what you have bought to it over the past 20 years. Imagine how limited you would have been if you had only used Czech writers and composers."

"I have always believed in cultural coexistence. I have tried to offer as varied a programme as I could."

"Yes, and look where it's got you. A half-empty auditorium most of the time."

"You know it wasn't always like that. It's the economy. People don't have the money."

"Have you not noticed the money they have for Mickey Mouse and Charlie Chaplin at the picture house? Or the way the Czechs are willing to queue for their latest masterpiece about their precious legionnaires. And you'll probably find my sister and Pavel and Tomáš at the head of the queue. God, I hate this awful place."

"We have had some good times here, haven't we?"

"You may have. I haven't."

Ernst walked slowly to his chair and sat down. He looked at Zuzana, who was still standing at the fireplace, leaning with her shoulders against the mantelpiece and her arms tightly folded. "Would you like to leave Eger then?" he asked her.

"Of course I would. I'd go tomorrow if I could."

"Where would you choose to go?"

"Berlin, Paris, Vienna..."

"Would you settle for Prague?"

She said nothing, but then looked at him, her mouth and eyes opening wide.

"Yes... why..?"

"Because I have been offered a post there."

Zuzana stepped forward and knelt down at his feet. She leant towards him with her hands on his thighs.

"What post? What do you mean? What post?"

"I wrote off a couple of weeks ago. I had been thinking about Otto. How little we see of one another. It's an assistant directorship at the National Theatre, starting in six months' time. I didn't think for a minute I had a chance, but somehow they want me. Without as much as an interview."

"Well, of course they want you, my love. Everyone knows how talented you are."

She leaned forward and kissed him on the lips, and then stood up and walked to the window with her arms raised.

"Prague. We're going to Prague."

"But wait a minute, Zuzana. There are things we have to consider. It will be wonderful to be with Otto when he graduates next summer, but what about Anna? It will break her heart to be away from Tomáš."

"Oh no, don't worry about that. I'll explain to her she'll have the pick of the boys in Prague. I still can't believe it, Ernst. I'm so happy."

"I do not think it's as straightforward as that, Zuzana. I have to consider Anna's feelings."

"Do you want her to stay here?"

"No, that's one of the reasons I want to leave. I want Anna away from any trouble."

"Why would Anna have any trouble?"

"She's Jewish, Zuzana. Feelings are running high here."

"But she doesn't even look Jewish. She can easily get away with it."

"That's not the point."

"Well, bring her to Prague then. Stop fussing, Ernst. Most of the people in the arts in Prague were Jews anyway when I lived there. No one cares in Prague."

She came over to Ernst and straddled his legs. Her dress rose up her thighs.

"Please, Ernst *Liebling*. Don't disappoint me now. Please say we're going."

He looked at her and smiled.

"Yes, Zuzana. We're going."

Chapter Thirty-Six

May 28th, 1934

"Open the door, Děda, for the Lord's sake," called Magda from the pantry. "How do you expect me to open it holding this?"

Michal pushed back his chair and moved quickly to help her.

"Now careful. You nearly knocked it out of my hands."

Magda emerged from the kitchen carrying a large iced cake covered in red, white and blue candles burning brightly in the shape of the flag of the republic.

Everyone stood and applauded as Tomáš helped his grandmother to place the cake in the middle of the table.

"There are fifty exactly," announced Magda. "Děda and I counted them three times, didn't we, Děda?"

"Fifty exactly," confirmed Michal.

Karolina had been determined to celebrate Pavel's landmark birthday, but with Ernst, Anna and Zuzana leaving Cheb the next day, she knew it was unlikely to be the joyous occasion she had hoped for. It was some consolation to her that her táta had recovered his spirits over the past few months, and for the first time for a long time he and Magda insisted the party should be held 'like in the old days' at the chata.

"Thank you both very much," said Pavel, as he stepped forward to kiss Magda and shake Michal's hand. "I feel honoured that you should go to so much trouble."

"You have to blow them all out, Uncle Pavel," said Anna. "All in one go."

"I'll need a week or two to get fit for that, I think. But here goes." And everyone laughed and applauded again as Pavel took three deep breaths before the candles were extinguished and only smoke rose from Magda's flag.

"Now I propose a toast..."

"Just a moment, sir, if I may..." interrupted Pavel. "I have something which arrived by special delivery from Karlovy Vary this morning. From Milan Musil." He bent down and reached into a bag he had stowed away in a corner. "Two special bottles from one of pan Musil's vineyards in France..."

"Champagne," exclaimed Zuzana. "Real French champagne..."

"Oh my goodness. I've got some special sekt glasses somewhere..." said Magda, disappearing again into the pantry.

The champagne was poured and Michal rose to his feet. "I propose a toast," he said, and although everyone made as if to object, it was a relief to them all to see the head of their family playing the role they feared he had forsaken forever.

"...a toast to someone who has earned the respect and love of us all. As a soldier, a friend, a father, a husband, and dare I say, as a son to Magda and me. So raise your glasses high to 'our Pavel'."

"Our Pavel..."

"Thankyou. Everyone. And thank you, sir, for saying such kind things," said Pavel, remaining in his seat. There was a silence before he spoke again, in a voice much softer than usual.

"These are strange times we share together, mixed with certainties and with change. Four days ago our beloved President was re-elected for the fourth time. His mere presence in our lives gives us security and confidence for the future. And once again our family gathers around the table of our dear Magda and Michal, secure and united beneath the love and generosity they bestow on us all."

Magda took Michal's hand and dabbed her eyes with her apron.

"And yet we are all aware that our world is not as settled as it was. We have to come to terms with more change than any of us would wish for, or are even ready for. But in the same way that I know President Masaryk will steer our country through these troubled times, so I am sure our family will sit here together again one day, just as we are now."

Pavel stood up and raised his glass of champagne. "My toast has nothing to do with my birthday, which I must admit, I thought more than once I might never reach." Ernst smiled to himself and nodded. "It is about family and friendship. May they always remain at the centre of our lives."

Everyone stood, except Magda, who kept hold of Michal's hand. "Family and friendship," they chorused.

"Tell everyone to start on the food, Děda," said Magda between her sobs. "I don't think I've got much of an appetite for it myself."

"Come on, Máma," said Karolína as everyone retook their seats. "Everything will be alright."

"But I'm losing my Zuzana again..."

"No, you're not. You'll come back to visit us, won't you, Zuzana?"

"Oh, I expect so."

"But what about my little Anna and Tomáš? What will they do without one another?"

"Don't worry, Babička," said Tomáš. "Anna and I have talked about it. I shall visit in the holidays if Uncle Ernst doesn't mind..."

"Not at all."

"... and next year I shall go to university in Prague and see Anna as much as we do now."

"So I won't see you any more either then," said Magda.

"Yes, you will, my love," said Michal. "They can all visit. And anyway, I can take you to Prague any time you like now the money's all sorted again."

"Sorted, Táta?" asked Karolína. "In what way?"

"Never you mind. Just rest assured your máma and me have nothing more to worry about."

"What have you done?"

"Never mind. It's enough for you all to know we have what we need now to see us through."

Karolína looked at Pavel, whose face showed as much bemusement as her own.

"So, Tomáš," said Ernst. "What will you study when you come to Prague?"

"Languages, Uncle. English and French."

"The languages of democracy. Do I see your father's influence there?"

"Yes," said Tomáš. "I want to understand other cultures and be able to communicate with people. I see here what happens when language separates people."

"Most commendable, Tomáš. And what will you do with your languages?"

"I'd like to teach, Uncle. And to write. Nothing as ambitious as you, of course. Short stories and poetry mostly."

"You should see some of the boy's poems," said Michal. "He has a proper way with words."

"I would like that very much," said Ernst.

"Can I show Vati some you have written for me, Tomáš?" asked Anna.

"Yes, of course, if you like."

"I suppose they're poems of undying devotion, are they?" said Zuzana.

"Yes, some of them express how I feel about Anna," said Tomáš.

"How sweet."

"That isn't the word Anna and I would choose. We love one another."

"But you are more like brother and sister."

"You know we are not, Mutti," said Anna. "You know how much I love Tomáš. We want to spend our whole lives together."

She took Tomáš's hand and brought it to her lips.

"We shall wait for one another for as long as we have to," she said.

"You may think so at 17, Anna, but wait until you see the bright lights of Prague..."

"What do you mean by that?" said Tomáš.

"I mean," said Zuzana, "that neither of you has much experience of life."

"I don't think you should say..."

"Now, now, all of you. This is what I was afraid of," said Magda. "People getting upset by it all."

"Sorry, Babička."

"That's alright, my darling boy. But I don't want anyone being upset. And no one's touched the dumplings yet. Come on all of you."

"It's all delicious, Máma," said Karolína. "As always."

"Yes, very good, Magda. Excellent."

"So, Tomáš," asked Ernst, "do you intend to write your poetry in French and English too one day?"

"Perhaps. But I'm happy to write in any language. I agree with what my father says. Language is just an instrument. It matters what you say, not what language you say it in."

Ernst looked over at Pavel who smiled knowingly back at him.

"I have to admit, Tomáš, it was your Uncle Ernst who taught me the truth of that some years ago. I didn't always think it."

"You and I have learned a lot from one another over the years, old friend," said Ernst.

"Yes, we have."

"I must admit now to something I got wrong many years ago," Ernst said.

"Just one? You'll have to remind me which one," smiled Pavel.

"It was a long time ago, back in 1918 when it looked as if Germany and Austria were winning the war, and there were plans for this area to become German Egerland. I believed then it would be a good thing. But I was wrong. Now I see Germany for the abomination it really is. With its book-burning and anti-Semitism..."

"I keep telling you, Ernst," said Zuzana, "your family is Austrian. You don't have to feel responsible for what Germany does."

"Bring back the emperor, I say," said Michal. "Things were better when we had our emperor in Vienna. He would have stood up to Hitler."

"Well, he didn't do a very good job standing up to the Kaiser, did he?" said Magda, who was now circling the table trying to fill people's plates. "He was like his little puppy dog."

"You're right, Magda," said Pavel. "And there's truth in what Zuzana says, Ernst. You cannot take the blame for what Germany does."

"But I embraced its culture as mine, Pavel. I lived off the glory of it. I must now share its shame. My old friend in Prague, Max Brod, says we must learn 'distanced love'. We must retain our love of the old culture but distance ourselves now from the country which produced it."

"Everything will be better when we get to Prague," said Zuzana. "When we can get away from all this unrest."

"The unrest will still be here when you have gone, Zuzana," said Karolína.

"But, Kája, please tell me you understand why we must leave," said Ernst. "We must go, for Otto and Anna's sake."

"Of course, Ernst. Don't worry. I do understand. Really I do."

The only sound was the clatter of cutlery on Magda's best Bohemian china.

"Things seem to be getting worse here," said Ernst. "I saw that von Stricker and his band of thugs again the other day, shouting abuse at Frau Blumstein and her daughter in the square."

"The authorities released him early on appeal," said Pavel. "Unfortunately, it's the price we must pay for democracy. To give people like him the same freedoms as everyone else. I hope you put the louse in his place, Ernst."

"To my shame, Pavel, I did not. I didn't want to draw his attention onto... you know... anyone close to me."

"We understand your situation, Ernst," said Pavel. "You have a new challenge in Prague, and Otto is there. It's right for you. But let me assure you all of something."

Everyone looked towards him.

"Nothing bad is going to happen here. Not in Cheb or anywhere else. Masaryk and Beneš will not allow it. Our government is more in control of events than people realise."

"And how would you know that?" said Zuzana.

"I shall tell you, Zuzana. I once heard Masaryk speak at length about the situation here. And I know he believes in the words on our country's crest. Truth prevails. Events will move in our direction, because we have the right moral attitude. Once again the Germans are showing their true colours, and once again the British and the French will not tolerate it.

And neither shall we Czechoslovaks. Right will prevail."

"Well said, my boy," said Michal. "I couldn't have put it better myself."

"And just in case our moral attitude doesn't impress the Germans, we also have a more practical solution. One of the most fortified, heavily defended borders in Europe. Only 10 kilometres from here."

"I told you something big was going on in those woods, Magda," said Michal.

"Some people say they've heard Frenchies out there in the forest. Is that true, Pavel?" said Magda.

"Perhaps, Magda. I cannot say."

"Are we building fortifications against the Austrians and Hungarians too, Táta," asked Tomáš.

"Not to the same extent, Tomáš. They're not such a risk."

"I should think not," said Zuzana, who kept cutting at her food without eating much of it. "Need I remind you all that Austria banned those Nazis you all dread so much, long before the Czechs ever did?"

"Only because they have their own Fascist government already," said Tomáš, "and don't want anyone else stepping in."

"I can see you are your father's son," replied Zuzana.. "Frankly, I do not see why you all object so much to Fascism anyway."

"Please, Zuzana..."

"No, Ernst. Everyone else is allowed to give their opinion. Why shouldn't I? Obviously I'm totally against burning books and laws against Jews and things like that, but Fascism itself doesn't seem such a bad thing. Sometimes a dictator is what a country needs. Look what Mussolini has done for Italy."

"He's stopped free speech," said Tomáš.

"People who are unemployed with starving families have more to think about than free speech, Tomáš. You might learn that one day."

"And he's stopped free elections..."

"Oh yes, free to elect one corrupt politician rather than another. The Duce has given Italians work, an organised life and a government the world listens to. And Hitler is doing the same for Germany. He is looking after his own people first. You all say it's good when families do it."

"But we don't beat our children because we don't like their religion, or lock them up when they disagree with what we say," said Pavel.

"I told you I don't agree with everything the Fascists do, Pavel. But even you have to admit that Hitler and Mussolini have inspired their people. You just don't listen to what I say."

"And you don't seem to understand, Zuzana, the real nature of these people. Your inspired German Fascists want total control of central Europe, including this area we live in. And I know they would use force to do it, if they thought they could get away with it. It's time you listened to what I'm telling you."

"Well, I've listened enough to all of you," said Magda, "and I'm calling a stop to it. We never seem to have a simple meal in this house without all this gabbling."

"Sorry, Magda," said Pavel. "I hope we haven't spoiled the party for you."

"It's not my party, it's yours. All I want is for you to enjoy the food, and this cake I've done for you. No one seems to want some."

"I think we all do, Máma," said Karolína. "It looks wonderful."

"Well, if all of you will excuse me, I am going outside for some fresh air and a cigarette," said Zuzana.

"Shall I come..?"

"No, Ernst. I prefer my own company, thank you."

No one spoke as Magda cut the cake and Zuzana closed the door of the chata noisily behind her.

"This is what I mean," said Magda. "Things would be a lot better if people filled their mouths with more food and less words. All this arguing just when everyone's going away."

"Poor Mutti," said Anna. "She always seems to say the wrong thing."

"No, dear child," said Magda, and she bent forward and stroked Anna's head. "I wasn't saying it was all your Mutti's fault. But it's true she has always had her own way of thinking about things. Ever since she was a little girl. Hasn't she, Děda?"

Pavel felt Karolína nudge his leg as Michal responded to Magda's prompt.

"Yes, Zuzana's always had her little ways, that's for sure. But she means well."

"What was my real mother like?" asked Anna.

Magda stopped cutting. Pavel held his plate motionless in mid-air.

"Why does no one ever talk about her?" said Anna, looking around the table at all the startled faces. "Well?"

"I think it's because we all loved your mother very much, and we still feel very sad about her," said Karolína.

"But if you all loved her, it should make you happy to talk about her. I always wondered if there was something wrong and you're all keeping it from me."

Ernst reached across the table and took his daughter's hand.

"No, darling Anna. There was never anything wrong. Your Auntie Kája is right. We don't mention your mother, because we have always been afraid of upsetting someone, especially you."

"I'm not upset. I hardly remember her. I *want* to talk about her."

She pointed to the photograph which hung on the wall next to her grandmother's green-tiled oven.

"That's a picture of her, isn't it?"

"Yes, darling, it is."

Karolína got up and brought the photograph over to Anna.

"This is your mother, when Uncle Pavel and I got married. Esther was my maid of honour."

"I've often looked at it," said Anna. "I always think she looks a bit like Otto there. How old was she then?"

"She and I were both 22. It was taken in 1910. And I have to tell you, Anna, that your mother was the sweetest, kindest person. Just like you."

"How did she die?"

Karolina looked at Ernst. He nodded to her.

"She caught influenza at the end of the war. Lots of people died from it. Uncle Pavel lost one of his brothers."

"I wish I'd been told all this before. Do you still get sad, Uncle Pavel?"

"Yes, Anna, I do. But I know my brother, Petr, would want me to be happy. So I try to be happy whenever I think of him. For his sake. And I know Esther would want you to be happy too. She loved you and Otto and your father very much."

"She did," said Karolína. "She loved all of us. You can keep the photograph, if you like, Anna, and hang it on your wall in Prague to remember us by."

"Thank you, Teta Karolína. And is that our cherry tree in the picture?"

"Yes, it was taken about this time of year. When all the blossom was out."

"Will you come outside with me, Tomáš," said Anna, "and sit with me now under the tree?"

Tomáš stood up and took her hand. Anna had the picture clutched to her chest when they met Zuzana at the door.

"I hope you're not leaving just because I've come in," she said.

"No, Mutti, of course not," said Anna, and she leaned forward and kissed Zuzana on the cheek. "Tomáš and I just want to spend some time together."

Zuzana came over to the table and took the wine Ernst offered her.

"Well, this seems more like a wake than a party," she said. "What's the matter with everyone?"

"I was thinking whilst you were out, Zuzana," said Pavel. "If I've been a bit too forthright tonight, I apologise."

"Good grief. An unsolicited kiss from Anna and now an apology from Pavel Kovařík. This is an evening to remember, I must say."

"We've decided to cheer up, Zuzana," said Karolína. "Let's talk only of happy things." She turned to her father. "So, Táta, what is this miracle you've brought about to get your money back?"

"Well, since you ask, Kája," said Michal with a smile, "I shall tell you. You all say the von Stricker boy is a thug and I believe you. But believe me, when I tell you his father is a gentleman."

"Are you talking about the Graf, sir?" asked Pavel.

"Yes, I am. The Graf has provided Magda and me with a secure future." He took Magda's hand and she placed her other hand on his forearm.

"What has he done?" asked Pavel.

"The Graf has given us enough money to see us out for the rest of our days, and a bit more for Kája and Zuzana when we've gone. And I won't be putting it in any bank either. You can be sure of that."

"And why has he done that, sir?"

Michal smiled an even bigger smile.

"He's given us the money and allowed us to secure it against the chata."

"Your Děda's been very clever," said Magda.

"I needed to be, my love. I let you down."

"The only time you let me down is when you have too much from that barrel. I know now why they've been calling all this a depression."

Michal patted Magda's hand and she rested her head against his shoulder.

"But what about Štasný Lake and the land?" said Karolína.

"Yes, that's secured too. But the Graf says your mother and me can stay here as long as we like. And when we've gone, you and Zuzana have the right to buy it all back if you want."

"And do you have this in writing?"

"It's not nice to be so mistrustful, Kája. The Graf is a gentleman. We've shaken hands on it. I am a simple man, but I know when I can trust someone. And you should too."

When Anna arrived at her new home in Prague, she hung the picture of her mother on the wall of her bedroom. Below it she pinned the poem Tomáš gave her as they sat together on her last evening in Cheb.

Ernst was pleased when Anna told him that Tomáš had not tried to persuade her to stay with him in Cheb. To make her choose between the two of them. When Ernst asked her if he could read one of Tomáš's poems, Anna took him to her room and led him to the poem on the wall. They stood and read it together.

My world will change tomorrow
I will eat and drink as yesterday
Hear talk and laughter as I did before
The lake will be the same, the forest unchanged
The summer sun, warm on my back, the same
As before, but all will be different tomorrow.

Tomorrow you are leaving
Your world will change, as mine
We shall not linger in the past we love
Nor dwell in lands of memory
We hold them dear, but dearer still
The future; embrace it with your heart.

Our worlds will change tomorrow
Our hearts will be the same
Unaltered by your leaving

Tomáš Kovařík
Cheb, May 1938

Chapter Thirty-Seven

November 14th, 1935

"Mr President, are you awake, sir?"

"What..?"

"The Foreign Minister is here for your meeting, Mr President."

"Eduard..?"

"Yes, sir. Dr Beneš is here for your four o'clock meeting."

"Show him in, Hájek. I must have drifted off. The heat of the fire..."

Masaryk raised himself from the armchair as Eduard Beneš walked towards him.

"Please don't get up, Mr President."

"No, Eduard. It does my old bones good to keep moving. How are you?"

The two men shook hands, and Beneš waited for Masaryk to ease himself back into his chair in front of the fire, before he sat down in the chair opposite.

"I am well, Mr President. But far more important, how are you?"

"The doctors say I can resume light duties. I thought it best to begin with a review of recent events from you."

"Will the prime minister be joining us?"

"I'm sorry, Eduard. I do not have the energy to listen to one of pan Hodža's lectures on a federation of central European states at the moment."

"He means well."

"I know, but we have such pressing issues, and I have so little energy. I know from you I shall hear about things that really matter."

"May I begin with the economic situation, sir?"

"Please."

"Our exports continue to rise month by month. So far this year they are back to 37 percent of their 1929 level. From a low of 28 percent last year."

"Good, good. And in Western Bohemia?"

"Not quite as high there. But that's hardly surprising since Germany imposed its trade barriers. It infuriates me. Just as there are signs of recovery the world's major economies block trade."

"Human nature, Eduard. Misguided people think they are protecting domestic industry. I remember the same thing happening in the slump of the eighties. They never learn."

"What concerns me, Mr President, is the boost the economic crisis has given to the Sudeten German Party in our border areas. I never thought I would see the day when they were the largest party in the National Assembly."

"We both knew the economic unrest would provide political momentum for such people."

"I'm afraid that's exactly what's happened with Henlein."

"But his party can never outnumber all the Czechoslovak deputies in the Assembly, Eduard, and no other party is likely to form a coalition with them."

"Hlinka's Slovak People's Party might. They polled a third of the vote in Slovakia and are just like the Sudeten Germans; refusing to accept government posts or any other concessions we offer them."

"Do their demands remain the same?"

"Yes, still the same. Autonomy for Western Bohemia and Slovakia within the Czechoslovakian state."

"Do you have any proof they are in league with Germany or Hungary?"

"Not yet. I think Hlinka is genuinely independent and loyal to Czechoslovakia. But I have my doubts about Henlein."

"I see he changed his party's name when told. The 'Sudeten German Party' is just about acceptable."

"Calling themselves the Sudeten German Homeland Front showed their real intentions in my opinion, Mr President. I am convinced their real aim is to become part of Hitler's Reich."

"But this man..."

"Henlein, Mr President."

"...he still gives nothing away?"

"We have reliable people monitoring him, and we have examined every speech and pamphlet leading up to the May elections. May I quote from a speech he made recently in Cheb? One of Souček's people there sent us a copy. It's fairly typical."

"Please."

"Henlein said, 'We seek fair and even-handed treatment for Sudeten Germans only within the democratic processes of the Republic of Czechoslovakia.' Clearly we cannot object to sentiments like that, but at the same time he does just enough to keep unrest in the Sudetenland simmering beneath the surface."

"By fair treatment he means..?"

"The Land Reforms, government contracts, the usual grievances. But they seem to think they live in a German enclave within our state. They see any Czech appointments in predominantly German-speaking districts as an act of incitement. It's intolerable."

"When I think how the Americans integrate everyone, Eduard. No German in America would dream of taking offence at being addressed in English."

"Or expect to live fully as a citizen without learning English."

"Do you know, Eduard," said Masaryk, staring into the fire, "my dear mother was Czech, but she only ever spoke German until late in life."

"But surely that makes the point, Mr President. Your mother was a citizen of Austria and spoke the language of her government. Now the government speaks Czech."

"Quite, quite..."

Masaryk reached for the glass of water on a side table. Beneš got up and passed it to him.

"Thankyou, Eduard. Thankyou."

"Would you like a break now, sir? I could return in the morning?"

"No, Eduard. Carry on. I need to know of your suspicions about this Henlein character. I believe you need to be wary of him. It is not natural for the leader of a successful party to turn down a role in government."

"It is difficult to know what Henlein wants, sir, but he has certainly been very clever so far. Although he claims to be pro-Czechoslovak and anti-Nazi in everything he says, he ran a campaign very much like Hitler did in '32."

"In what way, Eduard?"

"Anti-Jewish, anti-Communist. Plenty of banners, slogans and uniforms, calling on the spirit of front-line troops to follow him as their leader. He even styles himself 'der Führer', the same as Hitler."

"To attract the young and gullible, I expect."

"Yes, but the fact that he professes allegiance to Prague and doesn't use as much thuggery as Hitler, means our older, law-abiding German citizens feel they can support him too. Sixty-three percent of the Sudeten German vote is quite an endorsement."

"And where does he get his money for all this?"

"We think it must be coming from the Nazis. Probably from the Foreign Office in Berlin."

"Can you prove a link?"

"If we could, it would be all we need to move against him. Especially with Hitler making it so clear he wants to bring our German speakers 'home to the Reich'."

"You know, Eduard, I cannot understand why Hitler is being encouraged in all this."

"Encouraged, Mr President?"

"Yes. If no one opposes him... it amounts to tacit agreement. He took the Saarland back in March. The Poles let his Nazis operate amongst their German population. I begin to wonder who will stand up to him."

"You may rest assured, Mr President, that your government will never tolerate Nazism in Czechoslovakia. As soon as Konrad Henlein says one word in support of Hitler's claim to our Sudeten Germans, we shall arrest him for the traitor we believe him to be."

"I know how resolute you are, Eduard. But this has always been my greatest fear. That our German speakers would not embrace our democracy and might one day want to break away."

"Embrace it or not, Mr President, they will never break away. We won't allow it, the French won't allow it, and the League won't allow it."

Masaryk raised his hand from the arm of the chair. "I know, Eduard... I know..." He let his hand fall.

"I am sorry to say this, Eduard, when I know you have served the League so dutifully... as a member of its council and as its president; but the League of Nations has been one of the great disappointments of my life. It has stood by and watched Mussolini invade Abyssinia, and now it does nothing as Hitler rearms... in direct contravention of Versailles."

"There has always been a limit to its powers, Mr President."

"It would not need power if it spoke with authority and conviction. Looking back, I realise now the League was doomed in 1920 when the American Congress voted against joining. It broke President Wilson's heart. I truly believe he died from the disappointment of it."

"Then it's just as well we still have the French and the British with us, sir. And now the Russians."

"Your country owes you a great debt for securing the Russian treaty, Eduard. I believe even Hitler would not dare move against us, if it means bringing both France and Russia down on his head."

"Thankyou, Mr President. The German press and radio are trying to make the most of it, of course, saying we are aligning ourselves with Jewish Bolsheviks."

"Anyone who knows how we fought the Bolsheviks in Siberia will see that for the nonsense it is, Eduard. No, there is only one aspect of the treaty which concerns me."

"Only one, Mr President?"

"Please, Eduard, allow me in my final years not only to praise you for all you have done and continue to do, but also to pass on to you some reservations I have about certain of our allies. My reservations are unfounded in fact. They are the instincts of a tired old man, but I still feel I must share them with you."

"As always, you have my full attention, sir."

"This Treaty of Mutual Assistance with the Russians means they will come to our aid if ever we are attacked?"

"That is correct, sir."

"But only if France has already committed itself to our defence?"

"Yes."

"So France remains the key to our security."

"It always has done, Mr President. You have always agreed with me about that."

"And I still do, Eduard. I simply advise caution. As Germany has become more assertive, so I have watched the French become more circumspect. It is my belief that both she and Britain harbour a bad conscience towards Germany."

"A bad conscience, sir?"

"Yes, over the conditions imposed by them after the war. I would feel much more at peace if America were there to stiffen their resolve, but alas..."

Masaryk closed his eyes and lowered his head until his white beard rested on his chest.

"Is everything alright, Mr President?" asked Beneš.

"I hope so, Eduard. I do hope so."

He raised his head slowly and opened his eyes.

"I am tired, Eduard."

"Then we must continue this..."

"No, Eduard. I am in my eighty-sixth year. I am tired. I must stop. I can do no more."

"Shall we leave it..?"

"No, Eduard, you misunderstand me. I must explain. You must be the first to know, as you have the right to be. A month from now, on 14th December, I shall resign the presidency. And it is my dearest wish and my greatest hope that our legislature will choose you to be the next president of the Republic. No one deserves the honour more."

Beneš looked down and said nothing.

"My decision cannot come as a surprise to you, Eduard."

"No, sir, it does not. But we had all hoped..."

Beneš raised his head and looked at Masaryk.

"I am very moved by your confidence in me, Mr President," he said.

"I have known you since you were my student here in Prague, Eduard. We fought together to create this country, which we both love above all else. It can be in no safer hands than yours."

Masaryk got to his feet and offered his hand.

"Thankyou, Mr President," said Beneš. "There is no one who can ever replace you, sir, but if chosen I shall work by one principle: to always do for our people what I believe you would have done."

Chapter Thirty-Eight

Prague, 15th September, 1937

My dear Pavel and Karolína,

As soon as I learned yesterday of the death of Tomáš Masaryk, I had to write to you both to express my sincere condolences. I know the sadness of his passing is felt by people throughout the country and throughout the world, but I realise that Masaryk occupied a singular place in the lives of both my dear friends.

Kája, I remember a conversation you and I had more than twenty years ago. We were by the river with the children and with my darling Esther, and you and I talked about the war. I was angry that Masaryk was in Russia parleying with Austria's enemies, working to gain the freedom of Czech and Slovak prisoners of war. I believe I called him a traitor.

In the strictest sense of the word perhaps I was right. He was betraying the interests of a legally established government, of which he was a citizen. Yet for many years now I have realised I was wrong to see his actions in that light. For I believe that everything Masaryk did in his life was conceived with the simple end of securing freedom and democracy for his people, and adding to the general stock of humanity in the world. He was an upright man, whose humanism gave him an authority above the nationalities. How we could do with men of his stature now amongst the Great Powers of Europe.

Pavel, dear friend, I wonder if you will be coming to the state funeral in two weeks' time. I believe there is to be a call for legionnaires to act as pall bearers, and for many more to march behind the gun carriage. If you do decide to come to Prague, I must insist that you come to stay at my home. Visits between us have been far too infrequent over the past three years.

Did you by chance attend the 20th anniversary of Zborov here in July? I know that for reasons of your own you have not celebrated Zborov over the years. I looked for you amongst the thousands of legionnaires on the day. They were given a reception by the city the like of which I have never witnessed before. The army has become very popular here over recent months, as people's fears have grown. Smart young officers and airmen have become a common sight everywhere. They are often applauded in the streets.

I must say that I have never regretted coming to Prague, in spite of recent developments, of which more later. It has been particularly healthy for my self-regard to meet with fellow Germans who are decent and refined human beings. Many, of course, are long-standing friends, but some of my newest acquaintances are refugees from the evil that has overtaken Germany. Most of these are Jews, who have been stripped of all rights of German citizenship and have fled here in fear of their lives. No doubt you encounter many of the same as they pass through Cheb.

The relief these poor people feel, when they realise they are both welcome and safe in a country which recognises the value of every individual, is a humbling experience for a wretched German such as I. Indeed, sometimes I feel like a refugee myself, and I thank God for Czechoslovakia. Pavel and Karolína my dear friends, I embrace your blessed country with all my heart. The generosity it has shown me in granting me this position at the National Theatre still astounds me. If only the whole world could cooperate as people in the arts do. We put on productions here based on the worth of the work, not the nationality or religion of the writer or composer, (although I am happy to reassure you, Pavel, that Smetana, Dvořák and even Janáček always figure very prominently). It is a great compliment to our country, I think, that Thomas Mann, the greatest German writer of our time, has sought a Czechoslovakian passport to enable him to flee from the horrors of his homeland.

Our own President Beneš is an example to us all. I believe he is doing all he can to tread the same path as Masaryk. I hope you can tell me that the hand of friendship he held out to Henlein in the February Agreement is bearing some fruit around Cheb. He seems to be doing everything possible to calm the tensions in the border areas. Did you hear that President Beneš is coming to the New German Theatre here in January to attend a performance of Wagner's Meistersänger? I can think of no greater sacrifice he could make in the interests of Czech-German reconciliation!

Anna is looking forward very much to Tomáš's arrival in Prague next week for the start of his final undergraduate year. Time seems to be passing so quickly. It does not seem two years since he first came here. My dear friends, I must tell you how privileged I feel to know Anna and Tomáš. Of course, I take a father's natural pride in my beautiful Anna, and an uncle's natural interest in my fine young nephew, but there is something about the two of them together which exists beyond their worth as individuals. I wonder if I can explain it to you, and whether you feel the same. It is the constancy of their love, and their regard for one another which never questions, doubts or challenges. I find it a thing of beauty. I remember Esther telling me once that as soon as they became aware of one another as babies they formed a bond. And now that bond has lasted for more than twenty years.

Now some news of Otto which is both a source of great pride to me and of great sadness. In short, Otto is going to Palestine. Since he completed his doctorate I had hoped he would seek ordination here in Prague, but over recent months Otto has come under the strong influence of an old friend of mine, Max Brod (you remember me talking of Max, I'm sure – it was he who saved Kafka's work and saw it published). Max is a Zionist and believes young men like my Otto are needed to build the new Jewish state. I must admit that privately I had hoped Otto might not get past the quota system the British have imposed recently, but I suppose he is such a good catch. Is it so selfish of me to want to keep him safe by me here? I know our children must fly, but Palestine seems like another world and the stories one hears about the hostility of the Arabs worry me. Opa and Oma Lochowitz insist on paying his passage. He leaves in November.

My final piece of news is of something I would wish to keep from you, were it not inevitable that you would hear it anyway from other sources. I am afraid that Zuzana has left me. I could say that our parting was amicable and mutually agreed, but that would be a lie. Her admiration of German culture, which I realise first led her to me, has now taken her from me. Since we arrived in Prague she has become more and more infatuated with the New Order in Germany. It is true to say that she has been seduced twice; once by Fascism and once more by a young lecturer at the German University, who apparently represents to Zuzana the respectable face of Hitlerism. I regret to say that many of the students and teachers at the German University here are imbued with racialist ideology, whilst I am equally pleased to add that most Germans in Prague remain untainted by it.

I find it quite straightforward to forgive Zuzana for placing her love for someone else above any love she might have felt for me. I do, however, find it impossible to forgive her for joining with a cause which would cast my own children so low. Otto, God bless him, forgives her and professes to understand her. I cannot. My darling Anna still goes to see her Mutti and takes what love she can from her. I shall leave it with you, my dear friends, to decide whether to tell Tomáš about this before he leaves Cheb, or whether you think it best to let him learn it from Anna herself. I cannot think through all the implications at the moment. I only know that Tomáš's arrival will be the very best thing for my precious child. I shall also leave it in your hands to inform pan and pani Štasný, if I may. They may know already, of course, but either way I console myself by knowing they will not lend Zuzana's actions their approval.

You must forgive me if that last statement seems uncharitable. I am anxious that my friendship with you, Kája, and with your wonderful parents, does not make you judge Zuzana more harshly than you otherwise might. We had many good years together and she did her best to care for two children who were not her own. I owe her a great debt for that. Perhaps if I were to search my own heart I should agree to bear most of the blame for the failure of our marriage. For if I look into my heart even now it is not enough of Zuzana I find there, but rather my darling Esther. Perhaps it is I who should hope for people's forgiveness.

I remain, as always, your devoted friend,

Ernst

Cheb, 16th September

My dearest Ernst,

    We received your letter this morning and I have read it a dozen times and still cannot believe what has happened to you. Pavel has gone off to work and Tomáš is visiting friends, so at last I have the chance to sit down and put pen to paper.
    What can I say about my sister? I know you don't want me to apologise for her but I feel I must. Who is this man she has gone to? I wonder if you knew him or how long there may have been something between them. Zuzana has always been so selfish. She speaks and acts without any thought of how she may be hurting other people. Of all the people who do not deserve such treatment, my dear Ernst, you must be the first before any other. I feel so ashamed on behalf of my family. Máma and Táta will be heartbroken. They hold you in such high esteem, as we all do, but none more than I.
    I shall not tell them for the time being and hope we can keep it from them for now. I don't expect for a minute that Zuzana will bother contacting them. Táta has not been well recently. He is 76 now and suffers terribly from arthritis in his hands. It comes from working such long hours out there in the cold. They are finding life quite hard at the moment. The Graf has been demanding rent from them which was never part of the agreement they made. Pavel has asked a lawyer and it appears that my father signed a paper and the Graf owns everything now and can evict them if they don't pay. It's all very worrying for everyone.
    There is also a new law which puts all land within 25 kilometres of the border under military control so going into the forest is now very restricted.

And they say there are arms smugglers out there. Máma is too afraid now to go out picking mushrooms and berries and the like. She really thinks she might get arrested! Poor Máma, I shouldn't joke about it at all. She takes it all very seriously. I know you have more than enough worries of your own, Ernst, but things here in Cheb are really not good.

We are all broken hearted of course by the death of our dear Masaryk. It feels like the death of an old family friend who has always been a part of our lives. Pavel has been wearing a black armband which some Germans don't like at all. Tomáš brought home a copy of the Henlein newspaper, die Zeit, and in it they called Masaryk the great opponent of Sudeten Germans. Pavel was furious and we had to stop him going around to the SdP offices in the old Victoria Hotel to have it out with them. Some of them mumble about his black armband when he passes them in the street but they know Pavel and wouldn't dare say anything to him.

I am so pleased that you continue to enjoy your time in Prague, Ernst. I find it hard to tell from your letter how much this business with Zuzana has set you back. If you want to, please feel able to write to me again about it but only if it suits you. The one thing I am sure you must not do is blame yourself. To all of us you have always been a wonderful husband to Zuzana, and she always knew how happy you and Esther were in the past. I'm afraid Zuzana has acted selfishly like this all her life. I cannot forgive her.

Poor Ernst, so now you have the prospect of Otto going away. I wasn't even sure where Palastine was until Pavel showed me. Will it be possible for you to visit him there? I am sure he will be back in a year or two when he has done what he wants. Is he going to study whilst he is there? I know how much you will miss him because I miss Tomáš so much when he is in Prague. It helps so much to know that you and Anna are there for him. I found what you said about them very touching. I agree with you completely. Esther and I saw it from the very beginning. I used to find it so funny the way they used to talk when they were younger, starting a sentence in Czech and finishing it in German. Or the other way round. They didn't seem to know or care that they were speaking two languages at the same time.

Those carefree days seem such a long time ago. We have hundreds of people arriving here every week now from Hitler's awful Reich. None of the Jews stay here. It is so difficult for them. They get abused in the street. Some of the Germans I have known for years and went to school with behave in a way you wouldn't imagine. They have boycotted the Jewish shops so Zuckermann's and Levinson's have closed down in the colonnade. Even dear old pan Osanec where Esther and I bought our wedding dresses has been forced out. Nearly all the Germans here support Hitler now and are quite open about wanting to be part of Germany. They seem to suddenly be against all of us Czechs and they hate President Beneš. We heard he was planning to visit Cheb as some kind of goodwill gesture, but Pavel says it's not safe any more for him to come here. Everyone knows there are Nazi soldiers coming over the border here, because every now and then one of our soldiers or policemen disappears. It's really frightening to think of Hitler's storm troopers being so close to us here..

I'm sure I don't know where all the hatred here is taking us, Ernst. I even feel nervous speaking Czech when I pass Henlein's people, just as I used to back in the war. Pavel gets very upset by it all. He can be very outspoken as you know too well, and I worry sometimes he may do or say something foolish. He has several German refugees in his class now. Apparently their parents register them as Czech so they don't have to go to German schools where the Henleinist children would bully them. He keeps telling me our President has everything under control and that our treaty with France means there can never be another war, but I still worry, especially about Tomáš. I can't bear the thought of him going through the things you and Pavel went through. I know the war affects Pavel even now. He is going to Prague for the funeral, by the way. He says he would like very much to stay with you and will be in touch to make arrangements. I know he is looking forward very much to seeing you.

I must go now, Ernst. I promised Máma I would call on them this morning. Once more I send my regrets that someone as close as my sister should treat you so shamefully. I am so angry with her. I shall write to you again soon. You know that I always regard you with the greatest affection. Please tell me if there is anything I can do for you.

Your loving friend,

Kája

Chapter Thirty-Nine

May 20th, 1938

"Good afternoon, gentlemen. Thankyou for attending at such short notice. I have called this meeting of the Supreme Defence Committee because of disturbing news we received this morning. The news confirms a report handed to our Head of Secret Intelligence, Colonel Moravec, one week ago. Colonel, could you please inform our colleagues of the contents of that report?"

"Of course, President Beneš. Thankyou."

František Moravec opened a folder lying on the cabinet table in front of him. He sat straight-backed in his chair, with the bearing of a man who had spent more than half of his 43 years as a soldier. His voice was clear and his words precise.

"This report was received from agent A-34 at a meeting with Czech intelligence officers near the border with Germany during the night of 12th May 1938. With your permission, Mr President, I shall read from the report directly."

Beneš nodded his approval.

"The report from agent A-34 states, *'The Germans are preparing a campaign of provocation and sabotage which will erupt on the eve of the Czech local elections. Intelligence from local monitors over the last few days confirms that arms, explosives and munitions have been smuggled across the border into Czechoslovakian territory. Officials of the Henlein Sudeten Party have been instructed to listen regularly to German broadcasts. As soon as they hear an arranged password they are to declare a state of alert. This will be the signal for sabotage: destruction of railway lines, main roads and bridges, and armed attacks on frontier posts and Czech sentries. This action is expected to begin on 22 May. Shock troops, led by high-ranking officers of the SA and SS, and supported by Sudeten German Freikorps and SS troops, will then use the unrest to justify an invasion of Czechoslovakia to protect ethnic Germans.'* Report ends."

All six members of the Supreme Defence Committee sat in silence.

"Thankyou, Colonel," said Beneš. "And your counterparts in Paris and London have received copies of this report?"

"Yes, sir, as you instructed."

"Thankyou. So, gentlemen, I welcome your comments."

"I have only one, Mr President," said General Ludvik Krejči, Chief of Staff of the Czechoslovak Army. "Why have you waited one week before informing us of this report?"

"Because, General, since Hitler marched into Austria two months ago there is not one of us around this table who should be surprised by the information it contains. We all knew this was coming; it was just a question of when. I decided that none of us could be more prepared than we are already. We have been waiting during the past week for any further developments which might confirm its accuracy."

"And are we to assume then that there have been further developments, Mr President," asked General Jan Syrový, Inspector General of the Armed Forces.

"Yes. General. Colonel Moravec, could you inform the Committee, please?"

"Yes, Mr President. As you all know, on 12th May, the day agent A-34 made his report, Konrad Henlein left his headquarters in Cheb on a private visit to London. On his way there he stopped over in Berlin. We learned this morning that this was in order for him to receive his final instructions for the planned invasion, from Hitler in person."

"Good grief. Can there be a single person left who still doubts that Henlein is a puppet of the Nazis?" said Dr Kamil Krofta, the Foreign Minister and one of Beneš's greatest supporters.

"Yes, most of the damned British government," replied Milan Hodža, a Slovak who had been Prime Minister since the last months of Masaryk's presidency. "London and Paris still believe every damn word Henlein feeds them." He brought his right fist down onto the table. "A few good manners and softly spoken promises are all it takes to fool those idiots."

Krejči and Syrový muttered their agreement.

"Please, Prime Minister," said Beneš, looking across at Hodža. "Anger directed at our allies will get us nowhere. We all know our foreign policy is set. Now is the time to remain calm and retain our faith in the British and French. Please continue, Colonel Moravec."

"Thankyou, Mr President. As I was saying, we believe that Henlein was given his final instructions in Berlin for the invasion which is to take place this weekend. We believe now it could even take place tomorrow, the 21st of May. A day earlier than agent A-34 anticipated."

"Good God," said Syrový, "then we must mobilise at once."

"No, General, we cannot..."

"We must at least close our borders," said Hodža.

"Please, gentlemen..."

"And the air force should already be on full alert," said Krejči.

"Gentlemen. Please!" Everyone fell silent and Beneš lowered his voice. "This is precisely the reaction I feared. Strong words will not help us, gentlemen. At this time it is vital that we hold our nerve and act only in conjunction with our allies. We must do nothing alone. I assure you we are in close contact with London, Paris and Moscow..."

"And what are they telling you, Mr President?" asked Hodža.

Beneš put on his reading glasses and cleared his throat. He picked up two sheets of paper from the table.

"We received these communiqués two hours ago from the British and French ambassadors in Berlin. I regret to say, that they do confirm reports of German troop movements towards our borders in Saxony, southern Silesia and northern Austria..."

Moravec and Krofta sat motionless as once again Hodža and the generals demanded action.

"Gentlemen, gentlemen, please... I beg you to show restraint," said Beneš, as the protests continued. "Please. Please... Thankyou. I was about to add that our allies are responding to these reports on our behalf. At this very moment the British ambassador in Berlin, Mr Henderson, is at the German Foreign Office seeking assurances that there are no troop movements."

"This is the same Henderson, is it, Mr President," said Hodža, fixing his eyes on Beneš, "who told us we should emphasise the Nazi dictatorship less, and praise Germany's great social experiment more?"

Again Beneš spoke over the voices raised in support of Hodža. "Yes, it is the same man, Prime Minister, and believe me, I feel the same frustration as you at our allies' unwillingness to confront Hitler. All of us here agree they need to leave him in no doubt that if he touches the Sudetenland it will mean war. But they have chosen the path of appeasement and we have to live with it."

"Yes, and die with it too, if they abandon us."

"Our allies will not abandon us. I assure you all of that."

Beneš looked around the table at each man as he spoke, holding their gaze and addressing each for a few seconds before moving on to the next. "Look, gentlemen, I fully acknowledge the grave mistake the British and French are making in trusting Hitler, but the reality is that we cannot fight and survive without their support. We have France's formal guarantee against German aggression towards us. The French cannot... they will not renege on that. And when France declares, Britain and Russia will follow.

But we must wait for their declaration."

"But it could be too late by then," said Hodža. "We would be overrun before the French get here. They need to spell it out to Hitler now. If he attacks us, they will attack him."

"I cannot make them, Prime Minister," said Beneš. "We are doing all we can. Please tell him, Colonel Moravec."

All eyes turned to Moravec.

"I summoned the British and French military attachés in Prague to my office this morning. I explained to them that we see the German troop movements as a severe threat to our national security, and that they should remind the German government urgently of their guarantees to us. I think it is that which prompted Mr Henderson's approach to the German Foreign Office this afternoon. We are expecting word from the British ambassador in Berlin at any moment."

"But anything any of them say will be meaningless," Hodža protested. "The Germans will lie and the British will believe them."

"I insist you have faith in our allies," said Beneš. "The French and British *will* back us."

"But how can you be so sure? Look at what they did about Austria, Mr President," said Hodža. "Nothing. And what did the London Times report? Line after line about the joy that greeted Hitler and his army. But not one word about Jews being beaten in the street, of being made to scrub the pavements on their hands and knees. Do we want to see the same thing happening here?"

"Of course we all share your disgust at such things, Prime Minister," said Beneš, "but I can only repeat that we must remain true to our allies. The British and French helped us create our country. We must trust them now."

He was relieved to be interrupted, as the door opened at the far end of the cabinet room. Filip Souček approached him with a folded piece of paper.

"At last," said Beneš, "news from the British Ambassador in Berlin."

All eyes remained on Beneš as he read the report.

"It is good news," he said. "Henderson has received the personal assurance of General Keitel, Head of the German Armed Forces Department at the Ministry of War, that reports of troop concentrations on the German-Czech frontier are, and I quote, 'absolute nonsense' and he has given his 'word of honour' that no such thing is taking place."

"It's a joke," laughed Hodža. "They said exactly the same thing about Austria on March 11th, and the next day they were in Vienna."

Kamil Krofta looked at Beneš and saw the strain and frustration on his friend's face. "I do believe, Mr President," he said calmly, "that we need to satisfy ourselves that no moves are being taken against us. We cannot accept the word of a German general over that of a trusted agent. We need Colonel Moravec's section to get us all the intelligence it can before we decide how to react."

"Foreign Minister Krofta is right, Mr President," said Krejči. "If Keitel is bluffing and we do nothing tonight we will have lost any chance of defending ourselves. A partial mobilisation just to bring our border fortifications to full strength will take four hours. A full mobilisation will take eight. If there is a real threat we must act now."

"I understand, General. Thankyou," said Beneš. "What we must also take into account, however, is that even a partial mobilisation by us will be seen by Hitler as an act of aggression. He could use it as his excuse to invade. And both France and Britain will say we provoked him and brought it upon ourselves."

He stood up. "Gentlemen, this is going to be a long night," he said. "Colonel Moravec, please return to your office and bring us all the intelligence you can muster about what exactly is going on. I have asked for some food to be served in my office." He checked his watch. "It is now 18.20. We shall reconvene here at 20.00. At that time, gentlemen, we shall decide what action we must take."

Beneš stood with Krofta at one of the picture windows in the Office of the President, looking out over the River Vltava and the city. They drank coffee, but neither could eat. They both turned as Milan Hodža approached them.

"I do hope, Mr President," he said, "that I did not sound unsupportive in there." Hodža stood facing them with one hand holding the lapel of his dark suit. He was a stocky man, well dressed, with strong features.

"Not at all, Prime Minister," replied Beneš. "These are dangerous times. I need colleagues who voice their opinions openly. I know your views on my choice of allies are genuinely held."

"Our choice of allies is not yours alone, Mr President," said Krofta. "Most of the cabinet support you, as did President Masaryk in his time. You are the odd one out here, Hodža."

"I may be. But what has always worried me, Krofta, is that we share no common borders with France or Britain or Russia. I've always failed to see how they can help us."

"You must know it is the deterrent effect that President Masaryk and I always believed in," said Beneš. "If Hitler attacks us he will be faced with a war on two fronts."

"Yes, I understand that. But the difference between you as a Czech, President Beneš, and me as a Slovak is that you always look west, whilst I prefer to look about me. And I see Poland, Romania and Yugoslavia. I see Slavs who would support one another. I even saw Austria and Hungary as central European allies before the Anschluss."

"So you would have gone to war over Austria, would you?" asked Krofta.

"If we had been in a central European alliance with them it would have been demanded of us. But look at us now. We are faced with a solid Fascist block from the Baltic to the Adriatic. Our border with Austria has no natural defences. We cannot keep Hitler out now."

"What you and I do agree on, Prime Minister, is that we cannot win against Hitler alone," said Beneš. "I firmly believe the only thing that will stop him is the certainty that war with us will also mean war with Britain and France."

"Then all I can say is you must be deeply worried about the position London and Paris are taking," said Hodža. "You must admit, Mr President, they don't seem to be taking our side."

"They want us to make concessions to the Sudeten Germans, that's all. It is just a question of how much we concede."

"But Henlein's last set of demands at Karlovy Vary amount to a separate Nazi state in the Sudetenland. We cannot agree to that."

"Of course, we wouldn't," said Krofta. "You cannot possibly believe we would, Hodža."

"Who knows? The British Prime Minister and Foreign Secretary seem desperate to do any deal they can with Hitler. Chamberlain has already said we should cede some of our territory."

"I agree with you," said Beneš, "that neither Chamberlain nor Halifax has woken up yet to the true nature of Hitler or of Nazism."

"Not woken up? The idiots praise him more often than they ever condemn him. And some of the articles in English newspapers could have been written by Goebbels himself. You know, don't you, Mr President, that the owner of the English Daily Mail exchanges letters with Hitler all the time? He even visits him at the Berghof. He's a bigger Jew-hater than Himmler."

"We know all about Lord Rothermere."

"And Beaverbrook who owns the Express? He's a close friend of the German Foreign Minister."

"We know all about Beaverbrook and Ribbentrop too, Prime Minister. But newspaper proprietors do not make government policy."

"No, but they make public opinion. Most British people are fed the lie that Hitler has a right to our territory."

"I know. But it is important to remember that although Chamberlain and the British press criticise us for not conceding enough, they still say they could not stay out of a war in Europe which involved France. And we still have France's guarantee."

"But Daladier is leaving everything to the British."

"Yes, that is true. France's economic crisis has come at a bad time for us. But the next twenty-four hours will show how much France and Britain are behind us."

"Well, all I can say is I hope you are right about them, President Beneš, and that I am proved wrong," said Hodža. "God help us otherwise."

"Yes, indeed."

Beneš placed his coffee cup and saucer on a side table. Krofta noticed his hand was shaking.

"But would you please excuse me, gentlemen," said the President. "Colonel Moravec should be back soon and I must speak with the Chief of Staff before we reconvene."

Beneš made his way over to Krejčí and Syrový who were standing by the unlit fireplace beneath the portrait of Masaryk. Both men were in their general's uniform and both were remarkably similar in appearance; of medium height, rather stout as they both approached 50 years and both with strong, worn faces. Only the black patch over Syrový's right eye socket distinguished the two men from a distance.

Both had returned from Russia as national heroes; Krejčí for his heroism at Bakhmach Junction and Syrový as the commander of the Legion against the Bolsheviks and at Zborov, where shrapnel had claimed his eye. As the head of the army Krejčí had understood before most politicians the need for changes in the Czechoslovak military. He oversaw the building of the new fortifications and added motorised and armoured divisions to the army. An air force had been created and reservists trained, in order to bring the total strength of the armed forces in war to over one million men.

Syrový and Krejčí were in deep conversation as Beneš approached.

"Gentlemen, may I please interrupt you to put one very important question?"

"Of course, Mr President," the two men said together.

"General Krejči, can you confirm the present fighting status of our men, and tell me again the length of time we could hold out alone?"

"I have no hesitation in repeating, Mr President, that Czechoslovakia has the best trained, best equipped army in Europe. However, our exposure to the southwest along our former border with Austria is my greatest concern. We would now need to deploy most of our armoured divisions there."

"And how long could we hold out?"

"The fighting spirit of our men is second to none, Mr President. I believe it to be as high as our legionnaires in the war. Our only weakness remains numerical. Germany has so much manpower. I believe we could only hold them at our borders for up to three weeks. Employing a tactical retreat, I believe we could fight on in the interior for three or four months as long as the Poles or Hungarians did not move against us. We could last out much longer, of course, if Germany were also engaged on her western frontier."

"Thankyou, General."

Beneš turned as Filip Souček appeared at his side. "Colonel Moravec is here," whispered Souček.

"Thankyou. Show him in." Beneš stepped towards the middle of the room. "Gentlemen," he announced, "Colonel Moravec has returned. We shall reconvene next door."

The six men walked in silence into the cabinet room. They retook their places at the far end of the long polished table. Moravec sat upright in front of his folder. Everyone looked towards him.

"Please make your report, Colonel," said Beneš.

Moravec opened the folder and took a long pause before he spoke. "Thirty minutes ago we intercepted telegraphic reports from the British embassy in Prague to their Foreign Office in London. One report confirms that the 7th and 17th German infantry divisions are advancing in the direction of the Bavarian-Czechoslovak border. Other reports confirm a general movement of German troops in the direction of the Saxony-Czechoslovak frontier."

Krejči and Syrový looked at one another and nodded knowingly. Hodža uttered a loud sigh, and tears filled Krofta's eyes. Beneš did not react.

"Shall I continue, Mr President?" asked Moravec. "There is more."

"Yes. Please. If you will."

"There are reports from reliable sources in Asch, Karlovy Vary and Cheb of low-level flights by Luftwaffe fighter aircraft over Czechoslovak territory. There has been no engagement as of 19.55 hours. Additional reports confirm that members of the British and French Embassy staff in Berlin are preparing to leave, and in Prague it is reported that papers are being burnt at the German Embassy. My report ends."

Everyone looked to Beneš, but he did not speak.

"Mr President," said Krejčí in a calm, strong voice. "We have to mobilise, sir."

"I know, but not a full mobilisation."

"But, Mr President, we will need our reservists..."

"No, General Syrovy. A partial mobilisation only. There is still every chance the French and British will support us. A full mobilisation would be a declaration of war. The British obviously know as much about the German troop movements as we do. We must trust they are acting right now on our behalf. I will not be the one to start a war."

"But you heard the report, President Beneš," said Hodža. "The British and French are fleeing their embassies like rats."

"A partial mobilisation only," said Beneš. "That is what I said and that is what will happen. General Krejčí, can you confirm how many men you need to bring our border defences to full strength?"

"180,000 men, sir."

"How much notice would you need after a partial mobilisation to do that?"

"Four hours, Mr President."

"What else do you advise in the meantime?"

"Short of full mobilisation we should close our borders and put the army and air force on full alert."

"Please do so, General."

Both generals stood up.

"May we be excused, President Beneš?"

"Yes, of course. And you too, Colonel Moravec. Thankyou for your report."

"God, Eduard Beneš, I have known you a long time," said Hodža, when Moravec and the generals had left. "If your faith in the French and British leads to war tonight, may God forgive you. And you Krofta. And Masaryk too, may he rest in peace." He stood up. "Is there anything you want me to do?"

"No, Prime Minster. I shall call you if I need you. Goodnight."

Beneš and Krofta sat together for some time without speaking. When Beneš stood up he realised how rigidly he had been sitting in one position. His whole body ached.

"Come on, Kamil," he said, helping Krofta to his feet. "I would be very grateful for your company tonight, but let us at least allow ourselves to sit this out in comfortable chairs.

Beneš sat opposite his Foreign Minister in front of the fireplace, where he had spent so many hours in conversation with President Masaryk. Krofta could see the effort he was making to hold himself together.

"Don't take what Hodža says too much to heart, Eduard," he said.

"Thankyou, Kamil. But I can speak openly now with you. I can admit that I do not have the faith in the British that I professed tonight to Hodža."

"Perhaps the French will be more steadfast. After all, our treaty is with them."

"Yes, but you and I both know Daladier has abdicated responsibility to the British. There are some British politicians who understand the dangers Europe faces, but Neville Chamberlain is not one of them. He still talks about the Czech problem, not the German problem. He thinks we are the cause of all this, as if we had asked for three and a half million Germans to live within our state."

"But even Chamberlain must understand the problems in the Sudetenland come from Versailles, not from us."

"I think it suits Chamberlain not to remember it that way, Kamil. Hitler is so busy exposing the injustices of Versailles, and Chamberlain and Daladier are so busy nodding their heads at him in agreement, they conveniently forget the hatred they felt towards Germany back in 1918, when our borders were imposed on us."

"Our people understand, Eduard. The country is behind you as much as they were ever behind President Masaryk."

"If ever we needed Tomáš Masaryk, Kamil, I believe it is now."

"He would have handled this just as you are doing."

"Perhaps. But I think if he were still alive it would never have come to this. He commanded so much respect in America they would be at the frontline in our defence tonight."

"But Roosevelt offered the British diplomatic help with Hitler back in January and Chamberlain turned it down. You cannot be blamed for that."

"I know. Sometimes I wonder who is the greater danger to us, the German Führer or the British Prime Minister."

"Let me try to cheer you up, Eduard, with something Jan Masaryk said to me a few weeks ago. Apparently he is often referred to in London as either the Ambassador of Czechoslavia or Czechoslovenia. He says he spends most of his official time in 10 Downing Street explaining to the old man who lives there that Czechoslovakia is a country, not a contagious disease."

Beneš smiled. His handsome features and intelligent eyes were masked by anxiety and tiredness.

"I am sorry I cannot enjoy your story more, Kamil. I fear it is more tragic than comic. Any ideas we had of increasing our influence with the British by sending them the son of the father of our nation seem rather futile now."

"Do you think there is any chance, Eduard, that tonight will come to nothing?"

"I am sitting here saying one prayer after another, Kamil, hoping against hope that something will happen to stop it. But you and I know the reports must be accurate. A-34 is the best agent we have. We know Hitler has his plans ready to invade us. Until tonight we just did not know when. I think of our men manning our borders; and the Czech civilians just behind the front line. They are sleeping tonight not knowing how their lives could be about to change. I sometimes wonder..."

He looked across at his friend, who was ten years his senior and fighting to stay awake. Two and a half years before, on Masaryk's retirement, he had persuaded Kamil to give up the Chair of History at Charles University to become Foreign Minister and support him in the cabinet. Now he regretted placing such a heavy burden upon him.

Beneš opened the door to the anteroom and found Filip Souček still at his desk.

"Are there any messages, Filip?"

"Only from General Krejči's staff, Mr President, confirming that trains have been leaving the city all night. All border defences should be fully manned by regular troops by 02.00 hours."

"And there are no reports of hostilities?"

"Only from Asch and Cheb concerning incidents involving civilians. But nothing from across the border."

"Good. Please keep me informed at any time throughout the night."

"Of course, Mr President."

"And please come and help Dr Krofta into my private quarters, would you? He needs to rest."

"Of course, sir."

When Beneš was left alone he turned down the lights in his office and looked out over Prague. He was shocked to see the city in almost total darkness. Most of the lights in private houses were unlit as was normal at this time of night, but there were no lights either on the Charles Bridge or in the Old Town Square.

And then he understood why. Krejči had ordered them extinguished because of the risk of bombing. The thought of his beautiful Prague destroyed by German bombs made him almost cry out in protest. But at any minute they could arrive, and the families asleep in those houses would be totally unprepared.

Should he have forbidden even a partial mobilisation to save these people from any risk of violence? Better not to fight at all than for people to die and then their country be overrun anyway. Or should he have already mobilised every soldier-citizen with every weapon at their disposal in order to defend themselves against the Nazi monster, now holding most of Bohemia and Moravia in its open jaws?

He paced the room and stopped in front of Masaryk's portrait. What price he would pay to have five minutes in conversation with the man who had always guided him. To see all this through his eyes. He knew Tomáš Masaryk had been at heart a pacifist, but still he had ordered men to fight to fulfil an idea and create this country. Surely he would order them to fight now to preserve it, if it could be preserved.

But what was the essence of Czechoslovakia? Was it only its streets and buildings which would be destroyed by war, or was it the spirit of its people which could only be preserved through resistance to something they detested? Soon, it seemed, others would begin the fighting, and the only decision left to him would be how deeply to immerse his people in it, before he said 'enough'.

"Mr President, are you awake, sir?"

"What..?"

"A communiqué, Mr President, from one of our agents on the border."

"Is it war, Filip?"

"It's still not clear, sir."

"What time is it?"

"05.00 hours, Mr President. You've only been asleep for a few minutes."

"Our soldiers are not sleeping and neither should I. What does it say?"

"There has been an incident in Cheb, sir. Two couriers from Henlein's SdP failed to stop at a roadblock and were shot dead by a Czech policeman. Soon after, there were reports of small-arms fire and explosions. It seems the insurrection by Sudeten Germans has begun."

"Any incursions from across the border?"

"No, Mr President. But it is confirmed that German troops are at the border in force. In Saxony, Northern Austria, Southern Silesia, and now in Bavaria."

"My God. So they do intend to come. Anything from Paris or London?"

"Not as yet, sir."

"Very well, Filip. As soon as you hear anything, bring it to me. I shall not fall asleep again."

"Very well, Mr President."

Beneš went to the window. The sun was rising over the city, offering just enough light to distinguish the terracotta roofs of houses from the slate grey of the civic buildings, and the green and gold of the church domes and spires.

He questioned again his decision not to contact Paris or London during the night to plead for his country. 'No', he reasoned. 'They understand what is happening here as well as we do. One day we have to discover the strength of their commitment to our democracy. We must keep faith.'

Time was neutral in war, he thought. It passed at the same pace for everyone. German planes could appear across the sky, or the phone could ring with news that the British or French had intervened. It was simply a question of who did what first. "Damn the British. And damn the French," he said out loud. Hodža was right. There could be no excuse for the ambiguity they were showing when so much was at stake.

He watched Prague slowly coming to life on this beautiful Saturday morning and decided that its people could not be left at the mercy of such criminal prevarication. If no word came from their allies by 07.00, he would give the order for full mobilisation.

There was a knock at the door. Souček entered.

"News from our people in Berlin, Mr President."

"Quickly, Filip."

Souček read from the paper he held in both hands.

"At 06.00 hours the British ambassador in Berlin sought an emergency meeting with the German Foreign Minister, Herr Ribbentrop. We are informed that at that meeting the British stated that if France honoured its obligations to Czechoslovakia as a result of any aggression by Germany, Britain could not guarantee to stand aside."

"Could not guarantee... What the devil do they mean, 'not guarantee'..? Why can they not make it clear one way or the other? So now they are leaving it to the French. God save us from these fools."

The door to the President's private quarters opened and Kamil Krofta appeared.

"Do you wish to send any acknowledgement, Mr President?" asked Souček.

"Acknowledge the receipt of the message, Filip. No more. In ten minutes I want an update of the situation on our borders."

Souček left, and Krofta came and sat down in an armchair. His kind face was drawn and grey.

"I am so sorry, Eduard," he said. "I fully intended to keep you company through the night. I heard Souček's report."

"I might as well tell you, Kamil, I have decided on a full mobilisation. We have to force the hand of our allies. We cannot go on like this."

"How soon, Eduard?"

"I had decided on 07.00. Since there is at least some diplomatic activity, I shall delay until 08.00."

"Would you like me to contact the French Foreign Minister, Eduard? It seems we need something from them urgently."

"No. Thankyou, Kamil. We shall adhere to the policy we agreed. No pleading. We need to see what our allies are made of. It may as well be today as some time in the future. Besides, Bonnet is an even greater appeaser than Chamberlain."

"It's unthinkable that a great power like France would not fulfil its treaty obligations. It would be the death of diplomacy."

"It would be the triumph of dictatorship over democracy. The end of everything you and I and Masaryk believe in."

The door opened. Souček entered the room. His face was flushed.

"Stay calm, Filip," said Beneš. "Give me your report."

"I beg your pardon, Mr President. News from Ambassador Masaryk in London. The British Foreign Secretary, Lord Halifax, has been in direct contact with Hitler. It seems the British *are* backing us, Mr President. Ambassador Masaryk states, 'Hitler has been informed that the British will not stand aside if there is any precipitate action by Germany'.

Beneš cleared his throat. "Are there any reports from General Krejči?"

"Only to say that there has been sporadic gunfire throughout the night, but no incursions yet into our territory."

"Good."

"Any attack, Mr President, would come about now. An hour or so after daybreak."

"I know, Filip. Please get the general on the phone for me."

"Yes, Mr President."

"If it is war, Kamil," said Beneš, "at least it seems we shall not fight alone."

The phone rang. Beneš answered it and stood by his desk nodding his head, his jaw tightly clenched.

"I understand, General. I understand." He replaced the receiver. "That was Krejči."

Krofta stood up to face him.

"He reports that German troops have been observed dispersing from our borders."

Krofta slumped back into the armchair and put his hands to his face. "Thank God, Mr President," he said. "Thank God. You have delivered us."

Chapter Forty

September 12th, 1938

"What time is the broadcast, Pavel?"

"Seven o'clock, my love. Another fifteen minutes."

Karolína came in from the kitchen. Pavel was sitting in his usual chair by the fire. The light glowed behind the dial of the radiogram but the sound was turned down.

"I thought we bought that for music and entertainment, not for listening to Germans making speeches."

"The whole world will be listening tonight, Kája. Stop walking about and come and sit down."

"I can't sit down. All summer we've lived with this, never knowing if we'll wake up and find Nazi storm-troopers outside our door. It's all too much." She picked up some of Pavel's school papers from the sideboard and put them down again in the same place. "Ever since the May crisis no one ever talks about anything else."

"How could they, Kája, when everything's so uncertain?"

"I hate uncertainty."

"I know you do, my love."

Karolína stopped at the entrance to the kitchen with her back to Pavel. Her head hung forward and she rubbed the aching bone above her left eye with her fingertips.

"This is worse than a nightmare. It goes beyond anything I could ever have imagined, and yet it's all real. Henlein used to come into the shop, you know. And Frank. I talked to them about our family. Ordinary people. Right here in the colonnade. And yet they're traitors. They want to hand all this over to Hitler."

Pavel got up and put his arm around her. "Come on, my love. You know I won't let anything bad happen to us. And President Beneš will do the same for our country. Have faith."

He led Karolína to her chair. Her body quivered, and she stared straight ahead as she sat down. Pavel leaned forward and put her hands in his.

"You and I have both experienced worse than this, Kája, and we got through it. And we were separated then, but now we're together and we have each other."

"And Tomáš. He's all I really worry about. But he was only a baby last time. I knew I could keep him safe. Now he's a reservist... I don't know what might happen..."

"Tomáš will be alright, my love. He's safe in Prague. I keep telling you. He won't have to fight."

"But what about his last letter? About them handing out gas masks? And all the Jews leaving for France and England?"

"The masks are just a precaution, my love, and some people always overreact in a crisis. The main thing is that you and I do not." He looked into her eyes and smiled. "Will you be alright?"

"I suppose so." She smiled back and Pavel felt the tension release from her hands. "But I thought this Englishman they sent over in the summer was supposed to stop another crisis from happening," she said.

"Viscount Runciman, you mean? Chamberlain's mediator?" Pavel sat back in his chair. "What a waste of time he's been. You'll laugh about his latest idea. Or cry."

"What idea?"

"Runciman is apparently so impressed with Henlein's sincerity he actually suggested that Beneš should send him to Hitler as a peace envoy."

"No, Pavel. You're joking. The English can't be that stupid."

"They can. They have no idea what's going on here. Do you know where Runciman spent most of his weekends this summer, when it got too hot in Prague?"

"No."

"With the Graf von Stricker out at Reissig. Apparently most of the SdP people were there, including little Heinrich, of course."

"But he's a Nazi. Everyone knows that. Táta says he saw him again a few nights ago smuggling things through the woods."

"I know."

"I wish you and Táta would stay out of those woods, Pavel. It's not safe. And Táta can't do anything anyway. He can hardly move."

"Michal is a proud man, Kája. He wants to do his bit to help. Germans like von Stricker think they can get away with anything now they have the English in their pocket. But we won't let them. We'll make sure people like von Stricker are answerable to the law."

"Please don't take any more risks, Pavel. I need you with me. I used to hate it here in the war when you were away. The Germans were horrible to us then. I never told you this, but one night near the end all the windows at the front of our house were smashed."

"Why?"

"Because of the rumour you had joined the Russians against Austria. Tomáš and I had to stay away for over a week."

"I never knew, Kája. Why have you never told me?"

"You said we should put it all behind us."

Pavel went over to her and kissed her forehead.

"But the thing is," she said, "I think they hate us even more now than they did then. I don't understand how it's all gone wrong again."

Pavel sat on the arm of her chair. "It's Hitler, Kája. We know the Germans here never liked being governed by us Czechs, but they put up with it whilst things in Germany were bad. Now Hitler has everyone dancing to his tune they want to be part of the glory."

"But whatever we give them never seems enough."

"I know." Pavel stood up and put the back of his hand against the dial of the radiogram. "I think that's exactly what Hitler is telling Henlein to do. To keep demanding more and more and never be satisfied, so he can say how stubborn we are. I heard a very interesting story about President Beneš last week. Do you want to hear it?"

"If you must."

Pavel sat down in his chair.

"Apparently Henlein's people went for a meeting with the President at the castle with more ridiculous demands and Beneš simply handed them a blank sheet of paper. 'Write down everything you want,' he told them, 'and I give you my word in advance that I shall sign agreeing to all of it.' They were thrown completely, of course, and accused him of all sorts of trickery. 'No,' he said, 'I mean it. Anything you want.' They stormed out and complained to Runciman how impossible it was dealing with the Czechs. It just shows you what their real plan is."

"What?"

"Not to accept any agreement or compromise. All they want is a crisis. An excuse to make all this part of Germany."

"There you are, you see." Karolína closed her eyes and tried again to still her anxiety by rubbing the tips of her fingers over her forehead. "What would become of us, if that happened?"

"Don't worry, Kája. It will never happen. It can't. Beneš has secured a ring of allies around us. The English will see sense again, just as they did in May. You wait and see."

In the distance loudspeakers crackled into life and a cheer went up. A chant began. '*Sieg Heil! Sieg Heil! Sieg Heil! ...*'

"That's coming from the main square," said Pavel. He parted the curtains to look out. In the dusk of the September evening he saw only the deserted street and the river flowing under the bridge. He opened the window and the chants flooded the room.

"Close it, Pavel. Close it. I don't want to hear it."

He pulled the window to, drew the curtains and turned the sound up on the radio.

"If you put that on, I'm going to bed," Karolína said.

"But it's only seven o'clock."

"I don't care. I don't want to hear the voice of that madman in my own living room."

"But it's the Nuremberg speech. I told you, the whole world's waiting to hear what he plans to do next."

"I'm sorry, Pavel. You listen if you must, but I've had enough of it. I can't sit through any more of it."

"Alright, my love," he said softly. "You go upstairs or into the back room. I'll keep the sound down and let you know if I hear anything important."

Karolína opened the door leading into the hallway. She turned and attempted a smile as she closed the door behind her. Pavel lowered the volume on the radiogram and sat down in his armchair.

He sat for nearly an hour listening to Hitler's flat stage voice extolling the glorious achievements of the renewed Greater Germany. It was hard to concentrate through the monotony of it. He opened his newspaper. Just as well the audience in Nuremberg was handpicked, he thought, or the Teutonic messiah might have been greeted with a slow handclap by now, instead of the crowd's sheep-like 'Sieg Heils'. He sniggered. It was becoming comic. Each 'Sieg Heil' coming from the radiogram was followed by a slightly delayed and muted 'Sieg Heil' from the idiots in Cheb's main square.

Then, on the hour, Hitler turned to Czechoslovakia. 'That wretched state will not be allowed to sin eternally as it attempts to exterminate our Volksgenossen in the Sudetenland.' He rolled the words around his mouth and let them drift slowly and deliberately out over the crowd.

Slowly the mocking voice changed. It became angry and threatening. The words were being spat out now, sharp and venomous. 'That abnormal structure, that short-sighted enterprise conceived at Versailles, which ravages and rapes a mass of other nationalities'... The pauses became more frequent, and the audience in Nuremberg was no longer being obedient; it could hardly wait for every chance to play its part. Sieg Heil! Sieg Heil! Sieg Heil!

Pavel heard the anger in Nuremberg echoed in Cheb as Hitler's voice became ever more guttural and frantic. *'If these tortured creatures can find neither justice nor help by themselves, then they will receive it from us.'* Now the cheers and chants coming from the radio were drowned out by the noise coming from the town.

'That liar, Beneš, who manipulated the May Crisis to intimidate the citizens and stop the elections, can never count on Germany's moderation again.' Hitler now seemed beside himself with rage and so too were the crowds in Nuremberg and in Cheb. *'That criminal Beneš will learn that a great power such as Germany will not tolerate such a base incursion from him a second time!'*

The chants on the radio carried on and on as the German station manager obviously decided it would be inadvisable to cut them short. *'Ein Volk, ein Reich, ein Führer,'* they came, until Pavel got up and clicked the bakelite dial sharply to the left. The radio faded into silence and in perfect synchronisation the same chant filled the night air beyond the window.

"What's all that noise, Pavel?" asked Karolína from the doorway. "I've never heard anything like it."

"Come in, Kája. It's alright. He's just stirred them up a bit, that's all."

"That terrible chanting, Pavel. It's getting closer."

"They've probably decided to march around the town. I'll just..."

"No, Pavel. Keep away from the window. Don't let them see you. I'm turning out the light."

She came over to Pavel and clung on to him. "What did Hitler say to them to cause this? Has he declared war?"

"No, nothing like that. I knew he wouldn't dare. He knows how we can fight."

The noise of the crowd grew stronger as they reached the end of Krámařská Street. Some were still chanting but many more were screaming abuse at any Czechs who might be listening. Then came the first sounds of breaking glass, followed by cheers.

"Get behind the chair, Kája!"

Pavel pulled Karolína away from the window just as the first rock came through it. The heavy woven curtains billowed as first one rock and then two more fell to the floor behind them. Somewhere in the town the first *crack, crack, crack* of gunfire could be heard. Pavel put his hand over Karolína's mouth.

"Don't scream," he whispered to her.

The sound of breaking glass could be heard further up the street as the mob targeted the next Czech house. As Pavel edged away from the chair another rock bounced off the front door. He crept to the window and peered through a gap in the curtain to see a break-away section of the mob crossing the bridge on the way to Skalka and the woods.

"I think I ought to go and bring your parents here, Kája. They're very isolated out there."

"No. You're not going anywhere, Pavel. I won't let you."

"They've gone from here now, Kája. They'll target shops and government buildings next. I've seen how mobs work."

"Do you really think my parents are in danger?"

"Not really. But it's best if we bring them here."

"Will you be safe?"

"Yes, I know what to do. You stay here in the dark, Kája. No lights at all. Don't answer the door to anyone and stay in the back room. And don't worry about me."

He kissed Karolína. "Get my black winter hat and scarf from the bedroom, my love, and my black walking boots."

When Karolína left the room, Pavel went into the kitchen and took down his toolbox from a high shelf in the corner. From the box he took out the Nagant service revolver he had brought back from Russia. He checked the empty chambers and pulled the trigger. It made a healthy click and returned smoothly. He filled the six chambers, put a handful of bullets in his trouser pocket and put the gun in his waistband. He had just replaced the toolbox when he heard Karolína coming down the stairs.

"Pavel, where are you?"

"I'm here, darling," he said, appearing from the kitchen.

"I thought you had gone."

"No, don't worry. I wouldn't go without telling you. I'll be back soon with Michal and Magda. You just stay here and remain calm."

Pavel put on his boots and coat. He pulled the woollen hat over his ears and forehead and wrapped the scarf around his mouth and nose.

"Lock the door behind me, Kája, and don't worry."

The street was strewn with rocks and glass. Pavel saw a swastika armband on the ground and picked it up. He put it around his right arm, took the gun from his waistband and shoved it into his coat pocket. He hurried across the bridge and along the path to Skalka and the chata.

When he reached the turn-off to the chata, he caught the sweet smell of burning pinewood. He ran down the track towards the lake and saw the reflection of flames on the water and in the trees. At the edge of the clearing he stopped. The chata was a huge fire roaring 20 metres into the night sky. Its carved, painted wood crackled and spat, and the red roof

288

tiles exploded and spiralled out onto the floor of the clearing.

A group of a dozen or so people stood in front of the fire in a neat semi-circle, an audience riveted by the scale of the spectacle. At their feet Magda lay sobbing.

Pavel studied the figures lined up with their backs to him. By their clothing most were civilians. At least two were women. Only four wore the grey uniforms and kepis of Henlein's storm-troopers. He suspected they would be young and inexperienced. To his right, some distance behind the group, he noticed they had left their rifles and a box of grenades unguarded on the ground, keeping them away from the heat of the fire.

Pavel crept towards the weapons. He put two grenades in his pocket and carried the rest with the rifles to the edge of the forest where he threw them into the undergrowth. He walked back, pulling his scarf over his mouth and nose, and approached the group from the side. When the first of them saw him, Pavel waved in greeting.

"Grüss Gott," he said.

"Heil Hitler," replied one of the storm-troopers. It was Heinrich von Stricker.

Pavel took his place amongst the spectators a few steps from Magda, still on the ground, clutching her apron to her face and moaning. He waited a few minutes, studying the fire and nodding his head in approval. He bent down and tried to coax Magda to her feet.

"Leave the old witch down there," ordered von Stricker. "She'll be joining the old man in there in a minute."

"She's spoiling the fun with all her wailing," said Pavel. "I'll put her back here out of the way."

Before von Stricker had time to object, Pavel took Magda by the arms and dragged her to a spot behind the others. He bent down and put his face next to hers. "Magda, it's Pavel. Don't say anything. We've got to get you away from here."

When she seemed unable to take in what he was telling her, Pavel pulled his scarf away from his face. "Pavel," she said. "Pavel." She clung to him and began to cry again. "They beat my Michal. He tried to stop them.... but they killed him..."

"I know, Magda, I know. Can you get to your feet?"

"What the hell are you doing?" von Stricker shouted at him. "Leave the old hag where she is. Who the hell are you?"

"It's Kovařík, the schoolteacher," said one of the civilians. Pavel recognised Alois Krause.

Von Stricker took a step towards Magda. Pavel took the revolver from his pocket, stood up and pointed it at von Stricker's head.

"Step back or I'll shoot you dead, you Nazi bastard," he said. A familiar rush flooded his stomach. It rose into his chest, dried his throat and made blood course to his head.

Von Stricker stepped back. "Get the rifles, Weber," he shouted to a boy to his left.

"They are in the lake, you idiot," said Pavel. "With the grenades."

"He can't shoot all of us if we rush him," said von Stricker, looking quickly around him.

"No, but I can make one hell of a mess of you with this." Pavel took a grenade from his pocket, pulled the pin with his teeth and held the grenade above his head. He spat out the pin and kept one finger on the spring-loaded detonator. "You are going to let Frau Štasná walk away." He stepped towards Magda. "Go on, Magda. Get to our house as quickly as you can. These people won't bother you."

"I can't, Pavel. I can't leave Michal."

"You must, Máma. Think of Kája. She's worried about you. She needs you with her."

Magda got up and stumbled across the clearing. Pavel waited until the sound of her sobbing faded in the woods.

The heat from the fire was beginning to subside, allowing the group of Germans to edge closer towards it, away from the madman.

"I know every one of you," Pavel shouted at them. "Tomorrow when our police and army restore order here, all of you will be arrested for arson and murder, and tried according to the laws of Czechoslovakia."

One of the women started to cry.

"We were only watching. We didn't start the fire."

"This is my family's land," said von Stricker. "All these people have the right to be here. The old man had no right. He's been told often enough to clear out. It was his own fault."

Pavel took a step towards him. Von Stricker retreated.

"You people are wonderful, aren't you? You bully and bluster just like your precious Führer, but as soon as someone stands up to you, you can't back away fast enough."

"Don't think I'm afraid of you, Kovařík," said von Stricker. "One day all you filthy Slavs will be lying in the gutter, while our people walk over you."

"You Germans don't learn, do you, von Stricker? You can strut and bully for a while, but you can't win in the end. Decent people will fight forever to stay free of vermin like you."

Von Stricker laughed. "Do you think anyone will fight for Czechs? You're all *Dreck*. You mean nothing to anyone."

"Germany is in that direction, my brave little Nazis," said Pavel. He gestured with his gun hand towards the border. "If any of you stay in Cheb tonight, I'll see you're put in prison tomorrow, or I'll come to your homes and kill every one of you myself."

Magda arrived at the house by the bridge in a state of collapse. Her clothes were torn and muddy, her legs and arms cut and bloodied, and she was only able to tell Karolína that Michal was dead.

When Pavel finally got home he was relieved to find that Magda's need for her daughter's support had kept Karolína from breaking down too. She seemed able to cope with her father's death when he assured her Michal had collapsed from a heart attack before the fire started. Magda remained in a state of shock, and was too incoherent to tell them what had really happened.

In the morning Pavel went to the police station to report the fire and Michal's death. Karolína made a half-hearted attempt to dissuade him, but she seemed to accept that her job was to care for her mother and it was his duty to see the criminals were punished.

The police station lay on the other side of the square near the theatre. Pavel put on his overcoat and felt the weight of the Nagant in the right-hand pocket. He stepped out into a pleasant September morning and was surprised how quiet the town had become. He had hoped to find the town square full of Czech troops, but instead the whole place was deserted.

Swastikas hung from all the buildings. Broken glass littered the floor of the colonnade, and dribbles of white paint ran down from the daubing on the one window which remained intact. *'Jude'* it said, below a Star of David. But there was no sign of Henlein's storm-troopers, full of their usual self-importance, trying to claim the town as their own. They had melted away.

He walked diagonally across the square past the fountain. The smell of smoke grew more pungent as he reached Provaznická Street, which divided the row of old merchants' houses on the north side. As he walked up the street, the town theatre came into view. Along its elegant façade hung a swastika flag and a banner, *'Ein Volk, Ein Reich, Ein Führer'*. At the end of the street he stopped. To his right he saw the police station, its doors and windows smashed, and further along stood the smouldering skeleton of Cheb's synagogue.

"Pan Kovařík," he heard someone call out. "Can you believe all this, sir?"

Pavel recognised the young man in the light-blue uniform of the Czechoslovakian police. It was Johann Mestan, a pupil of his from five years before.

"Johann."

"Pan Kovařík, I'm the only one left."

Pavel saw tears in his eyes.

"What do you mean, Johann?"

"All the others are dead or missing. Two were killed here. Sergeant Marek was shot at the railway station. And three more went after the arms smugglers out at Skalka. I think they must have been captured and taken over the border."

"Why aren't the army here, Johann? Where is everyone?"

"Haven't you heard? Prague has declared martial law. We should have troops here by early afternoon."

"Where's Henlein's gang?"

"They're all at their headquarters by the station. It's like a fortress over there. There's nothing I can do."

"You're a brave man as it is, Johann, being out here alone in your uniform. Don't throw your life away by doing anything reckless."

"This is the end now, pan Kovařík. This is much worse than May. There can be no going back this time. We have to fight to stop this, or there's no rule of law. I can't even tell you how many civilian casualties there are."

"There's at least one. My father-in-law out at the lake. Von Stricker killed him last night and burnt down his home."

"I'm sorry, pan Kovařík. Pan Štasný was a good man. Everyone knows that. I haven't seen von Stricker this morning, but he's probably with Henlein and Frank just along there. But what can I do?"

"It's best if you and I wait for the army, Johann. Do you know if other towns are as bad as this?"

"I think Asch and Karlovy Vary got it even worse."

Pavel looked over at the synagogue. "At least our Jews got away in time, thank God."

"They wouldn't have stood a chance last night. What I don't understand, pan Kovařík, is why the English are still dealing with these people; still listening to them as if they made any sense. Can you tell me, sir, why they don't support us more?"

Pavel's eyes remained fixed on the synagogue. He did not reply.

"You always taught us to respect France and England, pan Kovařík. You always said our country should copy..."

"They *will* stand by us, Johann. When they hear about all this, they will have no choice."

Pavel turned to face the young man. He watched his former pupil kick away pieces of glass from the bloodied steps of Cheb's police station.

"Our allies backed us in May, Johann," Pavel said. "And I'm telling you, they'll back us again now."

In the early afternoon Czechoslovak troops entered the town and broke into the SdP's fortress headquarters next to Cheb station. They found it empty.

Two days later Henlein and his deputy, Frank, reappeared in Bavaria with Heinrich von Stricker, who had fled across the border in the night. Giving up all pretence at last that he was independent of Hitler, Konrad Henlein left behind in Cheb a proclamation to his fellow Sudeten Germans.

'We wish to live as free Germans! We wish to return to the Reich! God be with us.'

Realising his mission as a mediator was now pointless, Viscount Runciman also left Czechoslovakia. On his return to London he submitted his written report on the situation in the country for the attention of Prime Minister Chamberlain and the British Cabinet.

At the end of his report he stated that in the Sudetenland he had seen evidence of Czech colonists settled on land confiscated from the German population. Czech schools, he wrote, were built for the children of these *'Czech invaders'.*

'The rise of Nazi Germany,' he concluded, *'has given the Sudeten Germans new hope. I regard their turning for help towards their kinsmen, and their eventual desire to join the Reich, as a natural development in these circumstances.'*

Chamberlain was unable to read the report immediately. The day before Runciman returned, the British Prime Minister had flown from London to Germany in order to meet with Adolf Hitler at Berchtesgaden. His aim, he told the waiting press, was to find a solution at last to the problem of Czechoslovakia.

Chapter Forty-One

September 19th, 1938

The black Rolls-Royce Phantom 111 swept across Charles Bridge and climbed the narrow cobbled streets leading to Prague Castle. The two passengers in the back looked straight ahead and did not speak.

Guards in the uniform of the Czechoslovak Legion in Russia stood to attention at the entrance of the castle as the Rolls-Royce passed them. The car came to a halt in an inner courtyard where the two passengers, both dressed in morning suits and carrying attaché cases, were met by Filip Souček.

In his office President Beneš watched their arrival from a window. He returned to his seat behind the presidential desk, which had been repositioned in order that his two visitors would sit throughout the meeting beneath the gaze of Tomáš Masaryk.

Beneš stood up as the two men were announced.

"Their Excellencies the British and French Ambassadors, Mr President," said Souček, in a voice louder and flatter than usual.

Beneš stepped forward and offered his hand to each man in turn. "Please take a seat, gentlemen." He indicated the two upright chairs in front of his desk.

Basil Newton and Victor de Lacroix sat down without speaking. Newton's thin face was as pale as de Lacroix's was flushed. The Frenchman seemed close to tears. Neither of them looked at Beneš as he spoke.

"So, gentlemen. What news of Mr Chamberlain's meeting with Herr Hitler in Berchtesgaden?"

"President Beneš," said Newton in a tone suggesting arrogance, rather than the confidence he had hoped for. "I have here the conditions of the Anglo-French Plan for the settlement of the Sudeten-Deutsch problem."

"Surely, Ambassador, you mean you have the proposals?"

"Unfortunately not, President Beneš. The British and French governments have decided it is impossible for the districts mainly inhabited by the Sudeten-Deutsch to remain within Czechoslovakia without imperilling the interests of Czechoslovakia herself, and of Europe."

"And what do our allies therefore suggest?"

"That in order to maintain peace, and to secure Czechoslovakia's vital interests, the territory in question should be transferred to the German Reich forewith."

Beneš fought to keep his voice calm and measured.

"And how will you determine which parts of our sovereign territory you will present to Hitler, and when would any transfer take place?"

"This could be effected either by plebiscite or by direct transfer. The British and French governments favour the latter. It would include all areas with over 50 percent of German inhabitants."

"I see. And would Czechoslovakia's democratically elected government have a say in any of this?"

"Where necessary, frontier revision would be negotiated by some international body, which included a Czech representative."

"You are saying that our only involvement will be in the mutilation of our country? We shall have no say in trying to preserve it?"

"The British government is willing to join in an international guarantee of the new boundaries of the Czechoslovak State against any unprovoked aggression."

"But surely we already have such a guarantee relating to our present borders, do we not, Ambassador de Lacroix?"

De Lacroix broke down in tears. "*Je ne sais pas. Je ne sais pas.* The British and French governments do this together…"

Beneš turned to Newton, who was shuffling his papers.

"Your country supported us in May, for which I remain grateful," said the President, "but after a summer dealing with your Viscount Runciman, I am no longer surprised, Ambassador Newton, that the British are deserting us. You British love the underdog, and here you think the underdogs are the Sudeten Germans, but you are wrong. There is only one victim in all this."

He looked at de Lacroix, who shielded his eyes with his right hand.

"Do you not realise that what your governments suggest will leave 800,000 Czechs living under Hitler's dictatorship?"

Beneš found his words had a greater impact on himself than on his visitors. He struggled to catch his breath.

"Do you not understand the nature of this man? He hates us Slavs. You are stripping away all our border defences. We shall lose all means of protecting ourselves against him."

"You will have our guarantee of your new frontiers," said Newton.

"But what you have said here today, Ambassador, makes your guarantees worthless, does it not?"

Beneš waited for a response but none came.

"Do neither of you realise how our people have looked up to your countries? We Czechoslovaks have created our democracy in the image of France and Britain and America. We are a sovereign state with a treaty with France enshrined in international law. Coming here today with your conditions denies that and shames you both."

Beneš looked towards the French ambassador.

"At least Monsieur de Lacroix recognises his country's shame."

"We are here today to preserve the peace of Europe. Nothing less," insisted Newton.

"You are here today to save yourselves by sacrificing 12 million Czechoslovaks to a dictatorship. To pretend otherwise is a deception that only discredits you further."

"I must protest..."

"No, Ambassador, it is we who protest. Our country is nothing but an inconvenience to you British and French. You want to close your eyes to what we are, a democracy menaced by a totalitarian state which means to destroy us. We look to you now to support the principles of freedom we thought we shared with you, to stand up for the ideals which should bind us."

"We need to know if you will accept the Anglo-French Plan," persisted Newton. "Prime Minister Chamberlain has another meeting with the German chancellor the day after tomorrow. We need to know now."

"I'm not sure any more how democracy works in your country, Ambassador Newton, but you need to understand that when you deal with me, you are dealing with a constitutional president, not a dictator. I can agree to nothing without consulting my Government and Parliament. I shall do so as time permits."

Beneš stood up. He caught Newton's eye at last, but the British Ambassador quickly busied himself with his attaché case. De Lacroix still sat with his hand over his eyes.

"I shall detain neither of you any further," the President said.

On the way back to their embassies Newton and de Lacroix passed small groups of bewildered people gathered around the stalls of Prague's newspaper vendors. The terms of the Anglo-French Plan had been leaked by an official at the French Embassy and were now appearing in late editions of the main local paper, the *Lidové noviny*. *'Unacceptable'* ran its banner headline.

Total strangers turned to one another in the street and voiced their anger and frustration at the British and French betrayal. By the statue of St Cyril and St Methodius on Charles Bridge Tomáš and Anna stood with a group of people reading the latest news.

"It's unbelievable," said Tomáš. "Unbelievable..."

"What will Babička and Děda do? And your parents?"

"I'm worried about them, Anna. Not a word from any of them for over two weeks."

"Don't worry too much, darling. I'm sure Uncle Pavel will keep them all safe."

"It's him I'm worried about most. He had such faith in the French. He won't find this easy to take."

"We can never agree to the Plan anyway. It says here we would lose all our defences, and most of our factories."

"It will be war if we don't."

"Then it will have to be war. I'd fight if they let me."

"Well said, young lady," came a voice from behind them. "We stood up to them in May, and we'll do it again."

Murmurs of approval spread through the small crowd.

"Come on," said Tomáš, "let's go over there. Before they make you a general."

Anna and Tomáš walked to the other side of the bridge and stood at the parapet with their arms around one another.

"Everything has been going so well for us," said Anna. "My set designs for Figaro, and it looks as if you might have found a publisher at last. I don't want anything to change."

"Neither do I, darling."

They looked upriver towards the National Theatre and the Legion Bridge. The bright September sun setting over the wooded side of the valley to their right forced their gaze down onto the water.

"If you are called up, do you think you can ask to be sent somewhere near Cheb? I could stay close to you then," said Anna.

"I don't know. Reservists are treated the same as regulars. We have to go where they order us."

"I really would fight with you, Tomáš, if they'd let me."

"I know you would, darling Anna, but I would rather know you're safe here with your father."

"I shall have to do something. I'll drive an ambulance... anything. I know Vati will want to help too."

"Your father has nothing to prove." Tomáš took the newspaper from under his arm and showed Anna the front page. "No one associates decent

Germans like your father with this maniac."

"I don't know what it says, silly," she said, nudging him gently. "It's all in English."

"I was showing you the photograph of Hitler."

"Why is he on the front page of the Da....i....ly Ma....il?"

"The Daily Mail, silly socks. They think they've got a scoop. Their reporter in Berlin managed to get an interview with Hitler a few days ago."

"I wouldn't buy their stupid newspaper."

"I just want to see what the English are being told about everything, that's all."

"What does it say then? Translate a bit for me."

They both turned and leaned back against the parapet."

"It says, *'The Führer spoke in a tone of grim determination as he stated that this Czech trouble has to be ended once and for all.'* 'Czech trouble', that's rich... *'The Führer described it as a tumour which is poisoning the whole European organism.'* Cheeky swine... *'He protested that to set an intellectually inferior handful of Czechs to rule over minorities belonging to a race like the Germans, with a thousand years of culture behind them, was a work of folly and ignorance.'* My God..."

"But surely the English don't believe anything like that, do they?"

"I never thought so, Anna. Never. But now I'm not so sure."

Soon after Newton and de Lacroix left the castle, President Beneš called a meeting of his ministers, the leaders of the six coalition parties, and the chiefs of staff. They sat through the evening in the cabinet room discussing the Anglo-French Plan.

All had expected a German demand for autonomy in the Sudetenland, but none had expected their closest allies to demand the richest, best defended part of Czechoslovakia be handed over to a dictator who craved the complete destruction of their state.

"They are parents handing their young child to a ravaging monster," said Kamil Krofta, "so they might rest undisturbed."

The meeting continued throughout the night and into the following morning. Word reached the British and French embassies that only two options were being considered at the castle. Outright refusal or a call for arbitration. Both of these options, agreed Newton and de Lacroix, would mean a German invasion within hours.

Rumours spread quickly onto the streets of Prague. War had been declared. A full mobilisation had begun. German bombers were minutes away from Prague.

At seven forty-five in the evening Newton and de Lacroix were summoned back to the castle for a meeting with Czechoslovak Foreign Minister Krofta, who handed them the government's decision. The Anglo-French Plan was rejected. As Newton huffed and de Lacroix stared blankly through sore eyes, Krofta gave the reasons for the rejection.

His government had not been consulted, he said. The plan would not ensure peace. Acceptance would make Czechoslovakia unviable as an independent state, and the approval of Parliament would be needed for such a drastic revision to the country's borders to be constitutional. France, he reminded de Lacroix, had firm treaty obligations to Czechoslovakia. The whole matter, he concluded, should be placed before an international commission for arbitration.

Beneš went to bed that night for his first hours of sleep in two days. At 2 o'clock in the morning he was woken by Filip Souček.

"Mr President, the British and French ambassadors are here. They are demanding to see you, sir."

Beneš dressed quickly and made his way to his office. Newton and de Lacroix stood as he entered.

"Follow me, gentlemen," Beneš said, and he strode past them into the cabinet room. On the long oval table he spread out a large map of his country.

"Am I right in thinking, gentlemen, that your masters in Paris and London have sent you here at this hour to insist that we accept the Anglo-French Plan?"

"Yes, President Beneš," said Newton. "Your present position will lead to war as soon as Herr Hitler hears of it."

"I see. Before either of you says anything else, I want you both to listen to me. Firstly, I shall warn you once again that with Hitler you are dealing with a bully. If you give him what he wants now, you will destroy my country, shame yourselves, and still you will one day have to stand up to him. Like all bullies he will prey on your weakness until you show a willingness to fight. Show that willingness now and he will back down."

"We don't have time..."

"Do not dare to say to me, Ambassador Newton, as you plot the destruction of my country, that you do not have time."

Newton shuffled his feet and looked up at the ceiling.

"Now, I would like you, please, to look at this map of my country. You will notice these mountains which afford us a natural defence along our border with Germany. Throughout these mountains and forests we have constructed our fortifications. It is our own Maginot Line, Ambassador de Lacroix, built with the help and advice of your countrymen, our dearest ally. This is considered to be the strongest defensive line in Europe.

"Here, here and here lie our lignite and coal mines and most of our heavy industry. You are asking us to give it all away, along with close to a million of our citizens who must either move away from their homes and workplaces, or be swallowed up by a regime which detests them.

"Now, gentlemen, say what you need to say, but be in no doubt of the consequences for us if you renege on your obligations."

"I believe the British and French governments share the same position in this matter, President Beneš," said Newton. His eyes moved from the floor to the side wall to the ceiling and back again. "If your government continues to reject the Anglo-French Plan and armed conflict ensues as a result, the British government will not be able to offer you any assistance."

"I see. And is that your government's position also, Ambassador de Lacroix?"

"I regret, Monsieur le Président, that if you reject, we hold you solely responsible. *La France ne s'y associera pas.* "

"So, now we know once and for all where you both stand," said Beneš, as he rolled up the map. "As you know, I must consult my ministers and parliamentary representatives. You will hear from us later today."

"Not too late, I beg of you, President Beneš," said Newton, as he turned to leave. "Prime Minister Chamberlain is meeting Chancellor Hitler tomorrow to give him your response."

Beneš was about to reply, but paused. "Before you go, Ambassador Newton," he said. "Can you confirm something for me?"

"I will try."

"If we were to agree to the Anglo-French Plan, you are certain the British and French will guarantee our new borders against any further aggression?"

"Without question. If you agree to the Plan, nothing more could be asked of you."

"And the areas to be ceded are only those with a 50 percent German population or over? If we agree to that, no more territorial demands will be made of us?"

"Absolutely," said Newton, at last looking Beneš in the eye. "You have my government's word on it, sir."

"Thankyou. Then I shall meet with the cabinet and inform you of our decision later today. Good morning, gentlemen."

Within two hours Beneš had assembled the full cabinet and chiefs of staff at the castle. There was anger at the 'cowardice', 'treachery' and 'duplicity' of the French and British, and from all sides came opposition to acceptance.

General Syrový called upon the spirit of the Legions to once again overcome seemingly insuperable odds. "Czechoslovak legionnaires amazed the world with their fighting prowess," he said. "Now our soldiers and aviators are equipped with the best armaments of any nation in the world. Škoda guns and Avia and Aero fighters and bombers. Let our men fight for the honour of their nation."

General Krejčí agreed, but was more pragmatic. "However brave our soldiers and airmen are, and however resilient our citizens prove to be, we cannot win alone against such overwhelming odds. But what we can do is win the admiration of the entire world as we did in 1918. By holding out long enough in our fight against tyranny, we can shame our allies to the west and to the east into coming to our aid."

Below the castle in the streets of Prague normal life was suspended as people waited to hear their government's decision. The traffic stopped, shops closed, workplaces and schools emptied. Citizens milled around the streets and squares, waiting hour after hour to learn their fate.

In the cabinet room discussions continued throughout the morning and into the afternoon. After each speaker Krofta looked across at Beneš expecting at any moment some intervention from him. But the President stayed silent until by late afternoon every opinion but his had been heard. Finally at three o'clock he spoke.

"I thank you all, gentlemen, for your open and honest opinions on the most grievous crisis our young democracy has had to face. I think my proposal regarding our way forward will surprise and even shock you. I therefore ask for a chance to explain it fully before you respond."

He looked around the table.

"Gentlemen, I believe it is in our best interests to accept the Anglo-French Plan."

Beneš did not get the chance to explain his decision as voice after voice was raised against him. He waited until the last dissenter had stopped before he continued.

"Your reaction does not surprise me, gentlemen. Please allow me to explain my reasoning.

"General Syrový states, quite rightly, that it is not only the territorial integrity of our country which is at stake, but also its moral integrity. If we reject the Plan we may well lose the war, he says, but we shall retain our moral integrity as a nation. I applaud his bravery, but I also realise that, however courageously we fight, the advantage Germany has, and has always had, over us Czechs and Slovaks in terms of numbers and resources means we can never win alone.

"I believe that General Krejči's proposed strategy is a very good one. He suggests we fight alone, as fiercely as only Czechs and Slovaks can fight, and we shame our allies into supporting us. I believe it is this strategy which our citizens want and expect from us now. But I have looked into the faces of the French and the British, gentlemen, and I must tell you they will not support us if we reject this Plan and fight Germany alone, for these French and British governments cannot be shamed.

"No, gentleman, I have another strategy. We know Hitler means to take over our country, whatever concessions we or our allies make. We understand the Teuton attitude to the Slav. We have lived with it for centuries. The Russians, the Poles, the Serbs try to fool themselves, but in their hearts they know it too. The British think they can negotiate with Hitler, but we know him. We Slavs know we shall have to fight him sooner or later. The important thing, the crucial thing, is that we do not fight alone."

"But we cannot make the bastards fight with us," said Hodža from across the table.

"But I believe we can, Prime Minister. If we accept their Plan, I believe we can. Let me explain. The Plan is outrageous in what it asks of us, and that is what we can exploit. Even the British and French realise how outrageous the demands are and that no reasonable person could ask any more of us. Our willingness to accept it will retain their support.

"Chamberlain will go to see Hitler tomorrow to deliver the Anglo-French Plan agreed by us, believing it to be the end of Hitler's demands. I know the English. Chamberlain sees himself as an upper-class gentleman instructing an uncultivated German in the ways of diplomacy. He does not realise that Hitler has no respect for agreements and will always ask for more and more from us Slavs. When Hitler tells Chamberlain the Plan is no longer enough, diplomacy will break down. There will be war, but the British and French will be with us again."

"But what if Hitler doesn't ask Chamberlain for more?" demanded Hodža.

"We know he will. We have intelligence which tells us that yesterday Hitler had secret meetings with the Polish ambassador and the Hungarian Prime Minister at the Berghof. He did a deal with them both. If they remain neutral over the Sudetenland, Hitler has promised Teschen to the Poles and Southern Slovakia to the Hungarians. We expect Chamberlain to be told this tomorrow when he meets Hitler. The Plan will then be dead, and we shall regain our allies' support."

"But what if Chamberlain accepts the concessions to Poland and Hungary?"

"I do not believe even Chamberlain could be that dishonourable."

"But if he does?"

"Then, gentlemen, we shall fight alone."

When the government's decision to accept the Anglo-French Plan was finally announced in the late afternoon, armed guards were placed outside the British and French legations.

They were not needed. The reaction of the crowds in Prague, as news filtered down from the castle, was not one of anger, but rather of shock and sadness that the fine ideals of Masaryk and Beneš had been betrayed so cruelly by their allies.

Tomáš and Anna stood silently in a crowd of thousands in Wenceslas Square, watching loudspeakers being fitted to the lamp-posts, ready for a broadcast by the President at seven o'clock that evening. Some people were crying, a few raged, but most stared about them with a look of confusion and disbelief on their faces, unaware of the gamble behind their president's decision, and waiting for some explanation and guidance.

"We must get the train to Cheb tomorrow, Tomáš," said Anna. "We must make your parents and Babička and Děda leave before it's too late."

"But the Nazis won't take over right away. There's bound to be some sort of transition period."

"I don't care. I want to go tomorrow. Before it's too late."

Tomáš looked at Anna as she raised her head to watch the men fixing the speakers. Even at this terrible time her nearness made him happy. She was full of courage and life. She must be the only Czechoslovak, he thought, whose plan tomorrow was to go to the Sudetenland.

"They've got them working," she said. "What's the time?"

"Two minutes to."

The speakers crackled. In the middle of the crowded city there was complete silence. Then a voice, not the President's, was heard explaining the events of the past two days.

"Now you will hear a short message from the President of the Republic," the voice said finally.

There was a pause and Beneš spoke.

"My fellow countrymen and countrywomen, your government has been forced to make a decision which we all find intolerable. I shall not go further into the details now. They will become clearer over the coming days. Now I ask you only to keep faith in your government's decision. We had no choice, fellow Czechoslovaks, because we were left alone. We have been disgracefully betrayed."

Beneš's voice seemed to crack. There was another, longer pause. Tomáš could feel the crowd willing the President to continue.

"History will pronounce judgement on the events of these days. Let us have confidence in ourselves. Let us believe in the genius of our nation. We shall not surrender. We shall hold the lands of our fathers."

At the end of the President's address people in the crowd applauded politely, but everyone seemed too numbed to show any stronger emotion. Without any instruction or suggestion the whole mass of people turned and, as if directed by a collective will, walked solemnly towards the Charles Bridge and the castle.

Anna and Tomáš walked hand in hand.

"I don't understand, Anna. Why did the President say, 'We shall hold the land of our fathers'? That sounds as if we are going to fight. It doesn't make sense."

"I don't know, darling. I can't think at the moment."

When the procession reached the top of the narrow, cobbled Nerudova Street leading to the castle square, their way was blocked by a cordon of state policemen. Everyone stopped and waited. There they stood, shop assistants, students, workers in overalls, office workers carrying briefcases, and parents with their children.

They began to sing the national anthem, *'Where is my Home?'*, and the cordon of policemen stepped aside and mingled with them, as the people made their way into the square. There they stayed for hours, singing, willing their President to gain strength from their presence, until around midnight they drifted away, back to their homes.

The next morning Anna and Tomáš made their way again to Wenceslas Square. A government announcement would be broadcast at 10 o'clock.

"I don't like this, Tomáš. These people. It feels different somehow."

"I think it's the strike. They're angry. They want something to be done."

"I wish they would stop pushing. It wasn't like this yesterday."

"It's nearly ten, darling. They'll settle down in a minute."

"Stop pushing me," Anna shouted at the people behind her.

"Citizens of Prague," came a voice from the speakers. *"There will now follow an announcement from the Office of the President."*

There was instant silence. All movement stopped.

"At nine o'clock this morning Prime Minister Hodža handed to the President his resignation and the resignation of his government. In its place the President has appointed a Government of National Defence, which will have no party affiliations. The Government of National Defence will be led by General Jan Syrový. General Syrový..."

As soon as the crowd heard Syrový's name their cheers drowned out the rest of the announcement. Anna pulled Tomáš towards her to shout into his ear.

"Your father talks about him, doesn't he?"

She turned her head to allow Tomáš to shout back.

"Yes. He led them in Russia. He's a real fighter."

"Good. At last."

The crowd fell silent again as Syrový's voice came over the speakers.

"I guarantee that the Army stands and will stand on our frontiers to defend our liberty to the last. I may soon call upon you here to take an active part in the defence of our country, in which we all long to join."

A cheer rang out throughout the city as people at last rid themselves of their anger and disappointment and fear.

"There you are, Anna," shouted Tomáš. "I was right. We are going to fight."

"But it doesn't make sense, Tomáš. We have accepted the Plan so surely there will be no fighting."

"I don't know, Anna. All we can do is what my father always says, trust our President. He knows what he's doing."

Chapter Forty-Two

September 25th – 28th, 1938

Jan Masaryk left the Czechoslovakian Embassy in Grosvenor Square and set off on the two-mile walk to Downing Street.

He was well known in the Mayfair 'village', and many of the people he encountered when out walking took the trouble to greet him. Recently he thought he detected a note of sympathy in the way some spoke, while with others he was equally sure he detected embarrassment, or perhaps disapproval, in the way they regarded him.

Masaryk loved London. He felt more at home here than anywhere else, even Prague. The hectic pace calmed his restlessness, and the busy social life fed his need for conviviality and culture. It pleased him that his embassy had become a popular meeting place for the diplomatic community, and that his own piano recitals attracted an even wider circle from the world of cinema and theatre.

If he had stayed in Prague he knew the helping hand of his father would have been seen in anything he might have achieved there. Here in London he lived under no one's shadow, and it was due to his efforts alone that London society viewed Czechoslovakia through its embassy in Grosvenor Square as a place of wit, charm, erudition and culture.

The loss of his father one year ago had been a double blow to him. His pride in his country and his love for his father had always fed one another. Through his success as Czechoslovakia's ambassador in London he had been able to gain the approval of the great man, both in his formal role and as his son. It was the greatest disappointment to him that since his father's death the relationship between London and Prague had deteriorated so much.

"All the best to you, Your Excellency," said the doorman at the Connaught Hotel touching the brim of his top hat. "We all wish you luck, sir."

"Thankyou, Harry," replied Masaryk. "We live in hope." He raised his homburg and smiled.

Masaryk continued along Mount Street towards Berkeley Square. He undid the two top buttons of his overcoat and pushed the fur collar away from his neck. It was a beautiful Sunday afternoon and he was anxious not to appear hot and flustered when he arrived for his meeting with the British Prime Minister.

The day had all the hallmarks of a Sunday. The shops and offices were closed, and in the distance church bells rang. But the pavements were unusually busy and everyone walked with a sense of purpose. On the opposite side of the road a long queue stretched towards the entrance of Farm Street Church, which for today had been transformed into an Air Raid Precaution Centre.

The people of London were collecting their gas masks.

When Masaryk reached the bottom of Berkeley Street he crossed Piccadilly. To his left the windows of the restaurant and cocktail bar of the Ritz were being boarded up. Outside Green Park tube station a notice advised travellers of a 'temporary closure for repairs'. Masaryk guessed the truth. London's underground stations were being readied for use as air-raid shelters, as Chamberlain's government prepared for war.

Beneš had been right about the outcome of Chamberlain's second visit to Hitler at Bad Godesberg. The British Prime Minister had arrived with the Czechoslovakian President's signature on the Anglo-French Plan and dutifully delivered it to Hitler, who promptly told him it was no longer enough. Just as Beneš had predicted, Hitler demanded additional territory for Poland and Hungary, and insisted the Sudetenland be evacuated and handed over to Germany no later than the first day of October. If not, German forces would march in and take it. The Anglo-French Plan was dead, and the days to Hitler's deadline were counting down.

"Fleet mobilises," shouted the newspaper vendor outside Green Park. Jan Masaryk handed him thrupence for a copy of the Sunday Times. The British had mobilised the Royal Navy on Friday evening, followed by France's partial mobilisation of its monolithic army. In Prague, at 10 o'clock on the same evening, General Syrový had announced a full mobilisation of Czechoslovakia's army and air force, which within four hours had put one million men in the field. War was coming, Masaryk knew well enough, but Czechoslovakia, thank God and President Beneš, had France and Britain with them again.

Chamberlain had arrived back in London only yesterday with Hitler's new demands in his pocket. 'The Godesberg Memorandum' people were calling them. Masaryk had been informed officially of the contents of the Memorandum in the afternoon and knew at once that Beneš's gamble had paid off. No reasonable person could expect Czechoslovakia or its allies to accept Hitler's new, humiliating terms, demanding territorial concessions to Poland and Hungary and delivered with the threat of invasion.

Masaryk had immediately contacted his friends on the government's back benches, Leo Amery, Winston Churchill and Anthony Eden, the greatest critics of the government's policy of appeasement. He had intended to plead for their help in opposing acceptance of the Memorandum, but there was no need. They were as furious as he was at Chamberlain's willingness to indulge Hitler and his increased demands.

"I do not see how a British Prime Minister can forward such terms to a friendly government on behalf of a dictator," Churchill had said to Masaryk.

But forwarded they were. Only eighteen hours ago Ambassador Newton had handed the terms of the Memorandum to Foreign Minister Krofta at the castle. And now Masaryk was walking through Green Park with his government's reply in his pocket.

The park was full of workmen, which seemed so incongruous on such a pleasant Sunday afternoon. And what they were doing seemed incongruous too; defacing the grass, cutting long ugly trenches through it, and in three areas excavating huge pits, probably to build air-raid shelters, thought Masaryk, or something much worse. A dozen lorries were parked on the lawns, and planks and building materials were strewn over flower beds, scrutinised by a lone park keeper, who stood with hands on hips.

Similar work was going on in St James' Park, and anti-aircraft batteries were being set up on either side of the lake there. Masaryk reached Horse Guards Parade and stopped for a moment to catch his breath and compose himself. The clock on Big Ben said ten past three. His meeting with Chamberlain was at a quarter to four. He felt the inside pocket of his jacket again for the document he carried from his government.

He was not nervous. His breathlessness came from the despair he felt at the sight of a city preparing for war, knowing the same things would be happening today in Paris and in Prague. And he felt anger too, towards the Germans for making everyone go through this again, and towards the man he was about to meet for not seeing his weakness towards Hitler was making war more likely, not less.

He walked along Parliament Street. In front of him he saw a group of fifty or so people at the entrance to Downing Street. When they saw the dapper figure approaching, they cheered. "Stand by the Czechs," they shouted. "Good luck, Mr Masaryk sir," said someone as he came closer. Masaryk stopped next to him and shook his hand. "Thankyou. My country is very grateful for your support," he said. Above them a single Hurricane fighter patrolled the skies over the city.

Masaryk followed one of Chamberlain's personal secretaries up the grand staircase to the Prime Minister's study on the first floor. Chamberlain got up and nodded as Masaryk entered, and then waited for him to sit down in a winged-back armchair. Chamberlain retook his seat opposite. Between them stood a low coffee table on which were placed a jug of water and two glasses.

Masaryk had been in the room many times during his 13 years as Prague's ambassador in London, and had enjoyed many conversations in front of the hearth with Ramsey MacDonald and Stanley Baldwin. He was yet to enjoy a single conversation with the austere Chamberlain during the 15 months of his premiership.

Chamberlain looked exhausted, which was hardly surprising for a man of 70 who had spent most of Friday night trying to negotiate with Hitler, and then most of the 24 hours since his return to London in one hostile meeting after another. His grey hair and thick grey moustache were matched by the pallor of his face, but his eyes remained piercing and he retained the half smile which always made him look so pleased with himself.

Masaryk waited for him to speak. When he showed no sign of wishing to do so, Masaryk took out the letter.

"I bring my government's formal reply to the Memorandum presented to them by your government and the government of Germany," he said.

Chamberlain took the letter and read it. He put it down on the table in front of him. "This is as I feared, Ambassador Masaryk," he said in a pained voice. "It is a great disappointment to me that your government fails to see the broader picture."

"We see the picture very clearly."

"I rather think you do not. You fail to understand the need, above all else, to maintain peace. We are now so very close. I have Herr Hitler's absolute assurance that the Memorandum contains his very last demand."

"But he gave you the same assurance about the Anglo-French Plan, Prime Minister. There will never be a last demand. For years my government has tried making concessions to Henlein and Hitler. It does not work. You must realise he always comes back for more."

"But I have his word, don't you see? You must believe me, Ambassador, when I tell you I have developed a relationship of trust with Herr Hitler, man to man. I believe him when he assures me that his only wish is to look after his people in the Sudetenland."

"What can I say to you, Prime Minister Chamberlain? I can only tell you that Hitler's real aim is to enslave our people and plunder our country. And Czechoslovakia will not be the last."

"Now there you are, you see, that is the kind of statement I find most unhelpful. Wild exaggeration such as that only stands in the way of peace. Herr Hitler has explained to me that he desires only racial unity. It flies in the face of his basic philosophy to incorporate other nationalities into the Reich."

"That's nonsense. He will incorporate as many as you allow him to."

Chamberlain looked affronted.

"I must tell you I have worked very hard to gain Herr Hitler's respect. He trusts me and is willing to work with me. I ask only that your people should do the same."

Masaryk leaned forward, shook his head and looked Chamberlain in the eye.

"You know, Prime Minister, we Czechs have borne the proximity of Germany alone for years, but we have borne it for everyone who signed the Versailles Treaty. We have already agreed to give up our sovereign territory to Hitler. You cannot now ask us to hand over more to the Poles and Hungarians, simply because he demands it."

"I do ask. I ask you to accept the terms of this Memorandum. Or there will be war."

"Sometimes war can be the lesser evil."

"I do not believe that for one second. I am a man of peace before all else. The number of grateful people who write to me every day thanking me for my efforts in all this..."

"But you cannot ask Czechoslovaks to do nothing in the face of Hitler's threats."

"But do you fully understand the military realities?"

"I understand your government and the government of France agreed we should mobilise on Friday evening. That was clearly because you recognise we could never be expected to accept these new demands. They are the sort of ultimatum presented to a vanquished nation."

"I did not agree with your mobilisation. It was conceded by the Foreign Secretary in my absence."

"Are you telling me that even now you would bow to Hitler, when your own cabinet recognises that freedom in Europe depends on you supporting my country?"

"I do not know what makes you think you are privy to discussions in my Cabinet Room, Ambassador, but I can assure you I bow to no one. And I must tell you honestly that if another war is to be fought in Europe,

I strongly believe it should be over a larger issue than this."

"A larger issue..?"

Masaryk stood up so abruptly that his shin collided with the coffee table, knocking over one of the glasses. "I question whether you speak any more for your own people, Prime Minister Chamberlain," he said, "but I know I speak for mine. We Czechoslovaks would sooner go down fighting than accept Hitler's ultimatum. I tell you, sir, the nation of Jan Hus and Tomáš Masaryk will not be slaves."

Jan Masaryk looked at the pictures in the Times. A group of blind children being evacuated from London to the safety of the Sussex countryside; glum-faced members of Chamberlain's inner cabinet approaching Number 10. Alongside the pictures the full, brutal terms of the Bad Godesberg Memorandum made public, confirming the impasse and the inevitable countdown to war.

He turned to the paper's correspondence page, where prominence was given to a letter from his close friend, Leo Amery.

'Are we to surrender to ruthless brutality a free people whose cause we have espoused but are now to throw to the wolves to save our own skins, or are we still able to stand up to a bully?'

He folded the newspaper and threw it down onto the table next to his untouched breakfast. This whole business was the May crisis all over again. The same overriding issue again. Would Czechoslovakia's allies stand firm? Or would the fawning Chamberlain get his way this time and sacrifice a free people to the wolf? Would he never learn?

But the present threat was much greater than May. And there was longer to wait this time before his country's fate was known. Hitler's deadline for agreement to his demands was 2pm on Wednesday. Masaryk looked at his watch. Fifty-three hope-filled, painful hours.

Events unfolded quickly. Within an hour he received a report from his contact inside the French Embassy. General Gamelin, the French Chief of Staff, had arrived from Paris and was now in Downing Street. A second report at midday provided details of the General's discussions with the British inner cabinet.

The Czechs could not be expected to accept the Godesberg terms, Gamelin told them, and it was clear Beneš and Syrovy would resist an invasion. He confirmed the French guarantee to Czechoslovakia was reinstated and the French were ready to fight. When Hitler invaded Bohemia, the French would attack Germany in the west, drawing their troops away from the Czechoslovaks. What's more, Russia was ready to send troops through Slovakia in the east, as soon as the French went to the aid of their mutual ally.

It was the best start to the day. There was still hope. Hope that Britain would support the French and the Russians, and that Hitler would realise the forces aligned against him were too powerful, and at the last minute he would seek a compromise. Hitler's response would come that evening in a speech in front of 20,000 party cheerleaders in Berlin.

Just before seven o'clock Masaryk and the Czechoslovakian Embassy staff gathered in the Campbell music room to listen to the speech on the radio. Masaryk stood by the grand piano, while his 36 staff occupied rows of chairs in the middle of the room. The radio, specially adapted for musical soirées at the request of the ambassador, sent the *Reichsfunk* broadcast from Berlin directly to speakers hidden in four large corner cabinets.

Hitler began calmly, thanking Chamberlain for his efforts to secure peace, and reassuring the world that he desired only justice for his fellow Germans in the Sudetenland. The calm delivery was a hoax, Hitler's favourite device. Once his listeners were lulled by his moderation, the ranting began. He gained complete control of his Berlin audience, by seemingly losing all control of himself. He spat and raged against all Czechs, and saved his worst bile for Beneš.

'This Czech State began with a single lie and the father of that lie was named Beneš... I demand now after twenty years that Beneš at last be compelled to confront the truth. On the first of October he will hand over to us the Sudetenland... or we shall take it from him! Now two men stand arrayed one against the other: there is Mr Beneš and here stand I.'

Hitler delivered the words with such violence and menace that two of Masaryk's secretaries broke down. Masaryk went over to each of them in turn, putting his arm around them and trying to comfort them. For several minutes the crowd in Berlin delivered its customary chants of *'Sieg Heil'* and *'Führer befiehl, wir folgen'*, *'Führer command, we shall follow'*. The chants were familiar enough but the screaming frenzy of their delivery was new to everyone listening. In the Czechoslovakian Embassy the four speakers trapped Masaryk's staff in the middle of the venomous crowd.

The chanting stopped and Hitler began again, spewing each word with madness in his voice. *'I have made Mr Beneš an offer...'* he mocked. The crowd laughed. *'The decision now lies in his hands: Peace or War! He will accept either this offer and now at last give to the Germans their freedom or we will go and fetch this freedom for ourselves. We are fixed! Now let Mr Beneš make his choice."*

As the crowd laughed and cheered, Goebbels grabbed the microphone and shouted into it, *'1918 will never be repeated!'* Then the voice of Hitler was heard one last time. *'Ja!'* he screamed and the crowd's hysteria filled the Campbell Room.

"Turn it off, would you, please," asked Masaryk. In the silence that followed no one spoke. Now it was all down to the British.

The following evening Masaryk made his way to Winston Churchill's flat in Morpeth Mansions, Victoria. He was pleased to find Leo Amery there, and a young anti-appeaser on the left wing of the Conservative Party, Harold Macmillan.

"You may find us a little sombre, my dear Jan, now war appears inevitable," said Churchill, as his butler took Masaryk's hat and coat. "But we are also much relieved."

"In what way, Winston?"

"Not to be shamed and humiliated by bowing to a tyrant and deserting our friends."

Masaryk stepped into the drawing room and shook hands with the other two guests. Churchill handed him a whisky and soda.

"Good news from the Admiralty, Jan," said Amery. "The fleet being mobilised."

"Yes, it is very encouraging. But I hear Chamberlain is still blocking any mobilisation of the army. I wish he would follow the French."

"Typical of the man," said Churchill. "Neville made a half-decent mayor of Birmingham City Council, but he's like a maiden aunt in a docklands public house when it comes to dealing with dictators."

"I hear Sir Horace did a good job in Berlin this morning," said Amery. "Told Hitler to his face that when France honours her treaty obligations and fights, the United Kingdom will be obliged to support her."

"The mouse roars, eh?" said Churchill. "A strange choice of messenger, but the right message, thank God."

Masaryk knew Sir Horace Wilson, Chamberlain's chief advisor. He was generally disliked for his sycophancy and timidity, but nevertheless Chamberlain had sent him to Berlin in one more effort to save the peace.

"Hitler went puce apparently," said Amery. "Accused Horace of aggression."

The men laughed half-heartedly.

"Shall I warm up the crystals on the radio, sir," Churchill's butler asked, "and tune it to the Home Service?"

"Yes, if you would, please, Charles."

Masaryk checked his watch. It was seven fifty. Chamberlain was due to speak to the country in ten minutes. Only 18 hours now remained before Hitler's deadline expired and his armies prepared to march.

"I want you to be with your friends when the PM speaks tonight, Jan," Churchill had said to him on the phone earlier in the day. "I want you to rest assured we are all with you, and with your people."

The four men sat in armchairs with their drinks, and waited.

'This is London. You will now hear the Prime Minister, the Right Honourable Neville Chamberlain, speaking to you from Downing Street.'

There was a pause. Then came the soft, tired tone of Chamberlain's voice with its usual note of exasperation and disbelief at the way events were unfolding contrary to his wishes.

Much of what he said was familiar to Masaryk from his meeting with him two days before. There was the same self-congratulation at the number of letters he had received from a grateful nation. The same sympathy for Hitler's wish to do the best for his people, and his trust in the German Chancellor's assurance that the Sudetenland represented the limit of his territorial ambitions.

Masaryk watched the anger rise in the faces of Churchill and Amery.

"This will only encourage the Germans to go ahead..." said Amery in exasperation. "Did he not hear Hitler last night?"

'How horrible, fantastic, incredible it is that we should be digging trenches and trying on gas-masks here because of a quarrel in a far-away country between people of whom we know nothing.'

Churchill leapt up. "A far-away country..." he shouted. "The man's an imbecile." He sat down and reached his hand across to touch Masaryk's arm. "I'm so sorry, Jan," he said.

'However much we may sympathise with a small nation confronted by a big, powerful neighbour, we cannot in all circumstances undertake to involve the whole British Empire in war simply on her account. If we have to fight it must be on larger issues than that.'

"My God, Leo," stormed Churchill. "I do believe the bugger is preparing to scuttle."

They sat in silence listening to Chamberlain repeating his preparedness to accommodate Germany, with no word of sympathy for the plight of Czechoslovakia.

"What you said is right, Winston," said Amery when it was over. "If ever there was a man accustomed to dealing with citizens on a City Council, but incapable of thinking in terms of force, strategy or diplomacy, it is Neville."

"But he can't act against the wishes of the French and his own cabinet, can he?" asked Masaryk. "The policy is decided. My country has your renewed guarantees."

"Chamberlain is a law unto himself, Ambassador," said Macmillan. "His vanity allows him to believe he alone is in the right."

"Neville has always regarded opposing views as personal slights," said Amery. "That's his problem."

"But surely he cannot simply ignore his cabinet and his party in this way," said Masaryk.

"Do not despair, Jan," said Churchill. "I regret that Berlin will be much encouraged by what it has heard tonight. But our chance will come in the House tomorrow. I intend to have my say in the debate, and I believe in the present mood we shall, between us, be able to bring an end to Chamberlain's courting of Herr Hitler."

Wednesday 28th September dawned as the last day of peace. At 11am Masaryk took a call from President Beneš informing him that, if the invasion started when Hitler's ultimatum expired at 2pm, he was to remain at his post in London.

At one o'clock Masaryk set off for Westminster to hear Chamberlain's report to the House and the inevitable declaration of war. When he entered Parliament Square he saw a large, silent and anxious crowd. Some people recognised him and broke the silence with shouts of encouragement. He smiled and waved and, as he made his way through them, a gentle ripple of applause spread out around him.

He took his place in the Diplomatic Gallery a few seats away from Dirksen, the German ambassador. The green benches on the floor of the House were packed, and MPs were crammed together on the steps and by the doors. Churchill was in his usual place on the back benches at the end of a row, clutching the speech he intended to deliver during the foreign policy debate. Masaryk hoped to catch his eye, but his friend was deep in conversation with Leo Amery and Anthony Eden, the former Foreign Secretary, who had resigned over Chamberlain's recognition of Mussolini's conquest of Abyssinia.

Masaryk looked around him. The Press Gallery was packed too. Lord Halifax, the present Foreign Secretary, sat in the Peers' Gallery and in the Speaker's Gallery was the mother of the king, Queen Mary, dressed in black. The noise rising from the floor of the crammed chamber was oppressive, and Masaryk was pleased when the Speaker called for order. He looked down at the government front bench. Chamberlain was not there.

Fifty minutes passed, through prayers and departmental questions, before finally at two fifty Chamberlain appeared. Most on the government benches gave a partisan cheer and waved their order papers as he made his way to the dispatch box, while the opposition sat glum-faced and still.

The Speaker allowed the noise to subside and then called on the Prime Minister to speak. The deadline had long passed. The House fell silent. Chamberlain stood up. He looked tired and drawn.

"Today," he said, "we are faced with a situation which has no parallel since 1914."

Masaryk waited for the announcement that the invasion of his country had begun.

He waited, but Chamberlain made no mention of it. There was only the usual self-congratulation, as he relived the events of Berchtesgaden and Bad Godesberg. Only the usual support for the rights of Fascist Germany and not one word of sympathy or support for the democracy of Czechoslovakia.

He talked for an hour, and still Masaryk waited. At 3.50 MPs became distracted by activity next to the Speaker's chair. A sheet of folded white paper was being passed along the government front benches to Chamberlain. He stopped speaking and opened it. The news of the invasion, thought Masaryk. His heart pounded. War had come, but, thank God, Czechoslovakia would not be alone.

As Chamberlain read the note, Masaryk watched the colour return to the Prime Minister's face. Chamberlain smiled.

"I am now in a position to inform the House of a final, last-minute initiative of my own," he said, "which I undertook this morning to avert the disaster which confronts us.

"This morning I sent a telegram to Signor Mussolini asking him to use his good offices with Herr Hitler to intervene over the Sudeten Crisis. I am able to inform the House that as a consequence of this the German Chancellor has agreed to extend his ultimatum for a further 24 hours."

There was a collective gasp and sigh, of disbelief and relief.

"Furthermore, I am happy to tell the House that Herr Hitler invites me, together with Signor Mussolini and Monsieur Daladier to a four-power conference in Munich tomorrow to find a solution to the problem of the Sudetenland."

There were a few seconds of silence before everyone in the chamber was able to absorb the significance of the announcement. Then MPs on both sides of the House rose and cheered and shouted their congratulations to Chamberlain, who looked around him smiling and soaking up the acclamation.

"Thank God for the Prime Minister," shouted someone from the government back benches.

Winston Churchill tried to catch the Speaker's eye to intervene, but in the euphoria it was hopeless. He stayed in his seat and looked up towards Jan Masaryk in the gallery. Masaryk saw tears in his friend's eyes. Masaryk nodded and then looked away. A four-power conference, Chamberlain had said, not five. The wolf would be fed. He got up and walked to the exit. He took one look back at the jubilation on the floor of the House of Commons and left.

Chapter Forty-Three

September 30th – October 1st, 1938

"Anything to report, Kovařík?"

"No, sir. Nothing in the night, and nothing since daybreak."

"Good."

"The locals know it's more than their life's worth to set foot on that road, sir."

"So they should, Kovařík. Let me take a look."

Tomáš stepped back and Captain Mastny, an army regular, took his place behind the tripod and peered through the binoculars over the top of the dugout. He scanned the road below, and the woods on either side of it.

"You're right. Not even a dog wants to be caught out there."

"They won't stand a chance, sir."

"The Germans won't appear without you hearing gunfire from the border first, Kovařík, but remember... no firing here until you get my order. Even if a whole damn panzer division comes towards you. Understood?"

"Yes, Captain. Understood, sir."

Tomáš remained in his dugout, one kilometre south of the small town of Kaplice in Southern Bohemia; his machine gun post part of a defensive line urgently constructed after the German takeover of Austria six months before. The 80-kilometre line created a salient, surrounded on three sides by former Austrian territory, cutting off that part of Bohemia from the rest of the country.

Regular soldiers of the Czechoslovakian Army were on the border ten kilometres forward of Tomáš's position, manned mostly by reservists like himself. On the German side of the border three panzer divisions waited in battle formation, ready for the order to invade.

Most of the panzers would come up the main road from Linz. His section, and fourteen others, would hold the road as long as they could before falling back to Kaplice, where a Czechoslovakian armoured division lay in wait on a ridge overlooking the Malša River. There the main battle would take place.

Tomáš had been there for one week now. He was mobilised the

previous Friday evening. Everyone was expecting the call all day. When it came he went home with Anna to collect his kit and get into uniform. They walked together to the station where hundreds, thousands, of mothers, wives and sweethearts crowded the platforms, most in tears, but all behind Syrový's decision that their men should fight.

Saying goodbye to Anna had been the hardest part. She said she was going to Cheb the next day to make sure Babička and Děda and Tomáš's parents were alright. She was so headstrong that Tomáš knew it was pointless arguing. He just hoped her father had gone with her.

"Which one of you wants to take over for a while?" Tomáš asked Chalupa and Stich, the other reservists in his section.

"Me," said Jiří Chalupa, a waiter from Prague, who had thrown down his apron and the plates he was carrying on Friday night when his call came. "I wouldn't mind being the first to see the bastards."

"It's tomorrow they're coming, Jiří," said Vilém Stich. "The first of October. Hitler said."

"As long as they come, I don't mind when," said Chalupa. "I just want a chance to see what that beauty does to them." He gestured towards the heavy machine gun which rested on a cut-away section of the dugout, only the barrel showing above ground level.

"That won't stop tanks," said Stich.

"I know that, you stupid bastard. Our anti-tanks in the woods will take care of the panzers."

"What do you think, Tomáš?" asked Stich. "Do you think they'll come tomorrow?"

"They're bound to, Vilém. We won't back down, and Hitler won't lose face."

"I don't trust those French and English bastards though," said Chalupa, still peering through the binoculars. "I reckon they'd leave us in the shit soon enough, if they got the chance."

"They won't, Jiří," said Tomáš. "But it makes no difference if they do. Syrový will fight on anyway."

"I wish I was in one of those big forts up north," said Stich, "behind two metres of concrete. They say nothing can get through them."

"I tell you, those German bastards think they're going to walk all over us down here," said Chalupa, "but they've got one hell of a surprise coming."

"Too damned right, Jiří," said Tomáš. "My father told me what the Legions did in the last lot. The Germans got one hell of a surprise from them too."

"Was he in the Legion then, Tomáš? Your father?"

"Yes, in Russia. And he got through it alright. Against greater odds than we're facing."

"Where is he now then?"

"Back home in Cheb. Near the Bavarian border."

"If the poor sod's that close, he could end up fighting again," said Chalupa. "That's where they reckon the main thrust's going to be."

"I know, and I'm worried sick. My whole family's there. And my fiancée."

"Fiancée? You're engaged?"

"Yes. Since last Friday night. I gave her the ring at the station."

"Bit of a risk, wasn't it? How did you know she'd say 'yes'."

"I knew."

Captain Mastny appeared behind them. Tomáš and Stich jumped up. Chalupa remained at the binoculars.

"You can stop looking now, Chalupa," the captain said. "Kovařík, immobilise the KB-50. Then all of you get over to the command post. At the double."

"But, Captain…"

"Don't argue, man. Just do as I say."

"What the hell are the stupid bastards up to now?" said Chalupa as he gathered up their tunics. Tomáš took the firing pin from the machine gun.

"I don't know, Jiří," he said, "but I don't like the sound of it."

The eighty men of the forward defensive line formed up in front of their commanding officer.

"Men," he said in a strong, clear voice, "I have news I don't want to give you, and you don't want to hear. Yesterday a meeting took place in Munich, to which the likes of you and me weren't invited. The Germans, Italians, French and British were all there, but not one Czechoslovak.

"Even so, the people at this meeting decided they knew what was best for us and our country. It seems the French and British realised they couldn't wriggle out of backing us over Hitler's latest set of demands, so they decided to scrap those. And yesterday, men, they gave those same demands a new name and decided this time they would accept them, whether we like it or not. So now, men, we have the Munich Agreement, which gives all the territory you and I and our fellow soldiers are ready to defend, to Hitler."

"No! No! Fuck 'em..!"

"Silence in the ranks," commanded the captain. "I know well enough

320

what you're thinking, but you will remain silent.

"There's worse to follow. But you will make no comment until I say so. Now, here's the news none of us thought we would ever hear. Fifty minutes ago, at 12.30 hours, our government accepted the Munich Agreement.

"Be silent! You will remain silent whilst I speak." The captain waited. "The Agreement means our border areas will be occupied. The occupation will be staged over the next week and will proceed as follows."

He took a single sheet of paper from his breast pocket and scanned it as he spoke. "Tomorrow and Sunday, the 1st and 2nd October, the German army will occupy this part of Southern Bohemia. On the 2nd and 3rd they will take over Northern Bohemia. On the 3rd and 4th and 5th the districts of As, Cheb and Karlovy Vary. On the 6th and 7th, Northern Moravia. The occupation of all areas where the majority of the population are German-speaking will be completed by 10th October. A three-kilometre no-man's-land will be maintained between advancing German forces and Czechoslovakian forces, who will not retreat, but will withdraw in good order."

He screwed the sheet of paper into a ball, threw it to the floor and looked at the men. "A map will be made available to you all today to show exactly which areas of our country will, from tomorrow, become subject to the laws of Hitler's Reich. Those of you with homes and families outside these areas will remain in uniform and return to your barracks as ordered.

"Those of you with homes and family inside the areas have a difficult choice. You can stay in uniform and return to barracks, or you can return home at once. If you do return home you must get out of uniform before you enter an occupied zone. Anyone found in a Czechoslovakian uniform in Germany's new territory will be regarded as a combatant and treated accordingly."

Captain Mastny pulled his shoulders back and stood as tall as he could. "You have nothing to be ashamed of, men. We know how ready we were to fight here... but we have been betrayed." He looked down and cleared his throat. "Now, collect all your equipment, and those who have to stay, assemble here again in 20 minutes. Dismissed."

Tomáš walked with Chalupa and Stich back to their dugout. They were all in shock. Tomáš tried to grasp the implications, but for now he, like all the others, had only one question. 'Why did Beneš and Syrový not reject the Agreement and give the order to fight?'

"If we had no part in the Agreement," he mumbled, "why did we accept it?"

"Bastards they are. All fucking bastards."

"They didn't have to. Maybe without the French they thought... I don't know... But why did the French..?"

"Because they're all fucking cowards, that's why," said Chalupa. "And now they've made us into fucking cowards too."

"I reckon Syrový worked out we couldn't beat the Germans on our own," said Stich. "At least this way we stay in one piece."

"I knew you were a fucking coward, Stich," said Chalupa, grabbing him by the collar. "With a name like that you're probably a bastard German yourself."

"Cut it out, Jiří," said Tomáš. He took hold of Chalupa's arm. "The one thing we mustn't do now is turn on one another."

Chalupa released his grip and stood with his hands on his hips. He turned away from the other two, drew his head back and groaned. "It's the shame we'll always have to feel," he said. "We have to spend the rest of our fucking lives... knowing we did nothing to save our country. The bastards."

"But we'll always know we were prepared to do something, Jiří," said Tomáš, "and no one more than you."

Chalupa turned to him, opened his eyes and smiled. "It won't be enough, my friend," he said. "It will never be enough."

"Will you two go back to Prague?" Tomáš asked.

"Yes, back to barracks and see what they want to do with us. How about you?"

"I have to get back to my family in Cheb, whilst there's still time."

"Then leave everything here, Tomáš. Vilém and I will sort out all this junk."

"Thanks, Jiří. Thanks, Vilém. Good luck," said Tomáš, and he shook each by the hand and left.

Lorries took the men with families in the 'redesignated' zones back to Kaplice, where they were joined by many more from the armoured division. All the men were sombre, struggling to make the adjustment from the height of battle readiness to sudden flight. Although they gave one reason after another why they should feel anger, not shame, it was shame that intensified in them as they headed for the trains at České Budějovice.

At the station they were presented with travel passes, and bundles of civilian clothes, hurriedly collected from the local population. Some sought humour in their situation as they put on the ill-fitting clothes, but few could escape the feeling that seeking to hide their military status only increased their humiliation. Tomáš was relieved when the supply of clothes ran out and he was one of those asked to stay in uniform, since his home lay in a zone which would not become part of Hitler's Reich until two more days had passed.

At five o'clock, while he waited for a train to Pilsen, an announcement came over the station's loudspeaker. General Syrový, hero of Zborov and head of the Government of National Defence, would speak to the nation. For a brief time people's pressing need to be elsewhere was put aside as they stood and listened, hoping to find an explanation for their government's betrayal.

'I am experiencing the gravest hour of my life,' said Syrový. 'I would have been prepared to die rather than to go through this.'

"Well, die then, you old bastard?" shouted a soldier from the opposite platform.

'We have had to choose between making a desperate and hopeless defence...'

"No, you didn't."

'...which would have meant the sacrifice of an entire generation of our adult men...'

"We were ready, damn you..."

'...as well as of our women and children, and accepting, without a struggle and under pressure, terms which are without parallel in history for their ruthlessness. We were deserted. We stood alone.'

There were a few moments of silence; then a carriage door slammed and a baby cried and the station came to life again. Could that have been the same Syrový, whose defiant speech just one week ago had been greeted by the crowd in Wenceslas Square with such hope and passion? Tomáš stood back as people rushed past, some close to panic. For two hours he stood there, waiting for his train and seeing what people became when guidance and hope were taken from them.

Pilsen lay only 140 kilometres to the north-west of České Budějovice, but it took Tomáš five hours to get there. The trains were packed in both directions and stopped at every station. He stood at the end of the carriage, avoiding conversation and watching passengers getting off and on. Only confusion and anxiety united the people now. Some, he guessed, would be fleeing towns and villages shortly to have new Nazi rulers, and others, like him, were simply returning to their loved ones, to share their fate, whatever that might be.

At Pilsen station more anxious people jostled for space and pushed one another to gain a place in a queue or claim seats on a train. Gone was the quiet dignity shown by the citizens of Prague only eight days before, when they gathered at the castle to show their support for President Beneš. In only a few hours people had lost their faith in their leaders and in each other.

Tomáš got off the train at Pilsen and waited. "What's the matter with you soldiers? Don't you know how to fight any more?" an old man asked him, more in sadness than in anger. Tomáš offered no reply.

When he boarded the train to Pňovany, where he would get his final connection to Cheb, Tomáš found a seat in a corner and tried to make himself as inconspicuous as possible. He looked out of the window at the darkness, lost in thoughts of his family. He knew how heartbroken his father would be at the French betrayal. How difficult it would be for his grandparents to give up their life at the chata, and how worried his mother would be about everyone. Anna was the only one he did not worry about. They would be together again soon.

The train pulled into Pňovany Station at one in the morning. In the emergency the trains were running through the night, moving civilians and troops to ensure the phased occupation would take place without incident. The train taking Tomáš on the final leg of his journey arrived at Pňovany Station at five in the morning. The station was still crowded, but few people boarded his train bound for an area coming under German occupation and government in less than forty-eight hours.

The train made its way slowly north-west towards Cheb as the sun came up. For the first time he was able to see the changes taking place in the part of his country he knew so well. Nazi flags flew at every station and the Czech names of the towns and villages had already been painted over, leaving only the German. At the spa town of Mariánské Lázně less than 30 kilometres from Cheb a large banner had been hung between the gaslights on the station platform. 'Endlich Heim Ins Reich', it said. 'Home to the Reich at last', and the station sign told travellers they had arrived in 'Marienbad'.

Finally, at five forty-five in the morning, Tomáš reached Cheb. He was the only person to get out. At the exit he met the stationmaster who had known him since he was a baby in the arms of his mother.

"Be careful in the town in that uniform, Tomáš," the stationmaster said. "They don't like us much here any more."

"This is still Czechoslovakia for now, pan Čermák. I'm happy to remind anyone who might have forgotten."

The stationmaster smiled and handed him back his pass.

"And I'll be back with some paint later today," said Tomáš as he walked towards the town. "To correct your sign. This isn't Eger yet."

"Good boy, Tomáš Kovařík," said Čermák, wiping something from his eye. "Good boy."

Chapter Forty-Four

October 1st, 1938

Tomáš knocked just loudly enough to wake his parents without disturbing their neighbours. He thought he heard voices in the front bedroom, followed by movement on the stairs. Then everything went quiet. He waited and was about to knock again when a stern voice from the far end of the hallway demanded, "Who is it?"

"It's me."

"Who is it?"

"It's me. Tomáš."

"Tomáš," called out the voice, and the door was unlocked and thrown open. His father stepped forward, wrapped his arms around him, and then held him at arms length by the shoulders. "Come in, my boy," he said and ushered Tomáš into the hallway. Tomáš glimpsed a revolver lying under the small side table.

"Tomáš, my Tomášek," said his mother as they met at the bottom of the stairs, and he held her as she sobbed. She grabbed the sleeve of his tunic.

"You shouldn't be wearing this. You must take it off. Right away. Pavel, tell him he mustn't wear this."

His father took her gently by the shoulders, turned her towards him and put his arms around her. "I will, my love. Don't worry. I will. But he's alright here in the house. He's safe now."

Tomáš became aware of someone standing at the top of the stairs. She was wearing a white cotton nightgown which reached down to her bare feet. The nightgown was unbuttoned at the neck and her long hair hung loose over her shoulders.

"*Ahoy*, Anna."

"*Ahoy*, darling."

Tomáš climbed the stairs slowly; they looked and smiled at one another as he moved towards her. She held out her left hand with the engagement ring and they both laughed quietly. He stopped on the top step so their faces were almost touching. She put her arms around his neck, and he felt the soft shape of her body against him as they held one another.

"I was afraid you would go to Prague," she said.

"I knew you would come here."

"How?"

"Because you said you would."

A door opened and Anna pulled away. "I must get dressed," she said, and scurried back to her room.

"Tomáš. I thought I heard voices. I am so pleased to see you, my boy. How are you?" He offered Tomáš his hand.

"I'm well, Uncle Ernst. Thankyou."

"Kája and I will make some coffee for us all in the front room," Pavel called from the hallway. "Come down all of you when you're ready."

"Thankyou, Táta."

"Tomáš," said Ernst, "before you speak to your parents, you and I must talk. Come into my room for a moment."

Ernst pulled back the curtains to let in some light and offered Tomáš the chair by the window. Ernst sat down on the edge of the bed.

"Did you see any fighting, Tomáš?"

"No, Uncle. It was a debacle. From the state of the town I'd say there's been more fighting here."

"There's been a lot here, Tomáš. That's what I want to talk to you about."

"No one's been hurt, have they?"

"Yes, Tomáš. That's why your dear mother is suffering such a crisis of nerves. Three weeks ago there was a serious riot here following one of Hitler's speeches. In the course of the riot a mob attacked your grandparents' chata. Your grandfather tried to fight them off and was killed."

"Oh, my God."

"Your father..."

Tomáš got to his feet. "Where's Babička?"

"Let me tell you, Tomáš. Sit down... Your grandmother was rescued by your father and brought back here. But she had suffered a severe trauma and passed away two days later."

"Oh, my God, no..."

"She died peacefully here in this house. Your mother was with her."

"I don't know what to say, Uncle Ernst... what to think... Děda, Babička... How is my mother?"

"She needs rest and quiet, but I'm afraid it's almost impossible to provide it for her with all that's going on. Your return is the best medicine she could have."

"And Anna?"

"Anna is alright. She has been very upset, but she's strong, and she has you again now."

"My poor Děda and Babička. I can't believe it. Do they know who did it?"

"Yes."

"Who? Have they been arrested?"

"Their leader was Heinrich von Stricker. He's somewhere over the border now. The Germans here are making their own laws, Tomáš. You must have seen the police station when you arrived."

"I did, and the synagogue."

"A week ago a German Freikorps unit took the town over completely. I'm told the army had a struggle to take it back."

"My parents have been through all this? Why didn't they tell us?"

"Because they didn't want you here. It's too dangerous. And it's not safe for Anna, but she insisted."

Pavel called from the bottom of the stairs. "The coffee's ready."

"We're coming, Pavel," Ernst called back.

"Tomáš, it's very important that your mother stays calm. Your father can get very aggravated by all the news. I am sorry about your grandparents, dear boy, but do your best not to get emotional. You and I must stay practical."

"I understand." Tomáš stopped at the door. "Why did they attack the chata?"

"There was some nonsense about your grandfather being a spy, but we think it was really just random violence. Listen, Tomáš, I must talk to you about Anna. It's very important. Some time this morning."

"Of course, Uncle."

When Tomáš got to the bottom of the stairs, his father was waiting for him. He said nothing, but caught Tomáš's eye, took his arm and nodded towards the front room.

"It's alright," whispered Tomáš. "I know everything."

He went in to find the table laden with food. Buchty cake, fresh bread and cheese, ham and pickles, soup... His mother stood by the table waiting for him. She kept wiping the palms of her hands against her dressing gown, and her eyes followed his every move. For the first time he noticed grey flecks in her hair.

"This looks wonderful, Máma." He went over to her and kissed her. "But do you think we have time for all this?"

"Of course we do."

"Máma, I'm so sorry about…"

"Sit down and eat, Tomáš." Karolína stood behind him and smoothed his hair and kissed his head. "I promised myself that as long as you stayed safe, I would be alright," she said. "So I am."

"Won't you sit down, Máma?"

"Not yet. I want to see you eat."

Pavel, who had been waiting outside, came in and sat down at the table. Karolína poured them both coffee.

"So your officers just told you to walk away, did they?" he said.

"Only those of us with family in the zones. The rest have gone back to barracks."

"And what was the mood when you heard about Munich?"

Karolína sighed and went into the kitchen.

"Terrible." Tomáš lowered his voice and spoke quickly. "We were all ready to fight. They had totally underestimated us. None of us can understand Beneš and Syrový. They've just handed it to them."

"No, Tomáš. They didn't hand it to them. The British did."

"And the French."

"No. The French took the chance the British made for them. It was the British who kept going back to Hitler. In the end they couldn't rid themselves of us fast enough. Just to save their own necks."

"So you don't blame Syrový or Beneš?"

"I don't blame them for losing the support of the French. I blame them for not making you men fight."

"I was afraid you would say that. I swear we were ready."

Tomáš put down his knife and fork.

"Are you mad, Pavel Kovařík, saying such things to him?" said Karolína, appearing from the kitchen. "We have our boy home safe when we could so easily have lost him too. What else could possibly matter?"

"I'm sorry, Kája, I didn't know you were listening. Tomáš knows what I mean. You know I never wanted our young men to have to fight, but my God… our country…"

"Are we interrupting?" said Ernst, knocking gently on the half-open door.

Tomáš and Pavel stood up as Ernst and Anna came into the room.

"No, you're not interrupting," said Karolína. "It's just with all this chaos in our lives again, Pavel thinks everything would be better if Tomáš was out there in a ditch somewhere, fighting for his life."

"I didn't mean it like that, Kája. I'm sorry. Please sit down everyone and have some breakfast. Are you going to sit down, my love?"

"How can I?"

Pavel retook his seat. "I apologise to everyone," he said. "I'm finding it difficult today remembering what is really important."

"I'm not surprised, dear friend," said Ernst. "Your country has received a grievous blow. But you all need to remember that you haven't done this to yourselves. You are not to blame, especially not your young men like our dear Tomáš. It wasn't their decision not to fight."

"Thankyou, Uncle Ernst," said Tomáš, staring down at the table. Anna clutched his arm.

"But out of that decision has come something good," said Ernst. "Your country will suffer, but your young men are all alive, and they will be there to bring the wounded body back to life one day."

"Listen to Ernst, Pavel," said Karolína, "he's talking sense." She stood behind her husband and placed a hand lightly on his shoulder. "I know how bad you feel about this..."

"Do you? Does anyone?"

"Of course we do. But so many terrible things have happened over the past weeks, and at last we have our Tomáš back."

"I know. I know."

"And we could remember some good news, couldn't we?" said Ernst. "Tomáš and Anna are engaged."

"Yes," said Pavel. "I'm sorry. I'm very pleased."

"When will the wedding be?" asked Karolína.

"We haven't thought about it, Máma," said Tomáš. "We can discuss things like that when we're all safely in Prague."

"How do you know your mother and I will be able to get to Prague for the wedding?" said Pavel. "Am I the only one who realises the German border will be halfway between here and Prague after midnight tomorrow?"

"We know that, Táta. That's why we all have to leave here today."

"Leave? I'm not leaving."

"You have to. You can't stay here. You and Máma can't live under the Nazis."

"We lived under German rule for most of our lives, Tomáš. We can do it again."

"These people aren't the same, Pavel," said Ernst.

"I know how brutal the Germans can be, Ernst. We survived it before, and we'll do it again."

"You can't, Táta."

"I was born here, Tomáš. My parents and your mother's parents are buried here. One day Cheb will be Czech again, and I intend to be here when it happens."

"But Prague is staying Czech now. Come back when Cheb is free again."

"Tomáš, you're a grown man. You must know Prague cannot stay Czech for long after this."

"But the new borders have been guaranteed ..."

"Guaranteed? The Germans will be in Prague within three months. Don't you understand the Sudetenland is just a bridgehead for Hitler to take the rest of our country? As for guarantees..."

"I know. As soon as I said it I knew how ridiculous it sounded."

"I'll tell you what's ridiculous, Tomáš, my teaching you all your life to admire the democracies. I'm the real fool here."

"No one would ever think that of you, Pavel."

"I know it, Ernst. I'm the biggest of fools. Half my life I believed Russia would liberate us from the Germans. Instead they threw us into prison. For the other half I thought France and Britain guaranteed our independence from Germany. But in the end all the swines have guaranteed is our slavery. And we've damn well agreed to it."

Pavel pushed back his chair and went over to stand by the window.

"Táta, I understand how you feel," said Tomáš, "but we don't have time to dwell on these things now. It's vital that we all leave for Prague today."

"I'm not leaving, Tomáš."

"Do you agree with my father about Prague being occupied, Uncle Ernst?"

"It's a possibility," said Ernst. He tried to ignore the look Pavel gave him. "Perhaps you and I could talk in private about some of these things later."

"Why in private, Vati?" said Anna. "There's nothing that can't be said in front of all of us. Is it about me?"

"Indirectly, yes."

"Then we should all have the conversation together. We're all family and I'm 21. I'll be a married woman soon. I don't need to be protected from things like a little girl."

"There are some things I always want to protect you from, Anna."

"You mean being a Jew, don't you?"

"Yes, darling, I do."

"I don't mind being Jewish. I don't feel Jewish, but I'm proud to be the same as my mother. I tell everyone my brother's a rabbi."

"I know, darling. But we have to recognise how the Nazis treat Jews. I can't bear the thought of them being anywhere near you, and Prague will only be 60 kilometres from the new border."

"But I've always felt safe in Prague, Vati."

Pavel returned to the table and leaned towards Anna with his hands on the back of his chair.

"What your father is trying to tell you, Anna, is that tomorrow at midnight Nazi stormtroopers will be in this town, and the Gestapo will be in charge. Then, any Jews they find will be spat on, beaten or even murdered, and no one will lift a finger to help them. And that includes you."

"Pavel!"

"No, Ernst. Everyone's pretending our lives can go on, and somehow we can keep everything normal, but it's not true. The truth is, when the Nazis occupy Cheb on Monday, there is nothing to stop them being in Prague two hours later. And because we didn't fight, all we Czechs can do now is sit back and watch it happen."

He pushed his chair away and went again to the window where he stood with his back to everyone. "And if your father was truthful to you, Anna," he said, "those are the real reasons he doesn't want you to stay in Prague." He turned and looked at Ernst. "Isn't that so, Ernst?"

"Yes... it is."

"But where else can I go, Vati?"

Outside a rumbling sound could be heard in the distance.

"That's coming from the other side of the bridge. From the Františkovy Lázně road," said Pavel.

"What is it? What is it?" pleaded Karolína.

The rumbling turned into the roar of engines and the scraping of metal on the road.

"They're tanks."

"Oh, my God. Not yet, please."

Tomáš got up and joined his father at the window. "It's alright, Máma. It's only our troops pulling back from the border. This could be going on all day."

"What a waste," said Pavel. "Thirty divisions we had in reserve. And the best guns of any army in the world."

"Pull the curtains would you please, Tomáš," said Ernst. "Let's try to keep the noise out."

"The world has missed its chance," muttered Pavel.

"Where can I go, if I have to leave, Vati?" Anna asked again.

Tomáš came back to the table and took her hand. "Where can *we* go, Anna? Remember?"

"I don't know, darling," said Ernst. "France, England, America perhaps."

"America," said Karolína. "But I'd never see him again." She went to Tomáš and put her hands on his shoulders.

"I won't leave you, Máma. This is all exaggerated. We all just need to stay calm and get to Prague today and think everything through."

"Oh, for heaven's sake. Are you all blind?" said Pavel. "Can none of you accept what's happening? That is the sound of our army running away out there, of our whole country going under. Do none of you understand what's coming?"

Tomáš banged his fist on the table. "What's the matter with you, Táta?" he shouted. "Do you think you're the only one who feels all this? All you can do is huff and blame everyone for letting you down. We don't need your bitterness or self-pity. We need answers in our own lives."

Pavel did not turn around or speak.

"I think we all need to rest," said Ernst. "We're overwrought. I suggest we go to our rooms and think this through, as calmly as we can. You can have my room, Tomáš. We'll all come down here again at ten o'clock and decide what we're going to do."

Ernst stayed in the front room alone. The remains of the food, barely touched, still lay on the table. He had been sitting there for an hour when he heard the front door open and slam shut.

"Pavel? I didn't realise you had gone out," Ernst called out. "What's happening in the town?"

"A lot."

Pavel came in and sat down. "The trucks are still bringing our troops back from the forts."

Ernst poured him some coffee.

"The square is full of our soldiers, all waiting for transport out of here. At least it's keeping the local Nazis off the streets. So our army is doing some good at last."

"That's not fair, Pavel."

"The road to Prague will be very busy, Ernst. You ought to set off this morning."

"We shall."

"I've seen plenty of people packing up already."

"Will you and Kája please come with us? I have plenty of room in my flat."

"Thankyou, but I'm staying."

"Tomáš thinks you're being very stubborn."

"It's not that." Pavel stared into his coffee cup. "A lot of men died in Russia so that I could get back to Cheb, Ernst. And so many memories of my brothers are here. I don't intend to desert any of them. You can understand that, can't you?"

"Of course."

"Besides, I meant what I said about Prague. It won't be any safer there. The Germans will take it eventually. You know I'm right about that too."

"Yes I do know, but I'm afraid to admit it to myself."

"What will be left of our country won't be able to survive on its own anyway. We'll have no industry. No mines. Prague won't even have electricity or communication with the outside world, unless the Germans allow it."

"I know. I suppose I've been trying to deny it for Anna's sake. I've seen the Jews in Prague who escaped from Germany, Pavel. The stories they tell are terrifying. I've been sitting here trying to work out how I can get my Anna away."

"I think I may have found an answer to that, Ernst."

Ernst looked up and saw a smile on his friend's unshaven face.

"The reason I went out earlier was to make a couple of telephone calls. And I have what I hope will be very good news for you. Do you remember the Musils in Karlovy Vary?"

"You mean Milan Musil, the artist?"

"Yes. I've just spoken to his father. Victor. He owns vineyards in southern France and has his own winery and bottling plant there. He says he can find work for Tomáš. France won't let foreigners in without a work permit, but Victor Musil says he can arrange one quite easily."

"My God, Pavel, this is wonderful..."

"If you can get to Prague today, Tomáš and Anna could probably be married within the week, and then they can leave for France after that."

"Will pan Musil be able to arrange it so soon?"

"Yes, he's going to France himself in twelve days. He says they can go with him."

"Oh, thank God, Pavel. What made you think of it?"

"I listened to what Tomáš said earlier. He made me realise now is the time to look after our families. We can grieve for our country later."

"I've been sitting here for over an hour growing more desperate," said Ernst. He sat back in his chair, sighing with relief and running his fingers through his hair; then he froze. "There's still one problem, Pavel. What if Tomáš refuses to go?"

"Refuses to go? He won't refuse. Not when it's for Anna's sake."

"He might. Tomáš isn't convinced the Germans will take Prague. Even if he were, he probably thinks he can keep Anna safe there. And most of all, neither of them will want to leave Czechoslovakia."

"Of course they will in these circumstances."

Ernst sat forward, rubbing his left shoulder, and looked at his friend. "Don't you realise how much they both love this country, Pavel?" he said. "Tomáš talks about it with the same passion as you always have. And he has taught Anna to feel it too. Don't you see how hurt Tomáš is?"

"Not especially, no."

"That's because you feel no one is as hurt as you are. You think you've suffered a betrayal personal to you alone, but everyone is feeling the same, Pavel. And poor Tomáš not only feels he is a victim of betrayal. He thinks he's guilty of betrayal too."

"That's nonsense. Why should he think that?"

"Because he didn't get the chance to prove his love for his country in the way you did. He feels he has already run once. I'm afraid he might refuse to run again, and Anna would certainly back him up."

Pavel said nothing.

"You must persuade him to leave, Pavel."

"How can I persuade him?"

"My God, Pavel, you are a dear friend and an intelligent man, but you can be so short-sighted. I don't think you realise how proud Tomáš is of being the son of a man who helped create this country. But yesterday he was ordered to surrender that country without a fight."

Pavel looked straight ahead as Ernst spoke.

"Then his first thought is to come here to protect all of you, and you make him feel like a coward because he wasn't given the chance to do what you did. You tell me how you try to forget Russia, and I understand why you say it. But your life has been anchored on what you achieved there, Pavel. Those poor boys in the square, and that poor boy of yours upstairs, will never have that. They will never have Zborov. All they'll ever have is Munich."

Pavel knocked on Tomáš's door.

"May I come in?"

"Yes. I'm not asleep."

"I hope you've had some sleep."

"A bit."

"May I sit down?"

"Of course."

Pavel took the seat by the window.

"Tomáš, I have been talking with Ernst. We both think it's vital you get Anna out of Czechoslovakia."

"Anna and I have discussed it. We are staying in Prague."

"I have spoken with an acquaintance of mine this morning. He owns a winery in southern France. He will provide you with work and somewhere for you both to live, as long as you are husband and wife. You can leave in less than two weeks."

"Anna and I are Czechoslovaks. We will not abandon our country when it needs us most."

"You have nothing to prove, Tomáš."

"I know that. And if ever Anna and I did decide to leave, it would certainly not be to go to France. Not after what they've done to us."

Pavel leaned forward with his elbows on his knees and his head bowed.

"Tomáš, I have realised today, for the first time, that I am guilty of a terrible mistake."

Tomáš looked at him.

"What mistake?"

"I have taught you to love your country too much. I realise now that nothing is more important than the people we love and who love us. That was what brought me back here from Russia, and it is what brought you here to us today."

"But I didn't have to fight to get here."

Pavel looked up. "No, you didn't, but you have to fight now."

"What do you mean?"

"You have to fight to keep Anna safe."

"I can do that in Prague."

"No, you can't. These people who are coming will persecute Anna just for what she is. You will not be able to protect her."

"Our place is here."

"It's not. When we really want something, Tomáš... really believe in it, we should do everything we can to have it and hold on to it. And what you and Anna should want is not your country. It should be one another."

"We can have both."

"If you think so, Tomáš. If I cannot persuade you..."

Pavel stood up. "It's nearly ten o'clock. Are you coming down?"

"Yes, in a minute."

He stopped at the door. "You know, Tomáš, I don't believe for a minute that anything you might have been asked to do as a soldier would have frightened you."

"Don't you?"

"Not for a minute. I know my son. I know how brave and strong you are. There has only been one thing in your life that has ever frightened you."

"And what's that?"

"The thought that you could lose Anna."

When Pavel went into the front room, Ernst and Anna and Karolína were already sitting around the table.

"I've told Anna about France, Pavel," said Ernst. "She will not go."

"I don't think Tomáš will either. He's suffering from the confidence of youth."

"Or of his father."

"I hope not, Ernst."

"Well, I'm relieved," sighed Karolína. "I think we all have enough to worry about, without losing our children too. Perhaps later, if we really think it's necessary."

Pavel sat down and took Karolína's hand. "You may be right, my love. There may be time later, but can we really take that risk when our country is wide open to the Germans?"

Tomáš came in and crossed the room to stand in front of the fireplace. Everyone waited for him to speak, but he said nothing.

"Well, I'm not prepared to gamble with my daughter's life, Kája," said Ernst. "My darling Otto seems to be risking his life every day in Palestine. Everything is so uncertain for Jews there. I cannot tolerate the thought of the same thing happening here to my Anna."

Anna put her arm around her father's shoulders.

"Oh, Vati, please don't upset yourself. I'll be alright in Prague with you and Tomáš."

"I don't want to be parted from you, Anna, but I cannot stand the thought of you being at the mercy of those terrible people."

"Why don't Tomáš and Anna get married in Prague, and then if we think it's becoming unsafe, they leave then?" said Karolína.

"Who knows if the opportunity will still be there later, Kája?" said Ernst. "This could be the only chance." He hung his head and expelled all the air from his lungs. There was silence.

"I love you, Anna," Tomáš said.

Everyone looked at him.

"I think we should go to France. As soon as possible."

"Why, darling? What's changed your mind?"

"That has changed my mind. The love I have for you. And what I learned yesterday."

"I don't understand."

"Yesterday I learned there are forces at work in the world which you and I cannot fight on our own. One million men were ready to fight yesterday and to die, if they were asked to. And they were all betrayed with not one voice raised in their defence, and at a stroke they became powerless.

"If that can happen to a whole army, to a whole country, what chance do two people have? Let's save ourselves, Anna, get married, have children and bring our family back to our country when it's safe for them."

Anna got up and went to Tomáš and put her arms around him. "I'll go wherever you go, Tomáš. You know that."

Ernst stood and went over to them. He kissed Anna and shook Tomáš's hand. "I never thought I would thank the man who took my Anna away from me," he said.

Tomáš went over to his mother, who had started to cry. "I've prayed so hard over the years for this never to happen again," she said. "War took your father away and now it's taking you."

Tomáš knelt by her side.

"Come back to Prague with us, Máma. Come to the wedding. You can bring Máma back here later, can't you, Uncle Ernst?"

"Of course, Tomáš. Of course."

"Will you come too, Táta?"

Pavel shook his head. He looked at Tomáš and scanned his face and his body as if he were admiring a painting. He could still see the small boy, proud and determined, who had marched across the clearing by the chata on the day he returned from Russia.

"If times were normal, Tomáš, nothing would keep me away from such an important day in your life. Please know that. But please, I need your permission to stay in Cheb over the next few days."

"You have it, Táta. Of course you do. I know you always do what is right."

Tomáš and Anna went to the Church of St Wenceslas to pay their respects to their grandparents. When they came back, the car was packed and

Ernst and Karolína were ready to leave. Pavel stood on the doorstep to see them off. Anna and Tomáš embraced him together. "We promise you, Táta, that one day we'll come back with our children to live in our country."

"I know you will, and I shall be here to greet you. I shall always be here for you, Tomáš. Now go, before it all becomes too much."

"Goodbye, darling," said Karolína. "Please stay safe. I'll be back in a week or so."

They kissed and Pavel held her to him. "I love you, Kája. You and I will get through this again."

"I know we will. Can you just promise me we're doing the right thing, that Tomáš will be safe in France?"

"Yes, my love. The Germans are going east. Tomáš will be safe."

Ernst shook Pavel's hand. "We're off, old friend. Thankyou for all your help in this."

"I'll see you soon, Ernst."

Pavel went up the steps to the front door. The engine fired, and Karolína and Tomáš waved from the nearside window. At the last moment Ernst got out of the car and came back to the steps.

"Pavel, I hope you will excuse my impertinence, but there is something I need to say to you." He looked into his friend's face. "Do you remember the day many years ago when I went to see the Graf von Stricker about my Otto?"

"I do. Heinrich had been threatening him in the Turnverband."

"That's right. I was so angry that I issued threats of my own to the Graf. I said I would do to his worthless son anything he did to my Otto."

"Good for you."

"Perhaps. But today my threat would be hollow, Pavel, because people like von Stricker are amoral, and now they have all the power of an amoral state behind them. You cannot win against them alone, Pavel."

"I understand what you're saying, Ernst. But don't worry about me. Just have a safe journey. And please, look after our Kája."

Chapter Forty-Five

October 2nd – 4th, 1938

By Sunday afternoon all Czechoslovak troops and armour had left Cheb. In the evening Pavel waited for the Germans to arrive, but no one came. Delayed by the British request at Munich for a three-kilometre no-man's-land to be preserved between the two armies, the Germans did not enter Cheb until eight o'clock on Monday morning. It only added to Pavel's fury that the invasion of his country should be conducted with such good manners and observance of protocol.

Church bells rang on Monday morning and German householders were quick to hang swastikas from upstairs windows. Only the deserted houses of Germans who had supported the Communists or Social Democrats now stood unadorned and empty. From his bedroom window Pavel watched anti-aircraft batteries being set up on the banks of the River Ohře towards Skalka, and signs being erected at the bridge instructing motorists that in the Greater German Reich all traffic would drive on the right.

At midday Pavel ventured into the town. Even during the worst days of repression under the Hapsburgs he had not felt so alienated from the town of his birth. In front of the New Town Hall a podium was being built. Behind the podium two enormous swastika flags blocked most of the Town Hall from view. Between the flags hung a huge gold eagle with outstretched wings, carved from wood and clasping in its talons a gold-framed swastika. At five-metre intervals around the perimeter of the square soldiers in the field-grey uniforms and helmets of the Wehrmacht stood to attention, while young women in traditional Egerland costumes sought to impress them with their hysterical laughing and screaming.

"Morgen kommt der Führer!"

"Ja, nach Eger!"

"Er kommt nach Eger!"

"Der Führer!"

"My God, so Filip was right," said Pavel to himself. "The bastard is coming to Cheb tomorrow."

He walked back across the square to the colonnade. Groups of Sudeten brownshirts stood around in their usual pose, legs apart and thumbs hooked in their belts, but there were newcomers too; three men in the uniform of the Bavarian police, and two more in long grey raincoats and black fedora hats. They watched him as he approached the bakery of pan and pani Lanek. He paused to read the poster stuck to the window. *'Kauft nur bei Deutschen.' Buy only at German shops*. He shook his head, smiled and walked in. The shelves were full of unsold bread.

"Oh, pan Kovařík, thankyou so much. Those men out there are stopping everyone from coming in."

"Who are they, pani Laneková?"

"They're Gestapo thugs," said Vašek Lanek, appearing from the bakery. He shook Pavel's hand. "They arrived with the soldiers this morning. Now they've closed the Jewish shops, they're working on us. You're only the third person to come in since eight o'clock."

"I don't know what we'll do with all of this," said pani Laneková, pointing to the shelves.

"Don't worry, Marta. I've just been round to see Bruno Fischer. He's got people queuing down the street, and he can't bake it fast enough. I've sold it all to him."

"Well done, Vašek," laughed Pavel. "Give me two rye loaves before you run out then, will you? These Nazis make me smile with their stupid nonsense. Standing there posturing like that."

"They're nasty swines... pardon me, Marta. Watch out for them, Pavel."

"I will."

The men in the raincoats were waiting for Pavel when he came out of the shop. *"Ausweis,"* demanded one of them.

"I don't have one."

"Speak German, you Ivan shit," said the second man, and he pushed Pavel back against the wall. "Czech is a forbidden language and all you Ivans must have an identity card."

"What's your name and your address, you ignorant shit."

"Pavel Otakar Kovařík. Four Křížov Nická."

"What sort of address is that? Write it down. You can write, can't you?"

"Yes."

"Who else lives there?"

"My wife."

"What's the name of your whore wife?"

"My wife is called Karolína."

"You and your whore wife had better register at the Town Hall today.

If we find either of you out again without an identity card, you go to the *Zuchthaus* for a month. Understood?"

Pavel looked at him.

"Don't stare at me, Ivan. What's this?"

He took the bread and broke it open, letting the pieces fall onto the floor.

"It's a good job you weren't hiding anything in it. Now pick it all up *und hau' ab, du Arsch*. We don't want your sort here."

Filip Souček poured coffee for Eduard Beneš and Kamil Krofta in the president's office.

"Thankyou, Filip," said Beneš.

Souček did not reply. He nodded and left the two men together in their armchairs in front of the fire.

"He's like all the legionnaires. He's very angry," said Beneš. "I'm told some have been seen weeping openly in the street."

"It's probably true, Eduard. It is a bitter time for everyone. But you must not go on reproaching yourself like this."

"How can I not, Kamil? I keep looking at the portrait. It reproaches me. I ask myself over and over what he would have done. And I know the answer. He would have fought, and he would have won. But I don't know how."

"You know nothing of the sort. Masaryk was a pragmatist before all else."

"No, Kamil, not before all else. His principles came first. Remember, truth always prevails."

"Listen to me, Eduard. You, Masaryk, our people, did everything asked and expected of them. You have remained true to our democratic principles to the very end. The situation is simple. You were betrayed by the French and the British."

"Did you see the front page of Saturday's London Times, Kamil? It's there on the table."

Krofta took the newspaper and put on his reading glasses.

"'*No conqueror returning from a victory on the battlefield has come home adorned with nobler laurels than Mr Chamberlain from Munich yesterday.*' There you are, you see, Eduard. In the end it was just one man. Chamberlain. If he had kept his nerve for only a few more hours, the break-up of our country could have been avoided."

"But I still cannot understand why the British were so much against us, Kamil. I will go to my grave not knowing the answer to that."

"Jan Masaryk always said Chamberlain was parochial. He told me the man didn't even know where the Sudetenland was six months ago. And he's certainly not grasped the fact that it has never once belonged to Germany."

"But that's not what I mean, Kamil. Where was the British sense of fair play? Why did they side with a dictator in those talks, and not even allow us to be represented?"

Krofta shook his head and stared down at the table. "I don't know, Eduard. I simply do not know."

"Even worse is knowing the British and the French were both aware of our intelligence from A-34. They knew Hitler's generals and Admiral Canaris were ready to depose him if his attack on us led to war with them in the west."

"I think the British were afraid of the bombing."

"But not one German bomber was capable of reaching London and returning to Germany."

"I know."

"We could have held their forces here for weeks, and the French would have been far too strong for them in the west."

"As I said, Eduard, we were betrayed."

"I should never have accepted the Anglo-French Plan. It showed we were ready to concede."

"Do not keep reproaching yourself, Eduard. You did all you could."

"No, Kamil. I have destroyed my country. Even the Slovaks want to separate now."

"If we had fought alone, Eduard, our country would have bled to death."

"But we would have fought a virtuous war. Our national spirit would have remained strong and intact. No, my decision will haunt me for the rest of my life."

"Where will you go tomorrow?"

"England first. Then America perhaps. I feel shame at being driven into exile again."

"Any shame belongs to those who allowed Hitler to demand your exile, Eduard."

"I shall take this telegram with me. Prime Minister Lloyd George sent it to Masaryk in 1918. The President entrusted it to me when he left office. Will you indulge me for a moment, Kamil?"

"Of course."

"It is hard to believe what the British Prime Minister thought of us then. '*On behalf of the British War Cabinet I send you our heartiest congratulations on the striking successes won by the Czecho-Slav forces against the armies of Germany and Austria in Siberia. The story of this small army is one of the epics of history. It has filled us with admiration for the courage, persistence and self-control of your countrymen, holding the spirit of freedom in their hearts. Your nation has rendered inestimable service in the struggle to free the world from despotism. We shall never forget it.*'

Beneš held the paper in his lap. "But they did forget, Kamil. They did forget."

"Perhaps you could ask the Times to print it on their front page, Eduard."

Both men forced a smile.

"Are you determined to stay in Prague, Kamil?" asked Beneš.

"Yes, I shall serve the new president in any capacity he wishes."

"Syrový must only be temporary, Kamil. You must hold new elections. We must stay true to our democratic principles, even if the other democracies did expel us from their club."

"We shall remain true, Mr President, for as long as we can. I assure you of that."

Pavel was informed that Hitler was expected in Cheb some time after two o'clock on Tuesday afternoon. The Führer had apparently suffered a shock the previous day when he inspected the Czechoslovakian fortifications along the border. He had seen for the first time how strong the defences were, how serious the German losses would have been, and realised what a bounty had been presented to him at Munich. He had issued an immediate order to take every piece of Škoda weaponry to Germany for the use of the Wehrmacht.

Pavel made his way up Krámařská Street to await Hitler's arrival. It was a warm, bright day with not a cloud in the sky. The good weather meant he was unable to wear his heavy overcoat with the deep pockets. Instead he had put on his loosest jacket and his best trilby hat.

At the end of the street he was met by an impenetrable crowd and the sound of heavy military vehicles. He turned and made his way back past his house and along the river to the castle ruins. There he turned up the narrow Podvoki Lane to approach the square from the other end of the colonnade. It was crowded there too, but less so, and there was a way through.

The mass of people were already cheering wildly, although Hitler was not expected for another twenty minutes. Pavel forced his way into the middle of the crowd and found a clear view of the square. The podium where Hitler would speak was further to his left than he had hoped, and in front of it a phalanx of black-uniformed SS men in black steel helmets kept the crowd a good ten metres back.

More SS from Hitler's personal bodyguard were maintaining a thoroughfare through the centre of the square for a military procession to pass. Each man stood with legs apart holding the belts of the men to his left and right. Immediately behind them young women in their usual Egerland costume threw flowers onto the half-tracks carrying the German soldiers who had 'liberated' the town. All the women were laughing and shouting, and everyone in the crowd raised their right arm as the chant began, *'wir danken unserem Führer'. We thank our Führer.*

Pavel stood on tiptoe for a clearer view and was able to see the faces of young boys peeking out between the legs of the SS men holding back the crowd. He realised he needed to work his way through the crowd to his left, in order to get as close to the podium as he could. But it was impossible to move far to the left or the right. He decided to go back to the colonnade where he would be able to walk along more freely. He pushed his way through the crowd, smiling at people and feigning pleasure at the Führer worship. Several people recognised him and seemed willing to accept that he too had been seduced by the pure joy of the occasion.

At last he reached the colonnade again. It was almost empty because of the restricted view it offered of the podium. He started to walk along it and caught sight of the two men in grey raincoats. He darted behind a column. He did not want to be searched again. Not today. He forced his way once more into the crowd and received angry looks and curses as he sought sanctuary there. He had returned almost to his original spot when an enormous roar went up to his left. He made himself as tall as he could and, craning his neck, was able to glimpse a black open-top Mercedes car. Standing up in front of the passenger seat and holding on to a bar on top of the windscreen was Adolf Hitler.

At the sight of the Führer the carnival atmosphere turned to hysteria. The young women throwing the flowers, and many more in the crowd, began to weep as they screamed their love and loyalty and thanks. The SS men now dug their heels into the cobbles and leaned back against the throng behind them to ensure the Führer's progress.

Hitler did not smile. He looked straight ahead with a stern expression, his right arm raised like a man being sworn in at a criminal trial. Flowers bounced off the car. Some fell onto the bonnet, others found their way inside. Then a bouquet of roses thrown a little too enthusiastically struck the Führer on the side of the head. Hitler looked quickly in the direction of the thrower and then resumed his fixed stare into the far distance.

"Damn," Pavel muttered to himself. That was the answer. He had no chance with a revolver. He should have brought a grenade.

When the car reached the centre of the square opposite the podium, it stopped and Hitler got out. Pavel could only catch brief glimpses of him. He was wearing a long grey leather coat and peaked hat. He walked now along the thoroughfare, patting the cheeks of children and raising his right hand to his shoulder again in acknowledgement of the crowd. Behind him Konrad Henlein beamed his approval, and adjutants collected more flowers from the grateful crowd. Hitler and Henlein made their way onto the podium, and the noise around Pavel became so loud he found it hard to bear. Now that his plan had no chance of success, he wanted only to disassociate himself from the madness, but there was no way out. He was forced to remain a part of it.

On the podium he recognised the figures of Heinrich Himmler and Generals Reichenau and Keitel, the area's new military governor. Henlein stepped forward to speak, trying to emulate his Führer's passion and oratory with his thin, shrill voice. Then Hitler spoke, and Pavel heard the familiar guttural sounds fill the place which meant so much to him. His brain rejected the madman's words and instead provided images of better times; of Karolína crossing the square from St Wenceslas Church to sign the civic register; of being brought here by his parents when they registered the births of his brothers. Not knowing how much time had passed, he became aware the crowd was thinning and the podium was empty.

He felt exhausted and distracted as he retraced his steps slowly to Podvoki Lane and the way home, but he was able to catch snippets of conversation among the people around him. Hitler, it seemed, had gone into the Town Hall to sign the Town Book. Pavel looked back across the square. There were still several hundred people waiting for Hitler to reappear, mostly the SS men and the Egerland girls. It would be impossible for him to mingle with them. His chance was gone.

He had walked a short distance down Podvoki Lane, when someone called to him.

"Hey, you, Ivan, what are you doing here?"

"Stay where you are."

Pavel recognised the voices. Quickly he looked about him without turning. He knelt down on one knee, removed the gun from his inside pocket and dropped it down the storm drain to his right. He was relieved to hear the sound of it hitting the water.

"I said 'stay'. What are you doing?"

"You mean me?"

Pavel stood up and turned.

"Of course I mean you, you shit. What were you doing down there?"

The man in the raincoat looked into the drain.

"I was just tying my shoelace."

A fist landed on the side of Pavel's head as the second man reached them.

"Clever shit. Against the wall. Hands on your head."

The second man went through his pockets. Pavel felt the blood from his left eyebrow running down his cheek.

"So you had the sense to get an *Ausweis.*"

"I did what you told me."

Three SS men came up the street and joined the two in raincoats.

"Who's this?" asked one of them.

"An Ivan who thinks he's clever. He dropped something in the drain."

The SS man grabbed Pavel's jaw and stared at him. Pavel looked into his face and then at the two men standing either side of him. Their eyes studied him from beneath their black helmets. He recognised the look of men set on violence. But these men were not angry. They were not fuelled by the fear and passion of battle. Their eyes were calm and cold and lustful, anticipating pleasure. One of them took a large coin from his pocket, put the sharpened edge into the cut over Pavel's eye and turned it. Then he stepped back and another took his place, as Pavel bent forward clutching his face.

"*Der Führer kommt...*" someone shouted.

The three SS men turned and hurried back towards the square. One of the Gestapo men threw Pavel's identity card on the floor and snarled. "*Verpiss dich, Scheisskerl...*"

Pavel picked up the card and ran down the lane towards the river. Blood poured from his eye. When he had gone no more than twenty metres, he stopped and looked back. Coming towards him, talking animatedly and smiling, was Adolf Hitler on his way to the house of Wallenstein. A perfect target, thought Pavel, if only he had not thrown down his weapon and run.

Chapter Forty-Six

October 14th – 15th, 1938

Ernst sat in the car, watching Karolína approach her front door. She turned the key, stepped into the hallway, and his loneliness returned. It had been a long and difficult day and he was very tired. Pavel appeared at the door and came down the steps to the car. Ernst got out to meet him.

"Pavel, dear friend, how are you?"

"Well enough, Ernst. Kája says you had a bad time at the border. Here, let me take your luggage."

"Thankyou. What have you done to your eye?"

"I fell. It's nothing. You can have the same room as last time, Ernst. It's been aired. I think Kája is already in the kitchen preparing some food. She won't let me do a thing."

Karolína came out to the hallway to meet them. She had already put on an apron. Ernst saw an unforced smile on her face for the first time in two weeks.

"Would you mind if I took some time to freshen up before I eat?" he asked.

"Not at all," said Pavel and Karolína together.

"I'll be down in about ten minutes then."

Pavel and Karolína went into the front room and immediately put their arms around one another again.

"You feel so thin, darling," said Karolína. "And tell me the truth about your eye."

"Do I have to?"

"I shall know if you don't."

"I'll tell you in a minute, Kája, but first I want to know about Tomáš and Anna."

"You got my letter?"

"Yes, but tell me about after the wedding. Did they get away alright?"

"Yes, they flew."

"Flew?"

"Yes, to Marseille. Pan Musil always flies apparently. They were very excited. I didn't go to the airport. I couldn't have got through it. Every time I think of my Tomášek..."

Pavel kissed her forehead and stroked her hair.

"Don't upset yourself, darling. It's for the best."

"I know. I do know. Prague is so full of unhappy people. So many arrive every day, and then so many leave. It makes it easier somehow seeing other people going through it too. Is that a dreadful thing to say?"

"No, darling. It's only natural to want to share one's troubles."

"It was the only thing that kept me sane when you were gone. Knowing I wasn't the only one."

"Of course. Come and sit down."

"What has it been like here?"

"Hitler strutted in last week. The Germans have been barking like mad dogs. Gloating about our problems with the Slovaks, and more of our country going to the Poles and Magyars."

"That's not what I meant. Is it safe here?"

"There's no work. They've closed the Czech schools."

"We'll have to leave then."

"I could do some private tutoring."

"Is it worth it, Pavel? I know I said things were difficult in Prague, but there's no violence there. The Germans are mostly like Ernst. They hate Hitler as much as we do."

"I thought you were pleased to be back here."

"Not to Cheb. Only to you. I've missed you so much. When Tomáš left I needed you so much."

"I'm sorry, Kája. I had to stay."

"And what do you think now?"

"I'm not sure."

"And what did happen to your eye? It looks dreadful."

"I will be honest with you, Kája. I went to see Hitler arrive. Just out of curiosity. And some of the usual thugs didn't like the thought of a Czech being near their Führer, so they gave me this."

"Oh no, Pavel."

"Doctor Liška stitched it up for me."

"We can't stay amongst such people."

"Would you be happier in Prague, darling?"

"Yes, I would, but only if you were there."

"Then I'll leave, Kája. We'll go together."

Karolína took Pavel's hand and kissed it and held it to her cheek.

"Oh, thankyou, darling. Thankyou."

"Do you think it will be alright if we stay with Ernst until we find somewhere?" asked Pavel.

"Of course it will, dear friend," said Ernst from the hallway. He came in and stood behind his friends and placed his hand on Pavel's shoulder. "Please do not think I was standing there listening. I was just about to knock and heard..."

"We don't think anything of the sort," said Pavel. "We're very grateful to you for all you are doing."

Pavel stood up and disappeared into the kitchen. "Here we are," he said, returning with a bottle and three glasses. "I hope this won't upset you, Kája my love, but I kept a bottle of Michal's slivovitz. I can think of nothing more appropriate to toast our children's new beginning in France, and our new beginning in Prague."

Karolína nodded and smiled.

"And, of course, our dear Otto in Palestine."

"Thankyou, Pavel."

"So, I propose a toast to absent friends, and to new beginnings elsewhere."

"Absent friends and new beginnings."

The glasses were emptied and Pavel and Ernst exchanged approving glances.

"I must go and get something for us to eat," said Karolína, dabbing her eyes and hurrying into the kitchen. "Ernst has had nothing all day."

The two men watched her and sat down at the table.

"Did you have problems with the traffic then, Ernst?"

"No, all the traffic was coming the other way. They say over 100,000 have left already."

"That still leaves 700,000 Czechs living under the Nazis."

"I know. The problem today was getting back into the German area. They're very suspicious of Czechoslovakian citizens entering the Reich. We were more than four hours at the border. In the end they only let me through because of my Austrian German birth certificate."

"Ernst had to get a Sudeten German identity card," Karolína shouted through from the kitchen. "And I had to get a temporary Czech one."

"So you had to register as a Sudeten German, Ernst?"

"Yes, I am now officially a citizen of Hitler's Reich."

"I'm sorry, Ernst."

"It was the only way to get Kája back."

"I understand the sacrifice. I'm very grateful."

"There you are," said Karolína, placing a large platter on the table. "It's only cold, I'm afraid."

There was a loud hammering at the front door.

"Oh, my goodness, whatever's that?" said Karolína, putting her hand to her mouth.

Ernst looked over at Pavel and saw him close his eyes and wince. "I'll go," Ernst said.

Pavel heard him open the door.

"Are you Kovařík? Pavel Kovařík?"

"That's not him."

"My name is Neumann. Hauptmann Ernst Neumann."

"This is number four Křížov Nická?"

"Yes, this is my house."

"We believe a Czech named Kovařík lives here."

"He does. He's lived here for years," came the voice of Alois Krause from the street.

"Out of the way, Hauptmann Neumann. We're searching the house."

Pavel heard a scuffle.

"This is my house. I am a citizen of the Reich living here under the protection of our Führer..."

Pavel saw Ernst fall back and crack his head against the door frame of the front room.

"I'm in here," Pavel called out, and he went to the door leading into the hallway.

"That's him," shouted Krause. "That's Kovařík."

One of the men in a raincoat grabbed Pavel's arm. "Out you come, Ivan."

Pavel managed to glance back at Karolína and smile. He saw her eyes wide and staring, her hand still clasped to her mouth.

"Ever lie to me again, Neumann," said the man, as he kicked Ernst on the floor, "and you'll get some of what he's going to get."

Pavel was led in handcuffs up the steps of the Victoria Hotel by the station. The grey frontage still bore scars from the fighting on the night of Hitler's Nuremburg speech one month before. The front doors had been replaced and the insignia of Henlein's SdP removed. Inscribed on a simple brass plate at the entrance was the building's new designation, *'Geheime Staatspolizei. Eger'.*

Pavel was taken to the old reception desk in the entrance hall, where he was asked for information once asked of guests newly arrived from the station. Name, address, nationality. There were new questions. Religion, religion of parents and grandparents, political affiliation, next of kin. His pockets were emptied and his watch removed. His trousers were checked for belt and braces. For no reason he could think of, his house shoes were taken from him.

He was taken into a large room and ordered to sit in a high-backed chair in front of a large table. He heard the door close behind him. He turned and saw the two Gestapo men standing in front of it, still wearing their raincoats and fedoras. He checked his surroundings.

The room had a high stuccoed ceiling and was lit by three small bulbs in an old chandelier. The wallpaper was ruby red with a raised velvet motif. On the other side of the table was an office chair upholstered in red leather. Pavel recognised the room. It had once been the hotel restaurant. It smelled musty, although the carpet had been removed leaving bare floor boards. Only in the centre of the room, where he sat, was there a covering of thick rubber over the floor.

He remained there for fifteen or twenty minutes, and still nothing was happening. He thought of Karolína and imagined Ernst trying to soothe her nerves. Ernst no doubt knew what he knew, that he was going to take a beating for upsetting these people. He just hoped Ernst was not sharing that thought with Karolína. He would have to clean himself up somehow before he got home.

Through the wall to his right he heard people talking. There was some shouting and cursing and a door slammed, followed by silence for another ten minutes. They were giving him too much time to think. He turned to the men at the door.

"Why am I..?"

"Halt's Maul, Arschloch."

A door opened through the wallpaper to the right. Pavel had not even noticed it was there. A man walked to the desk and sat down in the leather chair.

"You are Pavel Kovařík?"

"Yes."

"Why did you attend the celebrations for the Führer in Eger on Tuesday, 4th October?"

"I was interested in seeing what all the fuss was about."

"Fuss? What do you mean 'fuss'?"

"I could hear the noise. I wanted to see what was happening."

"You are a Czech?"

"Yes."

"Do you think loutish Czechs are welcome when we Germans wish to honour our Führer?"

"I thought so. I was curious. I meant no harm."

"Harm? Why do you say 'harm'?"

The man raised his head for the first time. He looked as disinterested as he sounded.

"It was just an expression."

"What did you throw away when you were seen in Podvoki Street?"

"Nothing."

"You were seen disposing of something in a drain, minutes before the Führer was due to visit that area of the town."

"I didn't know your Führer was going to be there."

"We don't believe you."

The man opened the drawer to his desk. "Is this yours?" He put Pavel's revolver on the desk.

"No, I've never seen it."

"You are surprised to see it now, aren't you?"

"I'm surprised you say it's mine."

The man sat back and swivelled gently on his chair.

"You Slavs always amuse me. You think everyone must be as stupid and slow-witted as you are. Do you know what type of gun this is?"

"No."

"It is a Nagant. It was made in Russia, where you spent the years 1917 until 1920."

"It's not mine."

"You are surprised we have it, aren't you? And more surprised how much we know about you. Do you still deny it is yours?"

"Yes."

He gestured to the man at the door. The door was opened and Pavel heard someone approach the desk behind him.

"Do you know the accused?" the newcomer was asked.

"Yes, he's the schoolmaster Kovařík."

Pavel recognised the voice of Heinrich von Stricker.

"Have you seen this gun before?"

"Yes, it's the gun he used to threaten me on 12th September."

"How can you know that, von Stricker?" said Pavel. "You were too busy murdering a defenceless old man and terrorising his wife to notice anything."

Pavel looked around and von Stricker smiled at him.

"We have the report of that incident. The man Štasný was a spy, just like you. Is that not correct, Untersturmführer?"

"Yes, Herr Kriminalkommissar."

"Kovařík," said the man behind the desk, "the evidence against you is overwhelming. When the Führer visited Eger you intended to shoot him with this gun. When you were cornered like a rat you disposed of the gun, but were too stupid to realise what even a rat would know. That the gun would reappear at the end of the drain in the mesh which keeps detritus from the river. You will sign this confession."

Pavel was handed a blank piece of paper.

"I won't sign a thing."

"Very well. Bring the others from the house. His wife and Neumann."

"No, no. Wait."

"Wait? Why should we wait?"

"Because it was me. On my own. I admit it. I'll write a full confession and sign it, but it will say nothing about them. They weren't even here on 4th October."

"Very well. I accept. Here is the paper and pen. In your confession you will admit to your role as a spy for Prague, and to the assassination attempt. Do you understand?"

"Yes. You will need to remove the handcuffs."

The man stayed at his desk while Pavel wrote. He could feel the presence of von Stricker behind him. He wrote slowly trying to think clearly enough to find a way out. But there was no way out. He had thrown away his life for nothing, and put Kája and Ernst at risk. And Kája, poor Kája. How would she cope with his death after all she had been through? He closed his eyes and put his hands to his face.

"Don't think of your own skin, Kovařík," said the man. "Just write about the assassination attempt."

The bastard's right, thought Pavel. He had to subdue all emotion and think practically. The confession would save Kája and Ernst, and he knew Ernst would care for his Kája. And Tomáš and Anna were safe now, and he would live on through them and their children. Everything would be alright. His death would affirm his life. Nothing must matter, as long as they all remained safe.

A terrible realisation hit him. There was something else. He was falling into a trap. He stopped writing.

"Will I be tortured?" he asked.

The man at the desk smiled for the first time. "No, Kovařík. You will not be harmed at all."

"I'm not going to confess if you're going to torture me anyway."

"No, my brave little Slav, we will not hurt you."

"But I'm saying I did this on my own. It had nothing to do with Prague."

"We know you have been an agent of Prague for many years. We know you contacted your handler there two days before the Führer's visit."

"I won't write that."

"It does not matter. People will draw the proper conclusions at your trial."

"I'm going to have a trial?"

"Of course, very soon. You will be famous, Kovařík. The whole world will be interested in you. So we will keep you very fit and healthy."

"Thankyou. Because I really can't stand the thought of... whatever you do..."

Pavel heard von Stricker sniggering behind him.

"Have you finished it?" asked the man at the desk.

"Yes."

The Kriminalkomissar read the single sheet. "It will be enough. And you will confess to this in open court?"

"Yes. But I want you to order von Stricker not to beat me. And he must make sure the other two don't do anything either."

"Kovařík, you disappoint me. I always knew the Czechs were an inferior race with no stomach for a fight, but I never realised before just how cowardly and degenerate you really are. Von Stricker, you will take the prisoner downstairs and make sure no harm comes to him. Take Köhler and Bachmeier with you."

"Yes, Herr Kriminalkomissar."

Von Stricker took Pavel by the arm and led him out to the reception. The two men in raincoats followed. They walked him down the steps to the cellar. Wine, beer and food had once been stored in the dark, cold space. Now, on either side of the room, cells had been constructed from heavy planks which reached from floor to ceiling. The passage between the two rows was lit by a single bulb. Pavel counted four cells on each side. He was taken to the last one on the right. The heavy wooden door was opened and one of the men in the raincoats switched on a light from the outside.

Pavel hoped at least one of the three men would go in first, but he was pushed in alone. He sat down on his haunches by the wall next to the door. Before they closed it, he started to sob.

"Please don't hurt me. Don't leave me here."

Von Stricker came in to taunt him. "Look at this snivelling little Ivan, *Männer*. You're not so brave now you don't have a gun pointed at my head, are you, Kovařík?"

"I'm sorry. I didn't mean anything by it."

The two men in the raincoats came in to take a look and join in the fun. Pavel saw the three pairs of legs standing in front of him. He slowly raised himself to his feet, keeping his arms in front of his face to ward off any blows.

"Please don't do anything."

He saw one of the raincoats approach him. He stood to Pavel's left by the open door. "What a cowardly little Ivan shit you are," he said, as he landed a kick on Pavel's shin.

"Don't mark him," said von Stricker, "or we'll all be in trouble. Only legs and body."

"Please, no," begged Pavel.

The man stepped forward to land another kick on Pavel's shin and then retreated to the stone cellar wall, turning to acknowledge the approval of his partner and von Stricker.

In the moment he turned back Pavel took one stride towards him and drove the heel of his open palm up into the base of the man's nose, jarring his head back and shattering his skull against the cellar wall. Pavel kicked the cell door shut and strode towards the man's partner standing against the back wall next to von Stricker. Stunned by the suddenness and violence of the attack, both von Stricker and the Gestapo man stood rooted to the spot. Pavel took a second stride, planting his left foot, and, with a twist of his body released his right fist into the man's temple. The German's head snapped back, his neck broken.

Von Stricker raced for the door but, as he reached it, Pavel wrapped his left arm around his throat. Pavel's right arm went under von Stricker's right armpit and he spread his hand against the back of his head. He pushed von Stricker's head forward, closing his windpipe.

"Don't struggle, Heinrich, or I'll kill you even more slowly."

He released the pressure against von Stricker's throat, allowing him to gulp some air. Then he cut the supply off again.

"You will not terrorise one more Slav, Heinrich. You and I are going to die together today, but it will be me seeing you in the gutter, not the other way round. Do you want to say anything?"

Pavel released the pressure.

"Let me go... please... you can leave... "

"I don't want to leave, Heinrich. This is my own personal war against you little Nazis. Breathe deeply now. It will have to last you."

"Let me..."

"No, Heinrich. That was the last breath you'll ever take. Use it to think. Think about all the threats you made to Otto Neumann. Think about Michal Štasný and his wife. If you had left those people in peace, you would not be choking to death now. Think about that, Heinrich. Think..."

Pavel tightened his grip until von Stricker's body trembled, straightened, and went limp. He dragged him away from the door and searched the two Gestapo men for guns. They both had Lugers with eight rounds. He took a pistol in each hand, released the safety catches and opened the door. The corridor outside was empty. He walked to the stairs and saw a group of SS men at the top. He climbed the stairs slowly. Unable to believe that anyone would walk so obviously into danger, the SS men turned and stood facing him.

Pavel raised both arms and fired. Two men fell back screaming. Another stepped forward and fired into the stairwell. Pavel felt a blow to his chest. He tried to raise his foot to take another step but nothing happened. He felt more blows to his chest and shoulder. He felt himself falling back through the air, and then nothing.

The night Pavel was arrested Karolína thought she could lose her mind with worry. When he did not return home the next morning, she determined to go in person to the Victoria Hotel and demand to know the reason for his detention.

Ernst persuaded her that an enquiry from a Sudeten German might be better received, and it was he who went to the Gestapo headquarters in the early afternoon. A civilian worker Ernst had known for many years was behind the reception desk. She urged him to leave the building at once, and make no further enquiries there. She would meet him after work at the castle ruins to explain.

"There was a terrible tragedy last night, Herr Neumann," she told him later. "One of the prisoners killed two Gestapo men and an SS *Leutnant* in his cell. Then he took their guns and mortally wounded two more SS men, before he was shot dead."

"Do you know the name of the prisoner, Fräulein Niemeyer?"

"Not officially. They are trying to keep it all quiet, but I have to tell you, Herr Neumann, that I'm sure it was your friend the schoolmaster."

"Pavel Kovařík?"

"I'm afraid so. Are you alright?"

"It is a terrible shock, Fräulein Niemeyer. Terrible. I must recover his body."

"Herr Neumann, I could be in a lot of trouble for telling you this, but I think you and Frau Kovařík and anyone else at their house should leave here as soon as possible."

"Why?"

"Please, I beg you, Herr Neumann, do not whisper one word of this, but your friend was accused of plotting to kill the Führer."

"What?"

"I am only telling you because our two families go back such a long way."

"I appreciate that, Fräulein Niemeyer. I give you my word I shall not abuse your confidence or our families' friendship. You will understand if I return to the house as a matter of urgency."

Ernst knew there was no easy way of giving Karolína the news. She had been waiting for him for hours, and as soon as she saw him turn the corner by the bridge, she knew. She opened the door and looked at Ernst on the doorstep, and his face confirmed it.

If Karolína had burst into tears, or collapsed on the floor, or even been lost in hysteria, Ernst would have been less worried than he became as the evening wore on. Karolína had turned away from him as he stood on the doorstep, gone into the front room and sat down at the table. And there she stayed for hour after hour with her forearms resting on the polished surface, staring ahead and saying nothing. It was impossible to move her.

He had seen enough men in shock to know how dangerous it was. He talked to her, trying to bring her back, but there was no response. He brought her hot drinks and food, but she would touch nothing. After several hours she got up and went upstairs to her room. Without seeking permission he followed her in. She went to her dresser and took out a photograph of Pavel in a frame. She removed a small piece of folded paper from the back and read it. She looked over at Ernst and at last she spoke.

"He says he will come back to me."

"Pavel will always be with you, Kája. He will always be with both of us."

Karolína started to get undressed and Ernst turned away. He heard her getting into bed and looked back to see her in a white nightgown.

"I'm tired now, darling. I need to sleep," she said.

Ernst sat on the bed and stroked her head, as he had seen Pavel do. "Get some rest, Kája."

"Are you coming to bed too, darling," she asked.

"Not yet. Later." He kissed her forehead. "Remember, Kája, that I always love you."

"I know, darling."

Ernst went into his room and took down the suitcases to pack their clothes. Tomorrow at first light they would leave Cheb behind and find safety.

Soon after midnight he went to bed and fell into a fitful sleep, waiting and fearing another knock on the door. In the early hours he thought he heard movement and lay awake listening. He was convinced he had heard something or somebody at the front door. He got up and went out onto the landing. There were no lights on in the house. He went to Karolína's room and knocked gently.

"Kája, are you awake?"

He waited and knocked again. When there was no answer he went in. The bed was empty. He went to the bathroom. She was not there. He returned to Karolína's bedroom and opened the curtains. It was still dark outside, but a half moon threw light on the water flowing under the bridge.

Karolína looked down at the water. She loved the sound of it. On hot nights she and Pavel would lie in bed with the window open and listen to it as they held one another. The sound of the water and Pavel together. She leaned over the bridge, closed her eyes and took them both in.

From behind the bedroom window Ernst shouted to her, but she could not hear him. He saw her leaning further forward as if she was reaching for something, and then she toppled. For a second there was her hair and her white nightgown, and then she was gone.

He rushed out of the house and ran to the bridge. "Kája," he shouted at the top of his voice. "Kája." But there was only the water of the Ohře.

Treachery

I love thee, Wife
I love thee, Father
I love thee, Czechoslovakia
My Trinity

I learned your language, Albion
Lest I know not your ways of love,
Of fairness and tradition, ages-formed
Your ways of life-evolving laws

Land of Shakespeare

I learned your language fair
To write in soft poetic form
Of loves, of life and pain,
Of hopes betrayed.

I loved thee, England free.

By my father taught, with stories told
Of hero and of friend, my childhood faith
Imbued with thee, o treacherous State!
I write my last, I think my last –

Thy words spew false across the page.

Miluji tě, Manželka
Miluji tě, Otec
Miluji tě, Československo
Moje Trojice

Tomáš Kovařík
October 16th, 1938
Castiran, France

Biographies

Leo Amery (1873-1955)
Liberal Unionist and Conservative MP. An outspoken critic of appeasement. His speech in the House of Commons in May 1940 is widely held to have led to the resignation of Chamberlain as Prime Minister, and to the appointment of Winston Churchill.

Eduard Beneš (1884-1948)
Foreign Minister (1918-1935) and President (1935-1938, 1945-1948) of Czechoslovakia.

Stanislav Čeček (1886-1930)
Leader of the Revolt of the Czechoslovak Legion in Russia (May 1918). Commander of the Czech Legion on the Volga front. Promoted to General of the Czechoslovak Army and chief of President Masaryk's Military Office.

Jan Černy (1874-1959)
Prime Minister of Czechoslovakia (1920-1921 and 1926)

Neville Chamberlain (1869-1940)
British Prime Minister (1937-1940). Main proponent of appeasement. Led Britain during the first 8 months of war. Member of Churchill's War Cabinet. Died 6 months after resigning as Prime Minister in 1940.

Winston Churchill (1874-1965)
Conservative politician and leading opponent of appeasement in the 1930's. Prime Minister (10 May 1940 – 26 July 1945 and 1951 – 1955).

Karl Hermann Frank (1898-1946)
Keeper of a bookshop in Karlovy Vary. In 1935 became Henlein's deputy in the Sudetenland German Party. Gauleiter of the Sudetenland in 1938 after Munich. Promoted to general in Waffen-SS and deputy to Reinhard Heydrich, Reichsprotektor of Bohemia and Moravia. Hanged in Prague in May, 1946

Konrad Henlein (1898-1945)
Leader of the Sudeten German Party. After Munich Agreement was briefly civil administrator of Protectorate of Bohemia and Moravia. Later demoted to Gauleiter of the administrative subdivision Sudetenland. Held post until the end of the war. Committed suicide in Pilsen in 1945.

Milan Hodža (1878-1944)
Prime Minister of Czechoslovakia (1935-1938) Proponent of Central European Federation.

Alexander Kerensky (1881-1970)
Held posts of Minister of Justice, Minister of War and Prime Minister in the democratic Russian Provisional Government after the overthrow of Tsar Nicholas the Second. Deposed by the Bolsheviks in the October Revolution of 1917. Died in exile in the United States.

Ludvík Krejčí (1890-1972)
Commander of the Czechoslovak Legion at Bakhmach Junction. Promoted to General of the Army in 1934. Responsible for reorganisation of army and fortification of borders. Promoted Commander in Chief of Armed Forces in 1938. Demoted to private by the Communists in 1953. All pension rights revoked. Rank of General restored posthumously in 1990.

Kamil Krofta (1876-1945)
Academic and diplomat. Ambassador to the Vatican, Vienna and Berlin. Foreign Minister (1936-1938). Member of resistance. Sent to Theresienstadt concentration camp. Liberated in May 1945. Died three months later from maltreatment received during imprisonment.

Jan Masaryk (1886-1948)
Czechoslovak Ambassador in London (1925-1938).

Tomáš Masaryk (1850-1937)
Academic, philosopher, teacher, politician. President of Czechoslovakia (1918-1935).

František Moravec (1895-1966)
Czechoslovak army officer, legionnaire and military intelligence officer. Helped plan assassination of Reinhard Heydrich. Left Czechoslovakia

after the Communist takeover. Settled in the United States and worked as an intelligence advisor in the US Department of Defence.

Milan Stefanik (1880-1919)
Slovak General in the French Army. Member of Czechoslovak National Council and Minister of War. Helped organise the evacuation of the Legion from Siberia. Died in mysterious circumstances as his plane attempted to land in Bratislava.

Jan Syrovy (1888-1970)
Commander of the Legion in Russia. Chief of Staff of Czechoslovak Army (1926-1933) and General Inspector of Army (1933-1938). Prime Minister during Munich Crisis (22 September -1 December 1938). Refused to join the resistance during the war and was arrested in May 1945 for collaboration. Sentenced to 20 years imprisonment. All military honours and pension rights revoked. Released in 1960 and employed as night watchman. Died embittered at his treatment, which he considered unjust.

Woodrow Wilson (1856-1924)
US President (1913-1921). Favoured neutrality in World War 1 and sought to mediate for peace. Succumbed to war faction in April 1917 after continued German submarine attacks on US shipping. Unable to secure Senate ratification of the Versailles Treaty. Awarded the Nobel Peace Prize in 1919 for his support of the League of Nations, but was unable to secure Senate support for US membership. Health declined after suffering a stroke while touring America to promote ratification of the Treaty.

Proof

Manufactured by Amazon.com
Columbia, SC
08 April 2017